WHEN DANGER CALLS

WHEN DANGER CALLS

TERRY ODELL

FIVE STAR

A part of Gale, Cengage Learning

Detroit • New York • San Francisco • New Haven, Conn • Waterville, Maine • London

Copyright © 2008 by Terry Odell.
Five Star Publishing, a part of Gale, Cengage Learning.

Set in 11 pt. Plantin.
Printed on permanent paper.

LIBRARY OF CONGRESS CATALOGING-IN-PUBLICATION DATA

Odell, Terry.
When danger calls / Terry Odell. — 1st ed.
p. cm.
ISBN-13: 978-1-59414-723-4 (alk. paper)
ISBN-10: 1-59414-723-X (alk. paper)
1. Single mothers—Fiction. 2. Montana—Fiction. I. Title.
PS3615.D456W47 2008
813'.6—dc22
2008037093

First Edition. First Printing: December 2008.
Published in 2008 in conjunction with Tekno Books.

Printed in the United States of America
1 2 3 4 5 6 7 12 11 10 09 08

To Dan, for all his patience, understanding, support and love.
And to Jess, our very own Peanut.

ACKNOWLEDGMENTS

I may sit alone at the keyboard, but the final product relies on the help and guidance of so many.

Thanks go to everyone at Novel Alchemy, my critique partners Dara Edmondson and Julie Salvo; to Roxanne St. Claire for her constant encouragement and sage advice; plus everyone at CFRW. And much love to the Pregnant Pigs who got me started and refused to let me quit. Thanks also to my agent, Kelly Mortimer, for taking a chance with me, and to my editor, Brittiany Koren, who knew what I wanted to say and helped me get those thoughts on the page.

Blackthorne, Inc. and Broken Bow, Montana are figments of my imagination, but technical assistance thanks go to Wally Lind and the entire gang at crimescenewriter; to MAJ Tom Fuller, United States Army; Commander Tom Stroup, Orange County Sheriff's Office, Orlando FL; and Tom Bennett, Jefferson County District Attorney's Office, Golden CO, for helping me base them on some semblance of reality. In the end, the errors are my own, either unintentional or deliberate for the sake of the story. It is fiction, after all.

Thanks to Jessica for her fight scene choreography, to Nicole for her music, and to Jason for getting me into this whole writing thing, even if it was by mistake.

CHAPTER 1

Some cakewalk. A routine mission turned into a straight-to-video movie. To Ryan Harper, it smelled rotten—even more rotten than the garbage piled in the alleyway they'd trekked through to get here.

Senses on alert, Ryan cast a furtive glance over his shoulder. Hair prickled on the back of his neck. Maybe it hadn't been smart to insist on a solo mission. Still, after the last one, he couldn't bear the thought of endangering anyone's life but his own. He waited beside Alvarez, his contact, while the wizened man unlocked the warehouse door. Alvarez clicked on a light. Two feral cats yowled and hissed, then bolted outside.

Ryan stepped into the hot, stuffy room. Grime covered the sealed windows, and the ammonia stench of cat piss filled his nostrils. Why didn't any of his assignments include rooms with air conditioning? Instead, they sent him to a deserted neighborhood in Panama—one the jungle desperately wanted to reclaim. "Where are the files, Señor Alvarez?"

"Here," Alvarez said around the cigar stub that seemed permanently clamped between his teeth. He closed the door behind them. "I show you everything. You have the money?"

"After I see the files."

Outside, a generator hummed. Three cats peered warily around upended tables and a maze of cardboard cartons. Avoiding broken glass, rubber tubing, and other assorted debris, he followed Alvarez across the room. A rusty gas stove stood at the

9

far end next to a small refrigerator and a laminate-topped table. In a blur, the cats disappeared behind the stove. Opposite, two file cabinets flanked a beat-up wooden desk and a cracked vinyl armchair. Like an alien presence, a flat-screen computer monitor sat atop the desk.

"Momento." Alvarez reached under the desk, and Ryan immediately grabbed for his weapon. A button clicked and a hard drive whirred. Ryan exhaled. Maybe this was a cakewalk after all.

The door slammed against the wall. Flash-bang grenades hit the floor. "Get down!" he shouted at Alvarez, who still fumbled with the computer. Covering his ears and squeezing his eyes shut, Ryan scrambled for cover behind the desk as the room filled with brilliant light and an ear-splitting report.

Deaf and half-blind from the blast, Ryan pointed his Glock near the doorway. Gunfire sprayed the room. Alvarez gasped. Blood flowed from his chest. He turned and pressed a metal tube into Ryan's hand. The ringing in his ears muffled the man's words, but Ryan watched his lips. *"Importante."* Alvarez clawed his way to the desktop. The computer exploded. Ryan's body slammed backward. Alvarez sagged to the floor, half his face blown off.

Shit. First Colombia, now this. Ryan jammed the tube into a pocket of his cargo pants. Blinking to clear his vision, he turned to engage his assailants. Three of them—one of him. Some fucking cakewalk.

The desk and file cabinets provided cover, giving Ryan the advantage. He fired. Two shots to the body, one to the head. Repeat as needed. Two men down.

The third guy, built like a grizzly, bared his teeth in a malicious grin. "You are mine, *señor.*"

"Sorry. You're not my type." Ryan pulled the trigger twice. His assailant fell backward, his weapon firing in a broad arc. A searing pain ripped through Ryan's shoulder. His arm jerked, and his gun clattered to the floor skittering between the file cabinets behind him. He fumbled for the knife strapped to his ankle. Blood, hot and sticky, ran down his arm, and his fingers slipped on the knife's hilt. He scrambled backward to the file cabinets to retrieve his Glock.

He groped for the pistol. The man on the floor struggled to his feet. *Body armor. Crap.* Ryan's gun hand was all but useless. The angle sucked. Holding the Glock in his off hand, he took a head shot. The man twitched, swinging his arm. He went down.

Ryan's satisfaction shriveled when a grenade rolled across the room, stopping under the stove.

"Fu—." Ryan burst through the door and dove for cover outside. He grimaced with pain from landing on his knee as the warehouse exploded in flames behind him. He struggled to his feet and waited, heart pounding, between two abandoned cars until he was certain no one else followed.

Still dazed, he moved into the jungle. When he didn't check in on schedule, an extraction team would rendezvous according to plan three days from now. No sweat. Couldn't be any worse than survival training hell.

It was. In survival training, no one shot you and then infected you with some nasty jungle bug. His meager rations were use-less—he could barely keep water down. His knee looked more like a melon than a joint. His shoulder screamed and his teeth chattered despite the jungle heat. Hiding by day, traveling by night, Ryan reached the extraction point and waited. He wouldn't be left behind. He only hoped he'd be alive when the chopper showed up.

The appointed time came and went. He fought to stay conscious. Ten minutes. Another five. He could hold on for one more. And one after that. The world faded in and out. Then from above, the welcome whup-whup of a helicopter sounded. Praying he wasn't suffering from fever-induced hallucinations, he crawled out of his hiding place to the tiny clearing. He squinted into the darkness at the hovering helo and flashed his light in the prearranged pattern. He'd never make it up a rope ladder. He had to.

The ladder dropped. A body scrambled down. Someone—a face he should recognize despite the camo paint—put a hand on his shoulder.

"Your limo's here, Harper." Someone lifted him onto a stretcher. "Relax and enjoy the ride."

A burst of fire shot through his shoulder as someone ripped his shirt open, then a sting in his arm.

And then nothing.

"Enter."

It was a command, not an invitation.

Ryan propped his cane against the outside of the jamb. He steeled himself and opened the door.

Squaring his shoulders, he did his damnedest not to favor his injured knee when he stepped into Horace Blackthorne's private office. The sleek, modern public reception areas downstairs contrasted with this room, a time warp from the fifties. The old-fashioned Venetian blinds were lowered against the late afternoon sun, blocking the view of the Golden Gate Bridge in the distance. Ryan squinted into the glare sneaking through the cracks. Although his boss didn't smoke, the office always smelled of pipe tobacco. He cleared his throat, surprised at its dryness.

"You asked to see me, sir?"

Blackthorne looked up from the sheet of paper he'd been reading. No pleasantries, not that Ryan expected any. When the man didn't gesture toward one of the two utilitarian chairs fronting the steel desk, Ryan held himself erect, squelching the urge to grab the back of one for support. He waited while the man placed the paper into a file folder, gave it a tap, then set it in the wire basket on the corner of the desk.

Blackthorne removed his half-frame reading glasses, snapped them into a leather case, and slipped them inside his jacket pocket. He pushed away from his desk and levered himself to his full height.

At six-three, Ryan usually looked down on people, but he adjusted his gaze upward to lock eyes with his superior. Blackthorne disguised his emotions well, but over the last ten years Ryan learned to eke out the subtlest signals. A shift in the eyes, the twitch of a jaw muscle, a minuscule shoulder shrug— these were flashing neon signs. Today, the man stood stock-still, like the bronze statue of Old Whatshisname in front of City Hall back home.

Ryan waited out the silence, his eyes moving up Blackthorne's furrowed brow to the salt-and-pepper hair, neatly parted, still thick. He resisted the urge to run his fingers through his own hair, hanging in unruly tendrils over his collar.

"You met Alvarez." A statement, not a question. "Where are the files?" Blackthorne leaned forward. His gaze bored into Ryan's. Did he detect a glint of eagerness in his boss' eyes?

Uncertainty spread outward from Ryan's middle like ripples on a pond. Two weeks in the hospital kept him out of the loop, but not so far he didn't know about the rumors—all blaming him for the screwups. That a leak existed at Blackthorne, Inc., and he was suspect number one.

He balled his fists, keeping his hands away from the flash drive in his pocket. The intel. Mr. Alvarez's list of stolen artworks. Nothing worth killing for. But a sleazebag like Alvarez might be dealing in more than smuggled art. Was there a connection between Alvarez and the failed Forcada mission in Colombia? Ryan had to find the leak, and he'd do whatever it took to prove his innocence, even if it meant investigating Horace Blackthorne himself.

He kept his gaze steady. "The grenade destroyed the computer, sir. Along with the entire building."

Blackthorne hesitated. Cleared his throat. Nodded, the barest twitch of his chin. "Finish your rehab, take some extra leave."

"I'm fine, sir. Give me the weekend. I'll be ready for a new assignment on Monday."

"Two fouled missions. You're no good to me, the firm, or yourself now. I read your medical reports. I spoke with your doctors. We're not negotiating, Harper. Six weeks personal leave while you finish your rehab, plus any vacation time you've accrued, if you need it. Three months on security detail, and then we'll discuss your future as a field agent."

Security detail. A Blackthorne euphemism for chaperoning spoiled offspring of arrogant aristocrats or media hotshots. Why not say, "You're fired." His gut clenched. That's precisely what his boss had in mind.

Ryan reached for his wallet. He pulled out his ID. Ryan Harper. Six-three, brown eyes, brown hair, two hundred pounds. Not much had changed. True, he was thinner since his illness. He focused on the photo. The face of a younger man, fresh and optimistic, stared back at him.

The soft click of the laminated card landing on the scarred steel desk echoed through the room.

Ignoring the card, Blackthorne sat down and reached for the file folder on his desk.

Ryan pivoted, disregarding the pain in his knee. The one in his belly hurt worse. He retrieved his cane on the way to the elevator. On the ride down, he flipped open his cell phone. If there was anyone left he could trust, it would be Dalton. His ex-partner was out of the country on assignment, but even on his voice-mail recording, the Texan's easy drawl loosened the knots.

He waited out the message, concentrating on keeping his voice steady when he spoke. "It's Harper. Call when you can."

The elevator doors opened. He snapped the phone shut. Outside, sunlight bounced off the buildings, but its warmth eluded him. In the building's grassy courtyard, a group of young children chased around an abstract sculpture, one that always reminded him of a bunch of asparagus. He hated asparagus. He tuned out the giggles, but he couldn't turn off the image of Carmelita. His fingers ached, and he released his death-grip on the cane. On the way to the parking garage, he passed a wire trash bin. Without missing a step, he flung the cane inside.

Ryan sat behind the wheel, his mind replaying the afternoon in the warehouse, pieces falling into place. The smells he'd attributed to the cats. The clutter on the floor. At the time, he'd disregarded the Spanish writing on the cartons. He remembered one now, tilted on its side. *Éter.* Ether. An abandoned meth lab. With a sense of purpose, he put his Mustang into gear.

Ryan crammed his clothes into an oversized duffel and his other essentials into his backpack. He'd taken great pains to make sure he wasn't followed to the bank after he left Blackthorne's office. If someone at Blackthorne wanted him gone, he'd disappear—but on his own terms.

His laptop signaled it had finished burning the CD. He ejected the disc, slipped it into a jewel case and after wiping any trace of the file from his hard drive, shut down the machine. He scraped most of his scrambled eggs and toast supper into the garbage disposal and hit the switch. He walked through the apartment one last time, mechanically turning off lights and closing curtains as he'd done before countless missions. Duffel over his shoulder, pack on his back, he locked the door behind him, void of feeling. Nothing about this place had ever said home.

Ryan stood on the ranch house porch, rubbing his shoulder. An owl hooted in the distance, and something rustled in the trees. The night air smelled of pine and damp earth, layered over the smell of horses and manure. The familiar scent carried a tangle of emotions he couldn't take time to sort. He turned his gaze upward. Clouds blanketed the stars, but even so, the glow of the full moon cast everything in pewter.

He shifted his weight to his right leg, trying to ease the ache in his left knee. He should have traded in his manual transmission for an automatic, but that would have meant giving up his Mustang and admitting his knee wasn't ever going to be one hundred percent. Damn, letting a car shift whenever it felt like it wasn't *driving*.

He grazed his knuckles against the wooden door. Waited. Tapped again, harder. He counted to ten before lifting his hand again. This time he knocked, loud and clear. A shuffle of footsteps approached from inside.

Wrapped in a flannel robe, Pop appeared leaner in the legs, and thicker in the chest. He had the same full head of hair, the red Ryan remembered faded to a dull orange. The chest hair peeking out from the V of the robe was pure white.

"You coming in?" Not so much as a lifted eyebrow. As if showing up after being gone for more than ten years was a normal, everyday occurrence.

Pop's voice hadn't changed either. Not much, anyway. Maybe more gravel to it. Or maybe Ryan had gotten him out of bed. He looked at his watch. Twenty-one-thirty. Not that late. Shit. He'd forgotten the time zone switch between California and Montana. It was twenty-two-thirty here. Make that ten-thirty. He was a civilian for now.

"Sorry if I woke you, Pop." He took a step into the room. Instead of Rusty, the familiar Irish setter at Pop's side, a large German Shepherd curled its lip and growled. Ryan froze.

"He's okay, boy," his father said. "Friend."

The dog lifted his eyes. A slow wag of his tail said, *If you say so, but I have my doubts.*

Ryan extended his hand, knuckles up, to the dog's muzzle. A sniff, a lick, and an energized tail wag followed.

"Wolf," his father said. "Be fine once he gets to know you some. You gonna stay awhile?" He scratched the dog's head.

"I've got some things to work out. Taking a little time off, you know. It's kind of complicated. I don't want to bother you. The getaway cabin? Is it . . . still Josh's? I mean, if he's using it, I could . . . but he's away a lot." Shit. His voice was cracking.

With a plaintive whine, Wolf nudged his muzzle under Ryan's hand. Reflexively, he rubbed the dog's ruff.

"Your brother is on a shoot somewhere in one of those countries that needs to buy a few vowels. Keys are on the hook by the kitchen door."

"Thanks, Pop. I really appreciate—"

"It's almost eleven. Tomorrow's soon enough. Your old room's always made up. Might as well use it. I'll see you at breakfast." His father scuffed toward the stairs. Wolf didn't move, except to lick Ryan's hand.

He poured himself a whisky and sat in the dark, waiting for the alcohol to take the edge off frazzled nerves. Wolf sat at his feet, watching. He'd braced himself for his father's anger, or at least resentment. Not this time warp, like he'd come home from the prom, late, but forgiven. Only the dog was different. Once Ryan thought he could sleep, he hoisted himself to his feet.

Boots in one hand, he pulled himself up the stairs, avoiding the third one from the top that always squeaked. Even after ten years, he needed no lights to find his way, although moonlight filtered through the window at the end of the hall.

Pausing outside the door to his father's bedroom, he heard Pop snoring—the lullaby of Ryan's youth. He crept down the hall to his old room, Wolf at his heels.

He gave the dog a pat. "Go to bed, boy."

The dog whined, cocked his head, then gave it a shake.

Ryan urged the dog to the door. "Go on." With apparent reluctance, the dog left his side for the hallway. Ryan heard his toenails click down the stairs, and he shut the bedroom door.

Pop had redecorated his room, an obvious guest room now, but a familiar comfort eked out. He stared out the window and the years peeled away. Like his father, the oak tree outside hadn't changed much. Leaving the curtains open, he sat on the edge of the bed and stripped to his briefs.

He pulled back the comforter, turned off the lamp and lay on his back, with his hands clasped behind his head, and watched the shadows from the oak tree pirouette on the ceiling. The smell of clean sheets carried him back to a time when geometry theorems and getting up the nerve to ask Pammi Calder on a date were his biggest challenges, and he drifted off.

Even in sleep, hairs prickled on his neck and the nightmare returned. Icy fingers reached inside his chest and grabbed his heart.

He hid behind the couch in the Forcadas' living room, the little girl trembling beside him.

"Shh, Carmelita. It'll be okay," he said, knowing damn well it was anything but okay.

She looked at him with huge brown eyes. Trusting brown eyes. "Si. Okay."

He peered underneath the couch into the room. Boots. Too many boots. Gunfire filled his ears. Smoke assaulted his nostrils. If he fired, he'd give away his position. Someone tipped the couch forward. A faceless man with a gun.

He tried to move. Tried to fire. When the faceless man pointed the gun at him, he tried to scream, but no sound would come.

In the shadows, a man, tall and broad, broke through the dream and knelt at his side, pushing the hair away from his sweat-soaked forehead.

"It's all right," a familiar voice said. "You're safe, son."

For the first time since the incident, the terror faded, and instead of waking with a pounding heart, Ryan slipped back into sleep.

Sunlight streamed in the window. From the foot of the bed, Wolf looked up at him. Ryan squinted and rubbed his eyes, staring at the closed bedroom door then back at the dog. A lump formed in his throat.

Thanks, Pop.

CHAPTER 2

Frankie Castor adjusted the bustier under her blouse and threw her stilettos into her tote. Not telling anyone where she was going wasn't the same as lying, was it?

"Are you going out again, Mommy?" Molly peeked into the room. "You said we would be together a lot when we came to Gramma's."

Frankie's heart tugged at the look of betrayal in her five-year-old's face. "I know, Peanut. And we will. It'll be spring break tomorrow, and we'll have lots of time together. Be good for Gramma, and I'll kiss you when I get home."

"Can you make macaroni and cheese?"

Frankie glanced at her watch, weighing the tradeoff of a speeding ticket versus being late again. Neither option was acceptable. She leaned down and kissed Molly's cheek. "I have to go. I promise we'll have lots of fun starting tomorrow. Why don't you get a story to read with Gramma? You can ask her about macaroni and cheese."

Molly stormed out of the bedroom, closing the door loud enough to voice her displeasure, but not hard enough to earn a reprimand for slamming, before her footsteps clattered down the stairs.

On her way out, Frankie took a moment to enjoy the sight of Mom and Molly, her snit apparently forgotten, snuggled on the couch. Brenda Donnegall, Mom's latest graduate student boarder, came into the room carrying a laundry basket of folded clothes.

"Molly sure likes that book," Brenda said.

Frankie nodded. "I had to make green eggs for her last week." She gave Brenda an apologetic smile. "Molly can have one glass of chocolate milk, but make sure—"

"She brushes her teeth. I know the routine. Everything will be fine. I've got a computer game I can show Molly, if you don't mind me using your computer."

"Fine," Frankie said. She had to get out of here.

"You going to remind me to brush my teeth, too?" Her mother looked up from the couch.

Frankie inhaled. "No, of course not." She crossed the room and kissed her mother's cheek. "But remember to take your pain pills. How's your wrist?"

Her mother lifted her arm with its pale blue cast. "Still broken, last I checked." She gave Frankie a disapproving stare. "Going out again, I see."

Guilt rose as Frankie skirted the truth. "Promised to help a friend with some decorating ideas. I won't be too late. Molly wants macaroni and cheese for dinner. Do you think you can fix it?"

"I won't be eating here. Bob's taking me to the Golden Griddle."

Bob. Mom's boyfriend—if that's what you called it at their age. One more headache. Frankie pushed it aside to deal with later.

"I'll do it, as soon as I put the laundry away," Brenda said. "Have a good evening."

Frankie stepped toward the door, then stopped. She looked over her shoulder. "Brenda? That computer game. Molly's not going to be blowing things up, is she?"

Brenda laughed. "No, it's a Barbie game. Completely nonviolent. You have a good evening."

Frankie opened the door, raced across the porch, and into the old Chevy Cavalier waiting in the driveway.

"Come on, baby. Start for me." She patted the dash with one hand and turned the key with the other. As the car wheezed into compliance, she longed for the company BMW she'd had to relinquish when she'd left Boston. Not to mention her office with a view of the Commons. But family came first.

Guilt followed her down the highway, out of Broken Bow, Montana, toward Stanton. Not that anyone in the Broken Bow PTA would come into a honky-tonk like the Three Elks, but her day job as an elementary school art teacher would be over if parents found out she worked there. And since she only got the job because the regular art teacher was on maternity leave, she couldn't risk being fired.

She swung into a parking slot in the alley behind the Three Elks, grabbed her tote from the backseat and raced inside.

"I'm here, Mr. Stubbs."

Mr. Stubbs, owner and bartender made a point of looking at both his watch and the clock over the bar. "I can see that." He gave her half a nod as she rushed into the employee break room, locking the door behind her.

Drained from a day spent helping third and fourth graders create a collage, she was already counting the minutes until her shift ended. She squirmed into her skimpy uniform. It's temporary, she reminded herself while she fussed with foundation and blush, with bright red lipstick and black eyeliner. But the money was good. She was already thinking of a new furnace instead of a repair job. Soon she'd have to tell Mom what she was doing, but not until she figured out how to talk about the budget.

She remembered her dreams of a life of adventure. Traveling the world, taking award-winning photographs. Sneaking in and out of dangerous places. Well, life happened, and keeping secrets from her mother, sneaking in and out of the Three Elks was as much adventure as she was going to get for now. Probably until Molly grew up.

With a sigh, she pulled her shoes from her tote and rubbed her feet. Mr. Stubbs, always looking for a gimmick, insisted the wait staff spend twenty minutes of each hour dancing with the patrons. It wouldn't be half-bad if he didn't insist on stilettos. She slipped into her shoes and took a few warm-up steps. Before unlocking the door, she pinned on her Gladys nametag. Satisfied, she opened the door and headed for the bar, strutting the way Mr. Stubbs liked.

"Right on time, Mr. Stubbs," she said.

"I told you, call me Stubby. Everyone else does."

Tall and lean, if ever there was a man who didn't live up to his name, it had to be Clarence Stubbs.

"Right. Stubby. Anything on special tonight?" She grabbed an order pad from below the marble-topped bar and hoped he hadn't come up with another gimmick. Last week's Chinese tacos had been a disaster.

"Two-for-one margaritas until seven," he said.

Frankie nodded, and gave a hello smile to redheaded Belle, who pulled beers at the taps. Patti, the other server, wasn't due in until eight, which meant more tables—and more tips—until then.

"You like to cut it close, don't you?" Belle asked. She glanced in Mr. Stubbs' direction, then touched Frankie's wrist. "How's your mom?"

Frankie gave a noncommittal shrug. "About the same."

Belle leaned forward, her D-cups swelling over the low-cut uniform blouse, and lowered her voice. "Look, it can be tough. I've been there. But sometimes a nursing home is the best, you know? Like, it's better than them forgetting to turn off the stove and burning the house down. Think about it."

"Mom's nothing like that. Just a little absent-minded."

"But you're at work all day and here three nights a week. What if something happens? You've got a kid."

Guilt rose again, and she tamped it down. "Brenda's there. Mom cut back her rent so she helps around the house and baby-sits."

Belle shrugged. "If you say so. She's still a grad student. My money says either school or guys are her top priorities."

"She's practically family," Frankie said. "Molly loves her."

Mr. Stubbs coughed. "Take table seven, *Gladys*. You've got section three tonight."

She looked up. Table seven held a party of six—three couples—wearing clothes that said they worked in an upscale office. The promise of decent tips lightened her step as she began her evening. "Hi, I'm Gladys. What can I get you?"

At nine, ready for a break, Frankie filled a mug with coffee and ducked behind the bar, her back to the customers. The antique gold-flecked mirror reflected distorted images, giving the room an underwater feel.

Belle's whisper penetrated the background noise. "Oh, great. Mr. Tall, Dark and Grouchy's here early."

It didn't take long to see who Belle was talking about. Over six feet tall, the man radiated a presence that said, "Hands off." He trudged to the far corner booth and slid into its darkness like a bear into its cave.

"What do you know about him?" Frankie asked.

"Nothing," Belle said. "He's been coming in almost every night, after your shift. Has a drink, messes around with a computer, has another drink, then leaves. Always alone. Pays cash. Reasonable tips. He's not looking for action, that's for sure."

The computers had been another one of Mr. Stubbs' gimmicks, less than successful. Why he thought anyone would come to a tavern to work was beyond her. The few who used them tended to nurse drinks and leave lousy tips.

The man glanced in the direction of the bar. Patti sighed and reached for her order pad.

"Wait," Belle said. "Give him to Gladys—five bucks says even she can't get him to smile."

Frankie took a last sip of coffee and adjusted her Gladys nametag, her own gimmick. Who'd want to hit on someone named Gladys? Just about anyone, she discovered her first night.

She watched the man, slumped in the corner as if the world sat on his shoulders. "A smile?" she said. "I'll take that bet." She pulled a five out of her tip pouch and set it under her coffee mug. Giving her uniform skirt a quick tug, she stepped across the floor, forgetting her aching feet.

"What'll you have, sir?" She leaned forward to light the candle in the red jar on the table, displaying her chest the way Mr. Stubbs insisted. Not that she had a lot to display, despite the bustier. Belle got the big tips.

"Don't," he said, his voice a harsh bark.

Frankie straightened, and in the match's glow, gave her customer a closer look. Long, wavy brown hair mingled with a full, scruffy beard that showed he didn't bother to shave. He kept his gaze low, his eyes shadowed behind half-lowered lids. Nostrils flared on a nose that looked as if it had been broken at least once.

She fanned out the match. There might be a chip the size of a redwood tree on his shoulder, but there was a pain in his eyes that reminded her of Buddy, an abandoned stray she'd tried to befriend as a child. "Things are always better in the light. What can I get you?" *Besides a shoulder to cry on.* Nobody should hurt that much.

25

His eyebrows moved up a few millimeters, as if he expected her to know his usual drink.

"Jack."

She flashed him her friendliest smile. "Hello, Jack. I'm Gladys."

The eyebrows went up an inch this time, but his mouth was set. "Daniels."

She tried again. "Sorry. Mr. Daniels."

He glowered. "Jack Daniel's. As in whiskey. Neat."

"Sure thing, Jack. Coming up."

She stepped back to the bar. Aware Mr. Stubbs was watching, she widened her smile and shifted her gait to the hip-rolling strut he preferred. "Knob Creek," she said. "Neat."

Mr. Stubb's eyes snapped up from her hips, back to her face, where they belonged. "He order that?"

"I'm sure that's what he said, Mr. Stubbs. If you want, I can go back and ask again."

He waved off her comment. "One Knob Creek coming up." He poured the drink and slapped the glass onto the counter.

Frankie picked up a round tray and added the drink and a bowl of peanuts. She glanced back at Jack's table. He fingered the unlit candle, as if the solution to all of life's problems could be found encoded in the plastic mesh covering the jar. When Mr. Stubbs turned to take another order, Frankie sneaked a basket of chips and a dish of salsa, and strutted back to the booth, using enough hip-wiggle to get Mr. Stubbs off her case for a while.

"Here you go, Jack," she said and placed the glass and snacks in front of him. "You want to run a tab?"

He grunted and pounded back half his drink. His eyes widened. "This isn't Jack. I'm not paying extra."

"Smile for me and it'll be covered. You don't even have to leave a tip."

He looked her dead in the eyes. "Tell you what, lady. You leave me the hell alone. I pay for the premium stuff *and* leave a little extra for you." He wrapped both hands around the glass and stared into its amber depths.

His voice was quiet, his tone even, but it said he was used to giving orders, and having them followed without question.

She felt Belle and Patti's eyes boring into her from opposite ends of the bar. The band segued into the opening strands of *Take it to the Limit*. She reached for Jack's hand. "Please. You've got to rescue me."

His back stiffened. "What?"

She took his hand. "I'll explain. Dance with me. Hurry. I won't bite." She tugged and he slithered out of the booth. Wriggling into the middle of the crowd, she turned and lifted her right hand.

Eyebrows raised, Jack assumed the dance stance, his hand at her back a feather touch, with a good six-inch gap between them. "Okay, lady. I'm here. Mind explaining why?"

He moved with the waltz rhythm.

"I'm avoiding one of the customers. My feet can't take another attack of his waltzing. He can handle two-two and four-four all right, but the man can't seem to count to three."

"And you assumed I could?" One corner of his mouth turned up.

Almost a smile. Another minute and she'd have Belle's five. "I figured I'd chance it. I'm very good at reading people, you know."

He drew her closer and she smelled soap and an underlying outdoors scent above the room's beer background. No cloying aftershave. Jack's graceful movements belied the way he'd stumbled into the bar as he led her around the floor. His hand at her back was warm through her thin blouse. The bet forgotten, she caught herself before she rested her cheek on his chest.

"What?" he said.

"I didn't say anything."

"You didn't have to. You're surprised I can dance. I'm not so bad at reading people myself."

Her face grew warm, and she gave thanks for the dim lighting. He couldn't have read *all* her thoughts, could he? How, despite her aching feet, she wanted the dance to go on longer? How she wanted to make the pain in his eyes go away?

"It's not that—really. I mean, most of the guys can handle a two-step, but they don't seem to do anything different when it's a waltz. Thank goodness the band doesn't play many. But you know what you're doing, and it's nice not to have to dodge feet and knees."

His eyes crinkled at the edges. "I'll take that as a compliment." As if teaching her not to jump to conclusions, he led her in a series of perfectly executed pivot turns.

When he settled into a basic waltz step, the gap between them was now a lot less than six inches. A long-forgotten tingling surprised her. She licked her lips and swallowed. "So, where did you learn to dance?"

"Part of my job," he said, and his face clouded. The music stopped. He dropped her hand and disappeared from the dance floor.

"Thanks," she whispered after him. She adjusted her skirt and went back to the bar, her heart beating faster than a waltz warranted.

"He *danced* with you. Did he talk?" Belle asked. "Said more than, 'Jack'? That's all anyone here has ever heard him say." She fished a bill from her tips. "That's worth a five, even if he didn't smile."

"Sometimes people need a friendly face," Frankie said. She snatched her own five from under her mug, and tucked it along with Belle's into her apron pocket.

A throat-clearing sound from Mr. Stubbs squelched the rest of the conversation. "Someone's cell phone is ringing in the back room. Anyone here willing to risk her job to take a personal call at work?"

Frankie edged toward the storeroom until she made out the distinctive ring tone of "The Entertainer." Her pulse jumped. She reserved that tone for family.

Heart in her throat, she hastened to the door.

CHAPTER 3

Ryan parked his Mustang behind Josh's place, where it couldn't be seen from the road. He retrieved his Glock from the glove compartment and shoved it into the waistband of his jeans. Circling the cabin, he checked for signs of any disturbance.

Visions of tonight's blonde waitress interfered with his routine checks. None of the others ever looked at him. They slapped down his drinks and left him alone, which is what he wanted. She—Gladys, he recalled—had not only looked at him, she'd been so damn . . . perky. Smiled. Talked. Teased. Called him Jack, for God's sake, although she had to know it wasn't his name. And that, "Rescue me," had scared the shit out of him for a minute. He half expected terrorists to crash through the plate glass window, AK-47's spraying.

He snorted. If she only knew. Rescuing fair maidens from clumsy dancers wasn't exactly one of Blackthorne's top objectives, although he *had* learned to dance as part of the requisite bodyguard duty camouflage. But dancing with an ambassador's snooty daughter didn't feel anything like dancing with Gladys.

Her heavy makeup and severe hairstyle—like she was playing dress-up—clashed with the fresh, young scent that floated up when she'd bent over to light the candle. He'd actually responded with half his blood supply shooting south. And why not? She was a woman, her breasts were practically in his face, and he hadn't been with anyone in a very long time.

When they'd danced, there was another essence in her scent.

He hadn't recognized it at the time, but now it came through, clear as the night air. Elmer's glue.

At the bar, he'd considered spending the rest of the night dancing with her, even after that stupid show-off pivot turn had his knee complaining. And then she'd vanished into the back, come out, said something to Stubby, and disappeared. Good riddance. He damn well didn't need perky. Another image flashed in front of him. Of the frightened expression on her face when she'd talked to Stubby.

Shit, what was going on? He never got involved with women. He forced his attention to making sure everything was secure. Wolf trotted beside him. Wolf spent more time with him than he did with Pop now, but the man didn't seem to begrudge his companion's shift in loyalty.

Wolf growled. Ryan went still. He pulled his gun from his waistband. "Stay."

Wolf obeyed, but quivered in anticipation. After several long moments, a mother raccoon with three youngsters trailing behind her scuttled across the clearing toward the creek.

Wolf gazed up at him, begging to be allowed to give chase. He reached down and grabbed Wolf's ruff. "Sorry, fella. Not tonight." He scratched the dog behind the ears. "It's late. Let's go in."

Wolf whined and strained to get away from Ryan's grasp.

"No chasing coons. They can carry rabies. I'm tired, and I need to piss." The supplies he'd bought to repair and refinish Josh's front porch could wait in the Mustang's trunk until morning. Ryan started for the cabin. Wolf stood at attention a little longer, then shot past him.

Before Ryan got to the steps, Wolf danced at the door, tail wagging.

"Hungry, are you? Give me a minute." He grabbed the rail and put one foot on the bottom step.

With an excited yelp, Wolf nosed the door. When it creaked open and Wolf bounded inside, Ryan raised his weapon. His heart thudded against his ribs as he climbed the remaining stairs and stood off to the side of the now-open doorway, peering into the shadowy interior of the cabin.

Someone sat up on the couch. "No need for that. Thought we should talk is all."

Frankie raced into the emergency room, her eyes sweeping the rows of chairs, searching for her mother. Instead, she saw Bob Dwyer, her mother's current—whatever you called it at their age. Beau? Boyfriend? Leech? He rose from a chair in the corner, adjusted his navy blue sport coat and approached her, every strand of his silver hair in place.

"Bob," Frankie said, finally able to take a breath. "How's Mom? Where's Molly?"

"Relax. All's well. We didn't know how long it would take in the emergency room, so Brenda stayed with Molly, and I brought Anna. The doctor's with her now."

He gripped her hands. His were warm, soft, and smooth. Hers were icy and trembling. He guided her to a chair. "Sit. Relax."

She perched on the edge of the plastic seat. "What happened?"

"She was climbing the stairs," Bob said, still holding Frankie's hands. "She said she got lightheaded, and the next thing she knew, she was on the floor."

"Oh my God. Oh my God. Did she break anything else? Her hip?" Mom had a broken wrist—part of the reason Frankie had moved home. She felt the blood drain from her face. "Her back? Oh, not her neck?"

"Hey there. No—she was on the third step. Her head col-

lided with the newel post. But we thought it best to bring her here."

"Molly. Did she see it? How is she handling this?"

Bob squeezed her hands. "Molly was already in bed. Your mom was out for a minute or two. She swore she was fine. It was all we could do to convince her to get checked out. She refused an ambulance, so I drove her. And you'd better take some deep breaths, or they'll be picking you up off the floor next."

Frankie managed a smile. "Sorry. I've been doing the worst-case scenario playback in my head since I got the phone call. The cell reception was terrible, and I couldn't understand anything but 'Mom' and 'emergency room.' "

"Anna was adamant about that, too. She preferred that we not ruin your evening, so I told Brenda to call you after we left."

"Thanks. That sounds like Mom."

Now that her heartbeat had approached normal, she wondered why Bob would have been at the house so late, and if he'd been on the stairs when Mom fell. She was about to ask when she noticed Bob's gaze slide up and down her body. Good grief, she'd dashed out so fast she hadn't changed her clothes, and she was sitting in the ER looking like—like what she was tonight. A one-step-from-stripper cocktail waitress. She tugged on her skirt and gave the quickest glance possible around the room, praying that none of her students had come down with a bug. All she needed was to be caught in this outfit, and her teaching job was over. Only a few of the chairs were filled, and she relaxed when she saw nobody she recognized.

"Bob, you've got to promise you won't tell anyone, especially Mom. I've been moonlighting at the Three Elks in Stanton. If anyone finds out, I'm finished."

He opened his mouth, as if he were going to tell her what she

already knew, but instead, he nodded. "If that's what you want." He pulled a topcoat from the chair beside him and wrapped it around her. "If tonight is like any other ER visit, she'll be awhile. Why don't you go home? There's nothing you can do, and I'll be here."

She shook her head. "I'll be back right after I change, and then you can go. Thanks for bringing Mom in." Burrowing into Bob's coat, her head down, Frankie tried to keep a sedate pace out the door.

At home, Frankie hung Bob's coat on the hall tree and dashed for the stairs. Brenda appeared from the den, running her hands through her dark brown curls.

"How's your mother?"

"The doctor's with her." The thought swimming through her head surfaced now that she'd had time to think. First a broken wrist, and now this. Both times when Mom was with Bob. She remembered what her sister had said a month ago, when she'd called and dropped the bomb.

"James has a great job offer. But it's in London. Someone has to help Mom. And keep an eye on Bob. He creeps me out."

"Brenda, did you see Mom fall? Was Bob with her?"

Brenda tilted her head, squinted her green eyes as if replaying the event. "I'm not sure. They were in the den. I was in my room, working on my paper, and then I heard your mom fall. Bob was with her when I got there."

Why would Bob want to hurt Mom? And if he did, why would he have stayed at the emergency room? It didn't make sense. He'd looked genuinely concerned. But, if he was up to something shady, wouldn't he try to be the nice guy?

She couldn't deal with it now. "How's Molly doing?"

"She's been asleep the whole time. I've been using your computer so I could hear her if she woke up."

"That's fine. I'm going to change and get back to the ER."

Brenda's raised eyebrows said she'd noticed Frankie's unorthodox attire. What the heck. Bob knew. Better to tell the truth than have Brenda speculate and say anything to Mom. When she explained her moonlighting job, Brenda promised to keep her secret.

"Oh, and thanks for staying up," Frankie said.

"No problem. I have to finish two chapters before I leave. I've got an early flight, so I'll be gone before you're awake."

Upstairs, Frankie peeked into Molly's room. Her daughter's hair splayed over the pillow, shining red-gold in the glow of the night-light. As always, Mr. Snuggles, a once-white stuffed dog, lay in the crook of Molly's arm. Frankie tiptoed across the room and stroked Molly's cheek. "Sleep well."

Across the hall in her own bedroom, Frankie kicked off her shoes and stepped into the bathroom to scrub off her makeup. The mirror reflected stress, but all in all, she looked better than she felt. The internal flip-flops hadn't made it to her face yet. She unpinned her chignon, shook her hair loose and jumped into jeans and a sweatshirt—inconspicuous Broken Bow attire.

The shrill ring of the phone made her jump. Frankie rushed to the nightstand and grabbed the receiver. "Yes?"

"It's Bob. They're going to keep your mother overnight. They're doing a CAT scan, and want to check a little heart arrhythmia."

New worries surged through Frankie. She glanced at the clock. Eleven. "I'll be right there."

"There's not really any point. She's going to sleep through the night, and I'll bring her home in the morning. I think you'd be doing the most good by getting some sleep, and being there for Molly. Keep things routine."

Frankie sank to the bed. "Can I talk to her?"

"She's still in the ER, but they're going to take her to a room soon." He cleared his throat. "She asked for you to stay home.

I'll be here with her."

"Yeah. Sure. Okay. Thanks." She set the phone in the cradle. Her mother wanted Bob, not her. Frankie tried to digest that one. She looked at the phone. Mom said to stay home. Or had Bob? Frankie grabbed her purse.

"Pop. Shit, you could have . . . I might have . . ." Ryan slid his Glock into his waistband and waited for his pulse to slow. Damn, he was losing it. Blackthorne had been right. He had no business in the field. "How did you get here?"

"The usual way. I walked. Needed some exercise. Left you some grub in the fridge."

"Thanks. I've eaten." He went to the kitchen and flipped on the light. "You want a drink? Coffee?"

"Whatever you're having's fine."

He poured two glasses of whiskey and brought them to the couch. "Be right back."

He stumbled into the bedroom, emptied his pockets onto the nightstand, put his gun in the drawer, then stepped into the bathroom and relieved himself. At the same time, apprehension curled into his belly. Pop wouldn't have hiked two miles in the middle of the night simply to say hello. The man hadn't come by in the two weeks since Ryan had been here. He zipped up, then rubbed his tense neck muscles.

Standing at the sink washing his hands, he stared into the mirror. He'd looked worse, but there had always been reasons for it—like being on a two-week mission in some undeveloped country. Somehow, not sleeping on assignment wasn't as exhausting as not sleeping in his own bed. He grabbed his brush and ran it through his hair, wet a washcloth with cold water and pressed it against his red-rimmed eyes, bracing himself for whatever Pop wanted.

His father sat in the corner of the couch, leg crossed over

knee, his cowboy boots worn and dusty. Wolf lay at his feet. Ryan chose one of the wing chairs. "What do you want to talk about?"

His father downed half his drink, then set the glass on the table. "I'm getting old. I put the ranch on the market."

Ryan reached for his own drink. "The ranch? That's crazy, Pop. Why?"

"Not much family interest, I'd say. Lindy moved away when she got married. Was damn clear you and your brother didn't like the life."

"We were kids. It wasn't the work as much as the lack of choice. You assumed we'd follow along, mucking stalls, leading tourists on trips through the mountains four times a day when you stopped raising livestock. We wanted more. Maybe if things had been different, we'd have come back."

"Maybe so. But you didn't, did you?"

Damn. The boulder that materialized in his belly hadn't gotten smaller. "What do you want me to say?"

"Well, maybe it's my turn to go." Pop's chin jutted out and his eyes narrowed.

"Where would you go? What would you do?"

"Thought I might like to go somewhere warmer. Arizona, maybe. Or New Mexico. Hear Albuquerque's nice."

Ryan got up and paced the room, which seemed much too small to handle his energy. "Why didn't you say that before, when I first got here? Why wait until now?"

"You didn't seem to want much company." His father stood, and went to the kitchen to refill his glass. "Besides. Didn't think you'd want the place. Didn't think I needed to ask permission."

"No, of course you don't need to ask. But it might have been nice to tell me."

"Doing that now, ain't I?"

"Shit, Pop, I'm not ready to absorb this. It's late, I'm buzzed and—" He tugged on his hair. Wolf pricked up his ears, shifting his gaze from one man to the other, whimpering softly.

Ryan's voice was hoarse. "I know it's not my call. But damn it to hell, the timing sucks."

"Why?" His father raised his tone to a volume Ryan rarely heard him use. "You all but disappear for ten years, send a few Christmas cards, make a few phone calls, and then come strolling back and everything's supposed to be like nothing happened? Life don't work that way."

"Don't I know it? But what the hell. It worked for you, didn't it? Mom dies and it's like she never existed. Nothing that was hers in the house, not even a goddamn picture!" Now he was shouting too. "Everything else I had is gone, why should I be surprised to find out home—the one thing I thought would always be there—is being yanked out from under me?" He scrubbed his hands over his eyes.

"Who'd you lose, son? How?" His father's tone shifted to gentle. The voice from his nightmare. With a hand on Ryan's shoulder, Pop led him to the couch and sat next to him. "Ain't right to hurt so bad." He handed him the glass of whiskey he'd refilled.

Ryan took a slow sip. Then another, and another. When he thought he could talk, he spoke into the glass.

"My job with Blackthorne—sometimes things got messy."

"I kinda figured there was more going on than playing babysitter for rich folks."

That Blackthorne, Inc. had a covert operations side was something he didn't think his father had known.

"What makes you think that?" Ryan asked.

Pop gave him the same look he'd used whenever he or his brother had been caught in a lie. He shrugged. "No reason to shun family if all you were doing was hand-holding, or some detective work. Didn't figure you'd work the wrong side of the law. Covert operations made the most sense to me. Josh hinted a little, too—his path skirted yours a couple of times." He gave a little snort. "Besides. Can't see you wasting all that damn Navy SEAL time to baby-sit."

Ryan gulped his drink and tried to absorb what his father had said. He'd known what Ryan did, and accepted it. Even Josh had figured it out. Ryan's world shifted on its axis. "After the way you reacted when I joined the Navy, I didn't think you'd approve of my job."

"Approval wasn't my call. Disagreed maybe, but when you break a stallion to ride, you gotta do it without breaking his spirit. You knew what you wanted. I hoped it was what you needed."

"I thought I could do some good." Ryan sighed, his head hanging almost to his knees.

"I'll wager you did plenty." His father kneaded Ryan's shoulder. "Talk it out, son."

Ryan stared at the floor. "We were in—well, I can't tell you that. But a family—mom, dad, and two little kids—needed to leave. You were right. Blackthorne goes places where it would be . . . inappropriate . . . for our government to be involved. Three of us were sent to get them out. New identities, new lives. Totally top secret." The detachment that served him in his job returned, and he found he could relate the incident as if it had happened to someone else. Or was it the strength from his father's touch?

"Bushwhacked," his father said, his tone as detached as Ryan's.

"Yeah. It was ugly. The family died, and so did my team.

"A week later, they needed me again. This one was supposed to be a cakewalk. Turned into a total clusterfuck. I got out and waited for a chopper to yank me out of the jungle." No need to mention the three days of hell, or how he'd been sick enough to wish they'd never rescued him. Or that he had the intel he'd been sent to get.

His father leaned back. Nodded. Waited.

Ryan scratched his beard. "Nobody's talking about the leaks. Since I'm the only survivor in both places, I look like the obvious suspect."

"You gonna find who did it?" It was more statement than question.

He sighed. "I'm trying. It's tricky, because I don't know what sort of red flags I'll send up if I start digging." Unable to sit, he stood and refilled his glass. "My ex-boss might be involved. One friend I trust is digging through the places I can't go. But he's not in the country much. I'm looking for anything that will connect the two cases. I've been using the computers at the Three Elks. That way, there's no tracing anything back to me."

Pop gave a slow nod. "Didn't figure you for a melancholy drunk."

"You're something else, Pop. I know I shouldn't have stayed away so long, but it was easier than lying to you about what I did, or why I'd have to disappear with no explanation."

"Maybe so." Pop stood and clapped him on the shoulder. "You feeling better?"

"Yeah. I am. Thanks."

When his father grinned, Ryan felt like an idiot. "You're not really selling the place, are you?"

"Nope. Why would I do a fool thing like that? It's home. Gives the kids around here a place to work. Keeps me young. I can always go to Albuquerque for a vacation if the yearning strikes."

"So why come out here in the middle of the night to piss me off?"

"Had to get you riled enough so you'd talk. You always did bottle everything up. Needed some pressure to pop the cork."

"Dammit, Pop, I—"

Pop took the whiskey glasses to the kitchen and set them by the sink. "Good night, son."

"You're not going to walk home at this hour, and I'm too buzzed to drive. Take the bed. I'll sleep on the couch."

"I ain't too buzzed. Give me the keys to that flashy Mustang. You can pick her up tomorrow. Walk'll do you some good."

Ryan nodded and tossed the keys. His father snatched them from the air. He paused at the door, turning to face him. "See you in the morning, son." Whistling, he stepped onto the porch, closing the door behind him.

"Thanks," Ryan whispered. "For everything."

Ryan heard Pop's whistle fade away, then the engine of the Mustang. He stripped to his shorts and flopped onto the bed. He was no closer to knowing what had happened than when he'd walked out of Blackthorne's office, but he didn't feel alone anymore. He closed his eyes and relished the quiet drift toward sleep.

The crack of an explosion jerked him awake. Not a nightmare this time. He leaped out of bed, and had his jeans and boots on in seconds. Wolf barked at the door. Ryan yanked it open, and the dog raced down the trail. Ryan followed, punching 911 into his cell phone, praying for a signal. The sky glowed red. Smoke filled the air. And he saw his Mustang, engulfed in flames, wrapped around a pine tree.

"Pop!" Ryan's cry tore his throat.

CHAPTER 4

Her eyes glued to the winding green stripe on the floor, Frankie followed the directions the ER receptionist had given her, finally arriving in the lobby of the hospital that served Broken Bow and the surrounding communities. A tired-looking man in a gray jacket and red and white striped bow tie squinted up from behind the counter when she entered. His face was creased like a piece of crumpled tissue paper.

Head high, she marched past him, toward the elevator as if it were the middle of visiting hours, not the middle of the night. At the third floor nurse's station a heavy-set woman, her head bent over paperwork, didn't look up. Frankie located her mother's room and peeked through the view pane. Her mother lay in the bed, eyes closed, an IV drip in her uncasted arm. Relieved when there didn't seem to be any indications of a new injury, she pushed the door open and stepped inside.

She glanced around the room and into the small bathroom, but there was no sign of Bob. Not sure if she was glad he was gone, or angry that he'd deserted her mother, she sat in the bedside chair and touched her mother's hand. In sleep, Mom's face seemed less lined than at home, and Frankie realized the pain she must always carry from her arthritis. She'd have to talk to Dr. Sedgewick about adjusting her pain medication. Beside the bed, a monitor bleeped steadily.

"I'm here, Mom."

Her mother's eyes fluttered open. Frankie watched her

become aware of her surroundings.

"Frankie? What are you doing here?"

"You're my mother. Why wouldn't I be here?"

Mom shifted her position, her movements hampered by the IV and her broken wrist. "May I have some water? My mouth is *so* dry."

Frankie held the plastic container with its flexible straw to her mother's mouth. She brushed a stray lock of hair out of the way. Why hadn't she noticed how it had faded from blonde to white? She swallowed past a lump in her throat. Mom *was* getting older.

"Better," Mom said. "I don't know why they wouldn't let me go home. I got a little dizzy, that's all. It's happened before, and it passes right away."

Frankie almost tipped the water container. "It's happened before? When? Does Dr. Sedgewick know?"

"I don't bother him with little things like that. At my age, if I complained about every little thing, I'd spend half my time in the doctor's office."

"Mom, Bob said they did a CAT scan. Are you okay?"

"Just fine. They didn't find anything." She laughed. "Your father always said I had a head full of empty."

"You're smart as a whip, and Daddy knew it." Frankie set the cup on the bedside table. "Seriously, Mom. They're monitoring your heart. You have to tell the doctors when things don't seem right."

"My heart is perfectly healthy. I'm sure that's exactly what all this monitoring will show, and I'll be out in the morning."

"Bob said he was staying with you tonight." She hesitated, but decided not to mention that Bob said Mom hadn't wanted her around.

"I sent him away. The same way I'm going to send you away. What time is it, anyway?"

Frankie looked at her wrist. In her haste, she hadn't put on a watch. She found the clock on the wall. "Eleven forty-five."

"Well, you go home now and get some sleep. You have to work tomorrow. It's not good to need a substitute, especially when you've only been working a few weeks."

"Tomorrow's Saturday, Mom. And the start of Spring Break, remember?"

Mom blinked. "Of course—whatever they put in this IV has made my mind all fuzzy."

"Molly and I will be here as soon as you're released."

"Molly doesn't need to be here. I'm sure the hospital will scare her unnecessarily. Bob will pick me up." Her tone had taken on its school principal quality.

Frankie gave her mother's hand a squeeze. "He seems to care about you."

Mom settled into her pillow, and smiled. "Yes, he does. Does that bother you?"

Of course it did, but she'd analyze her feelings later. Forcing a smile, Frankie said, "Not if you're happy. Get some sleep." She kissed her mother's forehead and straightened her blanket. Before leaving the room, she listened to the bleeps from the monitor, comforted by their regular pattern. If there were heart problems, wouldn't they be erratic?

In the hall, the nurse glanced up as Frankie passed, but didn't ask questions. Frankie leaned against the wall while she waited for the elevator. By the time it arrived, she felt lighter. Back in control. On the ground floor, she found the green stripe and retraced her steps.

As she rounded the last corner, boots clumped, rubber soles squeaked, and people shouted medical terms she didn't comprehend. Paramedics rushed alongside a gurney, doctors and nurses materialized from double doors, and the smell of smoke mingled with the antiseptic odor of the room. A man, wrapped in a blanket, stood with his back to her, trying to hold the blanket around his shoulders and gesticulate to one of the doctors at the same time. She couldn't hear what he said, but there was a lot of headshaking, followed by some reluctant nodding. He leaned over the gurney, spoke to the man lying there, and then the doctors wheeled the gurney behind a curtain.

Curious, Frankie watched as the man spoke to the receptionist at the desk. There was another bunch of headshaking, but the clerk shrugged and clicked at her keyboard. The man leaned his arms against the counter for a moment, his head bowed into his hands. He signed some papers, turned, and her breath hitched.

It was Jack—or whatever his name really was—from the bar. His face was smeared with soot, giving his beard a piebald appearance. Someone spoke to him, nodded, then turned and disappeared behind a curtain. Silence filled the now-empty room.

Jack stared after the doctor, then slumped and sank into the nearest chair. His eyes caught hers, although she didn't think he was aware she was standing there. His world didn't seem to exist beyond whoever he'd brought to the ER.

Without hesitating, she crossed the waiting room and lowered herself into the chair beside him. He smelled of smoke, pine, and gasoline. His feet tapped the floor in a rapid staccato, seemingly out of his control. His fingers shook as he clutched the blanket around his bare chest.

"Do you want me to call the doctor back for you?" Frankie asked.

Still gazing at the floor, he shook his head. "No," he croaked. "I'm fine."

"I'm no doctor, but it's obvious that you're not. Can I get you some water, Jack?"

This time he looked up, and she knew those eyes—bloodshot and full of anguish—recognized her. In the harsh emergency room lighting, she saw they were the color of the whiskey he drank.

"Gladys?"

"Frances, actually. Frankie. Gladys is my bar name. What happened?"

"Car crash. My father."

He shuddered, and beneath the soot stains, his face faded to the color of parchment. Before she could call out, he clutched her forearm. Despite his condition, his grip was strong. She pried his fingers loose, but held onto his hand. It was frigid, and she cradled it, rubbing gently to transfer some of her warmth. He seemed oblivious to her touch.

"Well, then can I call someone for you? Your mother—does she know about the accident?"

With an uneven breath, he sat up straight. "She's dead."

"Oh, my. In the crash? I'm so sorry. I didn't think."

Shaking his head, he said, "No, she died years ago." He stared into space with hollow eyes.

"Let me get someone to help."

"No. No doctor. Need to catch my breath is all."

Still holding his hand, which she noted was warming slightly, she talked to him using the same tone she used to calm a rescued stray. "My dad died when I was a kid, too. Somehow, we think they'll live forever, and then something happens and you realize you'll be alone someday. But we still refuse to believe it, don't we? My mom was admitted tonight, but I know she's going to be fine. Same with your father. No way would they both leave us, right?"

Color returned to his face. He gave her a wry grin.

"Yeah. Pop's too stubborn to die. Not like this, anyway."

From the counter, the receptionist called Jack's name. He jumped to his feet, letting the blanket fall to the chair. Without giving Frankie a glance, he strode to the desk. Back straight, shoulders squared, probably unaware he wasn't wearing a shirt. Braced for the worst, Frankie thought.

A short while later, a woman in a white coat approached. She smiled, said something, and Jack lifted his head toward the ceiling. For several minutes they spoke in quiet murmurs Frankie couldn't understand. He shook the woman's hand, and she raised an index finger before pivoting and leaving the counter. Jack glanced downward, then leaned against the counter, and Frankie saw the deep breaths he was taking. The woman returned with a green scrub shirt and handed it to Jack. He shrugged into it and shook her hand once again.

When he turned toward Frankie, there was no disguising the relief in his eyes.

She smiled. "I told you he'd be all right."

"The doctor said it didn't look too bad, but they're going to keep him a day or two to make sure. Nothing I can do and I need to get out of this place." He swayed and grabbed the back of the chair.

Frankie took his elbow. "You're still shaky. I think you should stick around here, where someone can keep an eye on you."

His mouth narrowed. "No, I need to get away. It's complicated, but I don't want anyone to know I'm here." He stared over her shoulder, as if it took a long time for the words to line up before he spoke. "Can I impose on you for a lift to a motel? I'd like to be nearby."

He lifted his arms shoulder height, palms upward, and did a slow pivot. "I'm not armed. And I don't bite. Promise. In a few minutes I'll be out of your hair."

Logic said to give him cab fare. She checked her wallet, and didn't think three dollars would get him anywhere. She remembered his gentle touch on the dance floor. Right now, he was in no condition to do anything to hurt her, and she'd have him at a motel in a few minutes. Instinct trumped logic. "My car's outside. Can you walk?"

"Thanks. I really appreciate it." He stood, swayed, and she reached for his elbow again. He backed away. "I'm fine."

"Right," she muttered. "Follow me."

What on earth was she doing, agreeing to give a lift to a man she'd met a few hours ago? She pulled her keys out of her purse. Then again, this wasn't Boston. This was Broken Bow, Montana, where people left their doors unlocked. Nothing exciting ever happened in Broken Bow.

She headed for the cluster of motels beside the highway. At the Holiday Inn half a mile from the hospital, "No Vacancy" flashed in red neon above a "Welcome, ASM" sign.

"Looks like there's no room there," she said. "Let's check the next one."

Her passenger shifted in his seat and patted his pockets. "Problem," he said. "I seem to have rushed out without my wallet." He raked his fingers through his hair, looked at them, and wiped them on his jeans. "I know we just met, but if you could lend me enough to cover a night, I'll pay it back."

"I can't. I mean, I would, but I've only got a few dollars with me. Do you live far?"

He nodded. "In the mountains. Outside of Stanton. Little over an hour." One corner of his mouth twitched, but there was no humor in it. "Unless you've got lights and sirens."

"I'm about fifteen minutes away." What was it about him that had words falling out of her mouth before her brain kicked in? The pain in his eyes? Or the thought that giving a stranger a lift was as close to an adventure as she would ever see in Broken Bow, Montana?

"Thanks. I promise, I'm no bother. I'll wait outside if it'll make you more comfortable."

"You're not a deadly killer, are you?" she said with a smile.

It took him a beat to respond, a beat that sent a shiver down her spine. Then his expression softened and she saw raw honesty behind the pain.

"You're safe with me, Frankie."

For whatever the reason, she believed him. Besides, he had no way of knowing there wasn't a big, burly man in the house. Or a hundred-pound Rottweiler. With added confidence, she pointed the Cavalier toward home.

Aware of someone chattering beside him, Ryan clawed his way out of a nightmare. The lights he thought were explosions transformed into streetlights and car headlights. Bathed in sweat, he wiped his face with the back of his arm.

Damn, he'd been through a hell of a lot worse than this, and hadn't come apart. Losing someone who was *like* family didn't come close to almost losing someone who *was* family. The memory of seeing the crash site, thinking his father had died, made him shake again. The chattering continued, and he focused his attention on Frankie.

She glanced in his direction. "You're awake. I've got the heat on, but it's not very effective. Are you cold?"

"A little." He rubbed his hands together. "I left the blanket in the waiting room. No big deal—it belongs to the paramedics anyway."

"We're almost at my place." She chewed on her lower lip. "You like the Three Elks? They say you're in there every night."

"Passes the time."

"What do you do?"

Small talk. Cover stories. Keep it simple. "Between jobs." He watched as they navigated through Broken Bow's town center, past a park, and through a residential neighborhood.

Frankie pulled into a driveway and yanked on the parking brake. "We're here," she said.

His knee protested his earlier run down the mountain as he

slid out of the car. He shivered. The Cavalier's heater had done little to dispel the chill that had tunneled into his bones when he'd seen his Mustang in flames.

He stared at the large wooden house with its sagging porch. The weathered Victorian huddled under the oak trees didn't match the effervescent Frankie. "This is your place?"

"The old family homestead. Dad got a good deal on it right after Claire was born. She's my older sister. Anyway, it's been home ever since. Except I was living in Boston until Claire said Mom needed me, and she and James—that's her husband—moved to London so she couldn't live here anymore."

"Frankie."

"What?"

"You're babbling."

"Sorry. I do that when I'm nervous."

"There's no need to be nervous. I can sleep in the car. Or on the porch."

"No, that's stupid. You're shivering, and it's warmer inside. Come on." She trotted up the steps.

Inside, she pointed up a wooden staircase. "Up there. End of the hall on the left."

He hauled himself up the stairs with Frankie a safe distance behind him. He smiled. If she'd touch his screaming knee, he'd be at her mercy.

At the end of the hall, she moved ahead of him and opened the door. "Here you go." After flipping on the light, she crossed to the bed and shifted throw pillows to one side before folding back a floral comforter.

He zeroed in on an easy chair in the corner, sat and bent to unlace his boots. Without lifting his head, he pried them off, waiting for the wave of pain to pass.

"You need anything else?" she asked.

"A couple of aspirin would be nice, if you've got them."

"I'll be right back," Frankie said. "Bathroom's through there and there's an extra blanket in the bottom drawer of the dresser."

She disappeared, and he limped across the room to the bed, punching Dalton's number into his cell. His only coherent thought was someone had found him and sabotaged his Mustang. His best bet was for whoever did this to think they'd succeeded. For now, he was dead.

He hoped the medical staff would play along with his request to keep his father's accident off the radar. The clerk had been willing to register Pop as John Daniels, as long as the insurance information was right. Daniels. That name had come out of the blue when the paramedics and cops had arrived. He thought about Frankie. Maybe not totally out of the blue.

Ryan explained the situation, told Dalt where he was.

"Your daddy okay?" Dalton's easy drawl calmed him.

"Concussion. Cracked ribs. I told them to keep him an extra day, while I regroup. Dammit, Dalt. It might not have been an accident. In which case, it should be me in the hospital. Or worse." A shadow moved across the hall. "Gotta go."

"Hang tight. Lay low. I'll be there in the morning."

Ryan set the phone on the night table. Frankie came in carrying a glass of water. She handed him the water and dropped two blue capsules into his hand.

"I asked for aspirin. What are these?"

"Drugstore sleeping pills. Mom says one knocks her out. You're twice her size, so you get two."

"I don't need sleeping pills. Aspirin will be fine."

"You don't understand. I'll sleep better if I know you're sleeping."

"I'm not going to hurt you Frankie. If you thought I would, I'd still be at the hospital."

She looked at him, chewing her lower lip. Then she sat in the chair and crossed her arms.

51

"Sometimes I act before I think things all the way through. You looked like you needed a friend. But I don't really know anything about you, except you care about your father and you're a good dancer. And your name's not Jack Daniels."

He set the pills on the table. "You're right. But my knee is killing me, and my head aches. I'm going to get into bed, if that's all right with you. Then we can talk."

When he pulled himself to his feet and reached for the button of his jeans, she locked eyes with him, as if she knew he was testing her.

"You mind?" He twirled a forefinger in the air.

Instead of turning, she flicked off the light, leaving her backlit in the dim glow from the hallway. He shrugged and turned around, grabbing the bedpost for support. With his jeans on the floor, he slipped between the sheets. They were cool against his skin, and he glanced at the pills. Maybe a night of oblivion was what he needed. Then again, he had no idea what kind of pills they were. He let them lie beside his phone.

Frankie's voice came from the shadows. "You said you learned to dance for work. Are you a dance instructor?"

He laughed. "No. Navy man. Or I used to be."

"A dancing sailor." He could hear the smile in her voice. "Not a lot of call for that in Broken Bow. Or Stanton, for that matter."

"Nope. I came back to visit my father. I grew up on a ranch in the mountains."

She yawned, and he couldn't help but yawn in response. The post-adrenaline crash rolled over him like a tidal wave. The mattress seemed to envelop him. His eyes felt like they were filled with sand.

He blinked. "You're tired. I'm tired. We could both use some sleep, and I'll be gone in the morning." He blinked again, but his eyes didn't reopen.

"You're right. Pleasant dreams, Jack."

He heard the door close and relaxed into the mattress. "It's Ryan," he whispered. Sleep drew him in. . . .

. . . Until the nightmare came after him like a twenty-five-ton Bradley fighting vehicle.

Ryan fought toward the surface of the terror, to wake up and end it, but the images wouldn't release him. In the swirling darkness, a tiny angel appeared backlit by an amber glow. He knew he was dying. Or had the angel come for Pop? He tried to cry out.

Something tickled his nose. The angel spoke. "Here. Mr. Snuggles will make the bad dreams go away." The angel kissed him, a feather-soft brush on his cheek. Slowly, he drifted back to sleep.

CHAPTER 5

The aroma of fresh coffee trickled through Ryan's consciousness. Sunlight filtered behind his eyelids. Last night burst through the cocoon of sleep and he jerked awake, fumbling for his cell phone. He squinted at the display. No messages, no new calls. He punched Dalton's number. "Talk to me."

"I'm outside Missoula. Should be at your door in under an hour. Any word on your daddy?"

"No, but the hospital would have called if anything happened. I need to check on him."

"Understood. We'll take care of everything."

Ryan's protesting bladder insisted on being the next order of business, and he stepped into the bathroom. One look in the mirror explained Frankie's insistence on the sleeping pills. Covered in blood and soot, he was a scary sight. Last night, he must have looked ten times as frightening. Surprised she'd taken him in at all, he turned on the water for a quick shower.

Although he was stuck with his dirty jeans, he found a t-shirt folded at the foot of his bed. He shrugged into it and picked up the stuffed dog he'd tossed aside. Shaking his head in bemusement, he followed his nose to the kitchen.

Frankie had her back to him at the stove. Her hair, the color of summer honey, hung loose to her shoulders. He took a moment to admire the way her jeans hugged the curves of her rump before he surveyed the room. The kitchen was large and homey, with yellow walls bordered in floral wallpaper, and a pine table with six chairs. Fabric cushions tied to each seat matched the wallpaper.

From one chair, a young girl, her strawberry-blonde hair pulled into two ribboned pigtails, turned huge blue eyes toward him. For an instant, she wasn't fair-haired, but dark, and her blue eyes were deep chocolate. Carmelita Forcada's face blurred in front of him. He shook it off.

When he smiled at her, the requisite facial muscles felt stiff from lack of use. He cleared his throat. "Good morning, Angel. I think this might be yours." He held out the stuffed dog he'd been embracing when he woke up.

"I'm Molly, not Angel," the girl said. "And that's Mr. Snuggles."

"I'm . . . Jack," Ryan said.

The child gave him a serious stare, her eyes narrowing. "He makes my bad dreams go away. Did he work for you?"

"He did. Thank you." He put the dog in her pudgy hands.

"Molly," Frankie said. "I told you to stay in bed."

"But I had to go potty, and I heard the man having bad dreams, so I gave him my night-light and I let Mr. Snuggles sleep with him." She turned those cobalt blue magnets back at him. "I'm five, so I don't need him every night. Besides, I got to sleep with Mommy."

Frankie turned back to the stove, but not before a pink tinge flushed her cheeks. Hell, she shouldn't be embarrassed. Smart thing to do with a total stranger in the house. She probably had a baseball bat by the bed, too. He glanced at the table again. Three place settings. Her mother was in the hospital. No father? No husband? He glanced at her left hand. No wedding band. He tried to remember what she'd said about her family last night, but it was like trying to hold onto smoke.

He forced himself to focus on the child. "Thank you again."

She gave him a solemn smile, then began a mumbled

55

conversation with the dog.

Ryan stepped toward Frankie and lowered his voice. "Don't be ashamed of protecting your daughter."

She shrugged. "I've always trusted my instincts. They're usually right."

He couldn't help but notice the way her eyes darted to the large chef's knife on the cutting board. He smiled. "Well, I'm relieved to know I wasn't so pathetic that *you* gave me a night-light and a dog to hug. If you'll tell me where your washing machine is, I'll deal with my sheets. They're kind of grimy."

"Forget it." Her eyes went to his chest. "Sorry about the shirt, but it was the only one in your size. They gave everyone extra-large after the race."

Ryan glanced down. Filled with worries about Pop, he'd pulled it on without paying attention, pleased that it fit. A deep pink ribbon with "Run for the Cure" printed below it covered the front of the pale pink shirt.

"Nothing to apologize for. I should have one myself. That was how my mother died." Fifteen years, and the words still didn't come easy.

She must have sensed his discomfort. "Umm . . . how about some coffee?"

"Coffee would be great. Black is fine." He found a mug at a place setting on the table and brought it to the coffee maker. Frankie was pouring when the child spoke.

"Mommy, is 'fuckit' a bad word?"

Frankie stopped mid-pour. Her eyes snapped across the room to her daughter. "It most certainly is, young lady. Where did you hear that?"

"The man said it in the night." She held her hand out, palm up, smiling in apparent anticipation.

Shit, what did he know about kids? "Um . . . I'm sorry. I was having a nightmare."

"You have to give me a quarter." She looked at her mother. "Or is 'fuckit' a dollar word?"

"Oh, it's definitely a dollar word. But our guest didn't bring his money to breakfast. I'll get you a dollar later. It's time to eat."

The youngster smiled at him. "Mommy's making me happy pancakes."

Ryan, who was comfortable hiding in the jungle, trekking across the desert, or scaling a mountain, had never felt more out of his element than right now in this Mayberry kitchen. He turned, expecting Aunt Bea to wander in with a basket of fresh eggs.

"Sit down, please," Frankie said. "Juice is on the table."

Ryan pulled out his chair and sat. His orders were to stay low. Dalton was on his way. Meanwhile, he was starved, and when in Mayberry. . . .

Frankie opened the oven door, and using mitts shaped like chickens, pulled out a platter of pancakes. She set it on a padded mat, then slid into her seat at the other end of the table. She forked two pancakes onto her daughter's plate.

"Why don't you pass me your plate," she said to Ryan. "The platter is hot."

Ryan did as she asked, then gazed at three pancakes, each with two round eyes and a curved grin, staring up at him from his plate. His amusement must have shown, because Frankie laughed.

"Happy pancakes. It's one of my few specialties. You start the eyes and mouth and let them brown a bit before you pour the rest of the batter. I'm not much of a cook."

The child was busy eating, with obvious gusto. For about five seconds, Ryan thought of what it might be like to have a family. He quashed the idea. These homespun moments were few and far between to begin with, and too many people he cared about were gone. Getting attached brought nothing but pain.

"These are good," he said around a mouthful of hot pancakes drenched in maple syrup. "Although I'm not used to my food staring at me."

Frankie chuckled. "I usually turn mine over before I eat them."

The child pushed her empty plate to the center of the table. "I'm done. Can I watch cartoons?"

"After you brush your teeth. But only for a little while. We have to get Gramma soon."

Stuffing the dog under her arm, she skipped out of the room.

Ryan turned the coffee mug in his fingers. "Thank you for last night."

"No problem." Frankie got up and cleared the dishes from the table. When she bent over to put the plates in the dishwasher, Ryan let his gaze linger on her round behind again. One look, he told himself. In a little while, he'd be out of here and he'd never see her again.

The doorbell chimed. Frankie glanced at her wrist, a questioning expression on her face.

"That's probably my ride," he said. "I'll be out of your hair soon." He followed Frankie to the living room, feeling lighter than he had in weeks.

While she peered through the viewing pane, Ryan lifted a corner of the living room curtains. "That's him," he said.

Frankie nodded and opened the door. Dalton, wearing his standard off-duty attire of jeans, plaid wool shirt over a black turtleneck, and lightweight hiking boots, stood there, and Ryan felt a piece of his universe fall back into place.

"Frankie, this is Dalton. He's come to take me off your hands. Thanks again for everything." Without waiting for a response, he stepped out onto the porch, half-closing the door after him. "Am I glad to see you, man."

Dalton clapped Ryan on the shoulder, then shook his head, grinned, and pulled him into a bear hug.

"You do have a way of getting into things, don't you, pardner?"

Unexpectedly swamped by the concern in Dalton's drawl and the warmth of his embrace, it took Ryan a second to find his voice. When he did, the words came out in a rush.

"Before anything else, I need to know about Pop. Can you get into the hospital, check on him? Nobody knows I'm here, and the doctor last night said she didn't think it was serious, but—"

"But he's your daddy. I know. Calm down, and let's talk for a minute, okay?"

Behind him, the door opened and Frankie stepped onto the porch. Ryan wondered why he felt so protected now that she'd joined them.

"Ma'am," Dalton said. "If it's not too much trouble, I could use a cup of coffee."

Ryan wasn't sure how to interpret the flop in his belly at Dalton's request. Was it anxiety at the delay, or the way Dalton's eyes had raked up and down Frankie's body?

"Of course. I'll be right back." Frankie popped inside like a woodchuck into its hole.

"What was that about?" Ryan demanded. "We need to get moving. This isn't a coffee klatch."

"Cool your jets, Harper. We can't do much until visiting hours start, and this place should be under the radar." He gave Ryan a piercing stare. "Isn't it?"

"Yes. I wasn't so out of it that I'd have missed a tail." Ryan raked his fingers through his hair. "But it's Daniels, not Harper. Better for her not to know who I am."

"Daniels? Don't tell me. Jack."

He nodded. "That's what she called me. She knows it's not

my name, but she seems willing to play along. At least, she hasn't asked any questions."

"Shadows in the night, like always. But I notice you gave her *my* name."

"Only half of it." Ryan grinned and punched Dalton's bicep. "Man, I've been going fucking nuts."

"That's another dollar, Jack." Frankie came out onto the porch, carrying two coffee mugs.

Ryan glanced through the doorway, but no blue-eyed strawberry-blonde appeared with her hand out. "Crap. I forgot. Sorry."

"That one's only a quarter."

"Pay the lady, Dalt." He shook his head at Dalton's quizzical expression. "House rules. There's a kid."

Dalton nodded. He pulled out his wallet and extended a ten. "I'm not sure we're going to be able to break old habits, ma'am. Consider this a retainer."

Frankie set the mugs on the porch rail and smiled. "No charge today."

Dalton reached over, took a cup and settled onto a wooden bench. "Thank you."

"I'll leave you to your catching up," Frankie said. "I need to pick up my mother from the hospital." She disappeared again.

Dalton took a sip of coffee and balanced the cup on his thigh. "If you don't want anyone calling your daddy's room, we need to wait for morning rounds to be over before we check on him."

Ryan raised his eyebrows. Dalton was an expert at going anywhere, anytime, unnoticed. "I figured you'd put on some scrubs and blend right in."

"Not so easy in a small town hospital. You know what room he's in?"

Ryan caught himself before he swore. "He hadn't been admitted when I left. And I told them he was avoiding a vindictive ex-wife, not to put any calls through or give out his room number. Of course, that includes me. I guess my brain stopped a few floors short of the penthouse last night."

"Hang on a minute," Dalton said. "Is the little lady's mama at the same hospital as your daddy?"

Ryan nodded. "That's where we met."

"Think she'd help us? She's got a reason to be there. Nobody'd ask questions."

Ryan ground that one around for a minute. Dalton had a point. Would Frankie go along with it? He knocked on the door.

CHAPTER 6

Frankie watched Dalton cross the hospital parking lot toward her car, his long stride deliberate. Her nerves kicked into overdrive. She took a deep breath and tightened her ponytail.

Dalton tapped on the window. "You're up, little lady. It's carnations, with red and white heart balloons. You remember what to say?"

As if she hadn't been rehearsing it for the last twenty minutes. "Got it."

She opened the car door and slipped out. "Come on, Molly. Remember, quiet—"

"As a mouse. I know, I know. No running, inside voices." She climbed out of the car, Mr. Snuggles tucked under one arm. "Can I bring my book?"

"Sure. Maybe Gramma wants to hear it."

"Piece of cake, right?" Dalton raised his fist, and Frankie tapped her knuckles against his.

"Piece of cake," Molly echoed.

Dalton smiled and tweaked Molly's nose before heading to his car, where Ryan waited.

Inside the hospital, Frankie, with Molly dutifully in tow, went to the third floor and pushed open the door to her mother's room.

Molly darted inside, then stopped, apparently remembering the ground rules. "Hi, Gramma. Are you all better?"

"I am, Peanut. Come give me a kiss."

Molly tiptoed to the side of the bed and clutched the bedrail. "I brought *Green Eggs and Ham*."

"That's good. Did you bring me clean clothes?"

"Mommy has them."

Frankie leaned over and kissed her mother's cheek. "And your toothbrush. The doctor said you can go home, but he wants you to follow up with Dr. Sedgewick as soon as possible. He'll have your test results sent over."

"Such a fuss over nothing." Her mother peeked into the plastic bag Frankie handed her. She pulled out the red polar fleece blazer, then frowned. "Where's the elephant pin? I know I always leave it on the lapel."

"That's the way it was in the closet. You probably took it off when you had it cleaned and forgot to put it back."

"I don't remember sending it to the cleaners." She shrugged. "Maybe you're right. Maybe my head is full of empty after all."

"I'm sure it'll be on your dresser, or in your jewelry box," Frankie said. She looked toward the door. "I'll be back in a couple of minutes, Mom. I think I saw the mother of one of my kids down the hall. I should say hello. Molly, you stay with Gramma, okay?"

Her mother frowned. "I told you Bob was coming to get me."

"Why don't you call Bob and tell him not to bother? I'm here, and no need for him to make an extra trip." Not waiting for an answer, Frankie walked down the corridor, keeping her stride as purposeful as she could. Her pulse picked up. She chastised herself. This was hardly a big deal. Still, the relief she'd seen on Jack's face as the three of them had devised the plan had filled her with unexpected warmth. At each door, she paused and peeked through the viewing pane.

Near the end of the hall, she found what she was looking for. The huge floral arrangement, topped with big red and white heart-shaped balloons. She couldn't remember which television show she'd seen the ploy on, but Dalton had gone to the gift shop and bought the arrangement, asking the hospital to deliver it to Mr. Daniels. She inched the door open and edged inside.

A man, his skin creased with years of exposure to the sun, sat up in bed watching television. His hair, tousled in a serious case of bed-head, lent him an endearing quality. She closed the door and crossed to his bed.

"Mornin'," he said. "You don't look like you're going to poke me, or is the no-uniform look supposed to catch me off guard?"

"No, I'm not a nurse." She looked closer and saw a little of Jack around the eyes. "You must be Mr. Daniels?"

The man studied her. "Might be. Who wants to know?"

"Your son. You were in a car crash, right?"

He eyed her, still wary. "How about you tell me who you are, and why you're here, first?"

She nodded. Jack had made it very clear what she was supposed to say. "My name's Frankie. Your son, who's calling himself Jack Daniels for now, came with you last night. There was a car crash, an explosion. He can't come up himself because someone might think it was him in the crash, and he'd like them to go on thinking that. The ER doctor said she'd go along with it, which is why you're supposed to be Mr. Daniels." The man's expression didn't change. She recited her final line. "He said to tell you he's glad you're not moving to Albuquerque."

Concern replaced wariness. "How is he?"

"He's fine. Worried, though. My mom's being discharged this morning, and I said I'd check on you while I was here."

"Tell him I'm all right. It takes more than a bump on my head to put me down." He tapped his forehead and grinned. "Hard as a rock."

"He'll be relieved. Do you need him to send someone for you?"

"I'm here one more day, they said, and no. I got along without him for ten years. I can swing another day or two. Got plenty of my own friends."

"I'm glad you're all right, sir. I'll tell . . . Jack."

He glanced at her, then back at the television.

Frankie stepped into the hall and turned on her cell phone to call Dalton. She frowned at the display when there was no signal. Well, she'd be downstairs in a few minutes. Jack could wait a little longer for his good news. She put the phone back in her purse.

As she walked back to her mother's room, she wondered what would have kept Jack from his father for ten years. But then, she'd hardly seen her mother since leaving Broken Bow for college. Frankie shook off the old memories. She'd done what needed to be done, gotten her degree, a job, and the best daughter on the planet.

By the time she got back to her mother's room, Mom was dressed, sitting on the bed with Mr. Snuggles in her lap, listening to Molly read *Green Eggs and Ham*. Bob sat in the visitor's chair, a bouquet of flowers across his thighs.

"Good morning, Frankie," he said. "I can take it from here. We're waiting for the official wheelchair escort."

Crouched low in Dalton's car in the hospital parking lot, Ryan struggled to control his anxiety about his father. He checked his watch. Had Dalton only been gone seventeen minutes?

Last night Wolf had found Pop, unconscious, a good twenty feet from the car. In that frantic eternity while he had waited for the paramedics, his father drifting in and out of consciousness, his training had kicked in. He told the cops his father had swerved to avoid a deer, and about the flammables in the trunk. They'd filed their report, and arranged for the wreckage to be towed to Josh's place. Wolf he'd ordered home. The dog had refused to leave, staying at Pop's side until both men were loaded into the ambulance. Then he'd seen him trotting toward the ranch, where Ryan knew he would find food and water.

He'd done everything by the book last night. Talking to Pop, keeping him calm had been the glue that held him together. Until they got to the hospital and the doctors took charge, when every iota of control shattered, and he'd been at the mercy of a cocktail waitress with hair the color of honey and a smile that almost made the world right.

The way Dalton grinned at Frankie sent his hackles up. He reminded himself that Dalton's charm was an ingrained part of his personality, and the way he made people feel at ease was an asset to the team. He was this nice to everyone. Which didn't make him feel any better. Neither did the knuckle tap Dalton and Frankie exchanged before she and her daughter headed toward the hospital entrance.

He trained his eye on the hospital entrance, watching for Dalton's return. When he spied his friend's easy stride, he itched to meet him halfway and pump him for information. Instead, he waited for Dalton to join him. As if the car would be too confining, Dalton crossed to the far side of the vehicle and leaned against the fender.

Ryan opened the passenger door and slid out. With the door between them, he searched Dalton's face. "Any news?"

"Hang on. She and the kid are probably just getting upstairs now. We had to wait until they made a delivery run from the gift shop."

Ryan dragged his hands through his hair. "Right. It's—"

Dalton twisted to face him. "Tell me what happened. I've gotta say, I've seen you lookin' better on a six day surveillance in the jungle."

"I'm fine. Tired is all. You tell me what's going on."

Dalton didn't press. He never did. Instead, he looked at you, his eyes boring into your skull until you told him everything. How you ate out of habit, food nothing but cardboard which didn't always stay down. How you wandered through the forest, staring at leaves swirling down the current of a half-frozen stream. Or how you sat on the porch, counting the stars, afraid to face your nightmares, until a dog grabbed your pants leg and pulled you inside.

Somehow, Ryan resisted.

Dalton spoke, his drawl barely evident. "It's touchy. Nobody really believed you'd sabotage a mission, much less two, without a damn good reason."

"You're using the past tense. They believe it now?"

Dalton lowered his head, scuffed his boots along a stripe of the parking slot. "I don't know. But you walked out of there, and Blackie didn't stop you. In the business, it's—let's say that everyone's been tempted, and everyone knows that *they'd* never sell out, but they're willing to believe anyone else would."

Rage burned in Ryan's chest. "I worked with those people for years. Covered their sixes, trusted them with mine. How can they believe—?"

"Until we show them what happened, it's easier to believe that someone did, especially when that someone isn't around to defend himself."

Ryan didn't miss the "we" and allowed himself a flicker of hope. "What about Blackthorne?" Only Dalton called him Blackie.

For the first week, he expected a call from his boss telling him this was merely another covert assignment, and that he was supposed to be ferreting out the real leak. When the call never came, Ryan figured he was the scapegoat Blackthorne needed to keep his company's image secure. He could hear him talking to potential clients.

We had a minor problem, but it's taken care of now. You can be assured we're one hundred percent reliable.

He cast a glance over his shoulder toward the hospital. No sign of Frankie. He looked at his watch. He checked his cell phone before remembering they told her to use Dalton's number.

"What's taking so long?" Panic surged again. Had someone been waiting by his father's room and grabbed her? Was his father in the midst of a medical emergency? Ryan had tried to explain the need for subterfuge to Pop, but he wasn't sure how much his father had absorbed. He hoped Pop would remember he was supposed to be John Daniels.

"Check your phone, Dalt. You forget to charge it?"

"Cool it. Most of the job is waiting. You know that." Dalton's expression shifted. He reached for his pocket. After looking at the display on his cell, Dalton brought it to his ear.

Ryan's heart stopped while he tried to read Dalton's expression. Damn, the man had the best poker face on the team.

Frankie gave Bob a mechanical smile. "I know Mom said you could pick her up, but I think I should drive her home. I'm already here, and Molly wants to spend some time with her grandmother."

"Actually, dear, Bob and I are going to Lolo Hot Springs for a few days. We'd already made plans before this little setback. You dashed out so fast I didn't have a chance to tell you."

Frankie swallowed, trying to keep any look of shock off her face. "Um . . . are you sure that's wise, considering? What if something else happens?"

Bob crossed to the bed and took her mother's hand. "Then I'll make sure she gets help. It's not like we're going camping in the wilderness." Bob's tone was firm. Frankie looked at him, and he winked. "She'll be in good hands with me. Nothing to worry about."

In good hands. Frankie tried not to let her mind go there.

"That's right, dear," her mother said. "I've already asked the doctor, and he said fine. I can't see Dr. Sedgewick until next week, anyway. I made reservations at a nice little Bed and Breakfast, and we can enjoy the springs. Trust me, we won't be roughing it."

"But your wrist?" Frankie protested. "You'll get it wet in the springs."

"There's a clever invention called a plastic bag. I've been managing to bathe at home. Why should it be different?"

Because at home Brenda or I help you. Not Bob. And who's footing the bill for this little getaway?

Frankie vowed to look at the bank account again as soon as she got home. She studied Bob. Well-groomed, a decent haircut, but the clothes were probably discount-store issue. His trousers were a little threadbare around the cuffs, and she could see the worn crease in the collar of his polo.

Good grief. Three quarters of the people in Broken Bow dressed like that, especially on a Saturday. Comfort over style. Idle speculation was *not* going to get her anywhere.

Bob cleared his throat. "Tell you what, Frankie. If it'll make you feel better, why don't you and Molly take Anna home? You can help her pack, and I'll come by a little later." He stroked her mother's cheek. He spoke softly, but didn't seem to care that Frankie heard. "I'll stop and get some candles and a bottle of wine, my little Anna Banana."

"I guess that's the plan, then," Frankie said. *Anna Banana?* Mom was sixty-eight.

An orderly appeared, pushing a wheelchair. "Mrs. Castor? Time to get you out of here."

She gathered her mother's things. "I'll pull the car around, and Molly and I will meet you out front." She leaned down and kissed her. "See you in a little bit."

Molly dashed ahead and pressed the down button on the elevator. Frankie sorted through her thoughts while they waited. She thought back to her sister's warning before she'd left for London. *Keep an eye on Bob.* For what? Claire never could be direct. She must have missed the geometry class that said the shortest distance between two points was a straight line.

Okay, her mother was dating. Beyond dinner-and-a-movie. She pushed the images as far out of her head as she could. Could that be why Claire didn't trust Bob? Not because he was a shady character, out to exploit Mom, but because he was getting too close to her? Twelve years older than Frankie, Claire had known their dad a lot longer than she had. Maybe Claire felt betrayed. She couldn't imagine Claire coming out and saying she thought Mom was having an affair. Not Claire. Claire had trouble buying tampons without blushing.

Enough. In the lobby, Frankie brought up Dalton's number on her phone again. With one eye on the signal strength, she walked toward the exit, and as soon as she saw three bars, she pushed the button.

Dalton picked up after the third ring.

"He's fine," she said. Molly ran ahead to activate the automatic doors. "I'm on my way to my car."

"I see you. Hang on. I'll let you talk to—Jack."

With one hand, Frankie fished through her purse for her keys while waiting for Jack to come on line.

"I can unlock the door, Mommy." Molly snatched the keys from her hand and darted toward the Cavalier.

"Wait, Molly."

Jack's voice interrupted. "Did you talk to him? Is he all right?"

"Fine and feisty. Molly, slow down."

Molly skipped toward the Cavalier. A green car barreled through the parking lot, coming straight at her.

"Molly! Stop!" Frankie yelled.

She ran, flailing her arms to get the driver's attention, but the driver didn't slow. Molly kept skipping.

In a split-second that lasted an eternity, brakes squealed, tires skidded, and Dalton appeared, tucking Molly under his arm like a football. The green car sped off toward the emergency room entrance.

Frankie closed the distance to Molly at a dead run. She grabbed Molly to her. Trembling, she raised her gaze to Dalton's. "Thank you."

"She's fine." He set Molly down and patted her head. "Next time, sugar, you don't go into a street without a grownup."

"But it's not a street," Molly said, her voice petulant. "I know how to cross a street."

"Mr. Dalton's right," Frankie said. "Parking lots are like streets, only worse, because you never know which way to look. You should always hold someone's hand."

Molly pouted. "I had Mr. Snuggles."

"Mr. Snuggles is not a grownup," Frankie said. "You hold my hand now. Let's go say good-bye to Mr. Daniels." She half-dragged a reluctant Molly to Dalton's car.

Ryan leaned against the hood of the car, rubbing his knee. Ignoring the scowl on his face, she marched up to him. "Good-bye, Jack. I'm glad your father's all right. He said he'd find a ride home."

"Hang on." Reaching over his head, he pulled off the t-shirt she'd given him. "Here you go. Thanks."

Frankie didn't know where to look. His whiskey eyes were troubled, which triggered her maternal instincts. But when she lowered her gaze to avoid them, she saw his chest, dusted with light brown hair that didn't hide a well-developed six-pack, which triggered entirely different instincts.

"Please. Keep it. Consider it a gift—to remember your mother."

"I'll get my own," he said, his voice husky. He dropped it into her arms and got in the car.

Dalton slid past her into the driver's seat and started the engine. He tapped his fingers to an imaginary hat brim. "Take it easy, little ladies."

She watched the two men drive away, and thought about next Tuesday, when she'd be at the Three Elks again. Would Jack show up?

So what if he did? Men like Jack didn't want a woman with a kid. She'd learned that long ago. And she didn't need a man, unless that man wanted to be Molly's father. She and Molly had been on their own from day one, and were doing fine.

"Let's go, Mommy."

Frankie gripped Molly's hand until they got to her car.

Waiting at the hospital's patient pickup point, Frankie watched the orderly push her mother's wheelchair. Bob rested a hand on her mother's shoulder, and her good hand covered it. She was smiling up at him.

Bob pulled the passenger door open and helped her mother into the car. He leaned across and fastened her seatbelt. Frankie stared straight ahead.

"I'll see you in about an hour," Bob said.

Frankie twisted the key in the ignition, and the engine squealed.

"Can we go on a picnic, Gramma? Mommy said I could pick something special to do on vacation."

"Not today. But when we get home, you can help me pack my overnight bag."

"Are you going on a sleepover? I went on a sleepover to Katie Sue's house in Boston. We made popcorn and hot chocolate. And we had a sleepover yesterday with Mr. Jack. I gave him Mr. Snuggles to use."

"I'm sure your mommy will tell me all about it," Mom said.

Her school principal look was on in full force.

Frankie's face flamed. She fixed her gaze straight ahead. "It wasn't a real sleepover with Jack, Molly. He had his own room. You and I had the sleepover in my room, remember?"

"Are you and Bob going to have a real sleepover, Gramma?"

Frankie darted her eyes in her mother's direction. *She* wasn't blushing. Frankie drove out of the parking lot, trying to think of popcorn and hot chocolate instead of candles and wine. Or stuffed dogs. Or whiskey-colored eyes filled with pain.

CHAPTER 7

Ryan waited while Dalton dug through the trunk and emerged with a Longhorns sweatshirt. He tossed it across the seat.

"Thanks." Ryan pulled it on, only then aware he'd been cold.

"I kinda liked you in pink," Dalton said with a grin.

Dalton started the car. Ryan's heart still flapped against his ribcage like a pheasant caught in a snare. He'd seen Molly darting across the parking lot, and his damn knee had given out before he could get around the car. If it hadn't been for Dalton . . . damn kids. Always doing the unexpected. Hell, keeping people safe was part of their job, and in a split second, in a hospital parking lot, *for God's sake,* they could have lost another innocent life. Just because they weren't on assignment in the middle of nowhere was no reason to get complacent. Bad things happened everywhere.

Dalton's expression said he was thinking the same thing. "You're not going to charge me a buck if I swear, are you?"

Ryan shook his head.

"Crap. I can't believe she nearly got hit. Cute little critter, seemed too savvy to pull a stunt like that."

"I should have gotten to her," Ryan said, trying not to see Carmelita in Colombia. "Damn knee couldn't take the torque when I tried to get around the car." He rubbed the offending joint.

"Maybe we both had something else on our minds. Civilization makes you drop your guard."

"After last night, I don't think we can take that risk. Consider this an eye opener."

Dalton drove to the end of the parking lot. "Where to?"

"Left," Ryan said. "Then onto the highway. I want to take a closer look at the crash site."

"You have any idea who wants you dead? Assuming it wasn't an accident."

Ryan shook his head. "I was hoping you might shed some light on that one. Hell, I'm assuming it was one of those last two missions, but I don't know which one. My guess—it's a drug connection."

"Why?"

"The warehouse in Panama was probably a meth lab. But nobody'd used it in a long time. Still, it's a possible link between Alvarez and drugs, which *might* hook him to the Colombians. You get anything on the leaks?"

"I'm clueless. I did a little surreptitious digging, but there's nothing. Yet."

"So where are we?" Ryan asked.

"From where I stand, it looks like the tangos got what they wanted in both cases. Nobody alive, and the intel was destroyed." Dalton gave Ryan a piercing glare. "It was destroyed, right?"

Ryan couldn't see why terrorists would want a list of sources of missing art and artifacts, but he'd long since decided if it had been worth killing for, then the fewer people who knew it existed the better. Including Dalton.

"Alvarez blew up his computer. The grenade took care of the rest. The whole place was one big fireball. Who really gives a shit about smuggled art?" Before he'd come to Montana, Ryan had peeked at the files, and they appeared to be exactly what the informant had said they were. Names, addresses, and pictures of works of art. He rubbed his temples. Nightly searches using computers at the Three Elks hadn't shown anything otherwise.

"Headache? You still look like shit," Dalton said. "I got some aspirin in my pack in the trunk. I can pull over."

"I'm okay. Trying to sort things out." He made sure his voice would remain steady before he spoke again. "I'm glad you're here."

"After the last gig, I've got a few days."

"How'd it go?" Ryan wouldn't ask for details.

"Not bad. Sneak in, charm the natives, and wham, bam, thank you ma'am. Everyone's home safe and sound."

Ryan doubted it had been quite that easy. He missed the days when he and Dalt were on the same team, but separating them had created two almost invincible teams. Almost. Shit. "Rumors?" he asked.

"Some rumblings that the Phantom might be back."

"You're kidding." Ryan sat up straight and turned to Dalton. "I know I pissed him off in Saudi, but I didn't think he'd hold a grudge. It's been, what? Four years?"

"Can't say what makes him tick. You cost him plenty when you squelched his arms deal."

Ryan shrugged. "It's not like he intended to pay for the damn things. You think it's personal?"

"Who knows? For now, it's only a rumor that he's back. Nobody knows who he really is, so he gets credit when things go wrong. Or should I say, he gets the blame? If we listened to the scuttlebutt, he'd been in six places at once."

"Still, you think he's moving his operations to the other side of the world?"

"Hell, for all I know, he could be flipping burgers at a Mickey D's in Duluth. But I've got my ears open." He flipped open the console between the seats and pulled out a plastic bag. "Want one?"

Ryan smiled when he saw the familiar package, and extracted a butterscotch candy. The simple act of unwrapping the yellow cellophane brought a smile to his face. He popped the sweet in his mouth and a mental montage of interminable hours of waiting during assignments whipped through his brain.

"Thanks," Ryan said. "Haven't had one of these in awhile."

The two settled into the comfortable silence of people who had worked together until they knew each other's thoughts, and Dalton apparently sensed Ryan wanted to be alone with his.

About a hundred yards from the place where Ryan had found his Mustang wrapped around a tree, he told Dalton to stop the car. "Pull into that clearing, leave the car behind those trees. We can walk from here."

"You sure?"

Ryan caught Dalton's glance at his knee. "Walking will loosen it." He opened his car door and started walking as if to prove it, although he bit back a curse as he tried to avoid limping.

He looked over his shoulder. Dalton had the trunk open and was rummaging around. When he caught up with Ryan, he had a pack on his back, a Winchester rifle over his shoulder, and a collapsible hiking stick in his hand.

He offered the stick to Ryan. "Team's only as strong as its weakest link, and you need to give that joint time to heal. Cut out on rehab, didn't you?"

Ryan didn't bother to answer as he extended the metal stick and let it take some of his weight. After about twenty paces, the knee felt better, and the knot in Ryan's stomach loosened. Maybe he hadn't damaged the knee further after all. But Dalton was right—he needed to follow up with rehab if he was going to heal, and he had to stop being so stubborn about it. His attitude that rehab was for wimps, not ex-SEALs who had worked in black ops for the past seven years, wasn't going to cut it if he wanted full use of his leg.

To do what? Would Blackthorne take him back if he cleared his name, assuming he'd even want to go there? He refused the thought, filing it away to be dealt with once he solved his current problems.

"Tell me what happened." Dalton's voice cut through Ryan's pity party.

"I heard the explosion and ran. By the time I got here, I was too busy looking for Pop and taking care of him to examine the car. They towed it to my place, but I wanted to see if there was anything that might give us a clue as to who did this."

By now, they'd reached the site. A maze of tire tracks from the police, paramedics, and fire crew had obliterated anything that might have been on the ground. He strolled to the tree that his father had hit, noticing the bloodstains on the bark. Seeing the scene in daylight, Ryan's stomach lurched when he realized how close his father had come to serious injury—or death. He'd been hurled against the tree, but considering he missed a jagged boulder by mere inches on one side, and a forty-foot drop on the other, the tree had probably saved his life.

"Pop said the steering gave, and he jumped before the car went into the ravine."

Ryan scoured the ground where the Mustang must have swerved, and tried to backtrack along its logical trajectory. A glimmer of metal, half buried in the ground caught his eye, and he bent to pick it up, ignoring the protest from his knee.

"Whatcha got?" Dalton asked.

"Metal scraps. And a nut of some kind. Can't be sure if it came from the Mustang, or has been here longer." He handed the bits to Dalton.

Dalton studied the pieces of metal. "Can't tell. The nut might have come from a tie rod." He slipped everything into his pocket. "You said the car's at your place?"

Ryan nodded. "I couldn't see much last night. But there was

a gallon of turpentine, some wood stain and linseed oil in the trunk. Wouldn't have taken much to set it off. A piece of metal dragging against the rocks could have sparked."

"You think that's what happened?"

Ryan lowered himself to a boulder by the side of the road. "I don't know. My mind was mush last night."

"Understandable," Dalton said.

"Like hell. We go into firefights all the time. We rescue civilians, wipe out tangos, and things go south all the time. I've *never* lost it like that."

"It's never been your daddy," Dalton said softly. "And I reckon you weren't in the greatest place mentally to begin with. Losing kids is tough."

"Shouldn't matter."

"Rehab's for more than busted joints, pard. You gotta deal with the demons."

A hunk of granite filled his throat. He choked out the name. "Carmelita. She had huge brown eyes. Wrapped her arms around me. Scared to death, but I could see the faith she put in me. And I couldn't do a damn thing for her. Same age as Molly."

Dalton rested a hand on Ryan's shoulder. "Don't think of them by name. You know better. Keep 'em anonymous. You can't save them all."

Ryan knew detachment kept him from coming apart. But it hadn't worked with the Forcadas. And when he'd watched Molly—no, not *Molly*—the *kid*—racing across the parking lot, and he knew he couldn't get to her in time, a knife had sliced a jagged hole in his belly.

He swallowed hard. That was over. She was safe. Thanks to Dalton, not him.

"Let's get to it." He got up and wandered along the path the Mustang would have taken last night.

The packed earth left few distinguishable tire marks, but as far as he could tell, there was nothing to indicate Pop had been driving erratically. He'd had one drink last night, and a short one at that. And he knew this road well enough to drive it blind.

"Let's go," he called to Dalton. "I want to look at the car."

"Um . . . I think I've got a little problem here." Dalton's voice was low and even. Ryan turned and hastened toward the sound of his voice. That Dalton had spoken told him whatever the problem was, stealth wasn't necessary. Still, he regretted that his Glock was in his nightstand drawer.

Frankie's mother looked up from her dressing table when Frankie entered the bedroom. "Do you think Molly might have been playing dress-up with my jewelry?" she asked. "I can't find my elephant pin. Your father gave it to me for our tenth anniversary, and the stones are real. It's not a plaything."

"Molly doesn't take things that don't belong to her," Frankie bristled. "I'll call the cleaners." How dare her mother accuse Molly of going through her personal belongings. Realizing she was upset about Bob, she took a breath and smoothed her tone. "I'll ask Molly about the pin. What else do you need for your . . . getaway?"

"This is making you uncomfortable, isn't it?" Her mother stopped rummaging through her jewelry box and turned to face Frankie. "Would you rather I stayed home?"

"Of course not. I need to get used to the idea, that's all. When I was home, you were Mom, and the elementary school principal. Then I went away, you retired, and I guess I never made the transition from you being Mom to you being a single woman who deserves to be happy."

"Thanks for understanding. When your father died, I buried myself in you, Claire, and my work. But it's been a long time, and—"

"No need to say anything else." Frankie closed the small

suitcase and lowered it from the bed to the floor. "How long have you known Bob?"

"About three months—but it seems longer. We seem to complement each other. He's more . . . adventurous than I am. He makes me look at things with reckless abandon. Yet he's sensible, too."

Frankie eyed her mother's wrist cast. "Yeah, like ice skating. I can't remember you ever skating when we were kids."

"And I never did. But Bob convinced me to give it a try. He felt terrible when I fell—stuck with me all the way to the hospital, waited forever while the doctors did their thing. Like he did last night. He came by every day—helped me cut through lots of red tape with the insurance. And he convinced me to use on-line banking. James was already overseas, you were at work, and Claire was bustling around in twelve directions, getting ready to move."

"I thought James took care of the books."

"He offered to, but there was no reason to turn things over to him. I think Claire had him thinking no woman could manage a budget—she always was a bit of a flibbertigibbet when it came to finances. And, as Bob pointed out, with the on-line system, I didn't need to sign checks, so my broken wrist was no problem."

The doorbell interrupted before Frankie could ask the millions of questions that had formed. She pushed them aside for now. Next week, they'd sit down and go over everything. She realized she'd been acting as badly as James, assuming Mom and Claire were equally challenged in the financial department.

Bob ambled into the bedroom. "There you are. Ready?" He bent down and kissed her mother's forehead.

Mom stroked his cheek. "Almost. Why don't you wait downstairs? I'll be down in a minute. My bag's packed."

Bob picked up the suitcase and left the room.

"He walks into your bedroom?"

"Why not? He rang the bell, after all. Molly probably let him in."

She'd have to talk to Molly about that, too.

Her mother patted her hair. "Since you seem to be in the mood for interrogations, perhaps you'd like to elaborate on your sleepover guest?" Spock-like, her mother raised one eyebrow, a gesture Frankie had spent hours trying to mimic, to no avail. Her brows were inseparable.

"It was nothing. I met him at the hospital. His father had been in a car accident, and he needed a place to stay. He's gone now."

"You let a stranger spend the night? In *my* house? With my granddaughter here? Frances Marie Castor, what*ever* were you thinking?"

All three names. Ouch. "He was very polite. Even offered to wash the sheets."

Another eyebrow lift. Heat rose to Frankie's face. "I told you. He slept in the guest room. Molly slept in my bed. With me. I made pancakes. He left."

Her mother turned back to her jewelry box, and Frankie knew she was checking her prized pieces.

"Mom, your pin was missing *before* Jack showed up. He's not that kind of guy." She caught herself before she turned things around and accused Bob of taking it.

Her mother's school principal glare reflected in the mirror. "And you know this because?"

"Because I do. Kind of like the way you knew Bob was special, I guess."

"Oh, so this stranger is special?"

How had the conversation taken this twist? "No, not like that. He's . . . trustworthy, I guess. He was in the Navy. Polite, and . . . and I don't know. But I know he didn't take anything."

"Be careful." She closed her jewelry box, patted her hair into place, and stood. "You know what can happen."

Frankie recognized her mother's look reflected in the mirror. *You've got one daughter without a father.*

"Don't shoot," Ryan called to Dalton. "Wolf, it's okay. Friend."

The dog stood his ground, ears back, Dalton's rifle pointed at him.

"Lower the rifle, Dalt. Slow and easy." Ryan moved toward the dog, his voice calm, muttering reassurances that Dalton was no threat. "Once he gets to know you, he'll be fine."

Dalton let the rifle barrel drop, then crouched and set the weapon on the ground. "Hey there, boy. I'm a friend. Wolf, is it?"

Ryan grabbed Wolf's ruff. "It's okay. Dalton's okay. Friend."

Wolf whimpered and pricked up his ears, the only sign he was willing to give Dalton the benefit of the doubt.

Dalton extended his hand. Wolf gave it a perfunctory sniff, then pressed against Ryan's leg.

"I guess he's still upset after last night," Ryan said. "He's Pop's dog."

"I gotta tell you, he came out of nowhere and took ten years off my life. I might have pissed him off with the rifle, but it was pure reflex."

"He more or less latched onto me when I got here—guess he knows what a pathetic mess I am."

"Nothing wrong with having eighty pounds of muscle on your side." Wolf begrudgingly allowed Dalton to scratch his ears. "You about ready to check out the car?"

"I take it you didn't find anything significant here."

Dalton shook his head. "Rescue operations destroyed the scene."

Together, the men walked back to Dalton's car. Wolf insinuated himself between them, but wouldn't get in the car.

"Suit yourself, boy," Ryan said to the dog. "Why don't you go home? I'm sure Rosa will be in today, stocking the kitchen for Pop's homecoming. You might luck out and get something better than kibble."

"You talk to that beast like he understands."

Ryan looked into Wolf's deep brown eyes. "Sometimes I'm sure he does. Let's go."

As they settled into the car, Dalton turned to Ryan. "Would that Rosa you mentioned happen to be the Rosa you talked about while we were living on lizards and snakes in Yucatan? The one who made chocolate cake to die for?"

"The same," Ryan said. "Her pot roast is fit for a king." Ryan's mouth watered at the memory, his first recollection of wanting food in a long time. Or had sitting around a kitchen table eating pancakes with smiley faces pointed him down recovery road?

From the side mirror, Ryan watched Wolf stare after the car as he and Dalton drove off. They rounded a turn, and the dog disappeared from sight. As they approached Josh's house, anxiety snaked beneath his skin like a downed power wire.

Seeing the charred remains of the Mustang brought back last night's panic. Not until he felt Dalton's hand on his shoulder did he realize he was gasping for air. He jerked away, half-stumbling toward the car and leaned on what was left of the hood. The stench of smoke, gasoline and turpentine filled his nostrils. Nausea threatened to overwhelm him the way it still did after missions. He took a deep breath, rubbed his face with his hands and straightened.

"You ready to do this?" Dalton leaned against a nearby tree, studying his fingernails. Waiting, as he always did, for Ryan to pull it together.

"Yeah," Ryan said. As quickly as his panic had appeared, it dissipated, replaced by a numbness and detachment—not the exhilaration of a mission, but a hell of a lot easier to cope with.

"You take the back, I'll start in front," Dalton said. "This baby isn't designed for mountain roads. You sure it was sabotage? Might have snagged on a root or a rock."

"I've thought of that. I'd like to think I'd have noticed, but I was . . . preoccupied." He paused, waiting for Dalton to look up from the depths of the engine. "If someone rigged an explosive, I can't see them waiting around all night to detonate it in case I drove away. If they were studying me, they'd know I wouldn't leave until the next day, so a timer set for the middle of the night makes no sense, either."

"You think the explosion was a lucky side-effect?"

"That seems logical, but who knows? There wasn't much time between me getting home and Pop driving off. Given the nature of these roads, messing with the brakes or steering would be enough. Not a bomb."

"Guess we need to have a look-see."

What seemed like an hour later, Dalton crawled out from under the wreckage, tossing bits and pieces from hand to hand. "Between the fire, the water, and the crash, it's plumb impossible to tell what happened. But, far as I can tell, there's nothing here to indicate sabotage. You notice anything suspicious?"

"No. I've been here a couple of weeks, and nothing unusual's gone on."

"All the years in our line of work, we forget that accidents do happen, and these roads could shake something loose. How 'bout I take these parts back and use some of Blackthorne's high-priced techno-wizardry to check 'em out? Debbie owes me a favor." He winked. "Or maybe I owe her one. Either way, she ain't gonna talk. She might scream my name, but she ain't gonna talk."

Ryan rubbed his nose. "You ever think about settling down?"

"Like, with one woman? Forever?" He looked heavenward, as

if the skies held the answer. For an instant, his face clouded. Then he grinned. "Nope. Can't see it. Too many fillies out there."

Massaging his stiff neck, Ryan couldn't help but grin. Dalton assumed women would do his bidding—and they usually did.

"Tell me why the Phantom has the rumor mill grinding."

"Wish I could, pard. A couple of deals seemed to have his M.O. on them. But like I said before, that's an easy out. Unless he's got a clone or two."

Ryan mulled that one over for a few minutes. "Or he's recruiting? Training others in his methods?"

"Now that's a scary thought." Dalton stretched. "You got anything to drink inside? This is thirsty work."

They went inside, and Ryan opened the refrigerator. "You're in luck, Dalt. Pop delivered a care package the other night. No pot roast, but I've got turkey." He pulled out a six-pack of Heineken and set it on the counter.

"Help yourself to a beer." Ryan set to work slicing some turkey and assembling sandwiches.

Dalton hitched a hip onto the corner of the table. "You're lookin' better, man." He popped open two beers and handed one to Ryan. He raised his. "To answers."

Ryan tapped his bottle against Dalton's. "To answers." Despite the cold brew, he felt a warm glow flow through him.

"So, tell me," Ryan said around a mouthful of turkey. "If the Phantom isn't the likely suspect, what connects the two assignments? What does a high ranking government official's family in Colombia have in common with art smuggling?"

In Colombia, the Forcadas had been threatened into cooperating with Rafael, a sleazebag drug lord. Uncle Sam had been reluctant to get involved. Ryan comprehended the ways of the drug lords, and understood how those cases could escalate into areas the government didn't want to enter. And how Rafael would want very much to create an example so others wouldn't try to cross him. When everything went south, Ryan had been pissed, but that was always a possibility, no matter what the mission. It was losing the ones they'd been sent to protect that hurt.

But he wondered—not for the first time—or the hundredth—if he'd been too lax on his next assignment, thinking that the mission was trivial, that Blackthorne had given him an insignificant op, getting him back on the horse. Stolen paintings and antiquities seemed small potatoes given the global threats of terrorism.

"Talk to me, pard," Dalton said.

"I don't know much—and I had no reason not to trust Blackthorne. I was supposed to go to Panama, waltz into this guy's living room, he'd hand over some computer files that would provide information about missing art. For a modest price, of course. Said he'd spent the last twenty years compiling lists—people, places, stuff. You know—crap from the pyramids, paintings the Nazis stole, smuggled pre-Colombian artifacts. Lists of forgeries hanging in museums while the originals are in basements of the collectors. Low priority for Uncle Sam's finest, but a nice plug for Blackthorne, Inc.

"At the last minute, the contact calls me and says he has to move the meet. Like who the fuck is going to give a shit about him? But he insists on changing the time and place."

"Know the breed. Pains in the asses, all of them."

"So cliché, it would have been funny, we go to this abandoned warehouse."

Ryan shuddered at the memory. The man's eyes, so dark his irises almost disappeared into his pupils. The tobacco-stained teeth and fingertips. A thick brush of a moustache. The ever-present cigar tubes in his breast pocket. His breath, a mixture of cigars and stale beer.

"And then it was FUBAR. Door slams open. Flash-bangs. I can't see, can't hear. I duck for cover and wait it out."

"Longest ten seconds of your life. Been there."

"Yeah. My contact is screaming, messing with the computer. The intruders are spreading gunfire. I don't give a shit who they are, I shoot back. Got two of them." Ryan rubbed his shoulder. "Third one took a little extra."

He looked up. Dalton took another swig of his beer, waiting. Ryan exhaled and went on.

"Compared to the Colombia gig, this wasn't much."

"Hell it wasn't. You were alone. Why no backup?"

Ryan snorted. "My idea. It was supposed to be a simple transaction. After losing my last team, I insisted on doing it alone. In and out. Like you said, wham, bam, thank you ma'am. Then, when it went south, extraction was . . . delayed. Took three days.

"After I left Blackthorne, I tried to connect Alvarez to Rafael. I know I wasn't the leak." He stared at his Heineken. "I thought I could clear my name if I could find a connection between the two. But it's a stretch. Rafael's into cocaine, and Alvarez was using an abandoned meth lab. I haven't found anything to hook Alvarez to drug trafficking."

"Covered your tracks?"

"Of course. Used public computers at the Three Elks. Downloaded files to my flash so anything I did here wasn't on-line." He noted Dalton's quizzical expression. "And yes, I have spyware protection, and yes, I still have Blackthorne's magic program, although the best anyone could do would be to trace the searches to the bar." Ryan drained the bottle and set it down. "So, does anyone know what Alvarez's files were supposed to be if they're not smuggled art?"

"If anyone does, they're not talking. But I agree, knowing who's hiding some trinkets doesn't seem worth diddly in the grand scheme of things. Not that folks don't kill for less. Too bad the files were destroyed. If we had them, we might figure it out."

"Yeah. Too bad." Ryan stared at the ceiling for a while, not exactly sure why he didn't tell Dalton the truth. It could wait. "The good news is that they don't have them, either. Pass me another beer."

At some point, the beer changed to whiskey. Dalton kept the refills coming, reminiscences flowed with them, and Ryan remembered little else until sunlight pierced his eyelids and a cold nose poked his neck. "Go away, dog."

Ryan groped for his watch. Twelve-twenty, and unless he'd been transported above the Arctic Circle, it was noon, not midnight. He'd slept—damn, he didn't know how long he'd slept. At least twelve hours. His head felt thick, but blessedly, no hangover symptoms.

He picked through the tangle in his brain for the memories. He and Dalton, out on the porch, watching the sunset. Being helped into bed. No nightmares.

He stumbled into the shower. Revived, he got dressed and wandered through the living room. Everything was immaculate.

"Dalt?" In the kitchen, it was the same. As if Dalton had never been here. He caught the note propped up against the coffee pot.

Hope you slept well. You needed it. Got a 911 page about 2. Wheels up at 8. Had to dash. Will be in touch. D.

CHAPTER 8

"You almost ready, Molly?" Frankie took mental inventory of the picnic supplies and added a roll of paper towels, wet naps and a box of band-aids to a canvas tote. "Don't forget your jacket. And your red cap. It's cold up in the mountains."

After seeing her mother and Bob off yesterday, Frankie had tried to get a handle on the budget based on the few bits and pieces she found in Mom's desk. Molly settled for pizza and *The Little Mermaid* on video, with the promise that she could pick whatever she wanted to do on Sunday.

When Molly had proposed a picnic, Frankie jumped at the suggestion.

She ran her fingers along the pebbled surface of the camera she'd rediscovered in the attic while searching for the picnic basket. Surprised at how familiar it felt, how it seemed to mold to her grip as if she'd used it last week instead of years ago, she thought of her photos on the living room wall. She knew exactly where she and Molly would go.

"Ready, Mommy. Can Mr. Snuggles come, too? He said he likes picnics."

"Of course. Can you carry this for me?" Frankie handed Molly the tote. "Why don't you let Mr. Snuggles ride inside? Then you have both hands to carry it."

Molly nodded and arranged Mr. Snuggles so that his head and forepaws hung over the top of the tote. "Let's go."

With their supplies in the trunk, Molly secure in back, and

the camera bag up front, Frankie headed out of town, past Stanton, and into the mountains where she'd taken her award-winning photos. Okay, so maybe they were high school awards, but all that meant was that she could do better now.

Before they left Broken Bow, she stopped and picked up a supply of film. Black and white, although the clerk had to hunt for it. Digital might be the current trend, but Frankie couldn't separate the photography from the picture-making process. For her, manipulating images on a computer would never compare to watching an image appear, as if by magic, onto a blank sheet of paper immersed in the developer tray. She could almost smell the tang of the chemicals. She wondered if Mr. Anisman still taught at the high school, and if he'd let her use the darkroom. On impulse, she bought two disposable cameras for Molly.

By late afternoon, Frankie was comfortably tired. Their picnic had become secondary to the picture taking. Molly was enthralled with having her own camera, and learned that being quiet was rewarded with glimpses of wildlife, although Frankie thought Mr. Snuggles would be the focal point of most of Molly's photos.

"I'm all done, Mommy." Molly handed over her second camera. Her nose and cheeks were flushed pink with the cold. Frankie tugged Molly's knit cap lower, covering her ears.

"Almost time to go, Peanut. You've done a great job. I'll bet you have some wonderful pictures in here." Frankie slipped the camera into her jacket pocket and looked up.

Black and gray clouds billowed above, glowing with reflections that preceded sunset. Below, a stream, swollen with spring rains, twisted and turned its way down the mountain. A photo screamed out to her.

"Mommy's going to take a few pictures, and then I'll be done, too. Why don't you sit on that log, and be very, very quiet. Maybe the deer will come by again."

Frankie grinned as Molly did her best stealth tiptoe and settled onto a fallen log by the stream.

Finding a vantage point higher up the bank, Frankie screwed her camera into the tripod and attached the cable release. She stomped her feet and rubbed her hands against the calendar-defying cold. She'd forgotten what spring in Montana was like. Sun one day, snow the next, especially in the mountains. She tucked her hair into the hood of her parka and pulled the drawstring tight against the rising wind.

After snapping a couple of shots that would freeze the action of the water, mirroring the clouds above, she took a meter reading and adjusted the aperture and shutter speed for a long exposure. The rushing stream below would be transformed into a frothy blur, looking more like whipped cream than water.

Her eyes glued to the viewfinder, she composed the shot, framing the image with the overhanging branches above and a boulder below, and waited for the precise instant when the clouds and sun combined to give her perfect lighting.

A high-pitched shriek pierced her tranquil concentration. Molly! In Frankie's panic, the sound seemed to come from everywhere. Frankie whipped her head around, searching out the last place she'd seen Molly, but she wasn't on the log.

"Molly!" Her heart hammered hard enough to escape her rib cage. "Where are you?"

"Mr. Snuggles fell in! Mommy! Help!" The sound moved away, carried by the wind.

Cursing the stuffed dog, Frankie raced toward her daughter's screams. She caught a glimpse of Molly's red jacket being propelled downstream. With Molly inside.

"Grab something! Hold on! I'm coming!"

Frankie scrambled down the bank, slipping and sliding until she reached the streambed. The surging current, fed by the runoff of melting snow, no longer looked like the peaceful scene she'd framed with her camera lens. The water roared, or was it the blood pounding in her ears? She raced downstream, trying to get ahead of Molly.

"Hang on, please, hang on." Stumbling, trying to keep her footing on the slippery ground, a flash of brown fur bounded past her, sending her to her knees.

Oh, God. A bear? No, a wolf. It chased after Molly.

"No!"

She groped along the ground, seeking a rock, a stick, anything to keep the mad creature away from her child.

"Wolf!" A male voice cried out.

"I saw it. He'll get my daughter. Help me, please!" Her voice trembled, pitched two octaves higher than normal. Her fingers found a rock and she clutched it in her fist, her arm poised to hurl it at the beast. Someone gripped her wrist and pried it loose.

Without turning, Frankie screamed, "Give me that! What are you doing? That beast is going to kill my daughter!"

The man shoved her aside and raced past her. She scrambled to her feet and followed his hooded green parka.

Around a bend, her heart stopped when she saw Molly's red knit cap swirling in an eddy. Forcing her eyes to look beyond it, she saw Molly clutching a snagged branch.

"Hold on, Molly. I'm coming."

She plunged into the icy water. The current threatened to yank her feet out from under her. Submerged rocks and branches threatened what little footing she could maintain. She reached for an overhanging branch to steady herself. When she looked back at the stream, Molly was gone.

"Molly!" Her heart pounded in her ears. "Molly!"

She struggled back to the bank where she could move faster. Beyond the next curve, she spied the beast with Molly's jacket in its teeth, Molly in the jacket, the man close behind.

"Do something. Stop him," Frankie cried.

"Stay back." The man stood on a flat rock near the edge of the stream. "Wolf. Good boy. Bring her here."

Transfixed, Frankie watched the beast, not a wolf but a German Shepherd, keep Molly's head above water as it fought the current and dragged her toward the man.

"Good boy. A little more. Come on . . ." The wind caught most of his voice, but she heard the calm confidence in his tone.

Once Molly was close enough, he stepped into the stream and plucked her into his arms. "Okay, little one. You're okay."

Frankie splashed out of the water and up the bank where the man had placed Molly on her side. Molly choked, coughed up half the stream, and burst into tears.

"Peanut, you're okay. Mommy's here." Frankie knelt at Molly's side, clutched her to her chest and stroked her face. "You're safe now."

"Looks like she's all right," the man said.

Momentarily startled by his voice, Frankie's universe expanded enough to include the stranger. "You saved her life. I don't know how to thank you."

She gazed up into the man's face for the first time. In the dimming light, his face was cast in shadows. The cloud cover broke, and his whiskey-colored eyes caught hers. She squinted at him.

"Jack?"

Recognition flashed across his face. "Frankie?" He looked down. "Hello, Angel."

Molly's sobs subsided into hiccups. "Molly, not Angel."

Frankie swallowed. "You shaved. What are you doing here? Never mind. I'm so glad you were."

She looked for the dog, but it was nowhere in sight. "Was that your dog? I thought it was a wolf. I thought it was going to attack Molly. I thought she was going to drown, or—"

Strong hands gripped her shoulders. "Shh. She's okay. But we need to get her—and you—into warm clothes. Where's your car?"

Frankie whirled her head around, trying to get her bearings. "Off the main road. By the equestrian crossing." Her teeth chattered.

Jack removed his parka and wrapped it around Molly, who all but disappeared inside. "You have a change of clothes?"

Frankie shook her head. "Swimming wasn't part of the plan."

"My place isn't far. You can dry off there." He started walking. Frankie noticed he limped.

"I can carry her," she said. She reached for Molly, needing to touch her, to feel her breathing. To know she was safe.

"Faster if I do. Hypothermia can be a problem." He glanced over his shoulder. "You okay to walk?"

"I'm fine. Is Molly really all right?"

"She's shivering. Good sign."

Frankie jogged to keep up with Jack's stride as he traveled through the trees.

"Where are we going? The road's back that way, isn't it? Or did I really get turned around?"

"Shorter this way."

"She's going to be okay, isn't she? Do you think she needs to go to the hospital? I meant to give her swimming lessons in Boston, but I was so busy with work, and—"

"Frankie."

"What?"

"Save your breath."

"Sorry. But I tend to—"

"Babble. I know."

Despite the cold, her face burned. She clenched her teeth to stop the chattering—both kinds—and tried to keep Jack in sight as he set a brisk pace through the woods.

Ryan hoisted his shivering bundle over his shoulder and opened the front door. He'd sensed Frankie behind him as he'd hiked, and he trusted she'd keep up. She was freaked out enough without him adding his concerns that the child's tiny size had made her vulnerability to hypothermia a serious issue. Despite his attempts to engage the child in conversation, the most he'd been able to get out of her was an occasional headshake. She wasn't crying, but neither was she the outgoing child of their prior meeting.

She'll be fine. This is nothing like the Forcada mission.

Inside, he flipped the switch for the heat lamp in the bathroom and began peeling off her wet clothes.

"Hey. I'll bet you're cold, aren't you?" He held up a towel. "We need to get you dry."

She nodded.

Damn, he wasn't the team medic, although everyone had first-aid training. Only problem was, he'd been in nothing but hot climates for the past five years. Knowing how to treat heat stroke wasn't worth squat right now. He racked his brain for what he'd learned about hypothermia.

Warm her. Get her dry. That much was obvious. More filtered through. Check speech and motor functions.

"Can you talk to me?"

She gave a violent headshake and looked over his shoulder. He turned. Frankie stood in the bathroom doorway, breathing hard. She rushed to Molly's side. "Let me do that," she said, pulling of Molly's shirt. "Is she okay?"

"I think so. I'll get something for her to wear."

He got up, wincing at the pain in his knee and hobbled to his bedroom. He grabbed a sweatshirt and brought it to the bathroom. Molly's clothes lay in a puddle on the floor and she was wrapped in his bath towel, still shivering. Frankie reached for the sweatshirt.

"Wait," Ryan said. "Angel, can you come get the shirt?"

When she walked across the room on steady legs, he exhaled a breath he didn't know he'd been holding.

"She's got good motor functions. If she'd talk, I'd bet her speech is normal, too."

He leaned down, his hands on his thighs. "Would you like some soup?" he asked. Molly nodded. Ryan cocked his head at Frankie. "She doesn't seem to want to talk to me today."

"Molly, Mr. Daniels asked you a question. What do you say?" Frankie said.

"Yes, please." The words were tiny, but not slurred.

Ryan tousled the child's hair. "Hair dryer's under the sink. Get her settled, and then, I think you should get dry clothes for yourself. Bedroom dresser, second drawer. Help yourself to a hot shower."

"Jack, I can't begin to thank you. If you hadn't come along— Molly's everything . . . I'm a good mom—she was sitting right there, and then she was—I only took my eyes off her for an instant."

"Drop it. I did come along. Give me your car keys. I'll get your car. Take anything in the kitchen, but get something warm inside both of you as soon as possible. It's probably a good idea if she walks around some, too."

Frankie stuck her hands into her jacket pockets, frowned, and dug through her jeans. "Rats. They're in my camera bag." Her eyes widened. "My camera. Oh, my. All my shots. I totally forgot. They can't be ruined. I need them. It'll be dark soon, and what if it rains? Or snows?"

"Slow down again. Where's the camera bag?"

"With the camera. Near where Molly fell into the stream." Her eyes brimmed with tears. "What am I thinking? A camera?

Some pictures? I could have lost *Molly.* She's *my world.*"

He put his hands on her shoulders. Her tension vibrated through him. "Relax. I'll get everything. Make yourself at home. I won't be long."

He picked up his parka from the bathroom floor and shrugged into it. Not until he felt its weight did he remember his Glock was in the pocket. He marched from the house, leaving Frankie to tend to her daughter. Better that she dealt with the child.

Damn, the kid seemed like an innocent angel, with those huge blue eyes and open smile. But twice, she'd nearly gotten herself killed. There had to be some way to deal with kids—his theory was to put them in suspended animation with some sort of direct brain-feed education until they were eighteen. Thinking of himself at eighteen, he amended that to twenty-five.

Glad to be away from the confines of domesticity and out in the fresh air, he retraced his path and found Frankie's camera and equipment where she'd said they would be. Steadying the tripod, he peered through the viewfinder and wondered why it surprised him to find a well-composed shot. On impulse, he pressed the shutter before he unscrewed the camera and replaced it in the bag.

With the bag over one shoulder and the tripod over the other, he scanned the area. A few yards away, behind a rock, he found a canvas tote. A quick survey revealed paper towels, wet wipes, two bottles of water and a disposable camera. He felt around some more and pulled out a plastic bag half-full of stones, leaves, and a feather. The sorts of things a five-year-old might consider treasures. Assuming the tote was Frankie's, he replaced the bag and added the tote to his collection.

He wandered downstream to the point where Wolf had pulled her from the water, trying to see if either one had dropped anything else. Daylight had faded, and a storm was imminent.

He was about to turn around when he heard Wolf's whine.

Frankie didn't know whether to laugh or cry when she looked at Molly, standing barefoot on the bathroom floor, gnawing her thumb, virtually swallowed by Jack's sweatshirt. She'd never seen her daughter looking so contrite—or was it guilty? "Let's get your hair dry." She focused the warm air at Molly's head. "Hold still." When Molly fidgeted and fussed, her spirits rose. "You're feeling better, aren't you?"

Molly nodded.

Frankie shut off the dryer. She scooped Molly into her arms, then remembered Jack's words about having Molly walk, and set her back onto the floor. "Why don't you go out to the couch?" Frankie watched her move across the room on steady legs, and relief flooded her. She took the throw blanket from the back of the couch and wrapped it around Molly. "Warmer now?"

Molly nodded again.

Frankie sat down beside her and stroked her hair. "Jack said you need something warm in your tummy. How about some warm milk?"

"Okay," Molly whispered.

Frankie found what she needed. She nuked a mug of milk and brought it to Molly. "Here you go. Holding the mug will keep your hands warm, and the milk will warm you inside."

Molly reached for the mug and took a sip.

"Does your throat hurt, Peanut? You're not talking much."

A headshake followed by a fat tear running down her cheek. "Am I bad? You have an angry face."

Frankie set the milk aside and grabbed her close. "Of course not. I was scared. Everyone was scared. Sometimes people look angry when they're scared."

"Mr. Snuggles is gone. He saw a pretty leaf, but then he fell into the water and I couldn't catch him." The trickle of tears blossomed into hiccupping sobs.

For the first time, she noticed the absence of the ever-present toy. She stroked Molly's back. "Maybe we can find him tomorrow." Soon, she'd have to talk to Molly about using the dog to avoid blame for her escapades. "I want you to stay right here while I take a shower, okay? Drink your milk. Let's both be glad you're all right. Can you promise me?"

"Promise." The tone held little conviction.

Frankie kissed Molly's cheek. "That's a good girl."

Frankie found sweat pants and another sweatshirt in Ryan's dresser. She carried them into the bathroom, took a fast shower, dried off, and tugged them on. Outside, the wind howled. She padded to the window. White flakes danced in a light from under the eaves. She envisioned the photograph she'd been taking. Remembered her camera. If it was ruined, she didn't know what she would do.

Camera? How could she be worried about that? Molly was safe and Jack was out there, trying to help her. He'd already waded into the stream, carried her daughter goodness knows how far. And he'd been limping. No matter that he said it was nothing, guys always said that, didn't they?

"Mommy?"

"Coming." Frankie adjusted the drawstring on the sweats to fit her waist, found a pair of heavy socks in the dresser, pulled them over her now cold feet, and went to her daughter.

"I can't get glad, Mommy. Does the man have a timer? I need a grumpy time."

Frankie's heart twisted. She'd been wallowing in herself when Molly was the one who needed help. "I don't know, Peanut. Let's go look."

CHAPTER 9

Ryan left Frankie's Cavalier under a tree behind the house, away from the barbequed carcass of his Mustang. Bile still rose whenever he caught a glimpse of it. As soon as Ryan opened the car door, Wolf bounded out and raced up the steps. Ryan's pace was less exuberant. His knee ached again, along with almost every muscle in his body. He shivered, trying to ignore the growling from his stomach. He dragged himself up the steps, then stopped. Through gaps in the curtains, he saw silhouetted figures moving around the room in some sort of marching dance.

Good. He'd told Frankie to get the kid moving. He grabbed Wolf by the ruff, eased the door open and blinked. The two of them were stomping around the living room, pounding fists into palms, chanting a vocabulary that sounded most un-Frankie like.

"I'm mad, I'm angry, I'm grumpy. I'm grumpy, I'm angry, I'm mad."

A high-pitched voice rang out over Frankie's, and he bit back a laugh at her kindergarten curse words.

Until he heard *fuckit* added to the mix. He glanced at Frankie, but she didn't seem fazed by the expletive, which the youngster now rhymed with bucket.

"Hi," he said, hanging his parka on a peg by the door. "Can anyone join in?"

"Okay," said the child, not missing a step, "but only until the timer dings. Then you have to be happy again."

Bewildered, Ryan released his grip on Wolf, telling him to stay. The dog flopped down next to the door. Ryan crossed the room and sat on the couch. Familiar cooking aromas teased at the memory centers in his brain, but he couldn't quite identify them. Josh's kitchen timer sat on the coffee table, with about a minute to go.

Frankie gazed at him over her daughter's head, lifted her eyebrows and smiled, but kept on chanting and stomping. His sweatshirt dwarfed the kid, and the sweats Frankie had borrowed didn't fit her much better. She'd rolled thick cuffs on both the shirt and pants. Somehow she looked sexier than in her Three Elks getup—face scrubbed, almost every inch of her hidden beneath baggy cotton.

When the timer sounded, the show stopped. The two hugged, kissed, and he caught a glimpse of the friendly child he'd first met.

"Okay, Peanut. Time to go home," Frankie said.

"Um, I don't think so," Ryan said.

Frankie's head whipped around. "Is something wrong with my car?"

"No." Not if you didn't count the engine that missed every now and then, the temperamental heater, or the tires that could use a little more tread. "But you've both had a long day, it's snowing, and getting worse. It's not safe on the road."

He watched Frankie's expression go from indignation to frustration to—was it relief?

"We can't impose," Frankie said. "You've done enough already."

He heard the hesitation. "You two can have the bedroom. I'll take the couch. I'm sure the weather will clear by morning."

"A sleepover, Mommy. Like Gramma and Bob." The kid's smile faded and her chin quivered. "But Mr. Snuggles. I need him with me to sleep, or I might have bad dreams."

Yeah, Ryan thought. *Nearly dying could do that to you.* He mustered a smile. "You said that you didn't need him every night. Since you're five now."

She didn't look convinced.

"Tell you what," he went on. "How about if I let you have something better than Mr. . . . Snuggles?" God, how could a grown man say that out loud? He gave a low whistle, and Wolf trotted over. "This is Wolf. Do you remember him? He's real good at keeping the bad dreams away." He looked over Molly's head to Frankie, hoping he hadn't done anything against her rules. "He's well trained. He won't hurt her."

Molly hesitated. "Can I pet him, Mommy?"

"Go ahead," Frankie said.

Molly gave Wolf a tentative pat. He thumped his tail and licked her hand. She grinned, burying her face in Wolf's fur. "He likes me. Can he come to bed with me? A real, live doggie."

Ryan winced at someone calling Wolf a doggie. Frankie crouched next to her daughter and embraced the dog. "I think that will be fine for tonight. Let's get him dried off, though."

She looked at Ryan. "Towels?"

"Bathroom cabinet."

The kid skipped toward the bathroom, then stopped. "I don't have a toothbrush."

"There are some new toothbrushes in the bathroom drawer," Ryan said.

At Frankie's lifted eyebrows, he said, "This is my brother's place. He keeps it stocked." And then wondered why he felt the need to explain.

Too tired to move, he leaned back and closed his eyes, listening to the sounds coming from the bedroom as Frankie murmured to her daughter, praised Wolf. He envisioned her sitting on the edge of the bed, telling a bedtime story, brushing her lips against the kid's cheek, tucking her in. He wondered where the father was.

He flashed back to the car explosion, to his father. He'd convinced Pop to spend an extra night in the hospital, thinking he and Dalton might discover who—if anyone—was behind the crash. But they had nothing concrete, and Dalton was gone.

"Hey." Frankie stood above him. "I'd say 'penny for your thoughts,' but I think you've got more going on in there than a penny's worth."

He blinked, rubbed his jaw, surprised to feel stubble instead of his beard. "Not really. The kid settled?"

"Wolf's with her, but I think she's exhausted enough to sleep without a dog, stuffed or otherwise."

"I know the feeling."

"Oh. Of course. You're tired. I saved you dinner, though, if you're hungry."

"I can probably stay awake a little longer." He pulled himself off the couch and couldn't hide the grimace when his knee locked. He bent to rub it.

"Sit." She pushed on his shoulders, and he caught a whiff of soap. He knew it didn't smell that good on him. Come to think of it, right now, he was probably rank. He sank back onto the couch.

She hovered over him. "What can I get you for your knee? You have a bandage? Brace? Anything?"

"Ice, if you don't mind."

"Mind? You save my daughter's life and you wonder if I'd mind bringing you some ice? You stay right there. Don't move. I mean it."

"Yes, ma'am." She whisked away into the kitchen. He listened to drawers open and close, the clatter of ice cubes. And then she was at his side again.

"Here you go." She handed him a plastic bag filled with ice.

He set it on his knee, hoping it would take the swelling down. Or at least numb it enough so he could walk without swearing.

"Thanks."

"I meant to ask. Where's Dalton?"

So, she wanted to see Dalt. "He had to get back to work. Hope you're not disappointed."

Shit. He'd practically barked at her. He sounded like a jealous fool.

"Why would I be? I'll have your food in a jiffy," she said.

She hadn't noticed his reaction. Or didn't give a damn what he thought. He closed his eyes, dealing with the fact that he obviously wasn't stirring up her insides the way she was stirring up his.

He half dozed, listening to Frankie in the kitchen. He knew if he leaned forward he could watch her at work, but for now he was content to imagine her reaching into the fridge, stretching to reach a high shelf, or bending for a low cabinet. He sensed her return and opened his eyes.

"I brought you some dinner—not really dinner, but there wasn't much to work with, not that I can create much even with a full restaurant kitchen, but Molly likes it, and—"

"And it'll be fine." He sat up. Frankie moved away and he saw a bowl of tomato soup and two grilled cheese sandwiches. He stiffened.

"Oh, dear. You don't like it. I know it's kid food, but that's about all I cook."

"No. It's perfect. Absolutely perfect."

"It's . . . you didn't look all that happy when you saw it. And after what you did, it should probably be steak. Oh, dear. Wolf. He deserves steak, too."

"Frankie. Wolf is fine. He's with your daughter, and he knows he did good. And the food—it took me back, that's all."

"One of those childhood things? Mine, too. Mom always—

oh. Your mom?"

He nodded, unable to talk about how the memories had inundated him. How tomato soup and a grilled cheese sandwich made rainy days sunny, healed skinned knees and bumped heads, erased being the last one picked for the team, and made everything right in a gangly eight-year-old's world. Normal memories, but tonight they overwhelmed him.

"Sit down," he said. "Relax."

She wobbled, reaching behind her for the chair. "I guess . . . now that it's over . . . everything's okay . . . I feel kind of . . ."

Shit. She was white. "Sit down. Head between your knees. Now." He shoved the icepack aside and clambered to his feet.

"Oh, my," she said.

He caught her right before she hit the deck, eased her to the couch. He brushed a strand of golden hair from her face. With her blue eyes closed, he noticed her nose, tilted up just enough to give her an impish look. Her chin narrowed to a triangle, adding to the effect. But her lips. Rich and full, they were anything but impish.

Frankie opened her eyes. "Don't tell me I passed out." She struggled to sit up. "I've never passed out."

He held her down. "Stay there for a minute. It's not an unusual reaction. Your body was running on adrenaline, making sure everything was okay, and once everything *was* okay, it crashed for a minute."

"I'm so embarrassed."

"Did you eat?"

"I had a little soup with Molly. I wasn't hungry. Nerves, I guess."

He handed her half a sandwich. "Here. Eat."

She took a tentative bite, chewed it slowly. "Not bad." She giggled, and her eyes twinkled. She took two more huge bites, nothing tentative about them. When her tongue peeked out to sweep an errant crumb from her lower lip, he imagined that tongue on his lips.

"Feeling better, I take it?" The huskiness in his voice surprised him.

She nodded. "Now, you finish your dinner. Can't have you passing out, too."

Uncomfortably aware of his body's reaction to her nearness, he took his food to the chair. Frankie ate the last of the sandwich, licked her fingers, then leaned across to pick up a napkin from the coffee table. He found it hard to reconcile this carefree woman with the panic-stricken one he'd seen only a short while ago. Or the maternal one of a few minutes before, for that matter.

The lone sound in the room was the click of his spoon against the soup bowl. Aware that she was watching him as if she expected something, he broke the silence.

"May I ask what you two were doing when I came in?"

"That was our grumpy time out."

"I'm not familiar with the term." He picked up the sandwich and took a bite, the cheese still warm and stringy, and the buttery bread toasted crisp. Mayberry time again.

"It's something we do. Life's too short to waste time brooding about the negative. So, every now and then, we set aside a time to gather up all our anger, frustration, or grumps, as Molly calls them, and get them out in the open. It's amazing how hard it is for a five-year-old to stay grumpy for ten minutes—and after solid ranting, you can't be upset anymore." She lowered her head, and a flush rose from her neck to her cheeks.

He wiped his fingers on a napkin. "Does the ten minute thing work for you, too?"

"Most of the time. I've been called a Pollyanna, but truly, it's much easier to go through life happy."

"So nothing gets you down?"

She sobered. "Lots of things." Her smile returned. "But only for ten minutes."

He couldn't hold back a smile of his own. Frankie stood and gathered the dishes. While she was in the kitchen, he retrieved his Glock from his parka and stuffed it under the couch cushion. He sat, extended his aching leg and reapplied the icepack.

Frankie returned and flopped down in the chair opposite him with a sigh. "I totally forgot—did you find my things?"

Her eyes were full of hope, and he was damn glad he could give her a positive answer. "Right where you said they'd be. Got 'em before it started snowing. They seem fine."

She looked around, her eyes scanning the room.

He started to rise, but she interrupted. "Stay put. Tell me where they are, and I'll get them."

"Beside the coat rack."

She almost skipped across the room. "Thank you *so* much. I really owe you."

Seeing such unabashed optimism was payment enough, but he didn't know how to explain it—not without going somewhere he didn't want to go.

"Oh, you found my tote, too. I'm so glad. Molly's treasures were in there. At least she didn't lose everything."

She snatched the camera bag. After checking her camera, she set it aside and peered into the canvas carryall.

"And you found Mr. Snuggles! Where was he?" She held up the soggy and torn toy.

"Wolf found him. I'm afraid he's a little worse for wear. I didn't want to say anything. If he's a lost cause, I didn't want her to know."

Frankie examined the bedraggled toy. "A needle and thread, a trip through the washing machine, and I think he'll make a full recovery." She set the stuffed dog alongside the tote and crossed to the chair. Her step was heavy and her shoulder slumped.

"What's wrong?" he asked.

"I don't know. Molly seemed to be making the adjustment— the move from Boston was out of the blue, but she's a friendly kid, and seemed to be fitting in. But maybe she's unhappy. She's become so attached to Mr. Snuggles. She takes him everywhere. In Boston, he lived on her bed."

"It's probably just a phase. Lots of kids have security blankets, teddy bears, whatever."

She smiled. "And you?"

He scratched his head. "Pancho. Nobody could see him but me. I blamed an awful lot of mischief on him."

Frankie leaned forward. "I think that's what Molly's doing with Mr. Snuggles. She tells me that he wants to do all this stuff. As if she's using him to avoid the consequences of her actions. Like falling into streams. She told me Mr. Snuggles wanted to see a pretty leaf. I'm worried she's upset I dragged her away from her friends, and she's trying to fight back."

"Testing limits sounds like a normal kid thing to me, especially if you can blame someone—or something—else. But my knowledge of kids could be written on the head of a pin."

"I'll bet you can write really, really small." She got up and paced the room. "I should talk to her about it, but she was so scared this afternoon, I didn't have the nerve. I don't want to punish her, but I have to make her see that she can't hide behind a toy."

"It must be hard raising a kid. What about her father?" He stopped, aware he'd crossed a line.

Frankie tossed her head. "She doesn't have a father. I mean, of course, she has one, but he's out of the picture. It's Molly and me. And if anything happened to her—like today, I don't know what I'd do. How did I let it happen?" She paced at warp speed now, and her voice cracked.

He watched her make three circuits of the living room. "You're making me dizzy. Please. Come sit down."

She shook her head, and he knew ten minutes wouldn't be enough to get over this one. He struggled to his feet and limped to her side. When he took her hand, she followed him back to the couch and sat beside him.

"Don't worry. I'm not going to cry," she said. "I never cry."

He believed her.

She went on. "Crying wastes time when you could be finding the bright side. That's my specialty, you know. Finding the bright side."

When she burst into sobs, he reached for her and held her.

Frankie sucked in a deep breath and buried her face in Jack's shirt. She couldn't meet his eyes. He must think she's a total baby. She felt his hand stroke her hair.

She wheezed, hiccupped and pushed away. "I'm sorry. I've been nothing but trouble."

"I didn't check my watch," he said, "but I think you have at least nine and-a-half minutes of grump time left. Or don't your rules cover crying jags?" He thumbed a tear from her cheek.

Frankie traced her fingers over his hand, then took it in hers. He covered it with his other hand and leaned forward. Her heart pounded, and her face flamed. She jerked away. Then laughed. "I wouldn't know. I told you, I never cry."

He stared at her, then said, "I need a shower. Will it wake her if I get some clothes from the bedroom?"

Relieved that he seemed to be ignoring her embarrassment, she stood. "I doubt it, but tell me what you need, and where. That way, if she wakes up, I can get her back to sleep. Besides, I should check on her."

"There's a laundry basket in the closet. Bring out the whole thing. They're clean, but I don't seem to get to the putting away stage."

Frankie crept into the bedroom. Wolf raised his head. Molly's arm was flung over his back, her breathing deep and even. In lieu of a night-light, Frankie had left the closet light on and the door ajar. Opening it enough to squeeze inside, she hoisted the plastic laundry basket to her hip and returned the door to its almost-closed position. Wolf's eyes shone in the reflected light.

"Thanks again," she whispered. "Good dog."

He yawned and lowered his head.

She found Jack in the kitchen, pouring a drink. He turned when she entered.

"Want a nightcap?"

She lowered the basket to the table. "No, thanks. I'm not much of a drinker." At his hesitation, she hurried to add, "But go ahead. I have nothing against people having a drink."

Lifting the glass, he said, "Cheers." He downed it and poured another. "Sure you don't want one?"

She shook her head. "I want to thank you again. Molly's out like a rock."

He raised his glass again. "To the innocence of youth. May you sleep as well." He tilted his head back and drained the glass before grabbing some clothes from the basket. "I won't be long. Make yourself at home."

She pondered his toast as she roamed the living room. Remembering his father's accident, she decided sleep hadn't come easy for him lately. Worry would do that.

A padded leather photo album on the bottom of the entertainment center caught her eye. Hesitating a scant second, she carried it to the couch and started leafing through it. Instead of family photos, she saw unsettling, yet familiar images. The desolation of war. Hungry children. Before she could figure out where she might have seen them, Jack came back, barefoot, dressed in loose fitting black cargo pants, towel drying his hair.

It was much easier to look at him, lean, muscular and bare-chested, if she thought of him as a subject to photograph. For the first time, she took notice of the newly revealed angular planes of his clean-shaven face. There was a warrior look to him. Strength and confidence—qualities he'd kept hidden before. She could already see him, posed against a tree, Wolf at his side.

Then he smiled and the warrior disappeared. Warriors didn't have dimples.

"What are you looking at?" He gestured to the album and went toward the kitchen.

"Some photos. I hope you don't mind."

"Nah—unless you're going to make fun of the way I looked as a kid. I was awfully scrawny until high school." He pulled a sweatshirt over his head.

"No, these aren't those kind of pictures." She turned a few pages. Recognition set in. She looked, and looked again. Her pulse quickened. She flipped to the back of the album, then raised her eyes to study him.

"Who are you? What are you doing with an album of Joshua Harper's pictures? Not cut from magazines. Originals. With proof sheets."

As if he'd pulled on a mask, Jack's face hardened. A jaw muscle twitched. "How do you know those were taken by Joshua Harper?"

"I took photography in high school. I was hooked on photojournalism, and I've followed it ever since. His work is distinctive. For a while, I wanted to be that kind of a photographer—a photojournalist, showing everyone the truth. It seemed like such an adventurous life. Nothing like my dull Broken Bow existence. But that was a long time ago."

"Why did you give it up?" He relaxed a little, but his tone

remained guarded. Forced neutrality.

She pushed away the memories. She'd long since stopped regretting her decisions. "Things don't always go the way you want. You know how it is. Life is what happens while you're making other plans."

He nodded. The pain in his eyes was the same pain she'd seen in the bar. It had nothing to do with his knee. But tonight, without the scruffy beard, he seemed vulnerable. Like he needed something beyond tomato soup and grilled cheese.

No doubt he did, but despite the twinge below her belly, it wasn't her. She clasped her hands in her lap, resisting the urge to go to him. She had her own problems, and didn't need anyone else's.

"You're not Joshua Harper. I've seen him on the news. I know your name isn't Jack Daniels. So, who are you?"

He sank into the chair across from her and rested his elbows on his knees, his head lowered, for several heartbeats before he looked up. "Ryan. Josh is my older brother. But I wish you'd forget you know that."

"Why? Why is knowing you're Joshua Harper's brother a big deal?"

"It's not. But knowing me might be. Ryan Harper's not a very nice person. Definitely not the sort of person you want to be involved with."

She stared into his whiskey-gold eyes, seeing the pain. "Depends on what you mean by involved. I happen to like the person I met. I don't think Ryan Harper is that much different from Jack. I think we could be friends."

"Ryan can never be Jack." His voice was a husky growl. He got up and took the photo album from her, closed it and put it back on the shelf. He stood there, his back to her, hands balled into fists at his side. Without turning, he said, "Go to bed, Frankie."

113

For the first time since she'd met him, he frightened her, and she didn't understand why. She'd assumed he'd respond like a friend—which was all she ever wanted from anyone. He'd been acting like a friend, and now, when things seemed safe, with the pieces of her life ready to be picked up, she was trembling inside.

She mumbled a good night and went to the bedroom. Wolf looked at her, then jumped from the bed and trotted out the door. She closed it behind him. "He's all yours," she whispered.

Moving Molly away from the center of the bed, Frankie snuggled in beside her. She'd seen heat in Ryan's eyes, had almost allowed herself to feel some in return. And then he'd shut her out.

Men. They hit on you, but when they found out you came as a set, they ran for cover. Or assumed you'd leap at the chance to jump into the sack, because obviously, you'd done it before. Or worse, they brought your child presents, thinking they'd score points, but they were only pretending. Nobody wanted a ready-made family. They wanted a roll in the hay, and she'd learned the hard way it was *not* worth it. She listened to the soft sounds of breathing beside her. Except for Molly. *She'd* been worth it.

For a short time, she'd allowed herself to think Ryan was different. Then he'd dismissed her. Sent her away. Well, gruff and rude as he'd been, at least he was enough of a gentleman not to shove himself at her once Molly'd gone to bed.

Molly. Frankie replayed the afternoon. Ryan had rescued Molly without a thought as to who she was. He'd taken care of her, made sure she was okay. That they were both okay. But not once did she remember him calling Molly by name. He was no different from any of the other men she'd met. To them, a child was a nuisance. A thing. An obstacle to be shoved aside to clear the route to Mommy's bed.

Sleep came in fits and starts. Jack—no, Ryan—invaded her dreams, and they were most definitely *not* nightmares. She'd read about having sexual feelings after a life-threatening experience. That must be what was happening. She stared at the ceiling, trying not to disturb Molly.

By four a.m., she gave up. Tiptoeing to the window, she pulled back the curtain. The snow had stopped. She found her clothes, dry enough to wear, and wriggled into them. Warrior fantasies were one thing. Ryan Harper had no place in her ordinary existence.

Leaving Molly asleep, Frankie crept to the living room. Ryan lay on his back on the couch, snoring softly, with the whiskey bottle on the floor beside him. In the kitchen, she found a tablet of paper and a pen. Crumpling three false starts, she decided a simple thank you would have to cover it. She left the note on the kitchen table.

Frankie gathered her belongings, found her car keys in the tote, and eased the front door open. After putting her things in the car, she went back into the house and shook Molly awake.

"Time to go, Peanut. Be super quiet."

Molly lifted her arms, and Frankie picked her up, inhaling the sleepy-child smell that balanced her world.

"It's dark."

"Yes, we need to get a very early start. No talking until we get in the car, okay?"

From the dead weight in her arms, she knew Molly had fallen back to sleep.

She buckled Molly into her seat and turned the key in the ignition, staring at the house, praying the car would start on the first try. When it did, she patted the dash. "Thank you."

She peered into the rearview mirror. The faint glow of the closet light illuminated the bedroom window. The rest of the house remained dark. That was what she wanted, she told herself. Ryan didn't want her around, and she certainly didn't need his negativity.

CHAPTER 10

Ryan clutched his temples, afraid his head would burst. Shit, he hadn't gotten blind, stinking drunk in years. When he needed to, he could usually pace himself to keep a nice, numbing buzz on. And he never got drunk because of a woman. *Never.* Hell and damnation. A perky woman who scheduled her anger. A woman with a kid. No, it wasn't Frankie. She was the final shove that sent him over the edge.

He pulled himself off the couch, trying to convince himself. The bedroom was empty, his sweats neatly folded at the foot of the bed. He checked for her camera and tote. Both gone. Good riddance.

He staggered toward the bathroom. Standing under the shower's blast, he lowered the temperature until his head cleared. While toweling off, he decided a vague dream about sitting on the porch with a dog in the middle of the night must not have been a dream.

"Wolf?" No response. Pop should have named him Ghost. He groaned and stumbled into the kitchen.

"Thanks for everything. Frankie & Molly."

He crumpled the note and tossed it in the trash. *You're welcome.* Careful not to move his head, he managed to get the filter, water and coffee into the right places and flipped the brew switch.

Lust, he told himself. That's all it was. If he'd pressed, she would have given in. She'd been vulnerable; he'd been celibate a long time. He'd done the right thing. She didn't seem like a one-night stand sort of woman, and he wasn't a relationship man.

The pounding in his head started again, and it took awhile to figure out it was coming from the door.

"It's open," he shouted, regretting it as soon as the words left his mouth. Where the hell did Josh keep the aspirin? He braced himself against the counter, riding out a wave of nausea.

"Drink water." His father's voice floated through the haze.

Ryan started to straighten, decided it was impossible, and besides, his father undoubtedly knew exactly what was wrong with him.

"Morning, Pop."

"More like afternoon. You know what day it is?"

Shit. "It better be Monday."

"Yep." He set a cardboard box on the counter.

Ryan looked at it, looked to his father, who had retreated into the living room. He pried up the lid and peered inside. His heart stopped. The room spun, blood rushed in his ears, and it wasn't from last night's booze. Gingerly, he reached in, lifting first one picture, then another. Some still framed as he remembered them on the walls. Others loose in the box. A stack of pale yellow envelopes tied with a white ribbon, still emitting a faint lavender scent. His mother's handwriting, clear and bold. He blinked. Swallowed. Pinched the bridge of his nose. Cleared his throat.

"Pop . . . I . . ."

"Hurt too much to see her," came Pop's voice, gruff with emotion. "Thought you might want one or two of them. Help yourself."

Ryan leafed through the snapshots while he waited for the earth to start revolving again. He knew which one he wanted as soon as he saw it.

He remembered the day it had been taken, right after he'd won third prize at the fair with Dynamite, his pony. He'd been so sure he'd get the blue ribbon and hadn't wanted to pose for the family picture his grandfather insisted on taking. He was eight, Josh was eleven, and Lindy was barely out of toddlerhood, holding a wand of cotton candy. He saw the look in his mother's eyes, as she looked at him, not the ribbon, not the camera. So proud, she'd made him feel like he'd won first prize after all.

"Could use some help." Pop's voice from over his shoulder broke the spell. Ryan set the picture on the counter.

"Name it, Pop," he said, keeping his face averted.

"How about some coffee?"

"It'll be another couple of minutes."

His father edged around him and filled a glass with water. "Drink."

Ryan eyed the glass as if it were an implement of torture. Considering how his stomach felt, it was. Pop's eyes bored through him. He drank. His stomach churned, but he thought he'd be all right.

"Go sit," Pop said. "I'll bring the coffee."

Ryan walked across the room as if it were covered in eggshells. He lowered himself to the couch. Pop rummaged in drawers, then came over and set another glass of water and a bottle of ibuprofen on the coffee table.

"Anything you want to tell me?" Pop asked.

"Rough day."

"Looks like the night was rougher."

"I wouldn't know." He swallowed three tablets and downed the water. "What do you need?"

His father got up, went to the kitchen, and returned with two mugs of coffee. "It can wait."

A new churning roiled in Ryan's stomach. Pop never asked

for help unless it was to mend a fence, herd the stock or some ranch-related chore. But if all he needed was a hand around the place, he'd have come out with it, probably before he'd said good morning.

"No, tell me now." A flash of panic jump-started his pulse. "Did the doctors—they didn't find anything—I mean, you're okay?" Dammit, he was babbling like Frankie.

"I'm fine. Cracked a rib or two. Mild concussion. Been worse bustin' broncs. Too ornery to kick off just yet." He reached into a back pocket and dropped an envelope onto the table.

Ryan sipped his coffee, letting the hot brew sit in his mouth before swallowing. "For me?"

When his father remained silent, Ryan picked up the envelope. Heavyweight paper, addressed to Pop, a bank's return address. He reached inside and removed the pages.

Ryan skimmed the contents, his hangover forgotten. "Shit, Pop. Can they do this? Take away your access rights?"

"Apparently so. I talked to the lawyers this morning. I got no claim to the land."

"Can you buy them out?"

"Hell, no. I make a comfortable living, but ain't got that kind of cash."

"Without access to that stretch of land, the tours can't—is there another route?"

"Would either have to be half or twice as long—and not sure there'd be many takers. Two-hour ride was perfect for the city folks. The four-hour one was never a big draw—only did one or two a week." He grimaced. "That chunk of land's got some of the best vistas."

Ryan glanced back at the pages. "Six weeks? Can't they wait until after the season?"

"Could, I expect. Won't."

"Can't you work out the same sort of arrangement?"

"I figured you might have some ideas—I'm a hick rancher, you know. No way I can afford that spread, not worth it for access rights."

"Shit, Pop, you're no hick." He snapped the papers back onto the table. "What can I do that you can't?" The anger in Pop's eyes was new to Ryan.

"I don't know—thought you might have some idea—your life being a tad more . . . creative . . . than mine."

"Pop, I don't know. My field of expertise is a bit more . . . physical. Let me think about it for a bit." He worked past the throbbing in his head. "You have an Internet connection?"

"See—told ya you thought I was a hick. Broadband. And a website. How d'you think we snag the tourists these days?"

"I should have known."

There was a prolonged silence. "Could use you at the house, too."

Ryan studied his father. Pop hadn't sat down, and his stance was awkward. Ryan held up the bottle of ibuprofen. "You need some of these pills?"

A hint of a smile creased his father's weathered face. "Got some better ones at home."

"I'll be there."

"Truck's outside." He swiveled toward the door.

Ryan stood. The room swirled. He swallowed. "Be with you right after I puke."

Holding a tiny blue satin evening gown, Frankie trudged up the stairs toward Molly's room, shaking her head at the resiliency of kids. Molly had been up at dawn with a to-do list that started with French toast, moved on to French braids, help with a jigsaw puzzle and a search for the perfect outfit Barbie would wear on her upcoming date with Ken.

Frankie, on the other hand, ached all over, had barely slept, and hoped she wasn't coming down with something. When she was halfway up the stairs, the phone rang. Deciding whether to go back down to the kitchen or continue up seemed an impossible choice. Up. She grabbed the phone before Molly's hand hit the receiver. Molly snatched Barbie's dress and raced back to her room.

"Mom. How's Lolo? Are you having a good time? Any aftereffects from your fall?" She refrained from asking about Bob.

"Slow down, for goodness sake. Everything is wonderful. I tried calling last night, but you weren't home. Did you get my message?"

"Sorry. I forgot to check the machine. What's up?" Frankie heard country music in the background, muffled conversation and laughter. "Where are you?"

"We're still in Lolo—I wanted to let you know we're staying a little longer."

Thoughts of another accident crashed into her already aching head. "Mom, is anything wrong? You didn't have another dizzy spell, did you?"

"No, nothing like that. Bob's a bit of a history buff, and he's enjoying the Lewis and Clark trail sites. We lost time because of the weather, but since it's cleared up, we thought we'd extend our stay. I hope you don't mind."

It dawned on Frankie that her mother wasn't asking permission. "Of course not." Her hands got cold and her cheeks got hot. Maybe she *was* coming down with something. "Have fun. Molly and I will hold down the fort." She gritted her teeth and added, "Say hi to Bob."

Good grief. At sixty-eight, her mother had a better social life than she did. Heck, merely *having* a social life was better than what she had. She did *not* want to think about that. But when she stopped envisioning her mother and Bob, all she saw was Ryan Harper. She rubbed her temples and went in search of some painkillers.

Two hours later, standing at the checkout counter at the drug store, Frankie accepted the fact that she had a cold. A mild cold, she told herself. Nothing major. Armed with a sack full of cough drops, decongestants and nasal spray, she pulled Molly down the block to the camera store.

"I'll have to send these out," the teen-age clerk said. "We don't process black and white on site anymore." The look he gave her said nobody in their right mind did black and white anywhere anymore. Or even film.

He handed her five strips of paper. "Here are your claim checks."

Molly tugged on Frankie's arm. "I'm hungry, Mommy."

"One more stop. I need to take some pictures to a store in Missoula. I have an apple in the car for you." Frankie thanked the clerk, shoved the receipts into her purse and hurried to the car. With luck, the car wouldn't act up, and she'd get to the Photo Barn and back before dark. And before her head exploded.

Tuesday morning Frankie sat at the kitchen table, armed with a box of tissues and a mug of tea laced with honey and lemon, as she pored over bank statements. Too exhausted to do anything the previous evening, she'd made Molly macaroni and cheese for dinner, then napped on the couch while Molly watched videos. But yesterday's mail brought overdue phone and electric bills plus a maxed out credit card statement. Time to tackle the budget.

The last bank statement she found was two months old. Apparently Mom had switched to the computerized system after that. Frankie opened the checkbook and examined the register. The last entry was two months ago. All the notations were in her mother's neat handwriting. The payment column far outweighed the deposit column. Frankie recognized the Social Security income, and what looked like regular transfers from her mother's pension, but there was a recurring automatic deposit of three hundred dollars a month she couldn't account for. Probably James' contribution to the household.

She turned on the computer and went to the bank's website. Not sure if she should be happy or angry when her mother's account opened automatically, Frankie made a mental note to talk to her mother about leaving her password filled in. For now, she'd pay some of these bills.

A mixture of worry and relief drizzled over her. On one hand, there was enough money to cover the bills. But that raised the question about her mother's ability to manage the accounts. Had she forgotten to pay the bills? Misplaced them?

Answers would have to wait until her mother returned. She set up the payments, clicked "Submit" and sent a copy of the accounts to the printer. Brenda would be back Friday. She'd ask her to keep a closer eye on Mom.

"Mommy. Susie's outside. Can I go play?"

Frankie sneezed. "Outside where?"

"Her backyard. I see her playing with Buster. I like him, but he's not as nice as Wolf."

"Let me call Mrs. Winthrop and make sure it's okay with her." Frankie picked up the phone, peering out the kitchen window. Susie was throwing a tennis ball for Buster, who didn't seem too excited about returning it. Maybe the terrier next door would satisfy Molly's craving for a puppy.

"You sound terrible," Meg Winthrop said. "Of course Molly can come play. We were going to go see the new Disney picture, and then to Slappy's for pizza. We'd love to have Molly join us. As a matter of fact, why don't you plan to have her sleep over. Give that cold a rest."

At the mention of the sleepover, Frankie remembered that

with both Mom and Brenda gone, she needed a sitter for Molly tonight anyway, so she could go to work. She was getting as forgetful as her mother. "You are an angel of mercy," she said. "I will return the favor. All you have to do is ask."

"I'm sure things will even out. Greg and I have an anniversary next month."

"I hear you. Susie's welcome to stay here."

"To be honest, I think I over-planned Spring Break activities, but I can't back down now. Having Molly join us actually makes things easier."

With Molly off to play and the house to herself, Frankie changed into her flannel drawstring pants, her faded red sweatshirt with the frayed cuffs, and curled up on the couch with a quilt, her tissues, and Indiana Jones. She'd get a decent nap, her cold meds would work, and she'd be able to handle her stint at the Three Elks. Thank goodness Mr. Stubbs hadn't been serious about firing her, not after she explained the emergency. She'd make up her lost hour tonight. As a precaution, she set the kitchen timer before she focused on Harrison Ford. She attributed his morphing into a dimpled, bare-chested warrior to her cold pills.

CHAPTER 11

Home after an endless shift, Frankie trudged up the porch steps. She stripped off her Three Elks uniform, crawled back into her comfort clothes, and put on some water for tea.

She'd made better than average tips. Apparently, the customers liked her frog-voice. They said it was sexy. But she was glad she had tomorrow night off. She still hadn't decided if she was disappointed or thankful that Jack—no, Ryan—hadn't shown up.

While she waited for the water to boil, she checked the answering machine. Three messages. Wishing she had the mental fortitude to put them off until morning, she knew her curiosity would keep her awake. Bob and her mother would call on her cell if there was an emergency. Same went for Molly. Would Ryan have called? No, he was probably angry at the way she'd disappeared. Or glad. And why should she be thinking of him? He hadn't accepted her offer of friendship. And she didn't want more, not that he'd offered.

Good grief. She picked up the pen beside the phone and pushed the button.

Three words into a pitch for the investment opportunity of a lifetime, she hit Delete.

The kettle whistled, and Frankie stepped into the kitchen. The raspy voice on the machine quickened her pulse. She turned off the burner, raced back to the table and hit "Replay."

"This message is for Ms. Frances Castor. Um . . . Guess

you're not home. This is Will Loucas at the Photo Barn in Missoula. You were in yesterday. I'll call tomorrow—that's Wednesday—it's about those photographs you brought by. Thanks. Um, bye."

Her heart pounded. Will Loucas had accepted her two landscapes on consignment. This had to mean he had a buyer, didn't it?

If he sold them, he'd take more. He'd said so. The adrenaline rush cleared her head, and she happy-danced around the kitchen. Two sales wasn't much, but it was a start. Wait. Maybe not two. Who cared? Selling one picture in a day was better than she'd hoped for.

She stopped mid-pivot and took a deep breath. The message didn't say he'd sold anything. Wouldn't he have mentioned that in his message? It could mean he changed his mind about displaying them. But tonight, she was going to believe that he'd sold at least one of them. She would enjoy one night of feeling like a professional photographer.

The furnace groaned, and the empty house closed in around her. For the first time in she couldn't remember how long, she longed for someone to share her excitement. Heck, for the first time in she couldn't remember how long, she had exciting news to share. Even Molly was gone tonight. Knowing it would be a while before she could sleep, she went back to the couch and Indiana Jones.

"Hey, Indy," she whispered at the television. "I'm going to be a photographer. Isn't that great?"

Ryan pounded on Frankie's door, not caring that it was eight in the morning. How could she be involved in putting Pop out of business? The door opened, and he waved a sheaf of papers in her face. "What do you think you're doing?"

When he got no answer, he pushed his way past her into the

living room. "I can't believe you'd do this."

The door closed behind him, and he calmed down long enough to notice her bare feet and baggy flannel pants. His eyes moved upward, past the oversized sweatshirt, to her disheveled hair, red-tipped nose, and puffy eyes.

"Sorry if I woke you." As apologies went, he didn't think she'd buy it. So what. She'd be right. He'd spent the better part of a day tracking down the owner of the mountain property, and somewhere in the layers of paperwork, he uncovered an address. His blood pressure had skyrocketed when he realized it was Frankie's, that he'd misjudged her entirely. Like everyone else, she had a hidden agenda.

"Dammit, aren't you going to say something?" he asked.

She shook her head and pointed at her throat.

"What's that supposed to mean?" He looked at her more closely. The bright eyes. The pale face. The tremor in her hand. "Shit, Frankie. You're sick."

She rolled her eyes and gave him a crooked grin. "Got it in one, Sherlock."

Damn, she sounded like a baritone frog. His anger dissolved, replaced by a totally inappropriate physical response, one that defied all logic. Maybe not *all* logic. He'd been thinking about her on the drive over, trying to stay angry, but memories of her at the cabin—the way she smelled after her shower, the way her eyes lit up when he brought back her camera, the way she'd felt, all soft and vulnerable when she'd fainted into his arms—kept interfering with his fume. He'd come here to make her explain what was going on, to argue her into putting a stop to Pop's problem, and his body was overruling his brain, telling him to take her in his arms and comfort her. To feel her soft curves pressed against him.

"Coffee?" she said.

"Please," he said, ignoring the fact that he'd had three cups before he left and drained a thermos on the drive over. He sensed her behind him and tried to dismiss the way she enveloped his senses, even from five feet away. "Relax. I can do it."

In the kitchen, he found the coffee fixings on the counter and busied himself while he waited for things to settle down.

"The kid still asleep?"

She hesitated before answering. "Sleepover."

"Don't talk if it hurts."

She brushed against him as she reached for a teakettle on the stove. "I'm going to have tea." She twisted a knob and stepped back, pushing her hair from her face. "Be right back."

While she was gone, his cell rang. "Unknown caller" flashed on the display. He pressed the talk button. "Harper."

"Hey, pardner."

"Dalton? Where are you?" As soon as he uttered the words, he knew there was no point in asking. There was shouting in the background, he could hear a chopper, and what was probably wind whistling. "Never mind. What's up?" His pulse quickened in anticipation. Dalton wouldn't call from a mission unless it was important.

"Only have a second. Looks like the car accident was really an accident. Debbie worked her magic on the bits and couldn't find anything. Thought you'd rest easier knowing."

Before he could respond, the line went dead. He stared at the phone before pressing the end button. He pored over the papers again, trying to build up another fume, to no avail. The kettle whistled. He got up, turned off the burner and looked for tea bags.

"Left cabinet next to the stove, bottom shelf." Her voice, while still husky, sounded less like a frog and more like—like he imagined she'd sound in the throes of desire. He glanced over his shoulder. Still barefoot, but wearing faded jeans and a red pullover, she'd gathered her hair into a ponytail. He stared at the loose tendrils at the nape of her neck, wondering what she'd do if he caressed her there. Keeping his body turned away from her, he found the box of teabags, popped one into a mug from the draining rack, and set it on the counter.

"Sit," she said. "I'll do it."

Standing next to him, she smelled like soap, toothpaste, and cough drops. He enjoyed watching her pour boiling water into the mug, then stir in some honey. Another wave of lust crashed over him. She gave him an easy grin—an absolutely, totally, one-hundred-and-ten percent, innocent, 'let's be friends' smile.

Unable to resist, he leaned forward and touched his lips to her forehead.

She neither pulled away nor moved closer. She merely cocked her head in question. No reason to expect her to feel the same lust—and probably better that she didn't realize what she was doing to him. He was damn sure Frankie didn't do lust.

"Checking for fever," he mumbled.

"It's a head cold. No big deal." She poured a cup of coffee for him and sat at the table, her hands wrapped around the mug of tea.

"Now, what did I do to ruin your father's life? And what can I do to fix it?"

He'd come here ready for a knock-down, drag-out argument. Instead, he got—Frankie. Why had he expected her to fight him? He was dealing with a woman who considered problems pebbles in life's path, things to be kicked aside. Troubles were allotted ten minutes. As she smiled at him in anticipation, he mused that he'd been transported to some fairytale alternate universe.

He sipped his coffee, trying to remember the lines he'd rehearsed. Somehow, they wouldn't match the mood he'd come in with, or the one Frankie set.

The phone rang. Frankie jumped. Her eyes sparkled, as if she was hoping for good news, but she hesitated, as if she wasn't sure she dared answer it.

"Go ahead," he said. "I need to use your bathroom, if that's okay?"

She nodded, pointed toward the hall and rushed to the phone.

He vowed to focus on the reason for his visit, and to keep things impersonal. Frankie didn't need a guy like him, and he knew he'd only hurt her. For a lot longer than ten minutes.

When he returned to the kitchen, Frankie was grinning so hard, he thought her face would split. She raced to him, grabbed his hands, and practically jumped for joy. Then she threw her arms around his neck.

Her lips were close enough that he felt the warmth of her breath. For an instant, he thought he saw heat reflected in her eyes. Just as quickly, she blinked, and she was innocent exuberance once again.

He inhaled her scent before prying her hands from his neck, but he didn't let go of them. "Whoa. That's quite a welcome. I wasn't gone that long, and I've been reasonably competent in the bathroom department since I was four."

"I sold a picture. And he wants more. The proofs won't be back until Friday, and I'll have to see about getting a darkroom, or sending them to a lab at first, but I sold a picture and it was only up for a day. Isn't that fantastic? I'm not great, like your brother, but—"

He squeezed her hands, then released them. "That's wonderful, Frankie. I'm happy for you. Now breathe."

"I'm sorry. I'm so excited. I mean, it's not like the Photo Barn is a fancy gallery or anything, more like a tourist gift shop, but someone liked a creation of mine enough to pay for it. Maybe I'll be able to quit the Three Elks soon."

Who could dispute that optimism? "I'm sure you will."

She reached up and adjusted her ponytail. "Okay. Enough of this. You came here with a problem. Let's see if we can work something out."

He wished he shared her confidence. He sat down and slid the papers across the table. "What do you know about this?"

Frankie picked up the pages, leafed through them. As she read, her brow furrowed. She chewed on her lip. She laid them down and shook her head.

"I have no clue. What does it mean?"

Ryan sucked in a breath. Blew it out. "Your grandfather owned property in the mountains. My grandfather had some grazing land for his livestock, but he needed to cross your grandfather's property. They had a gentleman's agreement. My grandfather paid your grandfather a monthly fee, and your grandfather promised to notify him if he ever decided to do anything to the property that would deny that access."

"Okay," she said. "I'll take your word for that. I know that we used to go to the mountains when I was a kid. Family picnics, stuff like that. Dad called it 'our property', but I never thought about it. After he died, Mom never took us back. When I got older, I assumed she'd sold it. I'm not even exactly sure where it is. When you're twelve, you don't pay much attention to driving directions."

Ryan stared at her, but her expression didn't falter. He saw no deceit. "Then tell me why you were there taking pictures Sunday."

She sipped her tea, cleared her throat. "I'd been there in high school. For photography class field trips." She stood up, brought a box of tissues to the table, and sat down. After wiping her nose, she went on. "Come to think of it, Mom had volunteered to chaperone one trip. She probably picked the place. Honest, Ryan. One tree looks like the next one, and I don't remember if that's the same place. How much land are you talking about?"

"About two hundred acres."

She was quiet, apparently lost in thought. And, he noticed, she thought the way she did everything else. With one hundred percent of her being. Her fingers tapped the table. Her eyes squinted. Her lips moved in and out. Before he could dwell on what he'd like to do to those lips, she spoke.

"So, the places where we used to picnic could have been some distance away from where I was Sunday, right? I swear, I didn't know it was our land. I knew it would give me some great shots, that's all. But I still don't see what this has to do with your father's business."

"My father's been paying three hundred dollars a month for access to that land. He retired from raising livestock, but he has a flourishing trail ride business that passes through the piece of property your mother owns. The money's transferred from his bank to your mother's bank—has been for over a decade."

"Wait a minute." Frankie dashed out of the room and returned with a handful of papers.

"That explains these deposits to the account every month. I still don't see the problem. Can't your father afford the three hundred anymore? I'm sure if I talk to Mom, she'd be happy to make some kind of adjustment."

Ryan found the last sheet of paper and the letter from the bank. "Pop gets a stinking boilerplate letter from the bank telling him the property is being sold, that as a courtesy, he has six weeks to meet or beat the other guy's offer. Some courtesy. I've done some checking. This guy is a corporate hotshot who wants to build some fancy mountain retreat for his executives to play bonding games and meditate. No way is he going to want a string of tourists on horseback to come traipsing through his sacred domain."

"Oh, dear."

"Yeah. Oh, dear. Oh, motherfucking dear."

The back door to the kitchen slammed shut. "Hi Mommy. Hi, Mr. Man. Do I get another dollar?" The kid barreled in, clutching Mr. Snuggles and wheeling a pink and blue overnight case.

His face hot, Ryan reached for his wallet. "Good morning."

The kitchen lights flashed off and on. He looked up at Frankie.

"Lets Meg know she's inside," Frankie said. "Did you have fun, Molly?"

"Mrs. Winthrop said to ask if I can go to the merry-go-round in Missoula. I need to get a jacket because we're going to do a picnic. I promise I won't go close to any river. Is it okay?"

"Let me call her first." Frankie bent to kiss her daughter, then went to the phone.

The child stood at Ryan's side, and he handed her a dollar.

"Thank you," she said, then peered under the table. "Is Wolf here?"

"No," Ryan said. "He's at home taking care of my father today."

"Okay." She went to her mother and leaned against her leg. Frankie's hand lowered and stroked the child's hair. An unexpected longing coursed through Ryan's chest. His throat tightened. He couldn't be getting Frankie's cold already. When he'd become a SEAL, he'd pushed aside all things domestic. Working for Blackthorne had intensified the need for detachment. Until now, he never thought he'd been lonely.

Frankie kept her voice low, and Ryan shuffled through the papers. Moments later, she hung up and crouched to look her daughter in the eye. "It's okay for you to go. But I want you to try something for me, okay?" She grasped the child's hands.

From the serious expression on the child's face, Ryan guessed this was another of their rituals. Frankie's tone, while not threatening, clearly said, *You might not like this, but you're going to do it anyway.*

"I want you to have fun with Susie. But Mr. Snuggles has to stay home this time."

The kid was quiet for a few seconds. She clutched the dog to her chest. Ryan braced himself for tears, or a tantrum. At the very least, he expected Frankie to reach for the timer.

Raising the dog to eye level, the child said, "You have to stay here, Mr. Snuggles," her tone a perfect imitation of her mother's. "Like when I go to school. I'll come back and tell you all about the merry-go-round."

She trotted over to the table and flopped the dog next to him. "You can borrow him if you want. I'm going on a picnic." Clunking her case behind her, she dashed from the room.

Ryan bit the inside of his cheek to keep from laughing out loud.

"Did you brush your teeth after breakfast?" Frankie called toward Molly.

"Yes," came the reply, uttered with five-year-old indignation.

Frankie grinned and shook her head. "Can't help it. I'm a mom."

Her words ratcheted through his insides. She sure as hell was. And he did not get involved with moms. Moms came with kids. Kids created problems. He pushed back from the table and refilled his coffee cup, disregarding the acid buildup in his belly.

Frankie manipulated the papers in front of her. He took his seat and waited.

"I think I'll have to talk to Mom," she said. "I don't know what she's told this guy. Maybe she can back out. You've got some time left, right?"

"Yeah. A few weeks."

"You said your father couldn't afford to buy the property. Could he handle paying a little more each month? Maybe some extra cash would be enough to make Mom change her mind."

Her words neutralized some of the acid. "You think she would go for that?"

"I have no idea. Until you showed up, I didn't even know she owned the land. But I can give it a try."

In another whirlwind, the kid whooshed back, minus suitcase, dragging her jacket. She kissed Frankie, then darted around the table, stood on tiptoe and kissed his cheek.

"Bye, Mommy. Bye, Mr. Man." The door slammed again, and silence descended over the kitchen. Ryan sat, staring at the door. He touched his cheek, damp from the child's lips. Such innocence, to be so happy. So alive. Inwardly, he cursed at how fleeting life could be. He blinked, keeping his face averted from Frankie.

CHAPTER 12

Frankie watched pain and misery replace the surprise and confusion that had flashed across Ryan's face when Molly kissed him. She wondered what it would take to make him relax. Everything about him was tight, brittle, as if he'd shatter if anything poked him.

Back at his cabin, he'd let his guard down, but only for an instant. In that wink of time, she'd glimpsed the man she believed he was—strong, but not cold. Caring and unselfish. But when he put his defense wall back up, he reinforced it with steel and put barbed wire across the top. Electrified it, too.

He wasn't the sort of man she could tease out of his troubles. Was it because Dalton left? Or was it his father's predicament? She slid her chair back and walked around the table, stopping behind him. His head was lowered. If he noticed her, he gave no indication.

When she placed her hands on his shoulders, he stiffened, but didn't turn around. She kneaded the knots she found bunched up across his back. She moved her fingers up to his neck, pushing aside the hair to get at his skin. The silken strands contrasted with the tight muscles in his neck. He shuddered, but she merely increased the pressure. When she felt some of the tension ease, she worked her way back down to his shoulders.

"Relax," she said. "Tensing up won't make things happen any faster. When Mom gets back, we'll find out what's going on."

"Stop." His hand reached up and covered hers. "It's not . . .

just stop, okay?"

"Who are you, Ryan Harper? I think you owe me that much." She waited out his silence.

"I . . . I don't know anymore." His words were barely a whisper.

"Something bad happened to you. More than a car accident."

"I have to go," he said. He scribbled his number on the margin of one of the pieces of paper in front of her. "Call me when you talk to your mom." He shoved his chair back, making her jump out of the way. But he didn't rise.

She continued working her fingers into his shoulders. "You can't keep running away from whatever it is. Not if you want your life to be meaningful."

"Sorry, Frankie, but some things can't be solved by setting a timer for ten minutes."

"Who said anything about solving problems in ten minutes?" She heard the indignation in her tone, but didn't tamp it back. "You need to stop dwelling on the misery so your brain can find the answers. If you're wallowing in self-pity, you can't see them."

"Sometimes there aren't answers, Frankie." His tone matched hers.

Her hands dropped from his shoulders and she stepped in front of him. Gazing into his eyes, she saw something besides misery. There was heat. Need. In that instant, she knew her own eyes reflected the same. She lowered her head. Grazed his lips with hers.

Their softness surprised her. She felt his warm breath, scented with coffee.

He let her lips linger, then rose to his feet. "I can't."

She shook her head. "You won't. Why?"

His eyes flashed anger now. "Because I'm a man, dammit, and not a very noble one. Because I know there's a line here, one I shouldn't cross." His voice softened. "You're making that line very hard to see. It's not fair to you."

"Who ever said life was fair?"

"I've hurt too many people, Frankie. I won't allow you to be on that list."

"Isn't that my decision? How dare you assume that because I offered a kiss in comfort that I wanted to climb into the sack? I don't know what made me think you were different from any of the others."

"Maybe I'm not." Before her eyes, he retreated behind his wall.

"Get the hell out of there," she commanded. "Come back from your safe little mental fortress and let people help you, dammit!"

His eyebrows shot up and he actually grinned, dimple and all.

"What?" she said, refusing to succumb to his amusement. "You think I don't use those words? I prefer to save them for important things."

"Saving me from myself isn't worth it." The grin was gone, but so was a lot of the pain.

"Not your call."

"Not yours, either. You and the kid deserve more than I can give."

With that, her control snapped. "Say her name."

"What?" He looked genuinely confused.

"Molly. She has a name, and it's Molly, not kid."

"Of course she does. Molly."

"Why don't you use it when you talk about her? When you think of her, what do you call her in your head? The kid? The obstacle?"

"What are you talking about?"

Frankie couldn't stanch the flow of angered words. "I've met your type. Pretend the kid doesn't exist, not as a person anyway.

Put it to bed, farm it off with a sitter, get it the hell out of the way so you can get to Mommy."

"Frankie, slow down. It's—"

"It's what? Not that? Okay, so you'd be one of those who brings a stupid, totally inappropriate present for her, thinking it'll impress me that you like my daughter. Only you don't. The present is nothing but toll on the road to the bedroom."

"Shit, Frankie, I told you that's exactly why I wouldn't let you kiss me."

"No—you assumed there's no reason for a kiss unless it's a prelude to sex. You can't allow yourself a female friend, can you?"

"I could," he said softly. "But I'm not sure we're on the same page here. You want to be my friend. I'm not sure it can be the same for me."

Unable to respond over the twisting in her gut, she marched toward the den. After so many years of disuse, her female instincts must have atrophied. Flipping on the TV, she told herself it wasn't because she thought a relationship could possibly be in the cards for her and Ryan, but that she thought he needed help rediscovering his humanity.

When she sensed him standing in the doorway, she didn't lift her gaze. He entered the room and sat beside her.

"Indiana Jones? I prefer the third one, myself. With Sean Connery." His voice was hesitant, but she heard the apology in its tone.

"I watched that one yesterday."

"I'm not in a good place now, Frankie. Not for me, and certainly not for anyone around me."

"Bottling it up doesn't help," she said.

He gave a wry laugh. "You sound like Pop."

"Maybe you should listen to your father."

"Listening's never been my strong suit."

"Mom always says I never give anyone a chance to talk."

He put his hand on her knee, and a warm tingle spread through her. A fullness in her breasts. Heat. Familiar, yet distant memories of feelings she wasn't ready to accept.

"Carmelita," he said. The word came out as if it took every bit of strength to get it past his lips.

"What?"

"You asked me what I thought when I thought of Molly. Why I didn't use her name."

"She reminds you of someone named Carmelita?" She tried to reconcile how someone named Carmelita, who she immediately envisioned bearing dark Hispanic features, could possible remind Ryan of her strawberry-blonde, fair Molly.

Afraid to look at him and break the spell, she covered his hand with hers. "Tell me."

"She was Molly's age. Maybe a little younger."

At the use of the past tense, a fist clutched Frankie's heart. "Your daughter?" she whispered. She knew nothing of this man, she realized. Nothing beyond his pain, and that there was inherent good inside him, no matter what he thought. In her peripheral vision, she saw his head shake.

His hand tensed under hers. "She had big, round eyes. Brown, not blue, but innocent and trusting, like Molly. I couldn't save her."

"I'm so sorry. I'm sure you did everything you could."

"Everything's not always good enough." Anger, barely controlled, filled his voice. She squeezed his hand.

In one swift move, his hands were behind her head, pulling her toward him. His lips found hers, pressed against them, hot and demanding. His teeth scraped her lower lip. Startled by the abruptness, she gasped, and his tongue probed the depths of her mouth.

There was nothing gentle in the kiss. Its frenzy spoke of

anguish, of despair, of need. She sensed he expected her to pull away. Wanted her to pull away. Instead, she matched his heat. Her tongue met his. Danced. Prodded. Entwined.

He moaned, a sound from deep within, plaintive and urgent.

Her hands clutched his hair, refusing to let him break away. He was not going to intimidate her with his dominance. If this was the way through Ryan's wall, she would accept whatever opening he granted.

Slowly, the frenzy faded. He withdrew, planting gentle kisses on her lips, her nose, her forehead.

"That was uncalled for," he whispered beneath her ear. "I'm sorry." His eyes held unbearable sadness.

"Don't apologize for needing help," she said. She released her grip on his hair and ran her fingers down his cheek. "Do you feel better?"

A corner of his mouth lifted. "Don't tell Molly, but I like this better than Mr. Snuggles."

"I hope it was worth it," she said. At his questioning look, she said, "You'll probably get my cold."

Embarrassed and ashamed, Ryan drove his fingers through his hair. Never had he forced himself on a woman like that. And instead of pulling away, instead of slapping him, instead of swearing as he now knew she could, Frankie had returned his heated need. Not because of pity. Because she knew that's what it was. Need.

"If I do, I deserve it," he whispered.

"Who are you?" She repeated her question. The tenderness in her voice belied the frenzy of her kiss.

"You don't want to know, Frankie. I told you, I'm not a nice person."

"And I told you I don't think you know who you are."

He glanced around the room, seeing scattered evidence of

family life—books, a doll, a pair of slippers. Typical daily life clutter. Sweeping his arm in a broad circle, he said, "What would you do if I said to clear this room?"

She looked at him, then followed his arm. Shrugged. "Put the toys away, I guess. Straighten the magazines on the coffee table. Take the mugs to the kitchen. Why? You don't like my housekeeping?"

He took a breath, gathered himself. "I used to be a Navy SEAL. When I got out, I went to work for a private company that does a lot of the same kind of stuff. And a lot of hostage rescue." He turned to face her so that he was staring into her eyes. Why hadn't he noticed how blue they were? Or how they always seemed to care. He grasped her wrists. Too hard, perhaps, because those eyes widened, but she didn't pull away. He relaxed his hold but didn't release her. "In my job, if I clear a room, it means I go in shooting, and when I'm done, people are dead. I kill people, Frankie."

She didn't say anything for what seemed like an eternity, and he bowed his head, afraid to see what those blue eyes would reflect.

"What happened to Carmelita?" she whispered.

"She died. In my arms. In Colombia. Along with her brother, her mother and father."

"Did you kill the people who did it?"

"I did."

"I think—I think if someone tried to hurt Molly, I could hurt them."

When he looked up, a tear trickled down her cheek. He refused his own, though they stung behind his eyes and hung like a fireball at the back of his throat. The required visits to the shrink after the incidents had warned him that his feelings were likely to be near the surface. Some crap about repressed emotions. He'd discovered the diagnosis was correct, but that didn't mean he had to accept it. To him, all it meant was extra effort to maintain his detachment. And then along came Frankie. If he didn't get out of here in the next few minutes, he was going to come apart.

The phone rang, and he thanked God for the interruption. Frankie wiped her eyes, then got up to answer.

"I've got to go," he said. He held his hand to his ear, thumb and pinkie outstretched, and mimed calling before he retreated.

"Coward," he mumbled, when he sat behind the wheel of Pop's pickup. In his life, everyone had an alternate agenda. Not Frankie. With her, what you saw was what you got, and she had a way of making everything he'd buried rise to the surface. If he couldn't face himself, how could he let anyone else see him for what he was? A failure, going through the motions.

Maybe Frankie had the right philosophy. Self-pity didn't solve problems. Time to see if the old Ryan Harper was still around. He cranked the ignition and glanced at the house. Through the sheer draperies, Frankie's shadow paced, still on the phone.

As he drove, he tried to sort things. Answers had to be in his files; he simply hadn't found them yet. Where to start? The Forcada's? Panama? The Mustang exploding? One by one, he replayed missions, especially the ones that had gone south. Could the Phantom have anything to do with it? The man had an uncanny ability to show up at drug busts and arms deals, helping himself to the merchandise and disappearing without a trace. Not always on Blackthorne jobs, but often enough that it had made Ryan wonder if there was some sort of leak. And if there was a leak to the Phantom, could it be related to the leak that had nearly gotten him killed—twice?

Well, Googling "Phantom" wasn't going to get him anywhere, that was for sure. No, if there were answers, he needed to get his laptop back from the ranch and go to Josh's. He pressed harder on the accelerator.

At the ranch, he parked behind the house, opened the service porch door, and was greeted by the aromas of cooking. Onions, garlic, and spices. He stepped into the kitchen and found Rosa browning what had to be her pot roast. Potatoes and carrots perched by the sink, waiting to be peeled. Before he reached the stove, Rosa turned and wiped her hands on her blue-striped apron, giving him a white-toothed smile.

"Master Ryan. Your papa said you were back." She shook her head in disapproval. "Too long you've been away."

Ryan bent to give her a hug, lifting all five-foot-one of her off the floor. Gray hairs replaced much of the jet-black he remembered. New wrinkles creased her mahogany face. But her brown eyes still twinkled with life.

"If you knew how many times I wanted to come home for your pot roast," he said.

"Only my pot roast interests you?" She wriggled loose from his grasp. "Once you said I make the best oatmeal cookies ever."

"That you do. I don't suppose there are any—" He kissed the top of her head and wandered to the ceramic cookie jar and lifted the lid. Grabbing two, he turned and saw her beaming at him.

She picked up her wooden spoon and waggled it in his direction. "You go now, or my pot roast will burn."

"How's Pop doing?" he said around a mouthful of cookie. "Resting, I hope."

She nodded. "I tell him no dinner unless he takes a pill and a nap."

In the living room, Pop snored softly from his recliner. That his father still wore his robe and flannel pajamas sent a trickle of worry through Ryan's gut. He tiptoed to his father's side and picked up the pill vial from the end table. Recognizing the Percocet he'd taken in the hospital after his own injury, the trickle grew to a river. To have his father admitting pain—Ryan tried to remember another time and couldn't. Vague memories of Pop breaking an arm after being thrown by a bronc seeped through Ryan's brain, but in his mind, Pop hadn't slowed down despite the cast.

His eyes burned, and there was that damn lump in his throat again. Shit, all this domesticity was getting in the way of what he needed to do. With one last glance at his sleeping father, Ryan headed for Pop's upstairs office.

He retrieved his laptop from the bottom desk drawer where he'd left it after researching Pop's land problems and went back downstairs.

His father hadn't moved from the recliner. Wolf lay curled at his feet. The dog raised his eyebrows and thumped his tail but didn't get up. Ryan halted. Pop's snores were louder now, but regular.

Promising Rosa he'd be back for dinner, he climbed into the truck and returned to Josh's. He parked the truck off the main road, away from the house and walked slowly, keeping his eyes to the ground. Like the crash site, there was little visible evidence. Too much traffic in and out, what with the tow truck, the Mustang, not to mention Frankie's Cavalier and Pop's truck.

Okay, if there was no discernable beginning, then he'd start with his arrival in Montana, which should have been under the radar. He'd checked out of the hospital against medical advice, with a vague promise to continue with rehab. Automatically, he flexed his knee and rotated his shoulder, pleased when he felt nothing worse than dull aches. Any money Blackthorne owed him would go directly into his bank account. He'd paid cash for all his expenses on the trip. His next of kin was listed as an attorney, not Pop.

A rustling in the distant bushes caught his attention.

Probably another raccoon. He glanced around, half-expecting

Wolf to come charging out from nowhere. No, the dog was where he needed to be, and Ryan would have to adjust to flying solo again.

Remembering the night he'd encountered the coons, everything clicked. Maybe it was because he'd been in a shitty mood that night, or in a hurry to get inside, but now, he moved past the Mustang's remains and into the woods. He waited, letting his eyes adjust to the shadows. Not sure exactly what he was looking for, he wandered the path, checking the occasional side branch of a trail. Evidence of deer and the expected raccoons didn't surprise him.

The single booted footprint, revealed when a gust of wind blew some leaves aside, did.

CHAPTER 13

Frankie navigated the highway to Lolo Springs. Compared to her Cavalier, her mother's Mercury Grand Marquis was like driving a tank, but at least the tank had power steering. As she drove, she ran down her mental checklist again. It wasn't a Three Elks night. She'd get Mom settled, then go to Missoula and talk to Mr. Loucas. A call to Meg had made sure Molly was welcome a little longer if needed.

How could Bob have abandoned her mother at the Bed and Breakfast? What kind of an emergency precluded at least dropping her off at home first, or getting her a cab? Sure, Mom had probably told him to go take care of things, that she'd be fine— but what if Frankie hadn't been home? Or—there she went again. Relax. Everything *had* worked out.

Look on the bright side. She'd have Mom as a captive audience for the drive back, and would grill her about Bob. She exited the highway and followed the directions she'd Googled to the B&B.

She parked the Mercury in the small parking area and walked inside. The place must have been decorated by someone addicted to Bonanza reruns. She glanced around the living room space that served as a lobby and reception center. The aroma of apples and cinnamon wafted across the room.

"Good afternoon." A pudgy, gray-haired woman appeared, a gingham dish towel tucked into the waistband of her denim skirt. "May I help you? I'm Lucy."

"I'm here to pick up my mother. Anna Castor?" Frankie scanned the sofas, loveseats, and wingback chairs scattered throughout the room, but saw no sign of her.

"Oh, yes. She's in the lilac suite. Why don't you help yourself to some hot cider, and I'll tell her you're here."

"That won't be necessary. If you'll tell me where the room is, I'll save you the trouble."

The woman gave a polite smile, one that reminded Frankie of her Sunday school teacher when Marty Hopkins tried to distract her from the lesson. "I'm sorry, but that area is restricted to registered guests. We pride ourselves on privacy. Do have some cider. I won't be a minute." With another smile, the woman whirled around and trotted up the stairs.

The smell of the cider was irresistible, and Frankie stepped to a carved sideboard and ladled a cardboard cup of the hot brew from a steaming Crock-Pot. Inhaling the cinnamon scent, she carried the cup to the fireplace. The dancing flames wove a hypnotic spell, and as she sipped the cider, her anxiety left her.

"Miss! Miss, I think you should come up here."

The urgency in Lucy's voice sent panic surging through Frankie. She set her cup on the hearth and raced up the stairs, following the voice down a hallway to an open door.

Her mother sat on the edge of the bed, apparently resisting Lucy's assistance. Frankie stepped to the bedside. Her mother's eyes were unfocused, her hair was unkempt, and there was an unnatural pallor to her face.

"Mom. What's wrong?"

Lucy spoke up. "She started to get up, and collapsed. I told her to lie down for a bit, but she's insisting she's fine."

"And I *am* fine. Just a little groggy. If the two of you will give me a little breathing room, I'll be right with you."

With a look that said, *this is not my job,* Lucy retreated to the doorway. "I'll be downstairs. Call if you need me."

She sat down next to her mother and grasped her hands in hers. Frankie's hands were warm, and as they sat, she watched the color creep back into her mother's face. She stroked her cheek.

"Okay. I'm here. Tell me what happened? Why did Bob desert you?"

"Oh, stop fussing. He didn't desert me. He got a call at about three this morning about his sister and had to leave in a hurry. I told him I'd be fine, to do what he had to do. But after the call, I didn't get back to sleep."

"Why did you wait so long to call me?"

"I didn't want to wake you. I read for a while, and had breakfast downstairs—Lucy makes a fantastic Belgian waffle, by the way—and then I called. My wrist ached from packing, so I took a pain pill, and it knocked me out. End of story. Stop trying to run my life. Let me go fix myself up and we can leave."

While her mother was in the bathroom, Frankie plopped onto the bed and rubbed her neck. Mom wasn't a five-year-old. And Mom probably remembered her as her baby going off to college. Her baby who made one very big error in judgment. What Mom hadn't seen was how that error had propelled Frankie into a world of being responsible for a life other than her own. Time to think of Mom as an equal—and hope she'd do the same, because one way or another, Frankie was going to make Mom talk about Bob.

The bathroom door opened. Her mother came over to the bed and sat down next to Frankie, handing her a hairbrush.

"Can you help? This is one thing I can't seem to manage left-handed."

Frankie started brushing her mother's tousled hair, finding it comforting. Thoughts of Bob were tabled.

"You used to love to play beauty shop when you were little," her mother said. "You always had a gentle touch."

"I remember. I created some crazy hairstyles for you. But you never changed them—I think once you went to church with half your hair pinned up and the other half in a braid."

"You were so proud—I couldn't hurt your feelings."

Frankie hesitated, wondering where the thoughts whirling through her head were coming from. Or why the question leaped from her mouth.

"Mom. I have to know something. Do you . . . do you ever wish I hadn't been born? That I was a mistake you'd rather not have made?"

Her mother turned her head around. "Whatever gave you that idea?" Her mouth dropped open, her eyes widened. "Oh, baby. You're not thinking that about Molly?"

"No, no, of course not. I've never regretted having Molly. It's . . . well, you never really talked about it, but Claire . . . she's almost twelve years older than I am, and I know you were forty-two when I was born, and—"

"And you want to know if you were an unpleasant surprise?" Her mom smiled and kissed Frankie on the cheek. "Yes, you were a surprise, but not unpleasant. I had three miscarriages between you and Claire, and had given up on another child. And was going through the change—I thought. But I couldn't have been happier. Your father, either."

A burden she'd been unaware of lifted. "I guess I thought I'd messed up your life. And after Dad died, you were stuck with a little kid. You liked the grad students who boarded with us. I wasn't sure you wanted me. Claire kind of took over."

"Oh, baby. You poor thing. I had a lot of trouble adjusting after your father died. I suppose I did turn too many mothering responsibilities over to Claire."

Frankie chewed on her lip. "I thought I must be doing something wrong. That it was my fault you were unhappy."

"I'm so sorry. You were always such a perfect child, always

trying to do the right thing, to make everyone around you happy. I never realized—I never knew. Can you forgive me?"

She smiled. "Of course. And, on the bright side, it probably explains why I am the way I am."

Her mother's laugh was music. "That's my Frankie. Always finding the bright side."

"Let's get you home."

Once they were on the interstate, Frankie turned down the volume on the radio. Along with a tension in her neck and shoulders, Bob had worked his way back to the front of her brain, and she wasn't going to ignore him this time. How dare he treat her mother that way.

"Mom, where did Bob go?" She kept the irritation out of her voice. "I hope it wasn't anything too serious." Like heck. It had darn well better have been life-threatening for him to abandon her mother the way he did.

"I don't know, exactly." Mom fussed with her seatbelt. "He said his sister was sick and he had to get there right away."

"Where is *there?*"

"She lives in San Diego. Or was it San Clemente? No, I think it was Santa Barbara. Or is his sister's name Barbara? I was half asleep. It was one of those San-somethings in California, I'm sure. She's the only family he has left."

"Can you get in touch with him? I mean, to check to make sure everything is all right?" A glance in her mother's direction told Frankie she was treading on thin ice.

No. She was an adult now, not twelve, and the narrowed eyes no longer intimidated Frankie. Not much, anyway.

"I told him to go. He'll be in touch once things are settled. Now, if you don't mind, I didn't get much sleep last night, and that pill hasn't worn off." She twisted in her seat, tucked her sweater behind her head and closed her eyes.

"Wait, Mom. I was wondering . . . the mountain property,

where we used to picnic and stuff. Do you still own it?"

"Yes, technically. Someone made an offer. I thought I might take it. I have so many mixed memories of the place. Your father and I loved to go there."

She heard a dreamy quality in her mother's voice. She glanced over and caught a smile playing at the corner of Mom's mouth. "It was special for you, wasn't it?"

Her mother opened her eyes, revealing a twinge of sadness. "Yes, very. After he died, I hardly ever went back. The memories—made me miss him too much. But I didn't have the heart to sell it until now."

Bob again. Usurping her father's memories. "Umm . . . what about the rental, or whatever you call it? Access rights?"

"I told the bank to let them know they could match the offer. According to the old papers I found, that was what my father had offered, and I thought it fair to hold to it. What makes you bring this up now?"

She took a deep breath. "Well, you remember that man I met in the emergency room? You'll never believe it, but it turns out it's his father who was using the property and he needs it to make his living, and—"

"Frankie. Stop. My brain can't handle this now. We'll talk when we get home." She folded her arms across her chest and closed her eyes again.

She left her mother to her dreams, wondering if they were about Bob or her father. She tried to adjust to this new image of her mother, a woman trying to make the best of her life. But until she knew more about Bob, she wasn't going to stop watching out for Mom.

Ready to make a plan, Frankie let her mind drift, hoping one would appear. Since the land had meant so much to her, Mom would probably be open to some sort of agreement with the Harpers. She made a mental note to call Mr. Anisman about darkroom privileges and began visualizing her photographs as she drove. A little extra money from Mr. Harper, some photography income, and things were going to be great. She wouldn't think about Bob. Let him stay in California for a while. She smiled. Out of state, out of mind.

She glanced at her mother, relaxed in sleep, a faint smile playing about her lips. A layer of guilt washed over Frankie. Her mother obviously cared about the man, and if Bob disappeared, Mom would be hurt.

Once home, with her mother upstairs napping, she gathered everything she'd need to assess the budget and logged onto the bank's website. Confident she'd be able to juggle things and propose a new financial arrangement to Mom, one that would let Mr. Harper keep his business, she downloaded the most recent account information and clicked "print."

Once she'd set up a spreadsheet, she picked up the papers from the printer. Scanning the printouts, her heart jumped to her throat. This had to be a mistake.

Aside from the single boot print, Ryan had found nothing to indicate who might have been in the woods. Hell, for all he knew, some hiker had stopped to take a leak. Lots of innocent explanations. Like with the Mustang. But too many co-incidences made the hair on the back of his neck stand up.

He set up his laptop on the coffee table and went to the entertainment center where Josh stored his DVDs. His pulse quickened when he saw they lined up perfectly at the edge of the shelf. He'd left them staggered, very slightly, in a pattern he recognized. Telling himself it wouldn't matter even if someone had found his CD, that there was nothing earth shattering in its contents, he quashed the warning tension in his belly and pulled *Blade Runner* from the row. Opening the case, the sight of the strand of hair tucked behind the disc brought a sigh of relief.

Frankie had probably browsed the collection, looking for a movie to occupy Molly. She'd be the sort who'd put things back neater than she found them.

He popped the CD from the case and carried it to the coffee table. He moved the furniture so he could stretch his legs under the table and lean against the couch. As he lowered himself, his knee gave a quick twinge.

He might as well take his new slant on living all the way. While the computer loaded the disc, he crawled out of his workspace and found his duffel in the recesses of the bedroom closet. In it, still in its original package, was the elastic knee-support the physical therapist had given him. He removed his boots and jeans, slid the brace into place and grabbed the sweats from the end of the bed where Frankie had left them. Where he'd left them, as a reminder of her brief presence in his world.

He saw her in them again, stomping around the floor with Molly, getting rid of the grumps. Somehow, pulling on the sweats made him feel calmer. Warmer inside. Shit. *Enough.* He tried to ignore the damn lust that had burrowed into him like an unwanted tick.

Back in his makeshift office on the living room floor, he took a deep breath and pushed away the memory of what he'd gone through to get this data.

Despite the craziness and panic at the factory in Panama, Ryan held onto enough sanity to realize nobody used his last dying breath to give away a cigar, which was what he'd discovered in the tube Alvarez had given him. At the time, he'd thought the importance was inflated in Alvarez's mind, but he'd kept his word. For a few bucks, he had convinced a hospital orderly to mail it to him at his San Francisco PO Box.

Once he'd checked out of the hospital and retrieved his prize, he found it was no ordinary cigar. Alvarez had removed a good portion of the innards, replacing them with a small flash drive containing a single file. The best he could tell, the file was exactly what Alvarez had said it was. A list of names, addresses, and stolen or missing works of art, some with pictures. Nothing he recognized, but art had never been his thing. He'd checked names at random and cross-referenced them against a few of Blackthorne's databases while he still had access, and they seemed to be real people. People with no connections to Ryan's world. And when his internal red flags waved that day in Blackthorne's office, he lied about having the intel.

Maybe there was more.

He stared at the list on the screen until his eyes burned. He tried arranging the names in alphabetical order. By last name. By first name. Then by country. He searched for commonalities. He tried it from the other direction. Were there things that should have been here, but weren't? Since he was unfamiliar with the postal code formats for other countries, or if they even had postal codes, he couldn't be sure those were right. But the five he checked fit the pattern, so he eliminated that possibility. After two hours, he had nothing but a growling stomach and an incipient headache to show for his efforts.

He worked his way out from under his coffee table desk, surprised that his knee hadn't stiffened. Damn it to hell, if all it had needed was a stupid elastic bandage—

He peered into the fridge, trying to decide what he wanted to eat. When his cell rang, he rushed to the bedroom, finding his jeans where the phone hung from its case on his belt. Could it be Dalton with an update?

"Harper," he snapped into the phone. "Go."

"Ryan? It's Frankie. Am I disturbing you? I'm sorry to bother you—"

His resolve to dismiss her from his life vaporized at the sound of her voice. "Slow down. No, you're not bothering me." He took the phone to the couch, his head and stomach all of a sudden replaced by another demanding part of him. "What can I do for you?"

When ten seconds of silence elapsed, he said, "Are you still there?"

"Yes. It's . . . I don't know exactly . . . maybe I shouldn't have called."

Frankie at a loss for words? Instead of being amused, a thread of concern wove through his chest. "Whatever it is, Frankie, if I can help, I will."

"Before. When you said you were a SEAL, and then that other job. I wondered. Can you find things out about people? I mean, it sounded like you might know all that secret agent stuff."

He ran his fingers through his hair. Her voice had trembled. Something was very, very wrong. "Not really secret agent stuff. Tell me what you need."

"It's Bob—Mom's . . . boyfriend, if that's what you call it for . . . mature people. They were away, and then he left her, and her savings account . . . it's almost all gone."

"Okay, Frankie. Deep breath. Come on. For me." He was pacing the room now, his unoccupied hand clenching and un-clenching until he heard her exhale. "Did you ask your mom about the money? Maybe the bank made a mistake. Or she transferred it to another account."

"I can't. Not yet. She thinks I'm trying to run her life. We had this talk, and things were looking good, and I wanted us to be equals, and—"

"Okay, okay. Do you want me to come there? I can be at your place in under an hour."

"Yes. No. I don't know. I need to know all about Bob first, but Mom can't know I'm looking. Do you know how to do that?"

"If you give me some basic information, maybe. But wouldn't

it make sense to talk to your mother?"

"I told you, I can't. Not until I have more information. I can't say, 'Mom, I think Bob's a crook.' What if he isn't? And she doesn't know I'm looking at her finances. She'd never forgive me. Never trust me. You have to understand the way our family works. Castors don't interfere. We were always free to make our own decisions. Our own mistakes. I always respected that. It doesn't seem right to question her choices."

His mind raced. He could try to sneak into Blackthorne's system. "Can you come here? To the ranch, I mean. I can't promise anything. But I'll try." He hesitated, but only for an instant. "Molly's welcome, too."

He waited out an uncomfortable silence. Was she trying to pigeonhole him into her categories of men? And if so, where did she put him?

When she came back on the line, her voice was less tremulous. Basic Frankie. "I'll have to take care of a few things first. Is three o'clock too late?"

He glanced at his watch. One-thirty. "That's fine. Get me as much as you can about Bob. Full name, age, where he lives, was born—anything you can find out. Social Security number would be ideal." He gave her directions to Pop's ranch and hung up.

Once he realized he was wandering aimlessly around the cabin thinking about seeing Frankie, he went to the coffee table and popped the CD out of his laptop. He pulled the real *Blade Runner* disc from the drawer where he'd stored it and put it in its original case. Browsing the row of cases, he ran his finger along them, stopping at *Blazing Saddles*. No, if Josh came home unexpectedly, that would be one he'd likely watch. He moved down the row to *Gone with the Wind*. Taking a Sharpie, he wrote GWTW on his disk and swapped it out, yanking a hair from his head and tucking it in place.

He fixed a sandwich, gulped it down and told himself it was

perfectly normal to shower and shave in the middle of the day, and what was wrong with borrowing a little of Josh's aftershave? He put the elastic brace back over his knee, found a clean pair of jeans, changed his mind, and put on some khakis and a dark blue chambray shirt. God, he reminded himself of his sister getting ready for her first date.

But visions of him sitting in front of a computer terminal with Frankie leaning over him, her hair cascading over his shoulder, smelling like strawberries, her breath warm against his neck—okay, enough of that, or he'd need another shower. A cold one.

At two-thirty, he packed his laptop into Pop's truck and tried to keep what he knew was a stupid grin off his face as he drove to the ranch.

CHAPTER 14

"Sit down, boy. You're driving me nuts. Whatever it is you're waiting for won't get here any sooner for all your fidgeting."

Ryan stepped away from the window and turned to face his father, who sat reading in his recliner. So much for telling Pop he'd come to keep him company.

"How're your ribs?" Ryan asked.

" 'Bout the same as they were ten minutes ago. Is she pretty?"

Ryan's face flamed. He turned back to the window. He hadn't said anything to Pop about Frankie's connection to the access rights issue, and wasn't sure he should—not until he'd done his homework. Pop hadn't asked, and Ryan knew he wouldn't. Information was something to be dispensed when you had answers, not questions.

"She's got some trouble. I told her I'd try to help. You met her at the hospital. She's the one who took me in that night." At the sound of the recliner's footrest clicking into place, Ryan stepped across the room. "Let me help. What do you need?"

"Nothing. I'm going upstairs and I don't need help. Between you and Rosa, I'm fed up with hovering. Don't forget to call me when supper's ready. I've been smelling her pot roast all day."

His father's eyes twinkled, and one corner of his mouth lifted a fraction. Pop would make a great Blackthorne operative. Nothing escaped him.

The doorbell rang. Ryan's pulse quickened. Chiding himself for his schoolboy reaction, he controlled his pace and strolled to the front door. A quick glance over his shoulder told him Pop had gone upstairs. But he'd bet his father was lingering on the landing.

Ryan pulled the door open. Frankie stood there, dressed in black denims and a cream-colored blouse. Her hair hung loose around her face. A parka was draped over one arm. Her other hand rested on Molly's shoulder. When Frankie lifted her eyes, he swore they got bluer every time he saw her.

"Come in," he said, stepping back.

Molly, surprisingly quiet, followed two paces behind her mother, clutching a backpack to her chest. She gazed around the room, then leaned into Frankie.

"Hi, Molly," he said. "I'm glad to see you again. Did you have fun on your picnic?"

Her nod said yes, but her solemn expression denied it. She yanked on Frankie's hand. Frankie lowered her head and Molly whispered into her ear.

"Peanut, I told you I didn't know if Wolf was here. You have your backpack full of things to do." Frankie looked at him. "Is there a spot where Molly can sit and read. Or color? She knows she has to behave while the grownups have their time."

"Do we have guests?" Rosa's voice, bright and cheerful, told him she must have been nearby watching and listening. "*Ay, que linda.* What a lovely child." She crouched in front of Molly. "What's your name, little one?"

He saw the nudge from Frankie.

"Molly," she mumbled into her backpack.

"Well, Molly, in the kitchen I have a big table. Master Ryan used to color there. But maybe you want to help me. Do you cook?"

Molly looked up, her eyes wide. She shook her head.

"No? I need a helper. These two grownups will be no good. You come with Rosa, okay? We make chocolate cake."

161

When Molly got Frankie's nod of approval, the grin that spread across the child's face lit the room. As he watched her trot to the kitchen, hand in hand with Rosa, a spark lit in his chest as well.

He felt Frankie's eyes on him and faced her. She dropped her gaze as soon as he did. "She's in good hands," he said.

"I can tell." After an uncharacteristic silence, she said, "How's your father doing?"

"Fine. Grumbling about the enforced rest."

She nodded. "Did you tell him anything about what we talked about?"

He shook his head. "No point until we know something. Did you ask your mom?"

"No. I tried, but she wanted to rest. Pain pill."

"Yeah, same for Pop."

Damn, they might as well be talking about the weather. Frankie was obviously uncomfortable, but she wasn't babbling. That was a new one, and he ached to offer comfort.

He stepped closer. She stepped back. He waited. She looked almost as frightened as she had when Molly had fallen into the stream. Of *him?*

He cleared his throat. "I guess we should get started. The computer's in Pop's office. Upstairs."

"Right."

Lord, he wanted to wrap her in his arms. Tell her everything would be fine. She'd crumble if he did. He managed a smile.

"Look, if you want, you can give me everything you have, and I'll go to work. It'll probably bore you to death. You can stay down here with Molly and Rosa. They're going to be having a lot more fun."

She sniffed, then reached into the pocket of her parka for a tissue. She wiped her nose. "My cold," she said.

Giggles came from the kitchen. She turned her head, then

smiled at him. "I'm okay," she said. "I've got the papers in my purse. Mom was groggy, and I didn't want to push—she'd wonder why I was asking. Everything I have is here. I couldn't find his Social Security Number." She opened her black leather bag and handed him a large manila envelope. "If Bob ran off with Mom's savings, I don't know what I'll do."

He took the envelope, his fingers brushing against hers. He doubted a timer set for ten minutes would be part of her plan. "Let's not worry about that yet." He walked toward the stairs, sensing her following him all the way up.

"Take a seat," he said, pointing to the loveseat against the wall of Pop's office. He went behind the desk and spread the papers out.

"It was her savings account." She came up behind him, smelling altogether too good, and pulled out some pages from the pile. "Here."

"Okay. Let me see what you've got." Both disappointed and relieved when she left his side, he studied the transaction records. "Do you know anything about BLD Enterprises?"

Frankie shook her head. "Doesn't ring a bell." Her eyes snapped open. "BLD. Bob Dwyer? I mean, his name's probably Robert, and I don't know his middle initial, but—"

"It occurred to me. I'll check. Was your mother in the habit of using her savings account for making payments?"

"I don't know. I only started looking a few days ago, when I noticed some overdue bills in the mail. And then, with your land problem, I wanted to see if I could work out a budget, so I could tell Mom not to sell." Her voice grew softer. "Mom was proud of taking care of her own finances. Maybe I should have confronted her sooner."

If she had, they might not be sitting here right now. He didn't want to admit he could be that petty. "I need your mother's bank logon and password." He pushed away from the desk.

163

"Why don't you enter them, and I'll see if I can track down BLD on her payee list."

"It was automatic—she had it saved. Just go to the personal banking site."

She looked so eager, so confident. He did his damnedest to let her down gently. "That information doesn't carry over from one computer to another. We'd have to be at your place to use it that way."

He might as well have yelled, the way her face fell. A blush covered her cheeks. "I . . . I didn't think of that. I'm really not good for much here, am I?"

"Don't worry about it. Your hard copies give us current information." He found a tablet of paper and clicked open a ballpoint pen.

"Okay, Frankie. What can you tell me about Bob?"

Frankie sank into the brushed corduroy of the loveseat. For the first time since her mother had called her this morning, she could relax. Within seconds, Ryan was busy at the keyboard, his gaze shifting between the papers and the monitor. She answered his questions the best she could, but beyond Bob's name, his age and that he might have a sister in California, she didn't know much about him. Every now and then Ryan jotted a note. Sometimes he'd smile, sometimes he'd shake his head. When he finally glanced in her direction, she dared to interrupt.

"Is what you're doing . . . illegal? I mean, I don't want you to get into trouble."

He grinned like he was having fun. "Not exactly. I sort of borrowed a login from a buddy. His fault—I kept telling Grinch to pick a smarter password than his kid's name and birthday."

She felt herself blushing. She wasn't as bad as her mother, leaving logins in the computer's memory, but anyone could probably guess her passwords, too. She made a mental note to change all of them once this was over.

"So, what can you find out?" Frankie asked.

"I can use databases from my old job, and can get into a few . . . private ones. I wasn't the computer specialist, but I picked up a few tricks. I've run Bob through a criminal database, and I can't find a record."

"That's good, isn't it?"

"Means he hasn't been arrested is all. But, yeah, that's probably a good thing."

She studied his expression—there was something he wasn't saying. "Tell me what you're thinking."

He swiveled so he was facing her. "I'll need to work a little longer. You can go downstairs if you want."

"No. I'd rather stay. That is, if you think Rosa won't mind keeping an eye on Molly. Maybe I should go." Part of her wanted to relinquish motherhood for a little while. To watch this man at work, deep in concentration. She wished she had a camera. Another part felt guilty at imposing on both him and Rosa for her own selfish needs.

"Rosa loves kids. Trust me, having Molly around for an hour or two will make her day."

That was all she needed. "Thanks. I appreciate this. Really."

His smile made her forget all about Bob, and she relaxed into the cushions.

The warmth of a nearby presence and the scent of aftershave drifted through her consciousness, and she realized she'd dozed off. She opened her eyes and blinked at Ryan's form hovering above her.

"Oh, my. I guess I fell asleep. I didn't get much last night." She rubbed her eyes, then lifted her hair off her shoulders while she got her bearings. A smile played across his lips, and she remembered what she was doing here. "Did you find Bob? The money?"

He shook his head and tipped his head toward the cushion beside her. Asking permission, not demanding. "I've got a search running. It might take awhile."

She made room for him, but his thigh still brushed hers on the small loveseat. She tried to ignore the way the faint pressure aroused her. Her nipples puckered and she wished she'd worn a bulky sweater instead of a silk blouse. "How long was I out?"

"Not long. Ten, fifteen minutes, maybe."

She sighed and leaned into his chest. His arm reached around her, rested on her shoulder and she snuggled closer, listening to the steady rhythm of his heart. Just this once, she could borrow someone's strength.

His fingers brushed along her shoulder. Not even enough to call a caress. Certainly not enough to warrant the heat that surged through her.

His voice gentle, he spoke, "Tell me about yourself, Frankie Castor. What do you do when you're not serving drinks or taking pictures?"

Small talk. She could handle that. "For now, I'm a long-term sub at the elementary school in Broken Bow. Art. Mom pulled some strings, I'm sure. She used to be principal."

She felt, rather than heard, his chuckle.

"What's funny about that? I enjoy it."

"No, I was remembering the night we met. At Three Elks. You smelled like Elmer's glue."

She drew back, but he held her against him. "Don't pull away. I liked it. Tell me more."

"There's not much more. I have a degree in art, and I was a decorator in Boston before I moved, but there's not much call for that here. In Broken Bow, interior design means a trip to the building supply center and a couple of hours with HGTV. I moved back to help Mom when my sister left." The contented, safe feeling flew away, replaced by the too-familiar anxiety. "I'm not doing very well, am I?"

"Hey, none of this is your fault. From what you've told me, your mother is an independent woman. None of what happened—and we don't know for sure anything bad did happen—was your fault."

"But if she's broke—what are we going to do?"

"I'm sure it's going to work out. She's undoubtedly got other accounts in other places. Investments, retirement. Most likely, she was simply moving money."

She shook her head. "I don't know. My teaching job doesn't bring in that much, and I don't want to be away more than three nights—Mom still doesn't know about my Three Elks job. I got a hundred dollars for that picture, but I can't rely on that kind of income. I've tried, but there's no bright side this time."

"There is for me." He lifted her chin so that she had to meet his eyes. Oh, she knew that look. The half-lowered eyelids—why hadn't she noticed those long eyelashes before? The slight tilt to his head. His lips parted just a fraction. Her feminine instincts weren't that rusty. He wanted to kiss her. And she wanted to kiss him, too. Not smart.

Little footsteps clattered up the stairs. She held his gaze a moment longer, then pulled away.

He sighed, and his breath warmed her throat.

She adjusted the collar of her blouse. "Interruptions. Part of the mom thing."

Molly peeked around the doorway, her mouth ringed in chocolate. "Mommy, I baked a cake. And Rosa said I was her very best helper." She looked at Ryan, who had moved back to the desk. "She said you were good, too."

"That's wonderful, Peanut," Frankie said. "Now, I think we need to wash your face."

Molly grinned. "I licked the bowl."

Frankie turned to Ryan. "Where's a bathroom where I can

clean this little pastry chef? And then, I think we'll need to hit the road. You can call me and let me know what you've found."

Molly tugged on her sleeve. "Mommy, Rosa said I could help with the frosting. But the cake has to get cool first. I don't want to go home yet. Please? And Wolf's here."

There was no denying those pleading blue eyes.

Ryan clinched it. "Bathroom's down the hall on the left, and please stay for dinner. I'll tell Rosa to set two extra places. Besides, I might have news for you by then."

"That would be nice. Thanks." She scooted Molly toward the bathroom. "I'll call Gramma and let her know we won't be home for dinner."

The computer gave an insistent ringing sound. Frankie swerved. Ryan picked up the mouse, clicked a few keys and frowned.

"Ryan?" No response. "Ryan?"

"I'll be downstairs in a few minutes," he said, without looking up.

"Ryan? What is it?" Her pulse quickened, and not the way it had while she was sitting on the loveseat.

"Don't know yet. Let me work. I'll be down soon."

Before she could protest, Ryan's father poked his head into the room. "I hope my son's not boring you to death," he said. "He can lose himself in that machine."

She smiled. "Not at all, Mr. Harper. He's doing me a big favor."

"Call me Angus." Although his gaze quickly moved to Ryan, Frankie knew she'd been sized up.

"You think you can pull yourself away and tend to the horses before supper?" Angus said.

Apparently Angus' voice penetrated Ryan's concentration better than hers had, because he looked up immediately. His lips were set in a thin line, but they relaxed before he spoke.

"Sure. No problem." He glanced at the screen, clicked the mouse, and pushed away from the desk. Turning toward her, he said, "Would you like to tag along? Molly, too, of course."

"I'm sure she'd be thrilled to see a horse." Frankie didn't miss the way Molly had been added to the invitation as an afterthought, but the fact that Ryan seemed comfortable using her name made up for it. Maybe he was starting to recover from his loss.

"I'll go get her." She smiled at Angus. "I hope you're feeling better."

"I'm doing fine, ma'am."

"Please. It's Frankie."

"Very well, Frankie. I hope you and the little one will stay for supper. It's been a long time since there were youngsters at the table."

"Thank you. Ryan was kind enough to invite us."

He glanced at Ryan, who gave a sheepish grin, then he turned back to her. Angus' eyes, a deeper brown than Ryan's, were warm and friendly. She wondered if he'd be that cordial if he knew her family might be responsible for putting him out of business. Unless Mom's money reappeared, she didn't see how there was any other choice than to sell the property to that corporate executive. She hoped she could summon up an appetite. Even the smell of chocolate cake wafting up from the kitchen didn't unravel the knots in her belly.

169

CHAPTER 15

Ryan stood on the porch and watched the taillights of Frankie's car disappear around the curve. Molly had been leery of the horses until their old mare, Winny, nuzzled an apple slice from her palm. He chuckled. Now Molly was asking for a puppy *and* a pony. Frankie hadn't seemed too pleased.

At dinner, Molly's eyelids drooped until it was time for dessert, when she took great pride in describing every step in the baking process. Discussion skirted his searches on Bob, and the connection between Frankie and the mountain property. Pop did what he always did at the dinner table. Ate. Methodically, with pleasure, but not much conversation.

That had been Mom's department, he remembered, a little surprised at the warmth he felt instead of the usual pain. Mom had been the one to drag the daily events out of the three kids. Pop would grunt his approval for accomplishments, remind them of the chores for the next day, and retreat, leaving them to their household chores and homework.

After dinner, Frankie had insisted on letting Rosa go home early, claiming that doing the dishes would be small payment for the meal. Molly cleared the table, her pursed lips advertising her concentration on not breaking anything. Ryan picked up a dishtowel and took care of drying and putting away the things that couldn't be put in the dishwasher. Until tonight, he'd forgotten how comfortable it was being part of a family.

Now, Frankie was on her way home, and there was an empty

place inside him. An empty place that hadn't existed before he'd met her. Damn. He shoved the door open and jogged up the stairs to the computer.

Sitting at the desk, staring at the screen, he wondered if his contacts at the phone company knew he'd left Blackthorne. He might be able to sweet-talk one of them into pulling some of Bob's usage details for him.

Bob had accounts in the same branch in Broken Bow that Anna Castor did, and Anna had written him a few small checks. Nothing indicated they were consolidating funds, but the cancelled checks gave him Bob's account number. Although Blackthorne subscribed to some slightly less than approved methods of detecting bank information, Ryan wasn't ready to do anything to call attention to his actions. He needed better information about Bob.

He'd given Frankie what reassurance he could because he hadn't found any neon signs saying Bob was up to no good. That Bob did indeed have a sister in California made his story to Anna believable.

When Ryan volunteered to call the sister, Frankie quashed the idea, promising that she'd talk to her mother tomorrow. And, he thought, that was the only answer. Always better to go straight to the heart of the problem. He couldn't imagine Frankie not being able to mend fences with her mom.

Pop wandered into the room and eased himself down to the loveseat. Ryan pretended not to see him wince.

"Cute kid. Nice lady," Pop said. "You solve her problem?"

"Not really." Not much more he could do here. He started the computer's shutdown process. "Anything I can do for you?"

"Nope. Dinner was nice."

Ryan smiled. "Yes, it was." He waited. Eventually, Pop would say what he came for.

"Got a trail run on Friday. Thought you might want to lead

171

it. For old times' sake."

Damn, Pop must really be hurting. "Of course. What time? How many?"

"Ten o'clock. Three—got room for two more. Sammy could use some exercise."

Sammy. Their mule. Perfect for a kid. He shook his head. "You know, Pop, you don't have to beat around the bush. Hell, I'm surprised you didn't come out and ask them while they were here."

"Not my place to invite your friends."

"How bad are your ribs, anyway?" He unplugged his laptop and put it into the case. "You following doc's orders?"

His father grabbed the arm of the loveseat and started to push himself up. Ryan hurried across the room and supported him, concerned when he didn't resist.

"Ain't as young as I used to be, is all. And the damn pills fill my head with straw."

Once his father was on his feet, he removed Ryan's hand, but not without a gentle squeeze. "I'm fine, son."

"Take a pill at bedtime, okay?" he said.

"Yep. Straw's fine for sleeping." Pop took a few steps toward the door, then stopped. "Could use someone to make a recycling run. Bins are full."

"I'll do it first thing tomorrow. I've got some stuff at the cabin that needs dumping, too." He bid his father good night and made a quick detour through the kitchen for one last slice of Rosa's cake before driving back to the cabin. There, he collected the assorted recyclables and set them on the porch. Might be smart to do some laundry, too.

He went to his bedroom and stuffed the heap from his closet into a large plastic bag. He stripped and added tonight's clothes to the sack. After changing into sweats, he grabbed some clean towels from the top shelf, and his backpack tumbled down, hitting him on the head.

A depressingly painless impact, when he considered he'd put the important essentials of his life into it. He carried the pack to the bed and dumped its contents. He picked up his small notebook and leafed through the names and phone numbers that represented his former life. Too many were strictly work-related. But then, he didn't have time for friends outside of the job. Debbie's name and number seemed to leap off the page. They'd gone out for a beer once or twice when he was in town, but nothing had connected between them. That was Dalton's thing. He connected with everyone.

His own thoughts came back to him. Always better to go straight to the heart of the problem. Without knowing exactly why, he went to the phone and dialed Debbie's home number. She'd done the tests on the Mustang bits and pieces. Maybe she'd have some details Dalton's simple 'didn't find anything' call had left out.

When she answered he heard surprise in her voice.

"Ryan Harper. How are you doing? I thought you were—" Her tone was guarded.

"Were what?"

"Nothing. I mean, you were in those two snafus, and then in the hospital. I'm really sorry I didn't get by to see you, by the way."

"No problem." Hardly anybody had. He was over that.

"So why are you calling me?" He heard the unspoken *at home*. The hairs on the back of his neck prickled, and a vise clamped down on his gut.

"I wanted to know what tests you ran on the car parts Dalton gave you."

After a pause she said, "Dalton hasn't been here in weeks. He never gave me any car parts to test."

The vise twisted several turns. Had Dalton given them to

someone else? No, he'd definitely said Debbie. That he was going to keep it under the table, and he trusted her. He'd left in a hurry. Maybe he hadn't had time. But then why call to tell him everything was fine?

"My mistake, then. Sorry to bother you."

"That's all right. And if you see that Texan, you tell him he still owes me a steak dinner." The teasing in her tone was forced.

"I will." His mind raced. Hoping he could trust her, he asked her not to mention the call. When she agreed, he wondered if it was because she was afraid that associating with him, an apparent traitor in the eyes of Blackthorne, Inc., might implicate her as well.

Sometimes the covert ops policies about not sharing information could work in your favor. He wasn't sure this was one of those times.

He found a beer in the fridge and took it to the porch. Dalton had lied. No matter how he tried to rearrange the pieces, Dalton had lied. Why?

Forcing himself to look at everything since he'd arrived, ignoring the fact that it was Dalton, a man he trusted with his life, Ryan started from the beginning.

The boot print in the woods. Had Dalton been wearing boots like those? Around here, boots were the norm. If Dalton had sabotaged the Mustang, how perfect to be the one to volunteer to check it over. Remove the evidence, although he doubted that Dalton would have left any. Dalton couldn't have rigged a bomb in his car. If he had, Pop would be dead. Dalton knew what he was doing.

The clenching in his gut was genuinely painful now. He took another pull on his beer, staring into the distance. When Wolf appeared, he wasn't surprised to see him. The dog sat by his side, and Ryan scratched him behind the ears. His tail thumped, and he panted, giving a quick happy-dog yelp.

Wolf hadn't taken to Dalton. Then again, Dalton had pointed a rifle at Wolf, and the dog had instinctively gone on alert.

He went inside for another beer. As he drank, he paced, trying to ignore what was falling into place. No, he told himself. There were all sorts of innocent explanations. There had to be.

Wolf followed him once around the room, then flopped down beside the couch. Ryan set the empty beer bottle on the counter, remembering Dalton's visit. Dalton had offered comfort, support, and understanding. And plenty to drink. Or had he? He remembered several beers, some whiskey, and then being helped to bed. He'd slept like the dead that night, but woke with no hangover.

Afraid of what he'd find, he checked the level in the whiskey bottle. Over half full, and he and Pop had had a few hits from it as well. Not enough to knock him out.

Dalton's note. *Hope you slept well. You needed it.* Had Dalton drugged him? Dalton wasn't the domestic sort, yet the place had been immaculate when he got up the next day. He thought of his computer file. Intact, but if Dalton had searched his place, he wouldn't have left a trace.

He went out and rooted through the recycling, counting beer bottles. They'd been drinking Heineken. He counted five bottles. He pulled one out and sniffed it. Smelled like beer. Backtracking to the fridge, he checked, knowing they'd started with a full six-pack. So where was the other bottle?

He took a breath. There were at least two sides to every possibility. More than one way to interpret the note. Dalt might have taken a beer with him, or tossed the bottle outside. Maybe he'd slipped him a mickey so he'd finally get a decent night's sleep. Dalton could have killed him. He'd certainly had ample opportunities.

"Fuck!"

Wolf looked up and whined. "Yeah, mutt, I swore. Too bad.

You don't get a dollar." Instead, Ryan went to the kitchen, grabbed a scrap of turkey and tossed it to the dog.

He went back to the DVD collection and found his disc. If Dalton had copied the disc, would he have brought it to Blackthorne and utilized all their computer geeks? Or was he working alone? He waited for the disc to load, fighting the sick feeling snaking through him.

After she settled Molly in bed, Frankie stood in the hallway, trying to decide if confronting her mother would be easier after a good night's sleep. Knowing that if she put it off, it would be a sleepless night, Frankie flipped a mental coin. If her mother was asleep, she wouldn't disturb her. She glanced toward her mother's room, where a strip of light glowed from beneath the door.

Trusting her instincts would see her through, she tapped gently on the door. There was always the chance Mom had fallen asleep with her light on. Not likely. Not Mom. Her stomach sank when she heard her mother's, "Come in."

She twisted the doorknob and stepped inside. Her mother sat up in bed, reading. After all these years, she still kept to her side, as if she waited for someone to join her. Was it habit? Or loneliness? Or merely closer to the lamp?

Frankie smiled. "Hi, Mom. We're back."

"I see that." She marked her place in the book and set it on the nightstand. "Did you have a nice evening?"

"Yes, we did." Frankie sat on the edge of the bed, on her father's side, trying not to think of whether Bob had been there, and trying even harder not to begrudge her mother some companionship. After spending those hours at the Harper ranch, the lonely streak she'd thought was sewn shut had begun to unravel.

"Have you heard from Bob? How's his sister?"

Her mother took off her reading glasses and placed them on top of her book. "He called, yes. He was stuck in the Salt Lake City airport, but should be in Santa Rosa by now." She gave a tiny nod of satisfaction. "I got the city wrong, but I knew it was a San or Santa. And in California."

"And his sister?"

Her mother's expression, which had been open and curious since Frankie walked in, now grew pained. "She had a massive stroke. That's all he knows. He'll call me tomorrow."

"That's too bad. Do you know if she's older or younger than Bob?"

"She's his twin, as a matter of fact. They're very close."

"Oh, Mom, I'm so sorry. I hope she'll be all right." How could she segue this one into calling him a crook? She reached for her mother's hands and found them cold and moist.

Her mother stared at the ceiling, then back at Frankie. "Sweetie, this isn't the way I'd planned to tell you, but Bob has asked me to marry him. I said yes."

Frankie knew her mouth hung open, and she snapped it shut. "Isn't this sort of quick?" she said, and instantly regretted it.

Her mother didn't seem to take offense. "When you get to be our age, you don't buy green bananas. We've only got so much time left, and it seems silly to waste it."

"Oh, Mom, I didn't mean it like that. If you're happy—" She leaned over and hugged her.

"We're both happy. I hope you'll understand. I feel bad for you. You gave up so much to move from Boston, and now I'm throwing a monkey wrench into your life."

"Mom, what I had in Boston was a job. You're family."

Even as she spoke, Frankie's mind whirled. Where would Mom and Bob live? Where would she and Molly live? What about the mountain property? This was too much to handle after such a long day. Things would make sense in the morning, and she could talk to Mom about everything then.

Glad she hadn't walked in and accused Bob of being a thief, she kissed her mother's cheek.

"I'm happy for you, Mom. Truly. You shouldn't worry about me. I'll be fine, no matter what you decide to do. We'll talk tomorrow, okay?"

"I'll look forward to it." Her mother smiled and reached for her book.

Frankie half-staggered down the hall to her room. As she undressed, she tried to create a mental spreadsheet with all the possibilities. Maybe there was a bright side, after all. If Bob had stolen the money, he wouldn't be asking Mom to marry him. Maybe they were already combining bank accounts.

The other side of the spreadsheet filled with negatives. Bob could be stringing Mom along. Pretending they'd get married. No. Mom wasn't that easily fooled. Was she?

Frankie told herself she was jumping to too many conclusions. Mom must know what she was doing. Bob really had a sister in California. Ryan had verified that. Mom had found someone who made her happy. And maybe she and Bob would be willing to renegotiate the access rights with Angus Harper.

Before she crawled into bed, she grabbed her purse and dug for her cell phone. She plugged it into the charger and set it on the nightstand. The phone gave a quiet chirp, and the display light drew her in. She was exhausted, but it wasn't really that late, was it? Not even ten. Ryan wouldn't be asleep yet, would he? She told herself she was calling to let him know he didn't need to look into Bob's background anymore. No point in him wasting his time. She owed him the call.

Now that she'd convinced herself she wasn't calling merely to prolong the evening, she picked up the phone and punched in his number. She clicked off the lamp and settled under the covers while she waited for the call to go through. He'd smiled a lot today, and she enjoyed the memory. He'd seemed comfortable. In charge. Relaxed.

"Harper."

His voice sounded anything but relaxed.

"I'm bothering you. I'm sorry. I thought . . . I wanted to say we got home okay and you don't have to help us anymore because Bob is going to marry my mother, and his sister had a stroke, and—"

"Frankie. Stop."

Even in the darkened room, she knew her face glowed like a mountain sunrise. "Sorry."

The creak of wood and the faint chirps of crickets came though the phone. "It's okay. I'm getting used to it."

"Are you all right? You sound kind of depressed."

"Fine."

She knew he wasn't.

"You're outside, aren't you? Sitting on the log bench. Wolf's lying at your feet. Can you see the moon? Any stars out?"

His voice was husky when he answered. "Moon's a shade under half. Too many trees to make out the stars. Have to get up higher, or out to the meadow to see them."

"I'd love to photograph that someday. Maybe when the moon is full."

"Maybe . . ." His voice faded to silence.

"Tell me what's bothering you."

"Nothing I can't deal with."

From the hardness in his tone, she knew he'd barricaded himself again. "When you're ready, I'll listen. I'll let you go." When he didn't respond, she said, "Good night."

She had her finger over the 'end' button, and barely heard the "Wait. Please."

It was the voice she'd heard at the hospital. Broken. Naked.

She brought the phone back to her ear. "I'm here. What do you need?"

"Just . . . just talk to me awhile, okay?" He cleared his throat.

She curled on her side and pulled the covers over her shoulders. "Sure. What do you want to talk about?"

"Tell me about your mom. Did you ask her about the money?" His control had returned.

"Not yet. She said Bob asked to marry her. I figure they probably opened a joint account. She seems to love him. I can't deny her that happiness. It's not like he's marrying her for her money—she doesn't have much."

"Did you ask her about the land deal?"

"We're going to talk tomorrow. There's lots to figure out."

There was an empty silence before he spoke. "What about you? Will you stay in Broken Bow?"

"I can't think about that yet." She tried, unsuccessfully, to stifle a yawn.

"You're tired. I should let you go."

"I suppose."

"Frankie?"

"Yes?"

"I'm glad you called."

His voice was a warm caress. She envisioned him smiling now, with that dimple etched in his cheek. "Me, too."

"Oh, and I forgot. Pop said you and Molly should come out on Friday's trail ride. If you want to, that is."

In the mountains with Ryan—again. Of course she wanted to. She could see him on horseback, controlling a ton of horse-flesh between his legs. Good grief, what was she thinking? It wasn't smart. She wasn't looking for a relationship, she reminded herself. And definitely not one with someone like Ryan.

"Molly's kind of little for a horse, isn't she? I'm not sure."

"We have a mule she can ride—gentle as can be, and he'd be dallied to my horse."

"Dallied?"

"I'll have him on a rope around my saddle horn. It's safe. We do it all the time."

If he wanted her there, why didn't he say so? Or was this a favor to his father?

"I'll let you know tomorrow, okay?" For once, she wasn't going to jump in without thinking things through. Like she should have when he'd asked her for a ride at the hospital.

"It would be a good way for you to see what the rides are like—how they give folks a look at the countryside. Maybe help convince your mom not to sell."

So that was it. Nothing but a business deal.

"I'd already told you I'd help. You and your father don't need to convince me. It's a matter of finances."

"Of course." His voice dropped ten degrees. "Let me know."

"Good night." She mashed the button to end the call. Then she mashed her pillow. What was she thinking? She should have told him no as soon as he asked. Ryan was *not* the sort of person to get involved with. Molly needed someone stable. Someone who would be her father. A man with a nice, normal life. Not someone who, according to him, cleared a room with a gun instead of a vacuum cleaner.

CHAPTER 16

"Call it a night, son. You been staring at that screen all day. Most of last night, too. Can't be good for you."

Ryan rubbed his eyes and closed the laptop. "You're probably right." He'd gone to the Three Elks after Frankie called, downloading file after file for transfer to his laptop. Countless computer searches, countless dead ends, but he'd found too many coincidences. Too many times when Dalton's whereabouts coincided with the Phantom's. Finding out his best friend might be a ruthless mercenary at best, a traitor at worst, made him sick inside.

Part of him refused to believe it. That part shrank with each new piece of the puzzle. "I'll call it a night."

"Hit the rack—you need to be sharp tomorrow. Bunk here if you want."

Right—leading some tourists through the mountains, playing ambassador for Mother Nature. Normally, he enjoyed showing off the land. Frankie hadn't called, though, and he realized how much he'd looked forward to sharing it with her.

"No, I'll go to the cabin. See you tomorrow."

Despite every intention of crashing at the cabin, he turned left instead of right at the end of the ranch drive, and found himself sitting in the parking lot outside the Three Elks again. The sight of Frankie's Cavalier was enough to accelerate his pulse.

One look, he told himself. One look to make sure she was all right. He wouldn't even go in—one quick look through the half-curtained window.

Standing in the shadows outside the saloon, he watched Frankie bend low as she served drinks, sashay her hips as she walked between tables, nod and smile as men's eyes roamed up and down her body. One extended his hand, and Frankie took it in hers as he scooted out of the booth. The man led her to the dance floor. She followed, more stable on her high-heeled shoes than when he'd first seen her.

His fingers curled into fists in the pockets of his denim jacket. She was working. That was her job, and she needed the money. She couldn't possibly like it. The smiles she gave weren't real. Not like the ones she'd smiled for him. The ones that ignited a spark in his chest.

He was at the door, one hand on the metal handle. It opened, pushing him backward. A middle-aged couple breezed past him, arm in arm, laughing. The warm air, scented with beer, followed them out the door. He swore he caught a whiff of Frankie's scent. Impossible. He was exhausted, that was all. Little sleep and staring at a computer monitor for the better part of twenty-four hours led to mild hallucinations. Like hearing Frankie's voice above the music. He could walk to the bar a few blocks away, where he might find someone looking for mindless escape. *Stupid.* What he should do was get into his truck, drive back to the cabin, and sleep for ten hours. Or a week.

With a grumbled curse, he slipped inside before the door closed.

He paused in the entry, scanning the room, letting his eyes adjust to the dim light. Stubby gave him a quick nod, and the redheaded waitress approached.

"Jack," he said and went to the padded bench against the wall where he could see the dance floor. The small tables in front of the bench were littered with empty glasses and crumb-filled snack bowls. The waitress—Belle, according to her nametag—set his drink in front of him, clearing the remnants of the previous occupants and giving the table a swipe with a damp cloth.

She straightened the chairs. "You want to run a tab again tonight?"

He nodded, trying to see around her to the dancers. When she withdrew, his eyes picked Frankie out of the crowd. Her partner was short and broad, with a bad comb-over and a belly that spilled over his belt. Frankie smiled, nodded, and gazed into the man's eyes. Damn, she could at least look bored.

The man's hand strayed from Frankie's waist toward her bottom. Without breaking stride or losing her smile, she lifted it back to her waist. The man leered, the hand slid downward, and he whispered in her ear. She smiled, shook her head and once again moved it to her waist, anchoring it with her hand.

Ryan pounded back his drink. The whiskey burned all the way down. No upgrades from Belle. He stomped to the dance floor and tapped the man on the shoulder. "May I cut in?"

"I don't think so, bud. You can have her when the dance is over, but me and the lady are having a fine time. Isn't that right, Gladys?"

Frankie looked up at him, her face crimson. Was there anything behind that carefully guarded expression that said she was glad he was there? He felt as if he'd spent the last fifteen years of his life mopping floors for all the good his training was doing now.

The smile she gave him was no warmer than the one she'd been giving her customers. "Sir, no cutting is a house rule. But I'll be happy to save the next dance for you."

He nodded and clapped the man on the shoulder. "Fine, *bud*, but I strongly suggest you keep your hands where they belong."

The man met his gaze, held it for a fraction of a second, and Ryan saw the flash of fear he'd put there. Great. Now he was intimidating fat, defenseless civilians. He slunk back to his seat, where Belle had set another drink. Disgusted when he recognized his response to the man as jealousy, he shoved the glass aside and searched for hidden pictures in the scratches on the wooden tabletop. He didn't do relationships. How could he be jealous?

For the next fifteen minutes, Frankie went about her waitress duties without so much as an acknowledging glance in his direction. When he managed to catch her eye, the daggers she shot at him made him wince. He lifted his hands, palms up in apologetic supplication. After glancing around the room, apparently satisfied that she wasn't needed, she marched to his table.

"What was that about?" she said. "I'm at work here. I can handle myself."

"I know. I'm sorry. Please don't be mad at me anymore." He tapped his watch. "It's been over ten minutes."

He didn't get the smile he expected. Hoped for. Needed. The light was a little better here than on the dance floor, and he noticed the shadows under her eyes that makeup couldn't disguise. Stubby signaled from the bar.

She nodded to the bartender, then turned back. "I have to go. Maybe you should, too."

She approached the bar, and Stubby leaned forward, his hands on the counter. Ryan watched as Stubby glared in his direction, then spoke to Frankie. She shook her head, and her shoulders slumped. After a moment, she straightened her back, lifted her head and took a tray of drinks to a table at the other end of the room. Her dancing partner was nowhere to be seen.

Leaving his drink and a twenty on the table, he retreated into the night air, walking to the end of the block and back. Neither the air nor the exercise untied the knots in his gut.

Half an hour later, sitting on the hood of Frankie's Cavalier, he saw her descend the saloon's rear steps. Her head was down, and her hair hung loose, swaying as she walked. Dressed in khakis and a blue pullover sweater, she carried a denim tote, which he assumed contained her Gladys clothing. Although she'd parked her car under a light, there was none between the saloon's back door and where he stood. Even in shadow, he knew her stride, the way she carried herself.

Five paces from the car, she stopped and pulled a small pouch from the bag. Fumbling briefly, she extracted her keys and resumed walking. Although her gaze was on the pavement, he knew the instant she sensed him. Her head snapped up, and her eyes locked onto him.

"Why are you still here?" she said.

Her tone was flat, but at least there was no anger. He answered with as much truth as he was willing to admit. "I needed to explain."

She was doing all right with her plan to forget Ryan Harper, until she saw him. Why had he shown up tonight? And why had he waited? He could build walls to conceal his feelings. Maybe she should work on that herself. She steeled herself, trying to avoid the vulnerability in his eyes, a look she knew he rarely allowed himself to show.

"Frankie. I'm sorry. I don't know why I did that. He had his hand on you, and something snapped."

"Mr. Stubbs doesn't let things get out of hand." She kept her tone matter-of-fact. "I have to go home now. I think you should do the same. Maybe get some sleep. I don't need you interfering with my job."

"I'd like to talk to you. What about a cup of coffee?"

"In case you've forgotten, I have a child. The sitter's waiting, and time is money, Mr. Harper. And I might have a little more of it if *someone* hadn't pissed off one of my customers. He gave me a buck. Total. Rang up a sixty-five dollar tab for his table, I danced with him three times, and then you show up and I get one lousy dollar."

He had the decency to look chagrined. He reached into his wallet and held out a twenty. "Will that make up for it?"

She refrained from grabbing the bill and ripping it in two. "It's not about the money. You can't buy my forgiveness."

He lowered his gaze. "I wasn't trying to do that." When he looked up, his expression was contrite. "I'm not doing very well, am I?"

She banked her anger. He held out the bill again. "Please. I cost you your tip because I was acting like an idiot."

She couldn't hold back a smile. "I'll agree with you on that one. But I take money from customers as part of my job. I don't take money from friends."

He gave her a lopsided grin, and the dimple it revealed melted the last remnant of her anger.

He pocketed the bill. "Glad I fit in that category. So, how about that coffee, friend? I'll pay the sitter, okay? I assumed your mom was home."

She shook her head. "She's not, but that's another story." One she wasn't ready to get into. Not with Ryan. She hadn't dealt with it herself yet.

"My sitter has a curfew, and I have to get back." She cocked her head. "Think about that. I'm a mother. My time isn't my own. My life isn't my own. If you want to spend time with me, you have to share. You need to understand that right now. Please get off my car."

He slid off the hood and took the keys from her hand. "Allow me." He unlocked the door and held it open. Before she could get in, he grasped her wrist. Turned those whiskey eyes on her.

With a forefinger, he traced what she knew were purple

shadows underneath her eyes. "Are you okay?" he asked. "Did your mom explain the money?"

Mom. Who had been gone when Frankie awoke. Unable to talk, she shook her head. She wasn't going to cry. She never cried.

"Will you come to the ranch tomorrow, then?"

"Maybe." She lifted her chin and met his gaze. "If you tell me why I should."

He opened his mouth, then closed it. Ran his thumb along her jaw line. "Because I want to see you again." There was the slightest pause before he added, "And Molly."

His fingers spread, cupping her chin, and he raised her face higher. Lowered his. Her heart thudded against her ribs.

"I want one minute of only you, Frankie." His voice growled up from somewhere deep inside. His lips brushed hers, ever so gently. Nothing like the angry passion he'd shown the other day. She knew he'd release her if she pulled away. Knowing was enough.

She parted her lips. Invited him with the tip of her tongue. She heard something between a gasp and a groan as he pulled her against him. The sound of keys jingling to the ground was like celebratory music. His hands reached behind her head, fingers ran through her hair.

His tongue met hers in a mating dance. He tasted like whiskey. She hated whiskey, but couldn't get enough of the way it tasted mixed with Ryan. He hadn't shaved, and the stubble on his jaw scraped her cheek. His hands moved down, clutching her bottom, pulling her even closer to him. She felt his erection and ground her body against it. Their clothes seemed little more than a coat of paint between them as heat surged through her.

She pressed her chest against his, feeling the pounding of his heart echoing hers. Her nipples begged for his touch. Needing more, she reached behind her. She clasped one of his hands and placed it on her chest. His thumb found her, through her sweater, through her bra, and she whimpered.

Tentatively, she rested her hand between his legs. Somewhere, very far away, there might have been laughter, footsteps, conversation, but only their ragged breathing filled her ears. He moved against her hand, and she stroked him through the denim.

When she could no longer breathe, she broke away. His eyes were closed, and in the lamplight, she saw beads of sweat glisten above his upper lip.

"What time tomorrow?" she whispered.

With the sitter gone and Molly sleeping peacefully upstairs, Frankie stood at the window and gazed at the flickering shadows as tree branches swayed in the moonlight. In her hand she clutched her mother's note. No matter how many times she'd read it, it brought tears to her eyes. Knowing Mom couldn't write left-handed didn't take the sting out of the impersonal computer printout. The previous night, Frankie had finally managed to fall asleep shortly before dawn. When she got up, the note was on the kitchen table, propped against the sugar bowl.

Didn't want to wake you. Took a cab to the airport. Will be in California tonight. Don't worry. Everything's all right. I'll call.

Now she glared at the phone, willing it to ring. What did "everything's all right" mean? Bob's sister? The finances? Her happiness? Should she start looking for a place to live? If she did, that would mean no Brenda. She'd have to find suitable after-school care for Molly. Or could she convince Brenda to move in with her, make some kind of arrangement like she had here?

Until she talked to Mom, there was no point in trying to look at everything that could go wrong. What was going right?

She had a job—two, really—although she'd be glad when she could say good-bye to the Three Elks. Will Loucas at the Photo Barn would take her work on consignment. When she'd spoken with Mr. Anisman about using the school's darkroom, he'd said he'd look into her teaching night school photography, too. Forget that it meant sitters for Molly. If the classes were early enough, maybe she could come along. And selling a couple of pictures would cover baby-sitting expenses with money left over.

So where did Ryan fit into the puzzle? Never mind that merely thinking about him made her ache with longing. And kissing him wasn't like anything she'd ever experienced. But that was sex, and she'd been down that route.

Despite his recent willingness to include Molly in his invitations, she wasn't convinced he actually wanted a relationship, much less a ready-made family. She wished that she hadn't accepted the riding invitation. You'd think she'd have learned not to make decisions while she was . . . preoccupied.

Rubbing her cheek, still sensitive from Ryan's unshaven jaw, she went upstairs and searched for her old riding boots.

CHAPTER 17

Friday morning, Ryan gazed at the gathering clouds and turned on the news to catch a weather forecast before heading to the ranch. A thunderclap shook the windows. He sipped his coffee while he waited for the local update, able to think of little other than last night. He fought the stirring in his loins. If he was going to spend a few hours on horseback, that was the last thing he needed.

Scattered showers, possible thunderstorms, maybe in the morning, maybe in the afternoon. Or maybe the storm would miss this area entirely. He decided that the local weatherman would be hard-pressed to predict yesterday's weather and clicked off the set.

When Ryan arrived at the ranch, Pop sat on the front porch swing, a familiar stuffed dog on his lap and Molly beside him, her head bowed over a book. Her strawberry-blonde hair was gathered in a ponytail tied with a bright green ribbon. Wolf lay at their feet, inches out of swing range. Ryan slammed the truck door shut, and Molly looked up.

He hadn't taken two strides before she'd wriggled off the swing and run down the porch steps, throwing herself at him.

"Hi, Mr. Man. Mommy said I'm brave, and I'm going to go riding."

Without thinking, he scooped her up and gazed into her cobalt blue eyes. "That's right. If it doesn't rain." He tweaked her nose.

She kissed his cheek and giggled. An unfamiliar warmth spread through him.

"His name is Mr. Harper, Molly."

He looked up at the sound of Frankie's voice. She stepped onto the porch carrying a mug of coffee. Her hair was styled to match Molly's, down to the ribbon. Tucked into her jeans, she wore a ribbed green turtleneck, snug fitting enough so that he wondered if she was cold, or glad to see him.

Molly looked at him, then frowned and looked at Pop. "But you said the other man was Mr. Harper."

"Tell you what, Molly. You can call me Ryan."

She cocked her head and looked thoughtful. "Okay, Mr. Ryan. When can we go riding? Can Mr. Snuggles come, too? Mommy said I won't have a big horse." Her chin quivered. "I'm going to be brave."

Her voice faltered. He squeezed her and kissed her cheek. Her skin was silken, and she smelled like soap and chocolate. A closer look revealed the remnants of chocolate milk above her upper lip. He had to swallow before he could speak.

"You most certainly will. But if you don't feel brave, tell me, and you can ride on my horse with me."

"Really?"

He saw trust replace her uncertainty, and he blinked back images of Carmelita.

"Right in front of me, so I can hold you like this." He turned her around and held her around her waist, tickling her ribs. Her giggles erased Carmelita's face, and he gave Molly one more quick squeeze.

The phone rang, and he set her down, starting to jog for the house.

"Harper Trail Rides," said Pop.

Of course. He had the cordless on the porch. Ryan watched him nodding to the other side of the conversation, as if the caller could see him. Pop and telephones had never been buddies. Mom had always handled the business end of things. After a few unintelligible grunts, a couple of headshakes, he heard the word, "deposit." Another silence, then, "I understand. Thank you. Maybe another time."

He gave his father a questioning look.

Pop set the phone beside him. "It's thundering at the hotel where today's riders are staying, and they'd rather not ride if it might rain. They've cancelled." He turned to Frankie. "Guess you and Molly get a private tour." He got up from the swing. When it moved, he swayed, and Ryan resisted the urge to help him find his center of gravity.

"I've got errands in town." Pop said. "If I go now, maybe I'll beat the rain. Be back before two, I reckon."

"You sure you're okay to drive?" Ryan asked.

"Truck ain't like sitting a horse. I'm fine."

Frankie glanced at Ryan, a hesitant look on her face. "If you've got other things you should be doing, we'll understand. We don't expect you to spend your morning entertaining us."

Only her sedate tone told him how upset she was. Not being able to talk to her mother must be taxing even Frankie's optimistic attitude. The thought of her leaving sent his mood to match the darkening clouds above.

He shook it off and smiled. "No, my morning was set aside for the ride. But we can cut it short, or do whatever you like." He waited. Molly looked up from one adult to the next, obviously waiting for the grownups to make up their minds.

Frankie spoke first. "I'm happy to do what you decide. I know it doesn't sound very appropriate, but I would like to be in cell phone range. Mom still hasn't called me. And as long as I'm home by three. I have an appointment at the bank."

"Shouldn't be a problem. We can stay close." He saw concern in her eyes. "Did you check your mom's computer for BLD?"

"I did what you said, but there was no BLD on her payee list. That's when I called the bank. On the phone, they didn't sound too willing to give information to anyone but the account holder."

"Broken Bow's a small town. I'm sure they'll understand that you're acting in her best interest." He hoped so. The on-line bill pay feature was handy, but it also meant anyone with access to the account could log on, create a payee, and get the bank to send the money. And just as easy to delete the payee's information from the list.

They walked to the barn, Molly falling behind until Frankie took her hand. Ryan inhaled the familiar, comforting scents. Horses, feed, manure. His other concerns were forgotten. He turned to see Molly hiding behind Frankie.

"Come on, Peanut," Frankie said. "We talked about this, remember. You wanted to ride. You even wanted a pony."

"Over here," Ryan said. "This is Sparky. See. He's not so big." He patted the mule between the ears.

Molly shook her head. "My braves are all gone." She wasn't crying—yet.

Ryan crouched to her level. "Maybe if you watch your mom, some of your braves will come back. But you don't have to ride if you don't want to." He looked up at Frankie. "We can take a few turns around the corral and see if she changes her mind. I'm not in favor of forcing kids. They usually know when they're ready."

Frankie's eyes telegraphed her pleasure, but he was surprised to find it was the way Molly's had lost some of their wariness that warmed him.

Once Molly had agreed to watch, Ryan saddled Corky, his mount, and glanced down the row of stalls. "I think Hot Rod could use a little exercise." He wandered to a brown and white paint. The horse snorted and shook its head at Ryan.

"Um . . . it's been years since I've been on a horse. I kind of expected a Buttercup, or a Dobbin, or something milder than a Hot Rod."

Ryan laughed. "Don't let the name fool you. He's as docile as they come. Knows the trails better than I do."

She didn't look convinced, but he saw her glance at Molly and paste on a confident grin. "Okay, then. But let's definitely start in the corral."

An hour later, Frankie watched Ryan put away saddles and bridles, pitch hay, and curry the horses, all the while explaining everything to Molly, who was now enchanted and chock full of braves. After ten minutes of watching from outside the corral, Molly had allowed Ryan to settle her in front of him on Corky, and the transformation had begun. She'd gone from a death grip on the saddle horn to leaning forward to pat Corky's black mane. Before long, she was willing to ride solo, with Ryan walking alongside, one hand on Corky's bridle, the other on Molly's back. The heart-in-her-throat at seeing her little girl atop such a mass of power disappeared when she saw the way Molly smiled at Ryan—and the way he smiled back. Not once had he given her that *Look at me being nice to your kid* look she'd seen too often. As a matter of fact, he'd hardly paid her any attention at all since they started riding. It had all been focused on Molly. Now the lump was in her throat, not her heart.

She heard restless stirring in the stalls, and the occasional whinny. Seconds later, a thunderclap rattled the wooden structure.

"We'd better get back," Ryan said. He stepped out of the tack room wiping his hands on his jeans. "That sounded close."

They hadn't gone ten feet before huge raindrops pelted them. Ryan tucked Molly under one arm and reached for Frankie's hand with his other. The three of them raced back to the house, laughing and thoroughly drenched by the time they hit the porch.

He set Molly down and came close, tucking an escaped strand of hair behind her ear. "I guess I should see about getting you dry." His breath was warm on her face, and she took his hands. Wet and calloused, they were surprisingly gentle.

She leaned forward and kissed him, a soft, quick brush of lips. "Thank you."

"For what?" He looked genuinely confused, and her heart melted a little more.

"For . . . for helping Molly find her braves. That was very nice."

"I enjoyed it. She's a great kid."

"I know. And I'm glad you see it, too."

Molly sneezed, and Frankie pulled away. "All right, Peanut, time to dry you off." She looked at Ryan who hadn't budged. His gaze caught hers, and she had to force herself to break it. "We seem to be making a habit of this, don't we? Can we impose on you for some dry clothes? Again?"

He leaned closer. "What if I said there wasn't a dry piece of clothing in the house?"

She felt her face burn, but she kept her tone light. "I guess I'd have to sit around in these wet ones and catch pneumonia."

"Wait here. I'll see what I can find." He turned to go, but his hand slid down her arm, to her hand, to her fingertips, and even then, seemed to linger before he broke contact and jogged up the stairs.

She watched him until he disappeared around the landing. She wondered what he'd think if he knew she'd had her eyes on his backside for most of the ride.

Frankie and Ryan sat on the couch in the den, sipping coffee. Engulfed by one of Pop's red wool shirts, and fortified with hot chocolate and some of Rosa's oatmeal cookies, Molly sprawled on the floor in front of the television watching *Charlie and the Chocolate Factory.*

"As soon as the rain lets up and the dryer is done, we'll have to be going," Frankie said to Ryan. "Thanks for the interim wardrobe."

"Sorry about that. But Pop's robe never looked better."

She pulled the soft, plaid flannel a little tighter, all too aware of the absence of anything but one of Angus' t-shirts underneath. Ryan slipped his arm around her shoulder, relaxing and exciting her at the same time. She allowed herself a moment to enjoy the sensation before fishing her cell phone out of the robe's pocket. Although it was set to both ring and vibrate, she couldn't help checking for a magical missed call. She'd left a message for Brenda to call her as soon as she returned. If she didn't hear from her soon, she'd have to start lining up sitters.

She needed to be home where she could put things in order. She got up and checked the dryer, as if attending to the simple task would put her back in control. Sensing Ryan behind her, she turned before he could lean against her.

"What's wrong?" he said.

"Nothing. I've got the bank appointment, and Brenda's late getting back—probably got caught in traffic because of the storm. I need to line up sitters for Molly. We had a great time, but there's so much to do. My pictures should be ready, and I have to shop for dinner before I go to work tonight, and—"

His lips were on hers, stopping her mid-sentence. A coffee flavored kiss, deep and demanding, shut down everything except the need for more. He'd changed his clothes, but the scent of outdoors and horses clung to him. She reached behind him, twisting her fingers through his hair. Blood pounded in her ears, her heart drummed against her ribs. She heard bells. Reluctantly, she broke the kiss and looked him in the eyes.

"Dryer's done."

"It's still raining," he said.

"Not very hard."

"I'll follow you home. And I'll stay with Molly while you run your errands. If Brenda doesn't get back, I'll stay while you go to work."

"That's not necessary. I'll arrange something."

"I'm offering because I want to. I've had a good time today. I'd like it to last a little longer."

She ran down a list of possible last minute sitters and knew it would be a challenge, given it was the final weekend of spring break. She told herself that was the reason she'd agree to his offer.

Still, he could have had the decency to look surprised when she accepted.

CHAPTER 18

At the sound of a car in Frankie's driveway, Ryan snapped alert. Not that he hadn't been listening for the last twenty minutes. He lit the candles he'd bought on the way over, and poured wine into one of the two glasses he'd set out on the coffee table in the den. Frankie had said she wasn't much of a drinker, not that she didn't drink.

He heard her footsteps. She must still be wearing her heels, which meant she was in her uniform. Resigned to the fact that merely thinking of her sent his blood south, he didn't fight the sensation.

A light went on in the living room, and her footfalls grew softer—toward the kitchen, he guessed. Then closer. "Ryan?" Her voice was low. Curious, but with a sultry edge to it.

She came through the doorway, then froze. "Oh, my."

Well, it wasn't like he expected her to rush across the room into his arms. Imagined it, maybe. A little wishful thinking on his part. "I thought you might like to unwind a little," he said.

"I don't know what to say. This is . . . not what I expected." Now, she sounded nervous.

He stayed back, afraid if he moved closer, she'd bolt. Trying for an easygoing grin, he said, "And what did you expect?"

"I don't know, exactly. Dirty dishes, toys on the floor. Molly refusing to go to bed. Chaos, maybe? Everything looks so . . . orderly."

He couldn't help but laugh. To be honest, he'd been afraid of the same. "I'll confess that Molly stayed up half an hour later than your instructions said, but otherwise we stuck to the rules." *All four pages of them.* "She's sound asleep. I checked a few minutes ago."

Balancing on one foot, then the other, she removed her shoes. "Did you hear from Mom?"

He braced himself for the disappointment he knew he'd see when he told her no. "Sorry. Did the bank give you any information?"

"The address they sent the checks to. A post office box in Arizona."

The unspoken plea in her eyes threatened to overwhelm him. Why was it so hard for her to ask for help? "Would you like me to check it out?"

Her attempts at refusal were half-hearted, and he promised to do what he could, more to see the light return to her eyes than anything else. He could spare a little time tomorrow, and it shouldn't be too tough to get some basic information for her. Hell, he could probably just show her enough about using search engines and public databases, but he liked having an excuse to talk to her again. Or more.

"Thank you. Did Brenda call? Her car's not here."

"She left a message on the machine. Apologized for the delay and said she'd be back by Sunday."

Frankie raised her eyebrows. "Why did she leave a message? You should have picked up."

"Sorry. She called while we were gone."

"Gone?" She stepped toward him. "Where did you go? Molly had enough excitement for one day."

"Relax. We went to Dixie's Café for dinner, that's all. She wanted pizza, but we agreed that it was better to eat a healthy meal. She had chicken, mashed potatoes, and green beans, which she finished to the last bean, I might add."

"I'm impressed. She usually pitches a fit unless we go to Slappy's."

He tried to look nonchalant. "Maybe I did promise her ice cream if she ate everything."

Frankie's expression said she knew that wasn't all.

"Okay, and I told her we could go riding again." He winced, waiting for Frankie to give him grief for making a promise he had no right to.

"That might not have been smart," was all she said.

"I know. But I hope you'll both come again. I'm still getting the hang of managing a five-year-old."

"You're spoiling her, you know."

Tension sat behind her eyes. He took her hand, and led her to the couch. "Sit. Relax." He sat beside her, and she smelled a little like beer and grease and a lot like Frankie.

"Lean back," he said. She raised her eyebrows, but did as he asked. He massaged her temples, watching her eyes close and the furrows leave her brow. He found the elastic holding her French braid. "May I?" he whispered. When she nodded, he pulled it off, then ran his fingers through her hair, loosening the plaited strands. She sighed, almost in relief, he thought. As if whatever tensions had held her captive had released her.

"You're spoiling me, too," she murmured.

She tipped her head back, and he enjoyed the round swelling of her breasts above the low-cut top she wore. He resisted the urge to run his fingertip along their softness.

"You deserve it. I don't see how you manage. One day with Molly, and I'm exhausted. I can't imagine doing this twenty-four seven."

Her eyes snapped open, and she tried to squirm away.

Alarm bells went off in his head. Stupid remark. "I didn't mean it like that, Frankie. Wait. Please. I meant I admire you, and all you've done to make Molly the terrific kid she is. I'm

201

not sure I could do it, but that doesn't mean I wouldn't want to." Shit, he was getting in deeper. "We had a good time, and I'd like to do it again."

She settled down again, her eyes narrowed. "Go on."

He reached for a glass of wine. "Will you have one?"

With a long exhale, she nodded. "But only half a glass."

He poured and handed it to her, glad when her fingers slid along his as she took it from him. "I think I got myself into fatal guy-territory, and that's the last thing I meant to do."

"Fatal guy-territory?" She smiled now, and he leaned back onto the couch.

"You know. How does a guy respond to, 'Honey, does this dress make me look fat?' There's no safe answer to that one. I'm afraid you'll think I'm doing what you said you hated—being nice to Molly to make time with you, but I'm not. I like her for herself."

She gave him an evil grin. "Oh, so you don't like *me?* Don't want to—how did you put it? Make time with me?"

Warmth spread through his face. "I'm in way over my head here, aren't I?"

"A foot massage might extricate you from that pile of—stuff—you dug yourself into."

She shifted into the corner of the couch and laid her feet on his lap. Through the black nylon, he saw toenails painted a delicate pink, and a silver ring on the second toe of her left foot. He tried—but not nearly hard enough—not to let his gaze wander up her slender legs to where that scrap of a skirt ended. He was having too much trouble shutting off the little voice that told him Frankie was forbidden territory.

And then there was the other annoying part of his anatomy that had been reminding him of its presence all evening. He shifted her feet away from the evidence. When he pressed his thumbs into the balls of her feet, she moaned.

"Too hard?" he asked.

"Heaven." She took a sip of her wine and twisted around, trying to reach the end table behind her. Leaning forward, he took it from her before she spilled it. Her eyes glistened in the candlelight, and he hesitated, tempted to lean a little farther and nibble on her earlobe.

"So," she said, breaking the spell. "What did you and Molly do all afternoon?"

He set her glass on the coffee table and took a large swallow from his. So much for romantic seduction. He told himself that was a good thing.

"Play-Doh. Chutes and Ladders. We colored, and she made it clear that I didn't have to stay inside the lines and I could use any colors I wanted. That pictures were for imagining. We read." He paused. "She really can read. I thought she'd memorized her books, but I brought her a new one, and—"

"Wait a minute. You brought her a book? You bought my daughter a present?"

He looked at her, trying to read her expression in the candlelight. Had he screwed up? Was she back to lumping him with the other men in her life? She must have seen his distress, because she burst into laughter.

"I'm sure she loved it," she said. "She's been reading for at least a year. She picked it up on her own—with some help from *Sesame Street*, I'm sure, but she's almost always got a book with her. Probably because I was always reading—textbooks, mostly. She'd sit on my lap while I studied. Nothing like reading eighteenth century art history books to a baby—but you can make anything sound interesting with the right inflection."

Relieved, he moved his hands toward her ankles. "I didn't buy the book, though. It was one of mine. When she started reading it I figured she had a copy, but I didn't see one."

"What was it?"

"*Hop on Pop.* A family favorite."

"No, we don't have that one." She giggled. "I can see you sitting on Angus' lap, reading together."

"More like trying to pounce on him, but he was a good sport." He rubbed her calf now, digging his fingers into its firm muscles. When her eyes closed, he moved up a little higher, stroking, caressing. She had to know he wanted her. But she was an adult. All she had to do was say no.

Part of him—admittedly, a very tiny part—wanted her to give him the red light that would bring him to his senses, and send him on his way.

Instead, her quiet moan of pleasure aroused him further, and he shifted so he was propped over her. One hand sought her breasts. His lips kissed the hollow of her collarbone.

She tilted her head back, accepting his cautious advances, and he grew bolder, inching his kisses up her neck until he reached her lips. Soft and pliant, they welcomed him. No longer passive, Frankie returned his kisses, delving toward his soul with her tongue.

Her breasts sat, round and full, half-revealed by whatever contraption she wore under her blouse. Ignoring it, he lifted them, releasing them from their prison. She gasped as he fingered her nipples into taut, rigid peaks.

Her thigh pressed against his erection, and as she writhed, she drove him a little closer to madness.

"I want you, Frankie." His voice was more growl than speech. "If you want me to stop, say so now, and I'll walk away. I'm not sure I can promise that much longer."

"Upstairs," she whispered. "I want to do this in a bed."

She blew out the candles, then pressed her lips against his and wrapped her arms around his neck.

He would have carried her, but visions of his knee giving out rallied at the front of his consciousness.

Hands explored, as they moved across the room. Hers on his chest, then on his buttocks, drawing him against her. His, everywhere he could touch. By some miracle, they stayed on their feet. The kiss intensified as they navigated the stairs, then down the hallway to her room. Inside, he used his foot to shut the door. Still entwined, she reached behind him, and he heard the click as she locked it. For the first time, he felt that she was his, and his alone.

In the dim, gold glow from an outside streetlight, they crossed to the bed, and he sank beside her, trying to remember to breathe. She lay on her back and reached for him, almost as if she was afraid he might change his mind if she broke contact. Her fingers scrabbled for his belt, tugged at his shirt.

He grasped her wrists. "Slow down," he whispered, although every instinct told him to plunge inside her and claim her. No. This was Frankie, not a woman he picked up in a bar. She was a woman to be savored, not plundered. "What's your hurry?"

She turned her face away. "I thought . . . don't you want—?" Her voice quavered.

Sweet Lord, she was embarrassed. He leaned down and kissed her forehead. "Hey, of course I do. I want to enjoy you as long as possible, okay?"

When she nodded, he exhaled, glad for the brief reprieve that returned a modicum of self-control. Open curtains on the window above the bed weren't enough. He needed to watch her skin flush with pleasure, to see desire darken her blue eyes. But as he reached across for the bedside lamp, she protested.

"No. Leave it off."

"You're beautiful. I want to look at you."

She shook her head. "Please. I like it dark."

He stroked her cheek. "All right. I'll use the Braille method." He walked his fingers across her forehead, down her nose, to her lips.

She giggled and nipped his finger. He pulled it away and replaced it with his mouth. Heated kisses rekindled the passion. Blood pounded in his ears. He needed her. All of her.

He pulled her up so she sat astride him. His lips wandered down, suckling a bared nipple, teeth scraping along the taut peak. Her hands pressed behind his head, fingers threaded through his hair, squeezing him even tighter against her. With desperation replacing finesse, and welcome assistance from Frankie, he managed to extricate her from the body armor she wore under her blouse and threw both garments across the room.

"What the hell was that?" he growled.

"Bustier. No talking. Kiss me."

"My pleasure." His lips went back to work on her mouth. Tongues met, teased. Teeth nipped, scraped. Desire swelled in his groin. "Lie down."

She moved from his lap and settled on her back once again.

He stretched out beside her. His fingers caressed the softness of her breasts, meandered from one to the other, then ventured down her torso, along her warm, flat belly, to her navel. Her skirt, hiked up until it was barely a belt, posed no obstacle to his quest to know every inch of her. His hands roamed around her hips, back to her thighs, tracing along the sleek nylon of her pantyhose, pausing behind her knees, then up again.

Her whimpers of pleasure stoked his arousal. She squirmed, reaching for his belt again. He shifted, giving her free access. The confines of his jeans were painful now, and he ached for her touch. He held his breath as her hands released the buckle and popped the button at his waistband. The grind of metal against metal as she unzipped his fly was the only sound in the room.

She fondled him. Feather-light, her fingertips stroked his length, and he gasped, afraid his control would snap. All too accustomed to race-to-the-finish-line sex, somehow he found the inner strength to pull her hands away.

"No?" she murmured, confusion in her voice.

"Honey, if you do that now, it's going to be all over. Trust me, okay?"

He felt her head nodding against his chest. Her fingers moved up and fumbled with his shirt buttons. He took a few deep breaths and let her work, searching his mind for anything that would delay the inevitable. There was a shy and naïve quality about her, something unexpected, despite the passion of her kisses. He'd make this good for her, or die trying.

Both of them bare from the waist up, he lay on his side and drew her against him, skin to skin. Her breasts flattened against his chest like soft pillows. He stroked her back, from neck to waist, found the zipper of her skirt, and eased it down her legs. He worked his fingers under the waistband of her pantyhose.

"Wait," she said and pulled his hand away. "Last pair."

"I'll replace them," he said. He was losing his touch if she could still dwell on things like the cost of some tubes of nylon.

"It'll only take a second. Besides, there's no sexy way to get out of these."

He disagreed, but decided to keep his mouth shut. These little interruptions kept him from spontaneous combustion. He propped himself up on one elbow and watched as she rolled the nylon over her hips, then down her legs. As pale skin emerged from black nylon, his breath quickened. He hastened to shrug off his jeans, realizing too late that his boots were caught in their narrow denim legs. Cursing under his breath, he yanked the jeans out of the way so he could get the damn things off.

"Need some help, cowboy?"

"Apparently."

Frankie was already leaning over his feet, tugging off his boots and socks. Her breasts tempted, and he wiggled his toes against them.

"Pervert," she whispered. With an impish grin, she grabbed one foot and tickled the sole. He laughed, and remembering that Molly slept not far away, tried not to laugh too loud. In his entire life, not once could he remember sex being just plain *fun*.

He held out his arms. "Come here, you."

In a flash, she'd worked his jeans down his legs and added them to the puddle of clothes on the floor. She tilted her head. God, even in shadow, she was gorgeous.

"Is there a problem?" he asked.

"No. I guess I figured you for boxers, that's all."

At least his briefs were clean, was all he could think. On the job, he usually went commando. "We're not going to need them, are we?" He grinned and started to work them over his hips.

"Wait," she said. "Do you have . . . you know—"

"In my jeans. I'll get some." He rolled off the bed and found the condoms in his pocket. After sheathing himself, he optimistically dropped the rest onto the nightstand. When he looked back, Frankie had folded down the spread and was lying with the covers pulled up to her neck.

He slipped in beside her, and he felt her tense up. He put one hand behind her neck and drew her to him. Mouth against mouth. Flesh against flesh. Her heart pounded against his chest.

He ran his fingers along her jaw, touched the tip of her chin, and buried his face in the hollow of her neck. Her hair draped over him, sending a tingling feeling through him.

He nuzzled her earlobe and caressed her breasts, listening to her breathing grow ragged as he replaced his fingers with his lips once more. His kisses trailed down to her belly. He savored her scent, her taste. He stopped at the soft curls between her legs, seeking her center of pleasure. She jerked away and pulled on his hair.

"No . . . don't."

He retreated, probing with fingers instead, and found her hot and wet. Her hips tilted forward. His strokes grew deeper, and he matched his rhythm to hers. She writhed, straining against him, making sounds of pleasure. She clutched his back, pulling him closer. She parted her thighs.

He moved above her, the tip of his erection poised against her entrance. Fighting the urge to thrust inside, he inched forward. Despite her eagerness, she was tight—almost too tight.

"Relax, honey." He took her hand and placed it on his erection. "You do it. Take your time."

Her eyes opened, twinkling in the faint light. He lowered his lips to hers, kissed her gently. Waited. Her hands found him, guided him. She shifted her hips and took him inside— deliciously, agonizingly, slowly. Surrounded by her wet heat, the pressure for release was almost unbearable.

"Don't move," he commanded. "I need a minute here, or we'll both be sorry."

"Tell me what to do."

He gritted his teeth. Counted to ten. Twice. "Whatever makes you feel good, honey."

She raised her hips, then pulled back. With a groan of utter contentment, he followed her lead as they discovered their rhythm.

Frankie tried to concentrate on feeling good.

Had it been so long that she'd forgotten? Because the way Ryan treated her *did* feel good, nothing like what she remembered with Brent. She pushed those thoughts out of her head. Molly's father had no business in her life anymore.

Ryan had shifted and his tongue toyed with her nipple. The delightful torment sent electric thrills up and down her body and straight to her groin. All rational thought abandoned her. She moaned and moved faster, every sensation converging on one tiny portion of her body. She dug her fingers into his buttocks, trying to take more of him inside, to rub him against her core. New delights built, layer upon layer, as newer ones hovered on the periphery, promises of undefined pleasures yet to arrive.

She braved a peek at Ryan, poised above her, arm muscles straining. Sweat beaded on his forehead. Guys were supposed to like sex. He'd seemed to be enjoying it, but now he looked like he was grimacing in pain. His knee? She squeezed her eyes shut, praying she wasn't disappointing him.

"Wait." Ryan's voice whispered in her ear, his breath hot on her neck.

She froze, confused by his demand.

"I want you on top," he said, rolling their bodies as he spoke, without separating them. "I can last longer that way."

Straddling him, wishing she'd closed the curtains above the bed, she gazed into his eyes. She didn't see anything but desire reflected in their depths. He put his hands on her breasts and smiled. "Lean forward a little."

When she obeyed, he suckled one nipple and rubbed circles along the other. Reflexively, her hips twitched, and she discovered that in this position, the sensations were hers to command. Emboldened by this newfound power, she lifted her hips, almost breaking their connection. Slowly, carefully, she lowered herself, taking delight in Ryan's moan of pleasure. She adjusted her position so his hardness rubbed against the part of her that screamed for contact with every stroke, increased the tempo to meet its demands.

As she moved, all conscious thought left her. She disappeared, merged into some new being—part Ryan, part Frankie, yet more. From some far distant realm came the sounds of rough breathing, of the slap of flesh against flesh, and then the universe exploded in a flash of colors she could hear, of sounds she could taste, sensations that were brand new, yet instinctively familiar, and only Ryan's mouth on hers kept her from screaming in joy.

Vaguely aware of his hands clutching at her waist as he gasped and pistoned his hips, she collapsed, panting, onto his sweat-coated chest. *"Oh, my."*

"In spades," Ryan whispered, kissing her neck. His hands moved up and down her back in gentle caresses.

Unable to move, she listened as his heartbeat slowed. And then she must have dozed, because next she was lying on her side, curled into him, with his arm draped over her waist. She tried not to disturb him as she worked her way out of his embrace and went into the bathroom to stare at the wanton woman in the mirror. But unlike years ago, she felt no guilt. Ryan had released feelings and sensations she had never imagined.

She came out, her face scrubbed clean of smeared makeup, tossed on her robe and tiptoed down the hall to check on Molly. In the glow of the night-light, her daughter slept, cuddling Mr. Snuggles much as Ryan had held her moments ago.

A warm hand on her shoulder should have made her jump, but didn't. Somehow, she had become attuned to Ryan's approach. His scent, the cadence of his footfalls, slightly syncopated as he favored his injured knee. Had their lovemaking aggravated it?

Sex, she told herself. Not lovemaking. Wonderful sex, but she wasn't ready to go beyond that. Not yet, and not with Ryan. Tonight they'd both taken refuge from burdens they couldn't control.

"She looks like an angel, doesn't she?" he whispered. "Totally at peace."

He slipped his arm around her waist. She turned and rested her cheek against his bare chest, taking in the raw, male scent of him. He drew her closer, apparently at ease with his nakedness, and she traced the line of hair that ran down his torso, stopping at the nest of curls at his groin. He kissed the top of her head, and she felt as much at peace as Molly. Who should *not* wake up and see a naked man outside her door. Where were her brains?

Breaking the embrace, she closed Molly's door. She took Ryan's hand and led him back to the bedroom. The bedside lamp was on. "It's been wonderful, but you can't stay."

"I understand. I promise I'll be gone before she wakes up, but I don't want to leave yet."

She glanced at the clock on her dresser. After midnight. She should be exhausted, but she'd never felt so alive. "I guess a little longer's okay."

He lowered the robe from her shoulders. "Let me look at you."

She knew she blushed, but she stood still and let his gaze move up and down her body. Roughened by calluses, his fingertips were surprisingly gentle as they roamed the silver streaks at her breasts and belly. She fought the urge to cross her arms and hide the lasting evidence of her pregnancy.

"They're ugly. I know."

"Honey, don't be ashamed. You're not ashamed of Molly. You should be proud of these, too. Right now, I find them . . . erotic."

Dumbfounded, yet without embarrassment, she stood there as he walked around her, kissing her shoulders, her neck, running his hands down her back.

His fingers stopped at the base of her spine, exactly where she expected. "Now *that's* a surprise," he said. "I never would have figured you for the body art type."

"Does it bother you?"

He turned her around and placed her hand on his erection. "Not in a negative way, Frankie," he said in a husky tone.

She followed his gaze to the nightstand and the scattering of square foil packets. "Again? So soon?"

"What can I say? Stretch marks and palm tree tattoos seem to do it for me."

They seemed to do it for her, too.

Much the way she'd watched over Molly, Frankie watched Ryan, asleep beside her. Feeling brazen from the exciting new places he'd taken her, she studied his body without shame. In repose, his rugged features relaxed, and she saw a gentleness that made it difficult to believe he could be as hard and cold as his job demanded. The still-red scar at his knee, and others she'd seen, faded with time on his back, on his chest, half-hidden beneath the dark hairs, brought home the reality of who he was. He'd said he'd quit that job, but she wondered if he could stop being the person who used force to take care of things.

Well, he hadn't used any force tonight. Tender and patient, he'd shown her a side of him—and herself—that sent a warm glow through her. She brushed a lock of hair from his forehead. He snapped awake. The warrior, ever vigilant. For this night, her warrior.

"Hi," she said. "Nice nap?"

He sat up and raked his fingers through his hair. "Yeah. Guess someone wore me out."

She smiled, pleased that she'd satisfied him. Tonight had been one of mutual pleasure.

"What time does Molly wake up?" he asked.

"Usually by seven, although if she's as wiped out as she should be after her day, maybe eight."

"And how much sleep do you need?"

"Tomorrow—today," she corrected, after seeing that it was after one—"is Saturday. She knows how to fix herself a bowl of cereal and watch cartoons, but I don't like to leave her unsupervised very long. She may look like an angel when she's

213

asleep, but—"

"I get it. I think I found a little devil in her mother, too."

Her face burned. Before she could speak, he pulled her up alongside him.

He gave her the grin she loved, the one with the dimple. "Any chance of a midnight snack? My batteries need a charge."

"After I shower?"

He grinned. "If you'll let me wash your back."

"Now I'm really hungry," he said as they toweled off.

"I'm no cook," she said, "but I could probably scrape something together."

"There's ice cream in the freezer. Double chocolate chip." He picked up his jeans. She admired the view as he stepped into them. She also noted that his briefs still lay on the floor.

"I don't remember buying any ice cream," she said, trying not to laugh as Ryan lost his balance. "And I wonder how you figured out that was my favorite flavor. Could a little angel have told you?" All of a sudden she wondered what other secrets Ryan might have pried out of Molly while they were together.

He turned away, and she heard the buzz of his zipper. She shook her head. They'd been as intimate as two people could be, he'd walked down the hall in all his naked glory, but he had to turn away to get dressed. She stepped up behind him and wrapped her arms around his waist.

"I'll meet you downstairs," she said.

"I'd like fudge sauce on mine. It's on the counter by the microwave."

"You had this entire evening planned, didn't you? Candles, condoms and chocolate ice cream. What else could anyone ask for?"

He clutched her to him, giving her a kiss that curled her toes.

"The right person to share them with."

Downstairs, tucked side-by-side into the corner of the couch, they shared a bowl of ice cream in companionable silence. Frankie set the empty bowl on the coffee table beside the flickering candles.

"Did you pick up your pictures?" he asked.

How had she forgotten? This morning the pictures had been the most important part of her day. "Yes. Want to look?"

"Of course."

She'd glanced at the small prints as soon as she'd picked them up, but now she could study them in detail. Together, they leafed through her pictures. A glow of satisfaction welled up inside as she examined each one.

"You've got a great eye," Ryan said. "I can almost hear the wind in the trees in this one." He pulled out another. "Can I have an enlargement of this one? I love the way the bark patterns on the tree contrast with the smooth texture of the river rocks."

She took it from him. How had he known this was her favorite? "Of course." She put the pictures back into the envelope. "You seem to have a pretty good eye yourself."

"I guess you can't have a photographer big brother without some of it rubbing off."

She tapped the envelope against her hand, already eager to start printing. She told herself to slow down. Check with Mr. Loucas first. See if he agreed, before she spent a lot of time and too much money. He knew his clientele, and what they'd like.

Ryan took the envelope and set it on the end table behind him. He leaned into the corner of the couch and stretched out his legs, patting his thighs in invitation. She smiled and curled up on his lap. He draped one arm over her shoulder. With his other hand, he stroked her hair.

"How long were you married?" he asked a few minutes later.

For all the expression in his voice, he might have been asking about the weather. Her heart rate stepped up, and the dream-like quality of the evening snapped. Still, he deserved the truth, and she sighed. Afraid to meet his eyes, she faced away from him and positioned herself between his legs, reclining against him as if he were a comfortable chaise. His arms wrapped around her waist, confining as a seatbelt, but soothing.

"I wasn't," she said.

There was an extended silence. "I'm sorry. I assumed you were divorced."

"I can't say I'm proud of what I did. But I'm not ashamed, either. I was always the dutiful daughter. I needed everything around me to be stable. I was loved, but there was always this niggling fear that if I didn't do everything right, people would go away."

"Your father?"

"I think that had a lot to do with it. He died when I was little, and part of me was afraid I might lose Mom, too. Irrational, but I wasn't much older than Molly.

"I never felt like I fit in Broken Bow. I had bigger dreams. I wanted to study art and be a famous photographer. I worked for two years to earn tuition money, and I got accepted on a partial scholarship to NYU. There, I was a small town kid in the big city. The first year, I hid out. Not many friends, did all my work, felt obligated to prove I was worth that scholarship."

"That sounds like you."

Her mind flashed back to those days. Her goals, her plans. Everything had a purpose.

"It was. But in my sophomore year, I started poking out of my cocoon. Football games, a few parties, making new friends. Louise. She was from a small town, too. Her goal for college seemed to be to experience as much of life as she could. She convinced me to go to Daytona Beach with her on spring break."

"Sounds like a little R and R might have been good for you. All work, no play—you know."

She tried to move away, but he put his hands on top of hers and circled his thumbs over her knuckles. His touch reassured her, and she went on.

"Spring break was one big party. Louise had commandeered our hotel room, bringing in guys, getting drunk, and not much else. She set me up with a friend of whoever she'd found for one night. Brent. He was nice enough, polite, and the four of us went for a long walk on the beach. It was hot, and he had some beer. Fitting in became important, and I had a drink. And another. After the third beer, I was out of it, and we ended up in a tattoo parlor. You saw the result."

"A permanent reminder of your first spring break. Not that bad, really." He leaned forward and nibbled her earlobe.

She tried to laugh, but it emerged as a snort. "Well, there was one other reminder."

Ryan's fingers stopped moving. "Molly?"

"Yeah. I was buzzed almost the entire rest of the trip. For a while, I blamed Brent for keeping the beer coming, but I was the one who drank it. I wanted to party like everyone else. Little Frankie from Broken Bow, Montana was letting her hair down. Louise wanted the room, so Brent and I spent most of our time together, and . . . well, I gave in."

"You didn't use protection?"

"Yes, but those things don't always work." Her scalp prickled. "Tonight. Everything was okay, wasn't it?"

He smiled. "All intact."

He stroked her cheek. The comfort of Ryan's touch released her inhibitions more effectively than alcohol ever could. She let out a long breath and forged ahead. "I was a virgin. I thought . . . until tonight . . . until you . . . I didn't realize what sex could be

217

like." Her voice started to crack, and she swallowed. Ryan stayed silent.

"I thought it was supposed to be like that. Quick. With Brent, in the backseat of his car, it was all about him."

Ryan scooted himself up and worked his way out from behind her, tugging her legs around until she faced him. "You mean you never had sex again? Only that one time?"

She shook her head, trying to avert her gaze, but he lifted her chin, forcing her to look at him. In the candlelight, his whiskey eyes looked almost as pained as they'd been the first night she'd seen him. Tears burned as she realized the pain was for her.

"Not just that time, but only with Brent." And always the same, she thought. Five minutes of kissing, a few breast tweaks, and into the cramped backseat. "Honestly, I couldn't see what all the fuss was about, and after that, I was too busy."

"You didn't keep seeing him after you went back to school?"

She shook her head, afraid the dammed up memories would burst through and overwhelm her.

"But—didn't you tell him you were pregnant?"

"He was a fling. A stupid, drunken, spring break fling. The one time in my life I was reckless. I didn't know I was pregnant until after we'd gone our separate ways. When I finally tracked him down, I told him I was pregnant, but I didn't expect anything from him. He sent me one letter saying he thought it was a dumb idea, sent me some cash to 'take care of it'. I have no idea where he is now, and it doesn't matter. It wouldn't have worked out. He was more of a child than I was. Molly's mine. I returned his money, made up my mind to keep the baby, finish school, and I did."

"Your mom? Family? You went through it all alone?"

The huskiness in his voice undid her, and the tears finally came. He held her, rocked her until they subsided. He handed her a napkin, and she wiped her eyes.

"Sorry. I never cry."

"Hush," he whispered, stroking her hair. "It's okay."

"I couldn't come home. Oh, Mom would have accepted me, but it was easier being a single mom at school than it would have been here. I didn't want either her pity or her disappointment. And with her being the school principal, I figured it was better all around. I made my bed and all that. No pun intended." She managed a tiny smile. "God, what a cliché I turned out to be, saving myself for marriage, then losing my virginity and getting pregnant on my first spring break. Considering the way my mind was working at the time, it was a good thing Molly was a girl. If she'd been a boy, I probably would have named him Mustang."

She twisted to see his face, and he gave her his dimpled grin. "Well, I guess I can't totally hate the guy, then. He has great taste in cars." Kissing her, he added, "And women. But it's probably a good thing I don't know his last name. I'd hunt him down and make him pay."

"Why? Molly's the best thing that ever happened to me."

"That may be so, but he took what should have been the most wonderful experience of your life, and he cheapened it with his selfishness. I can't forgive that."

"I don't hate him, Ryan. It's over and done, and I have Molly. I can't help remembering how she was conceived, but I don't think of it as a mistake. I can't. And until tonight, I never knew how much I'd been cheated."

She snuggled back into him, drowsy and content. Relieved of a burden she thought she'd shed long ago.

"Why Molly?" he asked.

"What?"

"Why that name? It's old-fashioned. Certainly not the female equivalent of Mustang. A family name?"

She laughed. "No. But Brent always had an oldies station on

the radio. I lost my virginity to *Good Golly, Miss Molly.* Couldn't get it out of my head."

He chuckled and kissed her. Sweet and tender, but it sent a fresh surge of desire straight to her core. His hardness pressed against her thigh. No longer drowsy, she reached for him.

His hands were on her breasts. "If I set the alarm for six, can we go upstairs?"

The thought of an empty bed made the answer an easy one.

CHAPTER 19

Ryan wished for his Mustang as he coaxed the old ranch pickup down the mountain from his cabin back down to Frankie's the next morning. Her frantic phone call had sent his heart pounding, and it hadn't slowed yet. True to form, Frankie made absolutely no sense, babbling about Bob and Brenda, and then the damn signal had cut off.

All he got was that she and Molly were all right. Nevertheless, he shoved his Glock into the glove compartment before taking off. At eleven on a Saturday morning, the highway was clear, and he pushed the pickup to its limit. His pulse finally slowed, but his mind slammed into overdrive. It dawned on him that when he'd heard Frankie's frenetic rambling, his first thoughts had been of both Frankie and Molly. As a unit. The two had become inexorably linked in his mind. Maybe not only in his mind.

He refused the thought. He needed distance. It had been a marvelous night, but that's all it was. One night.

Frankie needed help. That's what he did. Helped people. No strings.

Then why was he sporting a two by four between his legs? He remembered how she'd transformed from a meek, almost frightened girl to a wild vixen, eager to learn and willing to go almost anywhere he took her. She'd ended up taking him places as well. Delightful places.

Reflecting on what she'd said about her earlier sexual experience, he clenched the wheel, still wanting to find Brent in some dark alley and teach him a lesson. What kind of a man didn't consider his partner?

He sobered when he realized his own recent encounters had been even shallower than Brent's. Hell, at least Brent had hung around for the week, not disappeared before dawn, never to return, the way Ryan usually did. But Ryan had never seduced a young, vulnerable girl—a virgin, no less. He seethed anew at the way Brent had treated Frankie.

He swerved into the turn onto Frankie's street and had barely stopped the pickup in her driveway before he was out and running up the porch steps. She met him at the door, throwing herself into his arms. He held her to his chest, her heart pounding against him. She smelled clean and fresh, nothing like the way he'd left her, slicked with sweat and carrying the musky scent of their lovemaking. He tangled his fingers in her shiny hair. After a moment she sighed, and he felt her relax against him.

"Okay, Frankie. Explain. Deep breath, and start at the beginning."

She took his hand and tugged him through the kitchen, down a short hallway and opened a door. Inside was a simple bedroom, a twin bed neatly made with a flowered comforter. A desk, a chest of drawers, and an easy chair upholstered in a narrow striped fabric completed the room.

"She's gone," Frankie said. "Brenda. I came in to air out the room, to put in some fresh flowers as a welcome home, and this is what I found." She swept her arm in a broad circle.

At the far wall a door stood ajar. He wandered over and found a bathroom with a pedestal sink and stall shower. Blue towels hung neatly on the racks, but not so much as a toothbrush indicated anyone had used the room.

Back in the bedroom, he roamed through the small space,

peering into the closet and dresser drawers.

"I already looked," Frankie said. "There's nothing in here. This is the way the room was when she arrived. She put pictures on the dresser, clothes in the closet, books—all the normal stuff any college student would. She wouldn't have taken it all to visit her family for a week, would she?"

He shook his head. "Doesn't seem likely. What do you know about her?"

"She was a grad student at the University. Business. She said she was from Arizona." Her face paled. "Arizona. BLD Enterprises. Brenda Donnegall. Not Bob Dwyer. I'll bet anything her middle initial is L."

Her face faded to the color of a cheap paper plate, and she sank to the bed. "You've got to find her. I was all wrong about Bob. Brenda stole Mom's money. Not Bob."

"Okay, Frankie. Let's not touch anything else in here." She was shaking. "How about some coffee? Tea?" Anything to distract her. "Let's see what we can do about finding Brenda." He slipped his arm around her waist and guided her to the kitchen.

Once he'd put the kettle on, he sat across from her at the table and took her hands in his. They were icicles. "Have you called the police?"

She shook her head. "I don't have any proof."

"Honey, finding proof is their job, not yours. And they have ways of tracking things, getting the bank to release information they won't give you. Is anything missing from Brenda's room? Something that wasn't hers?"

She chewed her lip and gazed at the ceiling. "I don't think so. Why?"

Ignoring her question, he pressed on. "Is your name on the bank account with the missing money?"

Her face sagged as the implications must have sunk in. "The

cops won't do much, will they?"

"I don't know. This is a small town. They might start investigating on your say-so. It's still a good idea to get the call on record. Meanwhile, maybe I can dig a little."

With a shake of her head, she got up and fussed with mugs, tea bags, milk, and honey, setting everything on the table. "I feel like an idiot. We treated Brenda like family."

Anger rose in her voice. The kettle whistled. She crossed to the stove and turned off the burner.

While she poured water into their mugs, Ryan saw her shoulders straighten and her chin lift. Her hands no longer trembled. He took the kettle and set it back on the stove, then wrapped his arms around her.

He lowered his face into her golden hair, inhaling its fresh floral scent. How he longed to make everything right. Kissing her wouldn't make it better, but damn, he wanted to try. Frankie had already proven she had the strength to handle whatever life threw at her. Hadn't raising Molly been enough? Molly. The interruption princess. He pulled back.

"Where's Molly?"

"Upstairs playing Barbies with Susie. I figured she needed someone more upbeat than me, and I owed Susie's mom for all the times she took Molly last week."

He turned her around and framed her face with his hands. "Do I dare kiss you without them wandering in?"

"How's kissing me going to help?" Her tone was serious, but her eyes twinkled.

"I have no clue. Why don't we try it and see."

With an ear cocked for the sounds of little feet on the stairs, he brought her lips to his. His fingers tunneled in her hair, and he lost himself in the softness of her mouth.

She was the one to break it off. "Your tea is getting cold."

"But other parts of me are getting hot."

"Cool them. I thought you were going to help me."

"I will. But first, call the cops."

"I guess you're right. What do I tell them?"

"Exactly what happened. Money's missing from your mother's bank account, and Brenda is gone."

"Okay. While I do, would you go upstairs and check on the girls? They've been quiet a long time."

Even he knew kids being quiet wasn't a good thing. Did she want him out of the room while she called the cops? Or out of the room, period? "All right, but I draw the line at playing Barbie."

She gave him a devilish grin. "I'm sure they'll let you be Ken."

Sitting at her mother's desk, Frankie hung up the phone. About the only thing that had gone right with the call was that she hadn't cried or gone hysterical when she'd been politely dismissed and told to call back if she had better evidence a crime had been committed. Maybe she should have gone hysterical. Maybe they'd have come out then. No, they'd probably have sent the paramedics to sedate her.

She lowered her head to her hands and began a slow count to one hundred, hoping to stave off a growing headache. Before she'd reached fifty, footsteps clattered on the stairs.

"Mommy!" Molly's voice rang through the house.

"In the den, Peanut. Please don't shout." She rubbed her eyes and looked up to see Molly and Susie, grinning like the Cheshire cat, holding up their dolls.

"Mr. Ryan knows how to braid hair," Molly said. She twirled around, revealing her now-braided ponytail, neatly adorned with a blue ribbon. "He did our ponytails, and our Barbies', too."

Frankie peered above their heads where Ryan stood behind

them, his face marked by a grin more sheepish than Cheshire.

"He gave mine *two* braids," Susie said, handing her doll to Frankie.

Frankie made a show of scrutinizing all four coiffures. "Everyone looks beautiful." To Ryan, she said, "Where did you pick that up?"

He shrugged his shoulders.

Molly chimed in. "On real horses. He used to braid their hair. For shows."

Frankie smiled at Ryan, then got up and hugged the girls. "Well, that makes sense. Horses have real ponytails, don't they?" She flipped their braids. "How about I fix you some sandwiches, and then Ryan and I need to talk."

"Peanut butter?" asked Susie.

Frankie sighed. "Of course."

"If you can handle the sandwiches, I can get started on your computer."

Grateful he hadn't said anything about Brenda or the police in front of the girls, she nodded and shooed them into the kitchen.

Once the two were settled, debating strawberry jam versus grape jelly, she loaded a tray with milk and sandwiches, and carried it to the den. "Will you eat a peanut butter sandwich? Grape jelly or strawberry jam. There's milk, but I can make coffee. Or do you want me to reheat your tea?"

"With peanut butter? Milk. No question." He didn't take his eyes from the screen.

She set the tray on the edge of the desk and picked up half a sandwich. "What are you doing?"

He turned and looked at her, a guarded expression in his eyes. "I'm searching the University's student list."

"That's right." She stopped, the sandwich halfway to her mouth. "You can probably find out her home address, or some sort of contact information, can't you?"

"Maybe." He cracked his knuckles and scanned the sandwiches, selecting a strawberry jam one. "What did the police say?"

"You were right. It's not a top priority, since Mom's not available to prove she didn't authorize those checks, and one missing piece of jewelry didn't seem to make much of an impression. They told me to go look behind the cushions or under the bed. They said to have Mom call. Maybe they'll come by tomorrow, but they didn't seem too concerned. I got the feeling they thought I was some poor over-reacting female."

"If you want, we could go to the station. That might speed things up. But the bank's probably a better bet."

"And the bank's not open until Monday." She stood behind him and looked at the monitor over his shoulder. The University logo filled the top of the screen, but other than that, there was nothing but the hourglass icon and a message that said, "Searching."

She frowned. "Are you doing that not-quite-aboveboard stuff again?"

"Do you care?"

She shook her head. "Not if you can find her."

"Right now, I'm a private citizen looking at what the University says I can. If she doesn't show, I'll see if I can boost the creativity."

"I take it she's not popping right up, is she?"

"Not so far. But their database doesn't show a master list of students, so I'm checking each department. Plus there are a couple of ways to spell her last name. If it is her real last name."

Frustration boiled over. "You know what? If she was legit, she'd have popped up right away. The fact that you're not finding her says enough for me." She lifted the hair from the back of her neck and let it float down. "And besides. None of this was my fault. Mom either sent the money, or someone else did. She's the one who left her password on the computer, and she's the one who ran off with Bob and hasn't bothered to call. Mom wasn't the one who asked me to move out here. Claire did. I like it, but if things fall apart, it's not the end of the world. I intend to enjoy what's left of my weekend. School starts Monday, and I'll have to deal with that, plus arrange for sitters, and try to figure out what the hell I'm going to do with my life."

Ryan twisted his head around and raised his eyebrows. "Quarter or dollar for 'hell'? Or should I ask Molly to bring in the timer?"

When he looked at her like that, his eyes crinkling at the corners with amusement, but with an underlying concern, everything inside uncoiled. Still standing behind him, she leaned over and put her cheek against his. Sandpaper stubble from his unshaved jaw rasped her cheek. "Can I run a tab?"

"Honey, your credit's good with me any time."

No results matching your search parameters popped onto the screen. Frankie put her hand over Ryan's on the mouse and closed the window. "Last night was special. Can we forget all our troubles for the rest of today, too, or does that seem selfish?"

"What did you have in mind?" His voice, rumbling from deep in his throat, resonated through her. He put his other hand over hers. Large and warm, it spoke of protection as hers disappeared beneath it. Memories of the previous night shifted her thoughts to regions well below her brain.

She nibbled his earlobe. He laughed and jerked away.

"You're ticklish," she said, remembering last night. "Any places I haven't found yet?"

He swiveled the chair and pulled her to his lap. "If there are, I'm not telling."

She dug her fingers into his ribs. His laughter brought the girls on the run, and within seconds, he was on the floor, gasping for breath, begging for mercy from all three of them.

The telephone rang, and Frankie went to answer it, leaving Ryan to fend for himself.

"Susie, that was your mom," she said when she came back. "It's time to go home."

Reluctantly, Susie peeled herself from the tangle of arms and legs. She gathered her dolls and shuffled toward the door. Frankie watched from the porch until she saw Susie enter her own house.

When Frankie turned to go inside, Ryan stood in the entry, tucking his shirt back into his jeans and displaying a questioning look.

"Reality beckons," she said.

"Can we postpone it a few hours? Come back to my place. We can ride, or hike, or sit on the porch and look at the stars." His hooded eyes said he expected more than stargazing.

Ryan checked the rearview mirror for the umpteenth time to make sure Frankie's Cavalier hadn't disappeared. Part of him wanted to race to the cabin and clean up anything embarrassing he might have left lying about. Another part feared she'd change her mind and vanish. Or worse, that he'd wake up and find her willingness to spend the day with him had been a figment of his imagination.

Glancing up yet again, he saw Frankie's lights flash twice and her right turn indicator go on. Reflexively, his foot tapped the brakes, and he maneuvered the pickup to fall in behind her. Her tires looked okay, and there were no unusual emissions from her car. The next exit was a good five miles away. Curious, he accelerated and drew up on her left, tapping his horn to get her attention. She seemed focused on Molly, not the road, and he had a quick panic surge. Was something wrong?

In the next instant, Frankie accelerated, leaving him stuck in his lane behind a semi, with two SUVs filling the gap behind the Cavalier. Trying to keep Frankie in sight, he almost missed the blue sign for the upcoming rest stop. In all the times he'd driven this stretch of highway, he'd never paid it any mind. He flipped his own indicator up and moved to the right, finally seeing Frankie's Cavalier heading into the rest area. By the time he found a parking place, half a dozen slots away from Frankie's, he saw her riding herd on Molly, who was rushing into the Ladies room. Kids. Leave it to Molly to delay a simple forty-minute drive. But instead of irritation, he felt a sensation he'd never felt before. Warm, yet jittery.

He ambled to the bank of vending machines and selected a cup of coffee, hoping it might distract him from the thoughts of Frankie that kept a stupid grin on his face. No such luck. Still smiling, he wandered back to Frankie's car. Leaning against the front fender, he watched the path from the restroom building. When a cluster of women headed toward the parking lot, it was as if all of them vanished except Frankie.

Molly tugged her arm, and he watched as mother and daughter exchanged some words, followed by a quick hug. Molly skipped down the sidewalk, an exuberant grin on her face. Warmth swelled in his chest, his eyes tingled and a lump filled his throat.

Damn it all to hell, he'd fallen in love with Frankie.

CHAPTER 20

Ryan sipped the sludge in his cup, trying to come to grips with the implications of his newfound awareness. He was in love with a Pollyanna with a five-year-old kid. What was he going to do about it?

Before he could get any farther along that mental train wreck, Molly picked up speed and barreled at him. He got the coffee cup onto the car's roof in time to avoid scalding both of them as she came to a halt at his side and wrapped her arms around his leg.

"Can I try to ride Sparky all by myself?" Her blue eyes sparkled in anticipation. "Mommy said you had to decide. I'm full of braves today." She looked to her mother, who flashed him an apologetic grin as she joined them. He stood there, afraid to meet Frankie's eyes in case his reflected desire to embrace her, to kiss her. To lose himself in her.

"Sorry about the stop," Frankie said. "Apparently all the fluids she and Susie drank filled her with something beside braves." She gave Molly a pointed look.

Molly tossed her head and rolled her eyes, a gesture that clearly said she'd dealt with this before.

"Let's get moving," he said. "Don't want to lose any of those braves, do we?"

Molly mimed locking her tummy. "Nope. They're all in there tight."

Frankie unlocked the car, and he helped Molly into the backseat. She buckled her seatbelt, gave it a tug and beamed at him. "All ready."

Frankie's expression was a little less bright as she adjusted her own belt.

He leaned into the car. "Are you all right?"

She tossed her head and tugged her ponytail tighter. "Fine. A little tired."

"Afraid you're running away from things you should be fixing?"

After a deep breath, she said, "I guess so."

"Nothing wrong with taking time for yourself. An afternoon in the fresh air can work wonders—give your brain a chance to regroup."

She chewed on her lip, then one corner of her mouth turned up. "You're probably right. Let's go."

"See you at the ranch, then."

He shut the car door and headed toward the pickup.

"Ryan. Wait!"

He pivoted, a split-second image of her racing to throw her arms around him disintegrating when he saw her standing by her car, holding his cup aloft.

"Your coffee."

"Right." He jogged back, letting his fingers slide over hers as he took the cup. Could she read his thoughts? She released the cup with barely a glance at him, and got back in the car. Apparently not.

Half an hour later, they were in the barn. Molly sat on a hay bale with Mr. Snuggles, telling Wolf about her upcoming ride. Corky and Sparky were saddled and hitched outside. He heaved Hot Rod's saddle over the gelding's back. Frankie kept her distance.

"I figure we should ride around the corral for a few minutes," he said. "Let Molly get the feel for Sparky. There's an easy trail that will bring us right by Josh's cabin."

"How long a ride?" Frankie asked.

He searched her face for any signs of reluctance. Damn, maybe he shouldn't have brought up a ride in Molly's earshot. He knew this part of the day was geared toward her.

"An hour, tops. But if you don't want to go, I can take Molly, and you can drive up and meet us."

"No, I'm fine." She scuffed her boots into the straw. "A little sore after yesterday's ride—and last night. It's been a long time on both counts."

"Oh, honey, I'm sorry. I should have thought—"

"No, no." She smiled. "It's a good kind of sore. Nice memories." She glanced over her shoulder toward Molly, who still seemed engrossed in her discussion with Wolf. When Frankie turned back to him, the invitation from her half-parted lips was obvious. He accepted, and met her more than halfway.

Hot Rod shattered the moment with a snort and a brisk shake of his head. Molly's, "Are we ready yet?" didn't help much, either.

Frankie placed her palms on his chest, over his pounding heart. With her eyes barely open, she murmured, "Would it really be all right if I skipped the ride? I have my camera, and I'd love a little time to take pictures."

Leaving him alone with Molly. When he realized how different his reaction would have been only days ago, and what it meant that Frankie trusted him, his heart kicked up again. "Sure. Molly and I will have a great time, and we'll meet you at the cabin. On one condition."

"Which is?"

"You make no judgments about me based on the state of the cabin. I hit the ground running when I got your call this morning."

"Deal."

"I can't remember if I locked the door." He fished in his pocket for his keys and handed them to her. "In case I did. Make yourself at home. I'll have one very sleepy little girl with me. See you in a few hours."

He watched her walk away, enjoying every swaying step. When she bent over to speak to Molly, he watched even harder. Hot Rod nudged him with his nose.

"Hey, a man can look, can't he?" He hoisted the saddle off Hot Rod's back. "Looks like you're not getting any action today, boy." Giving the horse's neck a pat, he said, "I don't think I will, either. But it's still going to be a glorious day."

After cranking off two rolls of film, Frankie parked her Cavalier behind Ryan's cabin. The burned-out remains of his car brought back the memories of their encounter in the ER. When she looked closely and realized the car was—or had been—a Mustang, she smiled. That's why Ryan said Brent had good taste in cars.

The thought took her into turbulent waters. Earlier, she'd waited around until Molly and Ryan left the confines of the corral for the trail. The way Ryan interacted with Molly, as if he enjoyed her, even cared for her, brought a lump to her throat. Molly was awe-struck and Frankie feared her daughter was growing attached to the man too quickly.

As if she herself weren't. Lust, infatuation, gratitude, she told herself. But why did her heart tumble in her chest every time she thought of him? And why did she think of him all the time? Because the alternative was thinking about her mother and Bob, and Brenda. Definitely not because she could be falling in love. Love didn't fit into her agenda.

She swung her legs out of the car and stood, knuckling her lower back, trying to unkink muscles stiffened by bending and crouching to get some macro shots of newly emerging wildflowers. She straightened her shoulders and strode up the steps to the front door. The door wasn't even shut tight, much less locked. A pang of guilt spread through her as she realized her phone call had sent Ryan flying. She pushed on the door, which swung open without a creak.

Well, well, Ryan Harper. You really did leave in a rush. Whatever were you doing?

Books rested in piles on the floor. DVD cases, some open and empty, lay next to the easy chair. The disks sat in a stack on the coffee table. She stepped around the mess and into the kitchen. Dirty dishes on the counter, the half-full trash can in the middle of the room. The bedroom wasn't much better, with clothes lying in haphazard heaps on the floor, and dresser drawers open with contents half in, half out.

"Bachelors," she muttered. She'd promised not to hold it against him, but she wondered why the place was such a disaster. It hadn't been anything like this the last time she'd been here. Maybe he'd been searching for something when she called.

If so, she owed him. Humming under her breath, she started in the bedroom. After making the bed, she picked up the clothes from the floor and piled them on top, automatically sorting them into lights and darks for washing.

In the closet, shirts hung half on, half off of hangers. She straightened them, tripping on a backpack. She assumed the items on the floor had fallen from the pack, and replaced them, looking to see where the pack might belong. Apparently on the shelf running along the top of the closet. Not quite able to reach, she stretched and half-tossed it upward. It took several tries before it settled into position. Scraps of paper floated down. A faded credit card receipt, a torn piece of lined paper with a phone number, and a cigar band. Ryan didn't smoke, did he? He'd better not—not around Molly. Shoving them into her pocket to deal with later, she closed the closet door.

Tackling the dresser next, she refolded his t-shirts and sweaters and put them away. The top drawer held socks and underwear, and she was tempted to leave everything in its current jumbled state.

Don't be ridiculous. It's laundry. Sort, fold, and put it back.

A smile escaped when she noted that in addition to a few pairs of utilitarian cotton briefs, he had some silk boxers. Red, black, and leopard print. Oh, no. She did *not* need to be tingling all over.

In the kitchen, she filled the sink with soapy water and stacked the dishes to soak, then went to attack the mess in the living room. She started arranging the loose DVDs alphabetically so she could match them to their cases. The odds were against her getting them back on the shelf the same way they had been. Same for the books. Well, Mr. Slob could deal with it, assuming he noticed.

When she finished, she ended up with an empty case for *Gone with the Wind* and a blank disk marked GWTW. Ryan or Josh must have made a copy. Come to think of it, it had been years since she'd seen the movie, and a little distraction would be welcome. When she slipped the disk into the DVD player and turned on the television, nothing happened. After fiddling with buttons on the unit and the remote, she decided it must be a bad copy—until her eyes spied Ryan's laptop.

"One more try," she muttered, her heart now set on an afternoon with Rhett and Scarlet.

Although she found no available electric outlet near the sofa, she refused to be thwarted. The bedroom would be even better. Curled up on the bed, a box of tissues by her side—maybe Ryan had some popcorn? What better way to spend a lazy afternoon. How long had it been since she'd treated herself to some personal time?

Anticipation rising, she set up the computer and went to the kitchen to hunt for a snack. The dishes in the sink glared at her, and she automatically started washing, then stopped, mid-dish.

"No. You can soak a while longer. My turn."

When the front door burst open, she started. Were they back already? Wiping her hands on a towel, she pivoted toward the living room.

"Ryan? I didn't expect—"

The black-clad man at the door was definitely not Ryan. Her heart pounded, but when he stepped further into the room and the light, she relaxed. "Dalton? Hi. I assume you're looking for Ryan. He took Molly riding, but he should be back in an hour or two. I was going to watch *Gone with the Wind*, but it won't play on the television, so—"

"Hello, Frankie. Still chattering on, I see."

"Sorry." She grinned. "Anything I can do?"

His eyes moved up and down her body, almost tangibly. Uncomfortably so. Had he looked at her that way before? Or did it bother her now because of the way she felt about Ryan? She wasn't supposed to feel that way about Ryan.

He gave her an easy grin. "Actually, I ran into Ryan. He wants me to bring you to him."

"Is anything wrong? Is Molly hurt?" Scenarios of Molly falling off of Sparky into a stream or down a ravine wound through her head. "Do I need a first aid kit?"

He chuckled. "Nothing like that, little lady. They're fine and dandy. They want you to join them is all. I've got wheels—we can be there in under ten minutes."

"Right. Let me get my purse and jacket." She moved toward the table by the door where she had dropped them.

"Let me help you," he said, and held her jacket. When she reached back to slide her arm into the sleeve, he grasped her wrist, and the next thing she knew, her hands were twisted behind her. Some kind of cloth bag went over her face. The weave was coarse enough to let some light in, but too dense to make out anything but flickering shadows.

"What are you doing? Let me go!"

"Sorry, darlin'. I need you to be quiet." His warm Texas drawl had grown colder than the stream Molly had fallen in.

She felt a sharp sting in her arm, and then even the shadows disappeared.

Chapter 21

Ryan woke to darkness, stiff and groggy, a pounding in his head distracting him from the roiling nausea in his stomach. With nothing but instinct to rely on, he knew he was someone's captive. Keeping his breathing steady, trying not to call attention to the fact that he was conscious, he assessed the situation.

The pain in his head faded as a growing agony in his shoulders swelled, especially in his recently injured one. He squinted into the darkness, the scrape of rough cloth over his eyes telling him he was blindfolded. The air smelled damp and musty, with no hint of a breeze or any warmth of the afternoon sun. Probably in a darkened room, he thought, or else he'd been out for hours.

Mentally, he worked his way down his body. Something hard pressed against his back, behind his knees, and the edge of his buttocks. A chair? Okay, he was secured to a point above and behind him, keeping him elevated enough so the seat didn't support all his weight. His legs dangled above the ground, unless he'd lost all feeling in them. Wiggling his toes let him know he hadn't, and that he was still wearing his boots. But his legs must be bound at the knees and ankles, because they moved as a unit, and not far. A little discreet wiggling confirmed this, quickly halted by the strain on his shoulders.

He listened for any signs that he wasn't alone. Nothing but his own breathing. His head cleared a bit, and he remembered the two hikers who'd come out of the woods while he and Molly—

Molly!

Where was she? Damn, his brain was fried. Whatever they'd given him had fogged his memory. Behind his blindfold, he strained to remember, to call up a mental image. A surge of adrenaline as he thought of someone harming her helped clear his head.

Hikers at the side of the road, packs at their feet. Staring and arguing over a map, one pointing one way, another shaking his head and pointing the other direction. Skin color? He blinked, as if it would clear the darkness that hung in front of his eyes. Long sleeves. Dark skin, but was it a clue to their ethnicity or simply a result of the sun?

Voices? Accents? He tried to play back the audio. The crackle of paper as hands slapped against the map. *No, no,* uttered in deep male voices, but no discernable accent. Hell, he could say *no* himself in at least eight languages and not give away his native tongue.

Another layer of fog lifted, and he remembered the third man. Or woman. He'd been ambushed by someone approaching from the other side. Before he could turn and focus, he'd felt a jab in his thigh. Someone yanked him from his horse. He remembered a struggle, and then the lights went out. But not before he heard Molly cry out for her mother.

He forgot all about stealth. "Who the hell are you?" Ryan screamed into the darkness. "Where's Molly? So help me, if you've hurt her, I'll—" He bit back the rest. Regroup.

Silence answered. His fingers had gone numb, and he clenched his hands in and out of fists to restore circulation. His shoulders throbbed. He worked his legs up and down, back and forth, trying to loosen whatever bound them.

Could be worse. He could be swinging like a side of beef on

a meat hook. At least his shoulders weren't supporting his entire body weight.

Damn if he wasn't looking on the bright side. Frankie had definitely wormed her way inside him. She'd be safe, back at Josh's. And when he didn't show up by dark, she'd go for help.

But this wasn't just about him. Molly was somewhere. Afraid for her and furious, he struggled against his bonds. Moving flooded him with nausea, and he took slow, deep breaths. Dammit, he'd been in situations like this before, but always as part of a team. Knowing a team never left someone behind made pain and uncertainty bearable. He fought the unfamiliar feeling of despair and focused on testing each restraint. He knew better than to struggle, that it would tighten the ropes.

If he got one foot high enough to pry off a boot, maybe he could slip through the bindings? *Be steady. Be methodical.*

Had his ankles moved a little further since the last time he tried? Small increments were still progress. Time lost all meaning.

Breathe. Move your foot. Don't lose your balance. Breathe again.

A creak sounded from in front and to his left. He felt a change in the air. Even blindfolded, he sensed increased light in the room. A door had opened. A faint odor of the woods, quickly masked by the acrid tang of sweat.

He froze.

"Too late, Mr. Harper. No need to feign unconsciousness. It's obvious you're awake."

A male voice, not a native English speaker, refined, but an indeterminate accent. Undoubtedly cultivated to obscure its origin.

"Who are you, and what do you want from me?" he asked.

From a distance, to his right, he heard a weapon being racked. Automatically, his muscles tensed. Two of them, then. The hikers?

"What do you want?" he asked again.

"Tell us where the file is, and we can talk about little Molly."

"File? What are you talking about?" Dammit, if he had anything someone wanted this bad, it must be important. The intel from Alvarez? What could these folks want with stolen art? But he knew better than to jump to conclusions. "And who's Molly?"

"Don't play games, Mr. Harper. We have the child. She was riding with you. However, if she means nothing to you, then there is no reason for us to care what happens to her."

Despite his experience, panic threatened. He'd never had to rescue anyone he loved. Detachment became an almost impossible objective.

Footsteps approached, and he heard a sound he recognized. Too familiar. Like a fist slapping against a palm as a warm-up to whacking someone. Not able to see the blow, not knowing where it would hit, only that it would hurt like a mother, he clenched already tight muscles even harder.

A punch to his solar plexus made him pitch forward. His shoulder screamed with the added strain, and he gritted his teeth to keep from crying out. He would *not* give them the satisfaction. The next blow was to the side of his head, then one to his bad knee, another one to the face, and he lost track after that, drowning in a sea of pain, no longer giving a damn about being quiet. He swallowed blood. He hoped his nose wasn't broken. Stars swam in front of his eyes, illuminating his private darkness. His ears rang. That creep had been using more than his fists.

"Enough." Mr. Manners' voice floated through the agony. "I know you enjoy your work, but you're not permitting our guest to answer my questions."

A grunt, and footsteps scuffed backward. Okay, Mr. Manners was calling the shots. Ryan turned his head to the side and spat blood in the direction of Mr. Muscle. A quick shuffle told him he had either hit his target or come close.

"I do apologize for my colleague's enthusiasm, Mr. Harper. Now, perhaps we can get down to business, yes?"

He sucked air through his mouth, the only way he could breathe. "Show me Molly."

"Surely you won't be so stubborn that you'd jeopardize her safety, Mr. Harper. Where is the file?"

Pain and fear for Molly congealed into a mass of uncontrolled rage. "What goddamn file, you motherfucker? Your goddamn intel is out of date. I'm not in the business. Got kicked out on my goddamn ass and I don't have any goddamn files."

"Tsk, tsk, Mr. Harper. Such language. Is it really necessary to be so . . . vulgar?"

"Put it on my tab," he muttered.

"I'm afraid I don't understand your reference, Mr. Harper."

"Inside joke."

The door opened again. He heard footsteps followed by a thud of an object dropped to the floor. Mr. Manners moved away, and after some hushed whispers, the door closed. When he spoke again, his voice was flat. Ryan shivered with its coldness.

"It appears I was partly mistaken, Mr. Harper. The file is now in my possession. However, the key is missing. I am sure our people will be able to decode it, but I'm afraid time is of the essence. If you will relinquish the code, you will soon be reunited with the child." Ryan heard a skidding thud, as if the man had kicked an impediment out of his way. "And perhaps someone else you seem to be fond of."

God, no. Frankie? Pop? "I don't know anything about any code, or key, or whatever you're talking about."

"You lied before, Mr. Harper. Why should I believe you now? Perhaps you would like a little time to consider the situation. I will be back."

"Not without Molly. I see her, or I don't talk."

Footsteps retreated, the door opened, clicked shut, and then silence. No, not total silence. He held his breath. No movement, but faint breathing sounds, barely audible. Someone else was in the room.

Frankie drifted within the darkness, slowly rising from the mist that surrounded her. It couldn't be time for work already. She hadn't prepared her lessons. "Ten more minutes," she mumbled under her breath. Aware she wasn't in her own bed—that she wasn't in a bed at all—she snapped awake, trying to remember.

She'd been in a car. But she wasn't moving, heard no engine sounds. Had it been a dream? Dim light filtered through the cloth covering her head. Her cheek pressed against a hard surface. Even through the cloth, it was rough and smelled like dirt and wood. A dirty floor. So, she wasn't in a car. Brilliant deduction. Hip bones and floor met in painful discord. She shifted. Thousands of stinging needles flamed in cramped limbs as the circulation returned. She gasped through her teeth.

"Who's there?" A deep voice, rasping and nasal, came from above.

Her head cleared a little. She couldn't see. Maybe the voice was another blinded captive.

A cough, a throat-clearing sound, and spitting. "I know you're there. Who the hell are you?" This time, the voice was clearer. Her heart lifted. Ryan.

"You owe me a quarter," she said, clambering to her feet. Dizziness kept her from following the sound of his voice, and she bent double, taking slow deep breaths.

"Frankie. God, are you all right? What happened?"

"Dizzy. Give me a minute. How's Molly? They didn't blindfold her, did they? She's afraid of the dark, especially in strange places."

The answering silence chilled like a glacier. Yanking the sack from her head, she blinked and scanned the space, searching for anything that might be Molly.

A single room. Some sort of storage shed? One window, partially boarded over, striped the floor with gold from the late afternoon sun. A wide shelf, about four feet from the floor, ran the length of two adjacent walls. Ryan hung from the roof, half-seated on the shelf. But no Molly.

Rushing to free him, she braced herself for answers she didn't want, and asked again, "Where's Molly?"

"I'm so sorry." His voice was a hoarse croak.

Her heart lurched. The room spun, and she grabbed the shelf. "No. No, she's not . . . she can't be . . ."

"Honey, no. They said she was all right. I am so damn sorry. I never saw it coming."

"What did you do to my daughter? I trusted you with her. How could you let anything happen to her? What kind of a man are you, letting someone steal a child?" Hysteria mounted, but she swallowed it. Screaming wouldn't bring Molly back.

Ryan groaned. "God, Frankie. I don't know. Please. Get me down. We'll figure it out."

She grabbed his legs, helping him get his feet onto the shelf. "Wait," she said. "Don't stand up all the way. You'll hit your head. We're in some kind of storage shed. You're on a shelf. The rope around your wrists goes over a beam or a rafter or whatever you call it, and it's a low ceiling to begin with."

"My blindfold. Take it off."

"Let me get this first." Right now, she couldn't deal with his eyes. His face, covered in blood, with purple bruises swelling on his cheeks, evoked a twinge of pity. She blinked. She didn't want to feel sorry for him. He'd lost her daughter. Stretching on tiptoe to reach his wrists, she fussed with the knots, trying to stop the trembling in her hands.

"Stop moving," she said, not disguising her irritation. "You're making it harder. Back up."

He slid his feet backward until he clunked into the wall. She sidled in front of him, frustrated by knots she could barely see. "Why isn't there a piece of broken glass, or a rusty nail? They always find those in the movies."

"Welcome to the real world," Ryan mumbled.

Her body pressed against his, and he exhaled explosively. He adjusted himself against the wall, giving her space. His jaw clenched.

"I'm hurting you," she said. "I'm sorry." How long had he been strung up like that?

"I've . . . been . . . worse." His words slithered out, one at a time.

"I think it's getting looser. The problem is, if you raise your arms to give me slack, I can't reach the knots."

"Check my pockets. Anything that will cut? Keys?"

Neither spoke while she reached behind him, patted his rear pockets, then checked his front ones.

"Nothing," she said.

"What about my belt? You can use the buckle."

"You're not wearing one."

"Makes sense. They knew what they were doing. Anything lying around?"

"No. It's clean—except it's dirty, if that makes sense."

"Perfect sense." He braced himself tighter against the wall. "Do what you have to do."

As she worked the knot, she tried to ignore the intimate way their bodies pressed together, the same way she tried to ignore her fear for Molly. Then she remembered what she'd heard as she awakened. Ryan, his voice choked with rage and compassion, telling them to bring Molly back and he'd give them what they wanted.

She couldn't blame him for this. Mothers protected their children. She hadn't been there when someone grabbed Molly. Ryan was a professional. If he hadn't been able to save Molly, what could she have done? He was experienced, and if they were going to get out, she'd have to rely on him. And as if that was the answer, the knot opened enough to get her finger under it, and it yielded to her demands. She yanked on the rope, bringing it down from the rafters.

Once his arms were released, Ryan collapsed onto the platform like a marionette whose strings had been cut. He yanked the blindfold from his eyes and cursed.

"Are you all right?" she asked. "You're all bloody." She swung her legs over the edge of the platform and sat there, stiff from working with her arms above her head for so long, and still a little disoriented from the drug.

"From my nose." He touched it with a fingertip. "Don't think it's broken after all."

He ran his hands down his body, checking and testing. "I'll be sore, but I'm all right. How about you?"

"I'm fine, I think. Fuzzy. A little queasy. Can't remember much."

"Feels like there was Versed or Rohypnol in whatever they drugged us with. Gives you amnesia. Things come back, eventually."

Frankie took a deep breath and looked Ryan in the eye. "All right. What do we do now?"

CHAPTER 22

"First," Ryan said, "we figure out what we're up against." He slid off his perch, biting back the curse as pain shot through his knee. Frankie grabbed his elbow in support.

"Should you be walking?" She slid her arm around his waist. "I heard them talking—at least I don't think I was dreaming—and they said they'd be back. Won't they bring Molly? Shouldn't we wait? If they come back and we're gone, they might . . . hurt her."

From the trembling in her voice, he knew she had already thought about the alternative. So had he. Carmelita's eyes hovered in his memory, and he willed them away. Thinking the worst wouldn't do any good.

"They said she was okay. We have to believe it." He hoped he sounded convincing. Right now, late afternoon sunlight streamed in through the window, but it would be dark in a few hours, and he had no idea where they were. "Can we get out? Did you try the door?"

Her eyes opened wide. "Stupid. I assumed we were locked in." She hurried to the door and unfastened the simple wooden latch. She yanked on the handle. Pounded on the door. Crestfallen, she turned to him. "And I was right."

His brain was still mush. The blood he'd swallowed threatened to come up, and he forced his mind elsewhere. He took a tentative step forward, then another. Frankie joined him and slid her arm around his waist, and he let her take some of his weight while he tested bruised and beaten muscles.

"Are you sure you shouldn't be resting?" she asked.

"Nothing's broken. Walking helps." He hoped so. He rotated his shoulders, worked his arms, rubbed his wrists. Frankie's growing impatience was obvious from the way she increased the pace of their stroll around the small shed. She must have had a lower dose of whatever knocked them out. Plus, she hadn't gone three rounds with Mr. Muscle.

She dropped her arm from him and paced. He limped along, grateful that she hadn't been hurt. After ten laps, he flagged her down.

"Take it easy, honey. You're giving me whiplash."

She stopped and leaned her back against the wall, oozing to the floor. She hugged her shins and rested her forehead on her knees. "I'm sorry. I have to move when I'm upset. What if they tied her up? Blindfolded her? She'll be so scared. They said wait. Maybe that's the smart thing to do. They could be right outside waiting for us to try to escape."

He stood across the room from her, gripping the shelf for support. Damn, he was still woozy. He lifted his head to the window, inhaling the fresh air flowing in, trying to work off the drugs.

"We can't rush blindly into anything. We're going to have to be patient for a little while and come up with a plan." His head cleared a bit, and he managed to string a couple of thoughts together. Although he doubted anyone was around, or they'd have come inside when they heard Frankie releasing him, Ryan lowered his voice to a whisper. "They think I have something they want. That's our bargaining chip. If they hurt me or Molly, they won't get it."

Her head snapped up and even in the dim light, her eyes flashed. "Well, then why didn't you give it to them already? What gives you the right to play God with my daughter?"

"Because I don't have a clue what the hell they're talking about," he muttered.

"What do you mean, you don't know what they want?" Frankie's voice was quiet now, as if she understood.

She uncoiled and resumed her circling, her feet scuffing up dust into motes that danced in the sunlight.

"My job makes me enemies. Those two thugs could be someone I pissed off years ago. Or hired by someone I pissed off."

"If you had to guess, what would it be?"

"Logic says my last job. Someone gave me some computer files he said were important. But I've looked. The only thing on them is a list of some stolen art, or forgeries—nothing particularly special."

"So give it to them."

"From what the guy said, he's got what he wants, but he needs some key. That's the part I have no clue about."

"Can you pretend to have it, or make up a story? So he'll let Molly go?"

He crossed the room and intercepted her, cradling her face in his hands. "Honey, you're going to have to trust me here. These people are not honest. Simply because they say they're going to release her is no reason to believe them. I'm sorry Frankie."

"You don't think they've already hurt Molly?" Tears glistened in her eyes.

"Listen to me. We are going to get out of here, figure out where the hell we are, and take it from there. I need you to do what I say."

She nodded, but didn't look convinced.

He hauled himself onto the shelf and checked the window. The boards were nailed from the outside, the one thing that had gone right since this mess started. If he could kick one or two away, Frankie should fit. He lay on his back, curled his fingers over the edge of the shelf behind him for support, and kicked against the planks. Pain shot through his left knee. His eyes watered. He kicked again, using his right leg. No point in escaping if he couldn't walk.

"Can I help?" Frankie asked.

"You're not tall enough. But I think I felt the board give."

Five kicks, and one end of a board loosened. Two more kicks, and he'd knocked it free. He stood too quickly, and gripped the window frame until the dizziness passed. Once it had, he wrenched the board from the window. He leaned out, grateful to see there wasn't much of a drop to the ground, and that the terrain beneath the window was level and not too rocky. And that nobody came running. The next board popped off readily. Maybe Frankie's presence was enough to create a bright side.

"Come here," he said. "I'm going to lower you out the window. Go around and see if you can open the door. Most of these old shacks don't have padlocks."

She took a shaky breath, then climbed up beside him. "Okay."

Seconds later Frankie pulled the door open. He blinked at the bright light.

"You were right. It was a board in a slot, not even a real lock," she said.

Once they were outside, he refastened the door. The window was at the back of the shack, away from the approach trail, so he didn't think anyone would notice they'd escaped right away.

"Let's go," he said.

"Where? Do you know where we are? Are you sure we shouldn't wait?"

"I have something they want. They have something we want. They're not going to relinquish their power and bring her back that easily. The important thing is to figure out where they are, and where they have Molly."

"We should go back to your place, or your father's. Or the

first place with a phone. Call the police. They can send the search parties, and the dogs, and helicopters, and—"

He put his finger to her lips. "We can't."

She wrested his hand away. "Why not? What can the two of us do in the middle of wherever we are? You're hurt, and I'm no woodsman—woodswoman—woodsperson. Whatever. I'm no good in the woods. The cops have experts. I don't mean you're not an expert, but there's only one of you. Come on. We have to get going." She headed down the trail, dragging him behind her.

"Frankie, stop."

"What do you mean? It'll be dark soon, and we need to get help. Fast. Down is the logical way to go, right?" She tugged at his arm.

He spun her around and put his hands on her shoulders. "I want you to trust me. I know these kind of people."

"I may not know them, but I'm smart enough to know I don't want my daughter anywhere near them a second longer. The faster we get help, the sooner they'll find her."

"Frankie, listen to me." His mouth went dry, and his throat tightened. God, he didn't want to hurt her. No matter how much he dreaded telling her, he couldn't find a way around what he knew was the truth. Her eyes, seconds ago eager with the thought of rescuing her daughter, signaled uncertainty. And fear. He rubbed the back of his neck.

"What?" she said. "Tell me. You said she was alive. They said they'd bring her back. Why do we have to go find her all by ourselves?"

He pulled her off the trail and sat on a log, lowering her beside him. He felt the tension, like a tightly coiled spring, where her thigh touched his. "Molly's not a child to these people. Not a person. She's a commodity. A bargaining chip to use to get me to talk. But I don't have the information they want. If she's useless that way. . . ." He searched for the words.

"They'll kill her. Is that what you're trying to say?"

Part of him wished that was all they'd do. A boulder sat in his belly. "She's young, she's got big, blue eyes and light hair. There are places where she'd bring a good price. They'd probably keep her safe for a few years, until she's older—"

Frankie jumped from her seat and paced. "White slavery? Or—God, are you telling me they'd sell her to some . . . man . . . some animal . . . who'd . . . who'd . . . with my *baby?*" Frankie whispered.

He tried to hold her gaze, but couldn't, and talked to the trees above them instead. "I'm not willing to risk it. I'd love to believe they're sitting around a fire, reading *Green Eggs and Ham* with Mr. Snuggles and drinking hot chocolate, but those aren't the kind of people we're dealing with. If they know someone's after them, the first whiff of cops, and they'll disappear, and take her with them."

She stopped in front of him, her lips white, her cheeks flushed. He stood, ready to gather her into his arms before she collapsed. She didn't. She swayed, then looked at him, chin raised and said, "Let's get the hell moving and find the bastards who have my daughter."

Frankie moved as fast as she dared down the trail, Ryan limping beside her. Dried blood painted his face, and his lips were parted as he sucked air. Good. He deserved to hurt, after what he'd let happen. Soon enough, she panted as well, part from exertion, part from panic.

She slowed, but Ryan forged on. Some of her panic left as she saw the determination in Ryan's face. Being angry at him was a waste of precious energy. If he could suppress his pain, she could do the same with her fears. Her anger. Let her turn her mind elsewhere. She wasn't certain they'd made the right decision. But for now, she followed him down the trail, putting her trust in his experience. Looking for the bright side. She was out in the middle of nowhere, some evil people had kidnapped her daughter, but she was with a man who knew what he was doing.

They reached the point where the trail met the road. It was narrow and unpaved. She noticed tire tracks in the dust. Ryan stopped and looked in both directions.

"Can you tell which way they went?" she asked.

He shook his head. "One lane road. But there seems to be more tire activity than I'd expect out here."

"Here? Do you know where we are?" She sucked in a few deep breaths, trying to loosen the bands in her chest.

He nodded. "If we bushwhack, about five miles from Josh's place. On the road, closer to ten. But we need to think about where they went, not about getting back."

She wondered if he'd stopped to let her catch her breath until she noticed his own labored breathing and took a closer look at his bruises. He must have sensed her concern, because he gave her hand a reassuring squeeze.

"I've been hurt a lot worse, honey. And today's nothing compared to how I'll feel tomorrow, so let's keep moving." He paused, and his eyes widened. At least one of them did. The other eye was disappearing behind purple swelling. He raked his fingers through his hair.

"Shit. I'm not thinking straight. Let's start at the beginning. At least three thugs are involved. They picked me up on the trail. The next thing I know, I'm hanging from the ceiling. They had to have put me in a car or truck. My guess is wherever they have Molly is going to be somewhere fairly accessible."

"But you said it would be faster to . . . bushwhack?"

"If I knew where they were going, we could take a shortcut through the woods, yes." Alarm rose in his eyes. He put his hands under her chin, lifted her face.

She pushed his hands away and rubbed her cheeks. "What's wrong? Did they mark me?"

"No, you look fine. It finally registered that they drugged you and dumped you in the shack, too. Where did they pick you up? Did anyone hurt you?" He ran his hands gently down her arms, as if feeling for broken bones. Picked up her hands, traced his fingers along her wrists. "They didn't tie you up?"

Her own memory hovered in the distance. She strained to remember more. "No, I had that sack—" she pointed to the burlap bag Ryan had tucked into his jeans—"over my head, but I wasn't tied. Just drugged."

The relief in his eyes was obvious. "Let's walk that way." He tilted his chin up the road. "There are more of these shacks. Old storage sheds, and places where the old timers could get out of the weather if they had to. There's a stream not far, and we both need to hydrate. We won't be any good to anyone if we collapse."

Until he said it, Frankie hadn't realized how dry her mouth was. Fear or dehydration, it didn't matter. She was suddenly very thirsty.

At the stream, Frankie crouched and cupped water into her mouth. Was this part of the same stream Molly had tumbled into what seemed a lifetime ago? At the time, she couldn't remember ever having been so frightened for her daughter. She didn't know how much deeper fear could burrow.

She drank her fill and splashed icy water on her face to clear her head. Ryan knelt a few yards away, using his blindfold as a washcloth, cleaning the blood, and pressing it against the bruises on his face. He rinsed the band of cloth, dipped it once more, and tied it around his forehead. As much to ease what had to be a killer headache as to keep his hair out of his eyes, she thought.

Battered and bruised, he was still a warrior.

She stood and stepped to his side. "Are you all right?"

He gave her a crooked smile. "I'd feel better if I had some kind of weapon. I'm afraid our captors are armed with more than a gunnysack and a few rusty nails. You wouldn't have an AK-47 in your pocket, would you? An M-16? How about a Swiss Army knife?"

"Don't think so." She dug through a front pocket. "I have two quarters, a dime and a rubber band." She laid them on a tree stump, before fishing through her other one. "ChapStick, some tissues and—oh, I found these in your closet. I was going to throw them away, but I forgot. He dismissed the scrap of paper and the credit card receipt, but took the cigar band.

"I didn't think you smoked," she said.

"I don't. It was a present from my last job." He turned the band around, then went rigid. His eyebrows shot upward.

"What? Is it important?"

"I don't know, but considering where this came from, it might be what those creeps are looking for. There are some numbers and letters written on the back." He slipped it into his back pocket.

Her pulse raced. "Then you can give it to them, and they'll give us Molly, right?"

His jaw clamped shut. His eyes moved to the ground.

She tried not to scream. "You said that's what they want. They said if they got the key, they'd give Molly back. You're going to give it to them, aren't you?"

His lips narrowed to a thin, white line. His brow furrowed and he rubbed his jaw. "I—"

"You what? You'd sacrifice my daughter for a bunch of art?" He couldn't be thinking about keeping the key, if that's what it was. It could be Molly's death sentence—or worse. Drawing a breath became an effort.

"What if it's more?"

She could barely hear his words. But the anguish came through loud and clear. "Oh, my. Like, plans for a terrorist attack?" Visions of explosions, of dead bodies—dead children—floated in front of her. She swayed. Her daughter or—? He couldn't expect her to choose.

"Let's go," he said. There was a new timbre to his voice. Anger, barely controlled. He pivoted and marched away, following the streambed.

Ice ran through Frankie's veins. She crammed everything back in her pockets and hurried after him.

"Too bad we don't have the horses," she said.

He stopped so abruptly she almost ran into him. He leaned over, picked up a rock and threw it against a tree. "Fuck." He grimaced and rubbed his forehead. "Sorry."

"Forget it. What's wrong?"

"My brain is worthless. Corky and Sparky will find their way home. Someone will know we're missing."

"Isn't that good? If we're missing, won't your father come after us? Will he call the cops? Oh, but if he does, and the bad guys find out, you said they'd—" She couldn't complete the thought. Every instinct told her to find Molly. Putting her faith in Ryan's experience meant she would be fighting her gut reactions every step of the way.

"Pop will look on his own, but not for a while. It wouldn't be the first time my horse beat me home. If I don't show up, he'll be pissed at having to take care of the animals, but I can't see him calling the cops for at least a day. He'll probably assume we're together and I got . . . distracted."

Frustration built. "So is it a good thing or a bad thing? Ryan, I'm scared. I want my daughter. Please. Tell me what you're thinking. You know about this stuff."

"I'm thinking things are not quite right, but I can't figure out why. Between the drugs and Mr. Muscle's handiwork, I've got too many short circuits. It'll come to me, Frankie. Meanwhile, let's keep moving."

Moving was good. Moving meant they were taking action. Ryan stopped and looked at a tree. He fingered its branches, then crouched down and picked up what looked like a shiny piece of paper.

"Now what?" she asked. "Did you find something? Are you tracking them?"

Without answering, he veered from the path along the stream and headed down a side trail.

"You did find something, didn't you? Please tell me."

"Candy wrapper. It's probably nothing. A piece of litter."

"You think the bad guys dropped it, don't you? We're on the right track?" She allowed herself an instant of hope. A rustling sounded from the bushes. She jumped.

Ryan grabbed her hand and yanked her from the trail. "Down. Quiet."

CHAPTER 23

Pain knifed through Ryan's knee as he landed hard, trying to keep his weight off Frankie while protecting her with his body. His shoulder didn't seem too happy about it, either. He held his breath, listening for any hint of an approaching visitor. Right now he hoped it was of the four-legged variety, although a grizzly wasn't high on his guest list.

He flattened himself into the landscape as much as he dared. Thankful that Frankie lay motionless and silent beneath him, he exhaled through his mouth, making sure to keep his breathing slow and steady. She was warm, and soft, and his body remembered what they'd done less than twenty-four hours ago. Not now, for God's sake. He was a professional. Until this was over, she was an assignment.

The rustling grew closer. Despite the pain, he took his weight on his knees and walked his fingers outward a centimeter at a time, searching for a sharp stick, a rock, anything that might be a weapon. All he found was dirt, but in the eyes of an enemy, it would buy him time.

He lowered his mouth to Frankie's ear. He felt her trembling. "When I roll off, move for the trees. Slowly. Stay low." A tiny nod told him she understood. "On three."

He waited. The rustling stopped.

"One." He shifted his weight to his good leg.

"Two." He clenched his teeth and prepared to roll.

"Three." He flipped over. He spared a momentary glance at

Frankie, long enough to see her slithering on her bottom toward a clump of trees. A flash of fur emerged from the bushes. He hurled the clod of dirt and the few pebbles he'd accumulated in that direction. From the silence, he assumed he'd missed. *Damn.*

Before he got his feet under him, eighty pounds of dog leaped onto his chest and licked his face.

"Wolf, dammit, you scared me to death. Off. Sit, boy."

The dog whined, still slathering Ryan's neck with cold-nosed dog kisses.

"It's not playtime, buster." But he wrapped his arms around the dog's neck and returned the greeting. "God, am I glad to see you." He struggled to his feet. "Frankie. Come on out. It's okay."

Frankie emerged from the trees, brushing dirt and leaves from her clothes. Wolf trotted to her, his tail sweeping back and forth like a windshield wiper. "Hi, boy." She scratched his ears and joined Ryan. Her eyes gleamed with hope. "Is this where we say, 'Find Molly?' "

"I don't know if he's much of a scent dog. He had some basic rescue training before Pop got him, and I know he'll attack anything that threatens Pop or me, but I'm not sure he's a wonder dog."

She crouched and cupped Wolf's muzzle. "Did you see the bad guys, Wolf? Do you know where Molly is?"

Wolf's tail thumped on the ground, and he licked her cheek.

"That's okay." She gazed up at Ryan. "Besides, didn't Lassie just go home and bark until someone followed her to Timmy?"

Ryan smiled. "He might not be a wonder dog," he said, "but Wolf is a formidable weapon." He thought of those teeth in the neck of one of his assailants. Yet formidable or not, Wolf was no defense against bullets. Stealth and surprise were their best hope.

Wolf barked and dashed down the trail. Ryan called after

him, but the dog ignored his command. A squirrel chattered from above.

"So much for the wonder dog," he said. "Prefers chasing critters."

The dog's continued barking had Ryan following. Frankie pushed ahead of him.

"Frankie. Wait. Don't rush off like that."

"There's a chance, isn't there? He saved her once before. What if Molly's somewhere and Wolf really is showing us?"

Frankie. Ever seeing the bright side. More likely, Wolf had scented a raccoon. Then again, sometimes the remotest possibilities actually happened. He stepped up his pace despite the pounding in his head and the throbbing in his knee.

Wolf sat at the base of a hemlock, staring into its branches.

When Ryan got there, Wolf stood and barked.

"He's found something, hasn't he?" Frankie said. "A clue?"

"Another squirrel, I'll bet. Or he's treed a coon."

Frankie's shoulders slumped. "I guess it was stupid to think Wolf would show up and Molly would materialize in a tree."

The single tear that trickled down her cheek twisted through his chest. He rubbed the back of Frankie's neck. "Don't ever stop hoping. That's when things go bad."

Ryan followed Wolf's gaze into the branches, wondering what he expected to find. About six feet up, a branch freshly broken, caught his eye. Wolf couldn't have noticed that, but Ryan scoured the area.

Snagged on another branch was a dirty blue ribbon. He yanked it down. Hair on the back of his neck prickled. Molly had blue ribbons in her hair today. He'd tied them himself.

"What did you find?" Frankie rushed over and snatched the ribbon from his fingers.

She stood, rooted, transfixed by the scrap of blue. Her tear was joined by another, until they coursed down her cheeks like silent raindrops on a windowpane. She wrapped the ribbon around her fingers, rubbed it against her cheek.

"What does this mean?" she whispered. "How did Molly's ribbon get up in the tree?"

Ryan cleared his throat. "We can't be sure it's Molly's."

She looked at him and shook her head. "You don't mean that. Don't sugarcoat things to spare me. How much of a coincidence would it be to find another blue ribbon in the woods?" She unwrapped it from her fingers and stretched it between her hands. It's dirty, but not old. Even I can see that. You can't tell me there were two people here recently wearing blue ribbons."

"No," he said. "The simplest explanation is usually the right one. But there's something wrong. There are no tracks, nothing to indicate how a ribbon from her ponytail got stuck six feet up a tree, three feet off the trail."

"Maybe someone was carrying her."

He moved outward in an expanding spiral and examined the ground more closely. "If they were, there'd be more than one broken branch." When he stood, pain stabbed him behind the eyes and the earth swam. He dropped to the ground, clutching his temples. Fresh agony shot through his knee.

Frankie crouched beside him. "You're hurt."

He clenched his teeth and waited for the pain to pass. "A twinge. I'll be fine."

"It might be a concussion."

He lowered himself to his butt and stretched his knee out in front of him, kneading the sore joint. "No time for that." He extended his arm. "We have your daughter to find, right? Help me up."

When Frankie's hand touched his, he knew he'd save Molly. As far as relinquishing the key—if that was what he had—he'd work that out on the way. Once his head stopped pounding, he knew whatever was bothering him would fall into place.

He whistled for Wolf. The dog trotted to his side and cocked his head in expectation.

"Frankie. Take Wolf to the stream. Have him drink. And, if you need to take care of any . . . personal needs, this would be a good time. We might be on the road awhile."

While they were gone, Ryan took care of his own needs, then worked his way back along the trail, still trying to piece things together. What was missing?

Suck it up. You've been hurt worse than this. Several times. Three days on your own in Panama, remember. You got through that, and you'll get through this. It's a headache. A bum knee. Deal with it.

He pulled the scrap of yellow cellophane he'd found earlier from his pocket. A candy wrapper. Dalton's favorite. But Dalton never left his trash. The man could walk across a mud flat and hardly leave prints.

Damn, he couldn't think through the pain.

"We're back." Frankie's voice sounded more optimistic than it had since she'd freed him in the shack. He swore he'd keep it that way. The world needed a few more Pollyannas.

"Give me the ribbon," he said. "Wolf, come here."

"Can he find her from that?"

"Longshot. Big longshot. I've touched it, you've touched it. I don't know a lot about tracking by scent, or even if Wolf was trained to do it."

"I get it. But it's the best we have, right?"

While the dog waited at his feet, Ryan pulled Frankie close. "We're going to do this." He allowed himself a few seconds to enjoy the way her body, tense at first, molded into his. Her heartbeat reverberated through his chest, the floral scent of her hair somehow calmed him.

He gripped her shoulders and she lifted her face. Cobalt blue eyes held his.

"Let's go," she said.

He held the ribbon out to Wolf. What the hell. "Find Molly."

Wolf sniffed, gave a yelp and trotted down the trail. Ryan lifted his eyebrows, wondering if he'd given the right command, or if the dog could track her even if he had. On their walks together, Wolf chased after wildlife at every opportunity. Was he after another raccoon or possum? Ryan took Frankie's hand and walked in the direction Wolf had gone.

"You think he's doing it?" Frankie asked.

"No idea. Keep your eyes open for anything unusual. Broken branches, footprints."

"Ribbons in trees?"

Wolf's barking grew louder and more urgent. So much for stealth and surprise.

"Slow down, boy. We're coming. Quiet." To Ryan's surprise, the dog followed his command.

Frankie's eyes darted back and forth, up and down the tree-lined trail, searching for anything that might be a clue. As if she'd recognize one. Unless it belonged to Molly. But it kept her busy. Kept her mind off the "what if's" thundering through her head until they blocked everything else.

Wolf zigzagged along. From time to time, he'd dart into the woods, then return. Ryan showed him the ribbon again, and Wolf gave it a perfunctory sniff before loping ahead.

"Was Wolf with you when they captured you?" she asked.

As if he hadn't heard her, Ryan studied the ground where a trail forked off. She came up beside him and put a hand on his shoulder. He exhaled a slow, deep breath and rested his hand on top of hers. Warm and dry, it contrasted with her cold, clammy ones. Jaw set, eyes reflecting steely determination, he stood in sharp counterpoint to the gentle lover she'd known last night. This was not the kind of man she'd ever dreamed about. But now, he was the man she needed.

"Did you say something?" he asked.

"I asked if Wolf was with you. Do you think he knows where they have Molly?"

Ryan took her hand from his shoulder, but didn't let it go. "He was with us when we started, but he did his usual thing—chasing through the woods. He'd come and go, but—"

She saw him straining to remember. "That's okay. Wishful thinking. Besides, he can't talk. What are you looking for?"

"Disturbances. Signals that say they went down a side trail. Otherwise, we keep moving straight ahead."

"Would be nice if they left road signs," she muttered.

"If you know what to look for, sometimes they do." He pointed to a branch lying across the trail. "If someone came by, they might kick that, or step on it, and we could see that it had been moved. That would tell us they turned here."

"But how do you know who 'they' are? Couldn't it be an animal?"

He kissed her forehead and his eyes softened. "I thought you always looked on the bright side."

As if there could possibly be one right now. A lump rose in her throat.

"Well, I have one," he said. "Those thugs aren't very good at their job."

"How do you know?" She brushed her fingertips against his jaw. "They did a good job on you."

"Which they will answer for when I find them. But look." He reached over her head and lowered an overhanging branch. "See how it's broken? Someone walked by here and shoved it out of his way, not very carefully. And these rocks were kicked aside. You can see the indentations where they've been."

"So how do you know it's not an animal. A bear, or a moose?"

"Because there are no footprints."

"Huh?"

"We've passed some damp places, where it's still muddy from the rain. A bear or a moose doesn't think about not leaving tracks. But these guys are avoiding the mud, and maybe sweeping their own prints in the dirt, although it's packed firm here.

"Now, if it had been my team we were tracking, we'd have our work cut out for us. Because we don't leave traces. In and out like the wind." He smiled, and hope rose like a bubble inside her.

"Your team." The memory came back like an image rising out of the developer. "Dalton. Wasn't he one of your teammates? But . . . oh, God, I just remembered. He's the one who drugged me at the cabin."

Ryan's smile faded, but it wasn't surprise that replaced it. Sadness, perhaps. Or wariness.

"You don't trust him, do you?" she said. "But you called him to help you. He seemed so . . . nice." Anger boiled inside when she thought about leaving Molly alone with the man. "I thought—"

"At the time, I thought so, too. I've known him for years. Can't begin to count how many times we've saved each other's butts. Now, I'm not sure what to think. I've got a strange feeling, but I can't put my finger on it. If Dalton's involved, this isn't like him at all." He pulled a piece of cellophane from his pocket. "Dalton likes these candies. But he'd eat the wrapper before he'd drop it on the trail. For Dalton, a candy wrapper, a broken twig or a misplaced pebble doesn't make sense. It's like he's leaving me a road map."

"But that's good, right? We follow the map to Molly." Almost lighthearted, she rushed down the trail. If Molly was at the end, they had to get there. Ryan would figure out what to do when they did.

"Wait, Frankie." He grabbed her elbow.

She slowed, but didn't stop.

"Let me go ahead," he said. "You might miss something."

Of course. Or she might obscure an important clue.

Be brave, Molly. We're coming as fast as we can.

She fell in beside him. He moved without speaking, his face reflecting worry as much as pain. She thought about discovering that Brenda had disappeared. How betrayed she felt after thinking of Brenda as family, even for a short time. How much harder for Ryan, to think a man he'd worked side by side with for years might have turned against him. And not only against Ryan. In their line of work, that meant against his country.

The trail narrowed. Ryan slowed the pace, then stopped at another fork. The trees cast flickering shadows as they swayed in the breeze. Frankie lowered herself to a log and worked on catching her breath. Nerves, combined with Ryan's tempo, filmed her body with sweat, and she shivered in the breeze as she waited for him.

She remembered waving good-bye to Molly, perched so proudly on Sparky. Her jacket had been tied to the back of the saddle. Had the kidnappers thought that it might get cold and brought it with them? And Mr. Snuggles. He'd been there, too. Would they have given a little girl a tiny piece of security?

Stopping was not good. Stopping meant too much time to think. With one final deep breath, she pulled herself to her feet and wandered over toward Ryan. He'd moved off the trail, and seemed intent on examining bushes.

"What do you have?" she asked, ashamed of the way her voice cracked.

"Not sure." He extended his hand, palm up, displaying a twig with an oval-shaped piece of faded red felt impaled on it.

Almost afraid to touch it, she fingered the scrap. Her heart galloped in her chest. "Mr. Snuggles had a tongue like this."

"I know."

"So we're on the right track?"

"I think so."

"You're worried about Dalton, right?"

His eyes clouded and he squeezed the bridge of his nose. "Two weeks ago, I'd have followed the signs without a thought."

"And today?"

"I'm thinking Dalton might be setting me up. That he might be in cahoots with the thugs." He kneaded his shoulder. "It makes no sense. When we were together, Dalton and I virtually shared a brain. He knows how I think. These bits aren't on the trail. They're far enough away so you'd have to be looking for them."

She pondered that one. "So Dalton, or whoever has Molly, must be weaving back and forth off the trail because the clues aren't obvious, right?"

"Right."

"So, maybe he's leaving the clues off the trail so whoever he's with won't notice. That would be good, wouldn't it? Unless he—or the other guys—figure you'd know something was wrong if they made the clues too easy to find." She paced small circles on the path. Ryan stepped back, as if he grasped her need to move.

She spoke, more to herself than to Ryan. "I'm an ex-interior designer, an elementary art teacher who wants to be a photographer. Oh, and a part-time cocktail waitress. You're the secret agent guy. I'm *so* out of my element here."

"You're doing fine, Frankie. It takes a while for the drug to wear off completely. I'm still functioning a few tacos short of a combination plate myself. Someone could have stepped into the bushes to answer a call of nature."

"How did you know where to look? If this is a trap, isn't Dalton taking a chance that you'll miss the clues if they're not on the main trail?"

"I'm working on that one."

His frown said he'd already come up with at least one theory. Did he think he was protecting her by not explaining? That she couldn't handle it? Not knowing was worse.

"Tell me," she demanded. She wrapped her arms around herself to ward off another chill.

"You're cold. Come here." Ryan's arms enveloped her, and she wondered how he could radiate so much heat. She didn't wonder long, simply leaned into his strength and absorbed what she could. He smelled rugged and male, sweat mixed with the outdoors, and a hint of evergreen.

"I'm fine," she said, feeling the lie before it left her lips. "And I'll get warm when we start moving again."

"We need to recharge. We won't be worth a damn if we're exhausted when we get there."

His hands moved upward, and he massaged her neck. She groaned as tension dissolved.

His fingers worked down to her shoulders, her back, and ended on her rump, drawing her against him, resting his head on hers. She felt his hardness, and her own body's response to his.

She angled her hips away. Her child's life was in danger, and she was thinking about how safe she felt in Ryan's arms. *What kind of mother was she?*

"We need to go." She avoided his eyes, but knew he could see the flush rising to her face.

"It's a normal reaction, honey. Danger's a rush. And last night wasn't that long ago."

Still, he increased the distance between them. Good. She didn't need a rush, and had no desire for danger.

"Thirty seconds. You're still cold." He rubbed her arms. "You smell good."

A hint of a smile crept to her mouth. "I was thinking the same thing about you."

He pulled back and looked her in the eyes. The swelling had gone down below his left eye, but the purple had intensified. His right eye twinkled. "You might need to see someone about your sense of smell. I've got to be ripe. I was sweating bullets while Mr. Muscle worked me over."

"It's worn off. You smell like a man in the woods." She folded her arms across her chest. "And you're avoiding my question."

"Which was?"

"How do you know where to look for these secret clues?"

"I'll show you. Let's go." He took her hand and led her along the trail. "See. This rock's been kicked aside. And there's an indentation that might be a footprint."

She looked where he pointed, but only saw more of what she'd been seeing since they started. Dirt, dead leaves, rocks, and bushes. But they were moving again, and had to be getting closer to Molly.

"And then there's Wolf," he went on. "When he goes off the trail, I check more carefully."

The trail was wide enough for walking abreast. He walked faster now, almost pulling her along. She adjusted her pace, wondering if she could keep up if he had two good knees. "You know where we're going?"

"Until the trail forks, they'd stick to it. Someone's sweeping behind them, but it's not eliminating everything."

"So whoever's doing it isn't very good."

"Or trying to make it look good and still leave a trail."

"Why would he do that?"

"That's what I don't know." He couldn't disguise the sadness in his one good whiskey-colored eye.

She stopped and entwined her fingers in his hair and lifted her face to his. "There's a logical explanation."

"Yeah. Like Dalton's a traitor. That's the one I keep coming back to. He's shown up in places where some really nasty people have been a few times more than coincidence would dictate."

The hurt and bitterness in his tone cut through her. She was almost sorry she said something.

Ryan jerked away. He stiffened.

"Well, don't let me interrupt you little lovebirds."

Frankie knew that voice. She'd heard it in the cabin. Then a clicking sound. And Ryan clutching her to him.

Chapter 24

Ryan pulled Frankie behind him, shielding her from the man who had to be Mr. Muscle. Although shorter than Ryan by a good six inches, the guy must have outweighed him by at least thirty pounds. He was a goddamn refrigerator, solid muscle, his belly flat above the belt of his cargo pants.

He'd met dozens like this guy—big, brawny, and an I.Q. about the same as his age. Good at following orders, but not much at independent thought.

"Let the woman go," Ryan said. "I have what you want. She's not part of this."

"Where's Molly?" Frankie shouted. "Give me my daughter!"

"Stay behind me," Ryan whispered. "And be quiet. Don't make him mad."

"Make *him* mad?" She poked her head around Ryan. "If you've hurt her, so help me—"

Ryan grabbed her wrist. "Dammit woman, let me handle this."

"The little lady, she is too much for you to handle?" the man said. "I'm sure I can take care of her for you." He leered, and Ryan clenched his fists.

"Leave her alone," Ryan said. "You've got her daughter."

"Yes. Her pretty little girl. Such big, blue eyes."

Frankie's fingernails dug into his biceps. At least she was quiet.

"I repeat," Ryan went on. "Give me the child, or there's no deal."

"First, you show me what you have."

The man stood, legs planted wide, one hand on his hip, the other holding a Remington rifle. Made sense. If they were supposed to have an accident, being shot with an assault weapon might bring too much law enforcement into the picture. The fact that he'd lowered the gun told Ryan enough. The man had his orders, and shooting them didn't seem to be on the list. Besides, this guy liked using his fists. Shooting wouldn't be nearly as much fun.

"I don't do business with subservient scum like you," Ryan said. The blank look right before the man's eyebrows furrowed told Ryan he didn't know what subservient meant. The scowl that followed said he understood scum just fine.

"In words of one syllable," Ryan continued. "I don't talk to you. I talk to your boss. Un. Der. Stand. That?"

Another scowl, and two steps in Ryan's direction said the man was taking the bait. Already choreographing his next few moves, Ryan locked eyes with his opponent. Two more steps. He flexed his shoulder. Shifted, loosening his knee. This was going to hurt.

Counting on the fact that the man's orders were not to kill the messenger, Ryan waggled his eyebrows in open invitation. "What's the matter? You afraid of me now that I'm not tied up and blindfolded?"

"I thought you said not to make him mad," Frankie whispered.

"Trust me. And get ready to run." Her hands squeezed his arms once more, then released, leaving him with an unexpected empty feeling.

With a smirk that revealed yellow-stained teeth, Mr. Muscle stepped closer, waving the Remington with his right hand. Ryan closed the distance between them. He grabbed the rifle by the barrel with his left hand and twisted it away.

Instead of letting go, Mr. Muscle swung his left fist towards Ryan's head. So far so good. As expected, the jerk was engrossed in holding onto the rifle at the expense of his defense.

Ryan sidestepped left and felt air as the punch buzzed past his ear. He grabbed Mr. Muscle's shoulder. Forced his elbow into Mr. Muscle's throat. He hooked his leg behind a knee of the now off-balance man and yanked it toward himself.

Ryan smiled as the thug's ass hit the packed dirt, the man still refusing to relinquish his hold on the Remington. Ryan kicked him in the ribs and wrenched the rifle from his grasp.

"Drop it, Harper. Turn around. Slow and easy."

Ryan froze at the sound of Dalton's voice. The one he used with tangos. Cold and flat, it brooked no nonsense.

"Please, Ryan. Do what he asks." Frankie's voice quavered from behind him.

A tidal wave of fury welled inside him. A glance over his shoulder showed Dalton, one arm wrapped around Frankie, the other holding a pistol to her head. Ryan relaxed his grip on Mr. Muscle's Remington.

From the other direction, another man stepped out of the woods, a hunting rifle slung over his shoulder. He swaggered forward and snatched the Remington from Ryan's hand. He grinned, and a gold-rimmed tooth flashed in the light of the setting sun. He prodded Ryan in the chest with the Remington's barrel.

Fists clenched, Ryan planted his feet, braced for a blow. But the man simply laughed and threw the rifle past him. Ryan listened for the impact, trying to judge where it landed. No sound of it hitting the ground. Definitely the sound of someone catching it. Dalton? If so, then he'd had to let go of Frankie. Or was there yet another assailant to worry about? He forced several deep breaths.

"You are a stubborn man, Mr. Harper. But consider the lives of the woman and child before you try anything stupid."

The voice was clearly that of Mr. Muscle's partner. Ryan heard Frankie's breathing, shallow and rapid. He kept his gaze focused on Mr. Manners. Tall and lean, the man was counterpoint to his partner. A neatly trimmed beard disguised a pockmarked face. His dark hair was combed away from his forehead. Intelligent brown eyes held Ryan's gaze. This one thought before he acted.

Hints of peppermint and cigarettes floated on the man's breath. Ryan raised his hands in surrender. "No tricks. Now take me to the girl."

"I believe we have been through this. First, I need what you have."

"If you think I'm carrying it around, you're not as smart as I thought you were. We get the child, and then I'll take you to this key you want."

He'd already made the mental switch to "the child." Not Molly. Keep it depersonalized. Keep the detachment. A hostage to rescue. Frankie's face swam before his eyes. Two hostages.

Mr. Muscle rose, wincing a little. Good. Hardly payback, but it was a start. Adrenaline kept Ryan's pain at bay. For now.

"You know my name," Ryan said to Mr. Manners. "I don't suppose you'd do me the courtesy of telling me yours."

The man guffawed. "I do so love a sense of humor. Why don't you call me . . . Mr. Smith? I believe that is a common enough American name."

"Right, Mr. Smith. Then your muscled colleague is undoubtedly Mr. Jones. He could use a few lessons in manners."

"Enough conversation, Mr. Harper. I will trust you for now. Please. That way." The man gestured toward the trees with his weapon.

"The woman comes, too."

"But of course. She will be behind us, with her own personal escort."

Ryan found the narrow trail from which Smith had appeared. Exaggerating his limp, he hobbled along, keeping his pace slow while he tried to ignore the gun aimed at him.

Before long, the trail opened into a clearing joined by several other trails. Ryan stopped. The gun poked into his back. In another lifetime, Ryan would have seized the opportunity to make his move. Not today. Not with two lives at stake.

"Which way?" he said.

"To your left, if you will."

"With your permission, Mr. Smith, I'd like to adjust my boot. I think I twisted my ankle while I was . . . engaged . . . with Mr. Jones."

Muffled laughter from Mr. Muscle-Jones. Ryan shuffled to a log and used a tree trunk for support as he lowered himself to a sitting position. He pulled off one boot and made a show of rubbing his ankle, wishing he had his hiking shoes. Dalton held both the Remington and his own pistol, although both hung at his sides. Frankie, her lips compressed into a straight line, raised her eyebrows in Ryan's direction. He gave her what he hoped was a reassuring smile. Apparently, there were only three men to deal with.

"Are you all right?" he asked, giving Frankie a fleeting glance. He couldn't handle her blue eyes right now.

"She is fine," said Smith. He stood a small distance away, relaxed, smiling, but his weapon remained trained on Ryan.

Stalling, Ryan focused on his boots again, watching feet move around the clearing. Jones' moved toward Smith's. A whisper, a grunt, and then Jones quick-stepped into the trees. Except for Frankie's presence, Ryan would have risked the odds.

He didn't look up. "If it's all the same to you, I'd like to hear it from her."

"What's the matter, pardner? Don't trust me?" The Texas drawl was back. Dalton's size twelves stepped closer with Frankie's smaller sneakers alongside.

"About as far as I can throw you, *pardner.*"

"Hey, sometimes a man's gotta do what works best for him. There's a tropical island with my name on it, and island beauties waiting. But I'll be too old to enjoy it if I stick with Blackthorne's payment schedule. Free-lance will have me sipping cold ones in no time."

Hearing the words from Dalton's lips almost had him on his feet and at the man's throat. Almost. Right now, this was about saving lives. He swallowed his rage. He'd deal with Dalton later.

"Are you all right?" he repeated to Frankie. "Nobody's hurt you?"

"I'm okay." Her voice was calm. He glanced up. She gave him a weak smile.

"Of course she is," Dalton said.

Jones clumped out of the woods, wiping his mouth, his face pale and sweat-sheened.

"Apparently a meal my colleague ingested did not agree with him, but we are able to continue now," Smith said. "Let us proceed." He moved toward Ryan. Ryan pulled on his boots and stood before the gun prodded him again.

As their procession began, Ryan caught a smirk on Dalton's face. The trail Smith indicated soon widened into a dirt road covered with tire tracks. Ryan glanced at the surrounding mountains, but saw no familiar landmarks. He surmised there was some kind of dwelling not far away, and that the child would be there. In what condition remained to be seen.

With the wider path, their little parade had become more of a cluster. Dalton stayed with Frankie, although he no longer restrained her. Once more, Mr. Jones bolted into the trees.

Smith slowed the pace until he caught up. They rounded a turn in the road, and a small cabin appeared off to one side, about twenty yards in the distance.

Wolf loped toward them, barking. Smith raised his weapon.

"Wait!" Ryan said. "Wolf. Down. Stay. They're friends."

The dog whined, as if he knew it was a lie, but obeyed, dropping to the ground at the side of the road.

"Good boy. Stay."

"If the dog moves, shoot it," Smith told Dalton.

"No problem," Dalton replied. "The beast and I don't see eye to eye."

Frankie moved toward the cabin, picking up the pace. Dalton let her go. Of course he would. She wasn't going to go anywhere except to find her daughter. Smith didn't protest.

From the outside, the cabin looked like a larger relative of the one he and Frankie had left. Frankie ran ahead and had one hand on the door handle before Ryan could stop her.

"Molly! Are you in there? I'm here." Powerful hands pulled Frankie away from the door.

"I don't think so," said the man Ryan called Mr. Smith. He gripped her arm. When she struggled to free herself, Smith released her with a shove that sent her stumbling to the ground.

Fear of what she'd find when she opened the door collided with her need to see Molly. Molly had to be alive. Ryan had said they wouldn't hurt her. She clung to that thought, and tried not to dwell on the reason.

The other man, Mr. Jones, hovered over her, a hand extended. She refused to take it. He grabbed her arm and yanked her to her feet. He lowered his head to hers, muttering in a language she didn't understand.

She recoiled. "You ever heard of mouthwash?" she said under her breath. "Or deodorant?"

Mr. Smith barked a command, and the man released her, but he winked and made kissing sounds. She stood her ground, fueled by anger now, not fear.

Ignoring Jones, she snapped at Smith. "Give me my daughter."

"She is unharmed, I assure you. Cooperate and she will stay that way."

Jones retreated to lean against a tree near the front of the cabin. He held his weapon casually in the crook of his arm, his lips curled upward in a confident smirk.

Mr. Smith reached out and ran a forefinger down her cheek. She shuddered.

"Perhaps you also know what we seek," he said. "You might save everyone a lot of trouble if you will tell us, since your gentleman friend seems reluctant to do so."

Tell them, and they'd give her Molly. A scrap of paper for her daughter. An even exchange?

Frankie's heart slammed against her ribcage. Ryan's warning replayed in her mind. These men were liars, not to be trusted. She tried to swallow, but her mouth felt like sandpaper. Her gaze returned to Jones. Forcing her eyes away, she met Mr. Smith's reptilian smile. She raised her chin. "Maybe—" It came out a croak. Hands on her hips, she found some spit and licked her lips. "Maybe I do. Show me my daughter."

"She doesn't know anything." Ryan burst forward, Dalton beside him. "Let her go. I've got what you want." Dalton's gun was pointed at Ryan. Ryan's eyes met hers. Was he going to tell them? If he did, would it save Molly?

She looked from one man to the next. Cold, menacing faces. Unreadable faces.

"Oh, this is beginning to sound very much like your American television shows," said Mr. Smith. "Each protecting the other. How touching." Grasping her forearm, he looked at Ryan. "I hope she was worth it."

In a terrifying flash of clarity, she understood. It didn't matter what she or Ryan said or didn't say. These men were not going to let them live. She scanned the clearing for Wolf. He hadn't moved from his position. Would he obey her if she commanded him to attack? If he did, one of the men would surely shoot him. This was *not* saving Molly.

Anger billowed into fury. With a shriek that seemed to come from outside of her, she wrenched herself from Mr. Smith's grip and slammed her knee at his crotch.

He dodged, but not quite fast enough. He grunted and staggered backward, falling to his knees. Ryan lurched forward. Dalton followed, pistol raised, and she watched, transfixed, almost as if it was in slow motion.

"Like in Afghanistan, pardner," Dalton said. "You remember that mission, don't you?"

Ryan jerked his head around. "Oh, yeah. Like it was yesterday, you scum." He yanked away.

She watched, horrified, as Ryan and Dalton clashed.

Dalton grabbed him by the wrist. "No you don't, Harper!"

"Like hell, traitor!" Ryan spun and hit Dalton in the jaw. Dalton spit blood.

"We don't need you, Harper," Dalton said. His voice rang through the clearing. "I found your little key."

"You're bluffing." Ryan punched him in the stomach.

Dalton doubled over.

Ryan grabbed him in a headlock. "How dare you betray your country for money, you motherfucker."

Dalton wrested free.

Ryan kicked the pistol from his hand, sending it flying across the clearing. Dalton raced after it. Ryan caught him in a flying tackle. Both men rolled on the ground, moving farther away from the cabin.

When it dawned on her that everyone's attention was on the fight, she inched away from Mr. Smith. Maybe she could sneak inside. Right. Even if she got in without being noticed, how would she get Molly out? She had to slow down and think ahead for a change.

Curses exploded through the air, and she watched Ryan and Dalton exchange blows. First Ryan was on top, then Dalton. Neither maintained an advantage. For someone with a bad knee and shoulder, Ryan was holding his own. She sidestepped another few inches from Smith. His breathing had evened out, and he was on his feet, but he clutched his privates with one hand, the rifle with the other. She should have kicked him harder.

In a blur of motion and a cacophony of shouts, Ryan and Dalton were on their feet.

Somehow, Ryan had Dalton's pistol pointed at Mr. Smith. "Get over here, Frankie. Now. Dalt, you go join your colleagues." He shoved him toward the others. Dalton took a position between Smith and Jones, glowering at Ryan.

She rushed to Ryan's side, glad to let him take command.

"Toss your weapons over here," he ordered. The strength in his tone raised her hopes.

"I don't think so," Smith said. "One of you, three of us."

"Well, gentlemen, the way I see it, by the time you get those rifles into position, I've fired three shots. One for each of you."

"I told you, you don't need him," Dalton said to Smith and Jones. "I've got what you want."

"And I told you what I think of traitors," Ryan said.

She heard the gunshot and covered her eyes. Seconds later, when she braved a peek through her fingers, Dalton lay on the ground, blood spreading over his chest.

"My God, Ryan!"

"The man sold out."

This couldn't be happening. In a minute, she would wake up in her own bed.

Ryan's touch to the small of her back said otherwise. She was wide awake in his world. With his rules.

Ryan whistled again. "Wolf! Come!"

Ears lowered, teeth bared, Wolf raced to Ryan's side. Barks and growls reverberated through the clearing.

"One word from me, and you're history." The cold edge in Ryan's voice made her shiver. "Do as I say, or you'll meet Wolf up close and personal." Ryan waved his gun again. "I said drop them, gentlemen." Smith and Jones eased their rifles to the ground.

"Kick them toward me. Easy."

Wolf growled. They complied.

"Hands on your heads, gentlemen. Oh, and I suggest you stand very still." Ryan gestured toward Jones. "Wolf. Guard."

Ryan gathered the rifles, slung one over his shoulder and handed the other to Frankie.

"Point this at Mr. Smith. If he blinks, shoot him."

Despite her quaking knees, she tried to duplicate Mr. Smith's sneer. The gun weighed heavy in her hands as her finger sought the trigger. She dug her elbows into her ribs to keep from shaking. God, she couldn't do this. She couldn't kill people. Her stomach roiled. She swallowed. No, she *could* do this. If this was the way to save Molly, she would handle it. A strange calm washed over her, masking her fear.

Wolf stood within leaping range of Mr. Jones, teeth bared, growling. At least Wolf's charge looked scared. Hers looked almost amused. She licked her lips and prayed her voice wouldn't crack. "You heard him. Don't move."

Jones spoke, his voice pleading. "Please. Tell the dog no. I—" He bent over, retching. Wolf took a step forward. Ryan repeated his command to guard, and Wolf stood his ground. Jones stood, wiped his mouth.

"To show you what a nice guy I am, you can sit," Ryan said. "Legs out in front of you. Get those hands back on your head." Jones lowered himself to a sitting position, eyeing Wolf warily.

Ryan approached the cabin door, ran his fingers around its perimeter, stopping from time to time to examine the surface beneath his hand.

Oh, God, maybe it was booby-trapped. She'd almost pulled the door open. She could have triggered something inside. Blown them up. And if Molly was in there—the rifle nearly slipped from her hands. How did Ryan stay so cool? If there was a bomb, he was right there.

The door creaked open. Ryan disappeared into the darkness.

She moved enough to see the cabin door and still keep the rifle pointed at Smith.

When Ryan emerged, carrying a hank of rope, her heart sank.

"She's in there, honey. Hang on another minute, okay? Let me get these two secured, and we'll all get out of here." He knelt beside Jones, yanked the man's hands from his head and tied them behind his back.

"She's all right?"

"I think so."

"You *think* so? Ryan—"

He cut her off. "Frankie, hang tough. You can do it. One more minute."

Hang tough? Her daughter was in there. And she was supposed to stand here and hang tough? Thirty seconds. She'd give him thirty seconds. "Yes, sir. Hanging tough, sir. But can you move faster?"

An eternity later, Ryan secured Smith's hands behind his back and took over guard duty.

Frankie raced into the cabin. What little daylight remained barely penetrated the dark confines of the single room. She crouched by a pile of blankets heaped in the corner. Blood rushed in her ears as she lifted a corner of the topmost cover. Tears sprang to her eyes and her throat thickened when she saw the frail form of her daughter. She ran her hand down Molly's cheek. Her skin was cool and dry.

"Molly? Peanut? Mommy's here. You're safe. Wake up."

Molly didn't stir.

Ryan came alongside and scooped Molly up. "We need to get somewhere safer. It's almost dark."

She nodded and squeezed Molly's hand under the blankets, alarmed when she got nothing in return. "She's going to be all right, isn't she? She has to be all right."

CHAPTER 25

Ryan studied the child in his arms. Her slow, shallow breathing worried him. He forced himself to regroup. Reacting without thinking got people killed. The need to keep Frankie and Molly safe had him disregarding the big picture.

He took another quick survey of the room, ran the options through his head. From outside, Wolf's low growls told him things were still under control. Gently, he set Molly down.

He blew out a long breath. "All right. There's a pack against the wall. Get it. I'm sure there's stuff in there we can use—or keep anyone else from using."

Frankie hefted the pack. "What's inside? It weighs a ton, and if I'm carrying it, I'd rather not worry about it blowing me up."

"Okay, let's have a peek." He tugged open the pack and peered inside, berating himself for not having done this sooner. He clicked on a flashlight. "Good news. We've got light, and it looks like they stuffed everything from my saddlebag in here, too."

When he got no response, he looked over his shoulder. Frankie crouched at Molly's side again, stroking her cheek, murmuring soothing words. A fist clutched his heart. He tabled the sensation to deal with later.

He rummaged through the pack, found his hiking boots. *Yes!* He sat down, yanked off his riding boots and laced on the more suitable footwear. His jacket was in there, too, and he pulled it out.

A quick check of the pack's outer compartments yielded some trail mix, a few chocolate bars and bottled water. And one more pleasant surprise.

He settled his jacket over Frankie's shoulders. "Put this on. It's getting colder. And look what else I found." He extended the tongueless Mr. Snuggles.

Frankie yanked the toy from his hand. "Look, Molly. Mr. Snuggles is here. Don't you want to say hello?" Her voice quavered.

He rested a hand on Frankie's shoulder. "We need to go." He pried the stuffed dog from her grasp and tucked it into Molly's arms. While the child's arm was exposed, he pinched a fold of skin on the back of her hand. Watching it flatten, relief displaced some of his worry. Not severe dehydration. That bought them some more time. He adjusted the blankets around her.

"We need to get Smith and Jones away from here. I think they're afraid enough of Wolf, but one of us is going to have to keep a weapon pointed at them. I can't do that and carry Molly."

"I can carry her."

"Better if I do."

"She's my daughter. She'll want to know I'm here when she wakes up."

"Trust me on this, Frankie."

"But—" She paused. "I get it. You think it'll slow us down if I carry her."

"She's dead weight, and I want to get at least a mile or two away." Her eyes widened, and the impact of his word choice registered. "Oh, God, honey, I didn't mean it like that. It just popped out."

"I know. Why can't we leave them here? They're tied up, aren't they?"

"I'm not convinced there aren't more of them on the way. They'd probably come here to rendezvous."

"Then give me the gun, and let's get going." The quavers had left her voice. She was a lioness now, defending her cub.

"Frankie—"

She tugged at a rifle, and he maneuvered it off his shoulder. She snatched it, holding it one hand on the stock, the other on the barrel, like a quarterstaff.

"Have you ever fired one of these?" he asked, gently pointing the barrel toward the floor.

"As a matter of fact, I have. I wanted to go deer hunting with my uncle. I was twelve, I think. Anyway, he made me shoot at targets nailed to a fence before he'd let me tag along."

"What happened?"

"I hit the fence every time."

Despite himself, he smiled. "This isn't quite the same."

"They took my daughter. They drugged her, and who knows what else. Are you afraid I won't pull the trigger if I have to?"

No, he had no doubt she'd defend her daughter to the death. He was afraid of what it would do to her if she did. Taking another life came with a price tag he wouldn't let her pay. All the years on the job, and he still threw up after he killed someone.

He helped her into the pack, adjusted the straps and leaned over to pick up Molly. "One second." He straightened and cradled Frankie's face in his hands. "We're going to be fine. All of us. Trust me."

Her eyes softened, said she did. As quickly, they flashed steely determination. "Let's do it."

Frankie preceded him out the door. Unlike Smith and Jones, she held the weapon in both hands, ready to fire. "All right. You. Jones. On your feet. Smith. Up you go. Start walking."

Frankie stared at the men shuffling along the dirt road in front of her. Wolf trotted between them, never more than a leap away from either captive. Ryan kept the flashlight trained on the path, sweeping it back and forth. Only the limit of its beam kept her from pushing to a run.

The sooner they got to wherever Ryan had planned, the sooner they could get help for Molly. The road forked and Wolf bounded to the right, barking. She slowed, waiting. Ryan stopped beside her.

"Halt," he commanded. Smith and Jones kept moving.

She pressed her finger against the trigger. "You heard the man. Don't move."

Smith and Jones halted. Warily, they turned back toward their captors.

Ryan tapped her shoulder and gestured with the flashlight toward a fallen tree beside the dirt road. "Wait here," he said to her, his voice calm and confident. She lowered herself to the log, aware of her pounding heart. He took her rifle, set it beside her and placed Molly in her lap. "This won't take long. I'll be right back."

She nodded, hugging Molly to her. Ryan's eyes never left Smith and Jones.

"Wolf. Stay," he commanded. Wolf sat at her feet.

"Let's march," Ryan barked at Smith and Jones. "This way. Double time."

The men disappeared ahead of the flashlight's beam. Soon there was nothing but flickering shadow. It didn't matter. Ryan would be back. Molly was alive, breathing steadily, and warm in her arms. She stroked her daughter's matted hair and sang *Hush Little Baby,* Molly's favorite lullaby. Between verses, she peeked in the direction Ryan had gone, trying not to think about what he might be doing to Smith and Jones. Visions of Dalton lying on the ground swirled before her eyes. She shuddered and tried to lock the sight away. Wolf inserted his muzzle between her hand and Molly.

"You want some, too?" She scratched behind his ears. "You're a good boy. Guess Ryan didn't want us to know what he was doing, hey?" Wolf settled his head on her thigh, and she went on with her song.

She had reached the verse about the cart and bull when car headlights blazed through the darkness. She clutched Molly to her chest. Ryan had said Smith and Jones might have reinforcements on the way. The car approached from the direction he'd taken them.

She crouched low, bundling Molly beside her, and grabbed the rifle. Where was Ryan?

Had those reinforcements shown up and captured him? No way the driver hadn't seen her. She'd been caught in those headlights like a deer. She braved a peek over the log.

The headlights flashed. The horn gave three quick beeps. "Frankie. It's me. Don't shoot."

Seconds later, Ryan was at her side, Molly in his arms. They ran to the car, Wolf at their heels. She scrambled into the passenger seat and Ryan set Molly in her lap. Ryan opened the back door and Wolf leaped in.

"How's she doing?" Ryan asked once he'd slid behind the wheel. He flicked on the dome light and put his fingers to Molly's neck. "Pulse is good. Breathing normal?"

"Yes, but she's still asleep. She doesn't move. Can we hurry to a hospital? I want a doctor to check her out." She wasn't going to ask about Smith and Jones. She couldn't.

"No doctor," rose from Frankie's lap. The words were slurred, but to Frankie, they were a Shakespearean sonnet.

"Molly. Peanut, you're awake." Tears of relief burned behind her eyes. "We're here. Everything's fine." She rested her hand on Molly's cheek.

Molly's eyelids twitched, then popped open. She squirmed in Frankie's lap.

Ryan's calloused hand covered Frankie's. "Hey, Angel. Good to see you again. You had a little nap, didn't you?"

She heard the huskiness in Ryan's voice and pulled her eyes from Molly's long enough to see tears glistening in his. She squeezed his hand, afraid she'd burst into tears if she tried to voice her gratitude.

Some of the confusion faded from Molly's expression, and she blinked. "Mommy? Mr. Ryan?"

"We're here, Peanut," she said. "How do you feel?"

Molly seemed to consider the question. Beads of sweat on her upper lip glimmered in the car's light. "I feel urpity."

He had the car stopped. "Does that mean what I think it does?" He was already running around the car.

"One minute, Peanut. Hang on." She yanked the car door handle, Ryan swung it open and helped get Molly outside.

She pressed her hand against Molly's forehead as she retched. "It's okay, Peanut."

When Molly's spasms stopped, Ryan handed Frankie a bottle of water and an unwrapped disposable moist cloth. She wiped Molly's face.

"I'm better now, Mommy. But my mouth tastes yucky." She reached for the water.

"Give her a couple of sips. Not too much," he said.

Frankie climbed into the backseat with Molly, who snuggled into her with one hand stroking Wolf. Mr. Snuggles lay forgotten on the front seat.

"We're going home now," Frankie said. "You tell me if you feel urpity again, okay?"

"I feel fine. I don't want a doctor. I'm hungry. Can we go to Slappy's?"

A suppressed cough came from the front seat. Ryan started the car again and drove off in the direction they'd come from.

"Hey. Where are we going?" Frankie asked. "We need to get

back to—you know." Despite Molly's insistence that she felt fine, Frankie wanted a doctor to check her out.

"Five minute detour, max. Then we're on our way. There's something I left at the cabin."

CHAPTER 26

"What could you have forgotten? We brought everything with us, didn't we?"

Frankie's voice was low, but Ryan heard the threat behind it. He pushed the accelerator a little harder and half-skidded into the curve to the cabin, sending a cloud of dust swirling through the headlight beams.

He'd barely stopped the car when the passenger door flew open.

"Haul ass, pard." Dalton lowered himself into the seat—gingerly, as if his ribs were broken. Which they might well be, considering how close he'd been when Ryan pulled the trigger.

"I'm not talking to you," Ryan said.

"Dalton?" Frankie's voice squeaked. "But—you—Ryan—he—"

"Kevlar vest, little lady. And a little stage blood."

"Hi, Mr. Dalton," Molly said. "I went urpity but I'm fine now."

"Will someone please tell me what's going on?" Frankie asked. There was no hiding her irritation this time.

"I'll second that," Ryan said.

"First things first," Dalton said. "You have the intel? The key?"

Ryan maneuvered the car back onto the road. "Maybe. I thought you had it." Then again, Dalton did have the best poker face on the team. He could bluff his way out of anything.

"Would you two stop ignoring me and tell me what's happening?" Frankie snapped.

"Hang on a sec. How's Molly holding up?" Ryan asked. "We might need to make one quick stop at my place."

"Perfect," Frankie said. "My car is there, and I'll leave the two of you to your secret agent business and say thanks for a really interesting afternoon. It's been swell, but Molly and I will be on our way."

Oh, she'd gone way past irritation. Despite the darkened car interior, Ryan glanced in the rearview mirror. Then again, he knew exactly what she'd look like—eyebrows scrunched together, blue eyes that would freeze a six alarm fire, and those soft, luscious lips flattened into a narrow white stripe. "Frankie, please—"

"Sorry, little lady." Dalton cut him off. "I truly am. It wasn't supposed to go down this way, but don't blame my partner. Ryan didn't know anything."

"Partner my—" Ryan bit back the expletive. "Ryan still doesn't know anything." And until Frankie and Molly were safe, it was probably better to leave things that way.

"Mommy, I'm hungry. Are we going to Slappy's?"

"Not now," Frankie said, stroking Molly's hair. "You can talk to Wolf. This is grownup time."

Dalton leaned against the window, eyes closed, his breathing shallow. Great. Between the two of them, they had half a body. Still, if Dalton could be trusted, the two of them, even operating at half-efficiency, could hold their own.

He felt the familiar adrenaline surge. The one that excited and focused the senses at the same time.

From the backseat, Molly sing-songed about five monkeys jumping on the bed. Soon, Frankie joined her. To Ryan's surprise, the long-forgotten rhyme surfaced, and he made it a trio. Dalton's lips mouthed the words.

"Here we are," Ryan said when they reached Josh's house. Torn between letting Frankie disappear—probably from his life—and subjecting her to possible danger if she stayed, he avoided looking at her when she got out of the car.

"My things are inside," she said. "I'll get them, and if you don't mind, Molly and I would like to use your bathroom before we go." Without waiting for a response, she dragged Molly from the car and up the porch steps.

Dalton grabbed his arm. "Don't let her leave. She's a target." He rubbed his chest. "Damn, that smarts."

"So, tell me. What the hell is going on?"

"There are numerous people of the not-friendly variety who want to get their hands on those files you got from Alvarez."

"No shit, Sherlock. What is so damned important about a bunch of hidden, stolen or smuggled art? I looked at the files, and that's what they are."

"Ah, and that's the beauty of the scheme. But can we finish this conversation inside? I'm feeling like the proverbial sitting duck here."

"First, tell me why Frankie is a target."

"She was in our company, pard. And if the tangos have seen her with us, they're likely to follow her when she leaves. They'll go after anyone they think has the information."

"They're here? Now?" Shit. He started to go after Frankie and Molly.

"Not right here, pard." Dalton held him back. "Those two goons you met were the first contingent to arrive. As you noticed, they aren't the best and brightest. The others are probably going to be more difficult. Speaking of Smith and Jones—you left them alive, didn't you?"

He nodded. "That was the idea, right? So they'll be able to report your death?"

"You got it. Beats the alternative, which would entail me

really being dead." He opened the car door. "Now, what do we do about the woman and kid?"

"Damned if I know. At this point, I don't think she'll listen to me. I can tweak her car so she'd have to stay, but shit, Dalt—she's no safer here than home."

"But here we can protect her. On the road, alone—and don't tell me you wouldn't be distracted, and I don't need a distracted partner."

Protect her. Like he'd protected the Forcadas. His skin got clammy. And what about Pop?

Take them to safety, and Dalton would be alone to face whatever might be showing up. Let them stay, they'd be caught in what could be another clusterfuck.

Headlights and car engines—big car engines—on the approach—made the decision moot. He bolted for the house.

"I'm right behind you, pard. Hardware's in the trunk."

"Wash your hands and face." Frankie squeezed into the small bathroom behind Molly. She tried hard not to think abut the emotions that had surged as she held two men at gunpoint. Instead of revulsion, she'd been excited. Ryan had been right. It was a rush.

Ridiculous. She was a schoolteacher. A mom. Her idea of adventure was shooting pictures, not people. She channeled her feelings to the relief that Molly was all right.

Molly whirled around. "I'm *hungry*. I want to go to Slappy's."

Frankie crouched down and held her daughter against her, afraid to let go. "We'll see if Ryan has a snack, and you can eat it in the car."

"Then can we go to Slappy's?"

"I don't know. I'll think about it."

The front door banged open, then slammed shut. The small

bathroom window rattled. Frankie squeezed Molly tighter.

"Frankie? Where are you?" Despite its even delivery, Ryan's voice carried a warning.

"We're here." She inched open the bathroom door and poked her head out. "What?" She clutched Molly's hand.

Ryan's eyes met hers, dropped to Molly and then back up. For an instant, she saw fear. She remembered Carmelita. The little girl he couldn't save. She touched his hand. "We'll be all right."

The muscles in his jaw clenched. "Stay put, okay?"

He bent low and picked up Molly. "Angel, I'm going to need you to do me a really, really big favor. Will you do it for me?"

Molly nodded, curiosity replacing her petulance.

"That's my girl." He set her in the big cast-iron bathtub. "Some of my friends are playing hide and seek. Can you hide in here for me, and be very, very quiet?" He handed her Mr. Snuggles.

Molly clutched the dog and looked back and forth between Ryan and Frankie. Her chin quivered.

Frankie pulled Ryan aside. With her back to the tub, she whispered in Ryan's ear. "She's been through enough. She's scared."

Ryan crouched down by the tub and held Molly's hands. "I'll bet you're super at hide and seek. Those people think they're the best, but you're going to be even better. I know you can do it. I'm going to talk to your mom for a minute, and then she's going to hide with you, okay?" He kissed her forehead.

Molly gave a solemn nod. "Okay."

Not until Frankie exhaled did she realize she'd been holding her breath.

"Okay, Angel. Your mom will be right back." Ryan slid the curtain shut and pulled her outside the door. "We don't have much time. There's at least one vehicle on the way, and I'm sure it's not the Avon lady. Dalton and I are going to intercept them and keep them away from the cabin."

Dalton appeared with Ryan's laptop and a handful of DVDs. He thrust them at Frankie. "Maybe you can find one to keep her occupied."

She took the computer and ducked into the bathroom. Almost immediately, the door reopened.

Dalton handed her a pair of headphones. "Might get a little noisy. Better she doesn't hear too much."

Frankie shifted her gaze to the headphones, then back to Dalton. Detached, professional eyes met hers. He projected a calm confidence.

"Can I do anything?" She realized the ludicrous question as soon as she uttered the words. Elementary school art teachers didn't do what these men did.

Ryan appeared with a Kevlar vest. "Take this." He shoved it into her arms. Taken aback by its weight, she stepped backward. Ryan disappeared.

"Wait. He should have this," she said to Dalton. "Not me."

"You keep it and stay with your daughter, little lady," Dalton said. "I need to know my partner's mind is on the task at hand, and if he's worrying about you and the kid, he can't do his job."

His job. Putting his life on the line for someone else. "I understand. You . . . be safe."

He flashed her a cockeyed grin. "It's what we do. You go watch a movie. Wish we had some popcorn for you." He pulled the door shut behind him.

She stepped toward the tub, searching for a way to keep this a game for Molly. She studied the line of sight between the door and the tub and opened the vest. "Look at this. Help me make a little wall, so we can hide behind it, okay? And look what Mr. Dalton gave you. Headphones, so you can hear the computer and nobody will know we're in here."

She found some towels and lined the tub before settling in beside Molly and booting the computer. She kissed the top of Molly's head, getting hints of Ryan's scent from the soap that Molly had used to wash her hands and face. "Here we are," she whispered. "Snug as two bugs in a rug."

"Does he have the *Barbie and the Little Mermaid* game?" Molly asked in a stage whisper. "Brenda showed me how to play."

"I don't think so, Peanut. Let's find something else. And remember, we have to be very quiet."

Brenda. Good heavens. She'd forgotten all about the missing money. And her mother running off with Bob. Not exactly. Mom left to help Bob with his sister, not really run off with him. She sighed. This morning, she'd been worried about her mother's love life and some cash. Well, Mom was free to live her own life, and they'd deal with what now seemed the trivial disappearance of Brenda later. She refused to accept that there wouldn't be a later. Not with two warriors on the other side of the door. Where it seemed far too quiet.

"Wolf," Ryan said. "Home." He opened the kitchen door. The dog cocked his head, whined, and sat at Ryan's feet. "No, boy. Home."

With another plaintive whine, the dog trotted outside and turned back toward the cabin. Ryan repeated his command. Wolf barked once, then dashed into the woods.

"You sure we can't use him?" Dalton asked. "He's got a good set of teeth."

"He's done his part. I won't have him shot."

"Gotcha." Dalton turned away. "You sure you can handle this?" he asked without looking at Ryan.

"Of course. Why wouldn't I?"

"Because you're loco in love with the woman in the other room, and her kid, too."

Ryan dragged his fingers through his hair. "It shows, huh?"

"Like fireworks on the Fourth of July. You want to stay in here with them?"

He hesitated, but only for an instant. Taking the fight away from the cabin was the safest measure, and Dalton couldn't handle things alone. "I'm with you."

"Okay, but remember. Detachment." Dalton opened a duffel he'd set in the middle of the living room. "Choose your weapons."

Ryan swallowed when he saw the assortment of firepower. "What the fuck is going on here, Dalton?"

"Long story, and we're short on time. The tangos should have been here already."

He closed his eyes and took a deep breath. With Frankie and Molly in the house, questions would have to wait. He shoved a pistol into his waistband, strapped a sheathed knife to his ankle, grabbed an AK-47 and wished he was wearing his standard uniform cargo pants. Jeans didn't have enough storage space.

Dalton pushed him aside, zipped the duffel and hoisted it over his shoulder. "You know the terrain here. My guess is that the tangos are waiting and watching. Where can we dig in?"

Ryan gazed at the closed bathroom door. "Nothing will happen to you," he murmured under his breath. With weapons in hand, the familiar pre-mission calm washed over him. He crept to the door. From the porch, all looked quiet. "This way," he said to Dalton. Clinging to shadows, they moved through the trees to higher ground as if they'd rehearsed the route.

A short while later, hunkered down behind a rock outcropping where they could see anything approaching the cabin, Dalton fumbled in the duffel and brought out night vision goggles, followed by two headsets. Ryan set a pair of goggles down beside him. He slipped on a headset, adjusted the earpiece and lip mic, wondering who the hell he'd hear on the other end when he switched it on. Before he did, he tapped Dalton's shoulder.

"When this is over, after I pound the crap out of you, you're going to tell me everything, right?"

Dalton stopped rubbing dirt onto his face. His white-toothed grin was visible, even in the dim light. "Ain't no way you can take me, but yeah, I owe you. And I'm sorry it went down like this."

"I can't believe you'd let anyone hurt a kid. She's probably going to need a shrink for years."

Dalton's expression sobered. "Nobody touched her. I made damn sure of that. She never saw a thing."

"You had her out the whole time?"

"Wasn't that long, and I kept the dosage light. She might be groggy for a day, but she's not going to remember anything."

Ryan clenched his fists. "Except now she's stuck in a bathtub. There's no way in hell she thinks she's playing hide and seek."

"Then let's end this quick and quiet." Dalton held his hand up. "Go ahead, Fozzie."

Ryan flicked the switch on his headset. Fozzie. Foster Mayhew, one of Blackthorne's controllers. How many missions had the unflappable Aussie talked them through? No way both Dalt and Fozzie had turned. A little more apprehension eased out of Ryan's gut.

"You alone, Dalt?" Fozzie asked.

"No, I picked up an assistant. The two civilians are holed up, but not secure."

Ryan adjusted the mic by his cheek. "Hey, Fozzie. Still pulling desk duty, I see." Of course, his 'desk' was usually in a helo, monitoring stealth equipment. "You up there?"

"G'day, Harper, my man. Welcome back. No worries. I'm telling my driver to plan on dinner and a movie when this is finished. The two of you can handle the six of them, no problem. No need to wake the neighbors."

"Six?" Ryan tried to stay calm. He took a breath. Fozzie was right. With the element of surprise, he and Dalt should be able to handle three-to-one odds. If they needed air support, any hope of keeping the local cops out of the mission was history.

Dalton's voice echoed from the radio and in Ryan's free ear. "Locations?"

"Two parked about half a klick north of you. They're on foot, paralleling the trail. One circled around and is coming from the east. Figure their ETA's about ten."

He reflexively checked his watch. Ten minutes could be an eternity, but it wouldn't give him enough time to get Frankie and Molly the hell away.

"You got ID on them?" Dalton asked.

"Those three are Palestinians. You got a couple of Koreans, and scuttlebutt has it that China might be in the picture. They're at least twenty out. Maybe longer. They're not moving fast."

Ryan shifted his gaze toward the east. "And the two we've already dealt with?"

"Independents wanting to sell to the highest bidder."

That helped explain their ineptitude. "We have backup?" Ryan asked. This still felt all wrong.

"Team Three's about to insert and take out the rest of the party. For now, you've got me, mates." Ryan's headset hissed and clicked. Fozzie was silent. When he came back, Ryan recognized the undercurrent of urgency in his tone. "Sorry, gotta back up Three. Hoo-Yah."

"The *rest* of the party? Would someone tell me what the fuck we've got that's so goddamn important?" But Fozzie was gone, obviously talking with Team Three.

"In a bit," Dalton said. "You mind the store. I'm going to set down a little welcome celebration." He grabbed a small pack from the duffel and trotted into the darkness.

Ryan poked through the duffel and assembled his arsenal.

CHAPTER 27

The computer in Frankie's lap came to life. A quick check revealed no games, not that she'd expected any. Maybe she could interest Molly in *Gone with the Wind*. Right. Wishful thinking. The classic would never entertain Molly, especially when she knew something was wrong.

Surprised when the screen displayed an image of a Seurat painting instead of the movie, Frankie manipulated the cursor and clicked through a series of works of art, some familiar, some she recognized only by style.

Molly tugged her arm and pulled off the headphones. "This isn't regular hide and seek, is it?"

Frankie stared into her daughter's trusting, yet too-wise blue eyes. "No, Peanut. But it's important that we're very quiet, like Ryan and Dalton said. Even quieter than inside voices. So we're going to whisper."

"Okay. Are there bad people out there?"

Frankie's heart skipped. "Why do you say that?" What had happened to Molly before they'd found her? She didn't dare ask, afraid to make Molly revisit it.

"Grownups don't play hide and seek," Molly said, a hint of uncertainty underlying her whispered words.

"Sure they do. A different way from kids, that's all." She squeezed Molly's fingers. "Let's look at some of these pictures, okay? We can make up stories about them." She clicked to another image. "What do you think is happening in this one?"

"I don't know. What's that in the man's hand?"

"Let's see. Wait a minute." She zoomed in on the image. "I think it's a flower. What do you think?"

Molly squinted at the screen. "I think it looks funny. All full of squares."

"That's right. Those are pixels. Tiny bits of the picture, like a puzzle. When you put all the pieces together, then make it small again, you can see the picture."

Ryan's laptop didn't have much of a photo editing program, but it would do to keep Molly occupied. She copied a few of the images and turned one upside down, made the sky orange in another, and with a little effort, changed a woman's dress from blue to green.

"Can you turn the dog into a duck?" Molly asked.

"Hmm. That's tricky. But let's see." She'd managed to create a two-legged creature when the realization that she had Ryan's secret file hit her like a battering ram in the belly. She shuddered. Moving back to the original file, she clicked through the pictures.

Molly grabbed at her hands. "I want the duck-dog back."

"Shh. Mommy needs to look at this for a minute." She scanned through the images. Something didn't seem right, but between Molly's tugs and trying to listen for anything happening outside, she couldn't concentrate. She needed some quiet and Photoshop, neither of which was available. She needed to get to Ryan and tell him what she suspected. He could take it to his people and they could run it through some fancy spy technology. Right. She'd simply get up, leave her daughter, and walk into the middle of a terrorist gathering.

What she needed was to get herself and Molly as far away from here as she could. Her car was outside. Ryan and Dalton were dealing with the bad guys. She and Molly could probably sneak out before anyone knew they were gone. But there was that terrorist thing again. She snuggled Molly closer.

Confident that Dalton would take out the two coming from the other direction, Ryan lay on his belly, burrowed into the mulch, his rifle pointed down the trail. Waiting. So much of the job entailed waiting. Quick and quiet. Blackthorne's specialty. He wondered what he was protecting, and decided he didn't give a damn. It had to be important, and that was enough.

When he settled into his mind-clearing rituals, he realized exactly what he was protecting, and it reverberated through him like a plucked guitar string. Frankie and Molly. Dalton and the rest had their objective. If saving the intel he'd been holding co-incided with keeping the two people who had entwined themselves around his heart safe, so be it. He'd do what he had to do, but if push came to shove, he wouldn't sacrifice them for some classified whatever he had. Fuck, anyone could get instructions to build a nuclear bomb off the web. Today's secrets were tomorrow's Internet downloads.

He slowed his breathing. He concentrated on the night sounds, listening for anything that signaled the approach of an intruder, all the while alert to an update from Fozzie.

Someone—or something—approached. He couldn't hear it, really, or see it, but he knew it was coming his way. He squinted into the darkness, the goggles giving everything an eerie green glow. A man approached, carrying an assault rifle, and he wasn't Dalton. Once Ryan had his target pinpointed, he yanked the goggles off, letting his eyes adjust. Wearing them, a strong flashlight pointed his way would blind him.

Calm now, immersed in the job, he took aim.

A tap to the head, and his target went down. He forced back the inevitable nausea and reached for the goggles. Scanning the area, he saw nothing. Heard nothing. Dalt must have intercepted his two. A peek at his watch told him they had about ten minutes before the second wave arrived. What had Fozzie said? Chinese? Koreans? Dammit, what were they holding, to bring out an international crowd?

His headset crackled. "Heads up, mates."

He whipped his head around. Nothing. Wait. In the trees. He focused on the movement. Goddamn raccoons. His palms sweated. One at a time, he wiped his hands on his jeans. Without conscious direction, his body performed the ritual moves, checking the knife strapped to his ankle, his weapons, and his supply of flash-bangs.

"Watch your six." Dalton's words came through the trees. "On my way."

He cursed under his breath and scrambled for the rocks again. Seconds later, Dalton slid in beside him, panting and clutching his arm.

"You're hit," Ryan said. He reached for Dalt's arm.

"Just a scratch. I'll be fine."

As if Dalton would say anything else, regardless of his injury. Before Ryan could press, gunfire sprayed their position.

Reflexes took over. Ryan followed the muzzle flashes and returned fire. So much for quick and quiet. Dirt spat. Rock chips flew. As if their last mission together had been yesterday, he and Dalton slipped into their rhythm, anticipating moves, passing loaded magazines as needed.

"There's more than three of them," Ryan said after a barrage of fire came at them from all directions.

"Seems Team Three let a few get by. Afraid I only got one of mine."

"Where the fuck is Fozzie?" Ryan asked. "We could use his lights."

"He'll be here. Meanwhile, we hold down the fort."

"Be nice if our fort had a few more soldiers," Ryan mumbled.

"Watch my six." He scanned the panorama in front of him with the goggles."

"Something's coming. Four o'clock," Dalton said.

Ryan swung around and squinted in the direction Dalton indicated. Trees. He pointed his rifle into the darkness. "I need more. Where? What?"

"Check the dead tree over there. Five feet to the left."

Ryan located the tree. He pinpointed three tangos and opened fire. Two went down. A boulder chip whizzed by his ear. He ducked. A series of explosions, then a fireball filled the sky. He squinted through a gap in the rocks. His heart filled his throat. His gut twisted. Bits of Josh's cabin drifted down through the smoke and flames. Only Dalton's vise-like grip on his belt kept him from racing headlong down the mountain.

"Watch it!" Fozzie's voice rang through the headset. "More headed your way. Two approaching from the west. More from the north."

"West is mine," Dalton said. "I'll flank them." He was already darting through the trees.

Gunfire came from behind Ryan. He pivoted, tried to locate a target. A tree above him shattered. His arm jerked. He fired, ducked and covered his face against the raining bits of wood and pine needles. The next shot was closer. Too much closer. "Damn, Fozzie, where the fuck are you?"

His headset crackled to life. "No need to swear, mate. Cavalry's on its way." At the controller's voice, relief surged through Ryan. An instant later searchlights lit up the forest. Visions of the cabin, of Frankie and Molly hung before his eyes. He shook his head. Blinked. Found his targets. In a cold, blind fury, he fired. And fired. And fired.

At last, silence filled the mountain. Leaving the aftermath to others, Ryan flew down the trail to the blazing cabin.

"Frankie! Molly!" He ripped off his shirt and tied it around his face. Stomping on flames, he fought his way through the smoke-filled living room toward the bathroom. Or where the bathroom had been. Tears streamed down his face, not all from the smoke.

He stumbled over a small hard object on the floor. He crouched below the smoke and felt for it. His hand jerked away at the touch of hot metal, but not before he recognized it as a camera. Frankie's. He yanked the shirt from his face, and using it for protection, picked up the Nikon. He choked back a sob. She wouldn't leave it behind.

"Outside, sir." A muffled voice echoed in his ear. Hands gripped his shoulders.

"Two more," Ryan gasped. "Inside. Woman. Little girl. Find. Them." Ryan's head swam. He tried to breathe, but collapsed in a paroxysm of coughing.

"Outside," the man repeated.

On limbs that refused to obey his commands to search for Frankie, Ryan was pushed into the cold night air.

He fought an oxygen mask, but the ape holding it against his face overpowered him. He struggled to remain conscious, finally understanding the words floating through the mist that threatened to overwhelm him.

"Easy, Harper. There was some sort of gas in the house. You've been out for almost ten minutes. A few deep breaths and your head will clear."

He pushed the hands away and stared into the blurred face of Hank Cooper, another of Blackthorne's operatives. Damn, whatever was in the house had knocked him for a loop. He clutched the mask to his face and sucked oxygen.

"Frankie. Molly. Did you find them?" he said as soon as he could get the words out.

"Sorry. Not unless Frankie was about six-three, two-fifty and had a beard. Nobody else was in there. But there's a lot of rubble."

His gut twisted tighter. "Great. Another FUBAR mission." But if they hadn't found bodies, maybe Frankie and Molly had escaped before the explosion. He allowed himself a scintilla of hope.

"Not exactly," came a Texas drawl. "Blackthorne twelve, tangos zero. Of course, there's still the missing intel."

He turned his head toward Dalton's voice and regretted it immediately when a hot knife of pain inserted itself behind his eyeballs. "Shit, what was that stuff?"

"Not sure, but you don't want to breathe much of it," Cooper said. He held out a canteen. "Here."

Ryan poured some water into his hand and splashed it over his eyes before swigging great gulps of the cool liquid. "Thanks." He passed the canteen to Dalton. "It's going to be a circus here in a little while." On shaky legs, he shoved away from his former teammate and walked to the clearing behind the house where Frankie would have left her car. Four slashed tires and a shattered windshield dashed his last hopes that she'd escaped.

Numb, he sank to his knees. Another bout of coughing jackhammered through his head. He clutched his throbbing temples.

He sensed Dalton behind him, but knew the man wouldn't intrude until Ryan could handle it. Which is what he did. Handled things. He scrubbed his hands across his face and stood. Dalton's arm sported a fresh bandage, gleaming white against the dirt that caked the rest of him.

Ryan met his gaze. "What now?" *God, please don't let him tell me they found the bodies.*

"You should go home. Get some rest. Let us take care of the cleanup."

"No. It's my place. The locals will want to talk to me. I'm surprised they're not here yet." Another piece of reality burst forward. "Pop? The ranch?"

Dalton closed the distance between them and put his hand

on Ryan's shoulder. "Never got close. Leave things to Blackie. He'll put his spin on it and keep the media at bay. A training mission, things got out of hand, flammables in your cabin. Your sheriff will probably be glad to have it off his plate. And that assumes the locals even find out what's gone down. We're off the beaten path out here."

"And they can explain away—what did you say?—twelve bodies?" Even as he spoke the words, he knew Blackthorne's clean-up crew would have whisked the bodies away. Dalton was right. The sheriff's department would prefer to look for poachers and trespassers, and not get embroiled in international espionage. Without manpower or finances, they'd accept the easy explanation, even if they knew it was an incongruous one. The media would be trickier, but he knew Blackthorne had ways of greasing skids. He squeezed the bridge of his nose. "Dalt—I don't have the energy to flatten you right now, but what do I—did I—have?"

"Genetic code for a chunk of mutated smallpox virus. They can splice it to a more common variety, make a new bug. All I know is it's double ugly."

Double ugly was right. A pandemic could devastate millions. "Shit."

"Yeah. Nobody'd want to release it until they came up with a vaccine, but they need the code first."

"And that's what Alvarez gave me?"

"Apparently so. I retrieved your laptop. I'll take it to the techies, but my guess is it's fried. Your DVD collection looks like that Dali clock painting. We'll check, but I don't think they could have salvaged anything."

Questions circled around Ryan's brain like horses on a carousel, but the brass ring remained out of reach.

Dalton tapped his headset and swung his mic into position. "Say again, Fozzie."

CHAPTER 28

Guided by faint moonlight and a lot of luck, Frankie picked her way to a passable hiding place. They'd walked for at least twenty minutes, she estimated, and even half-carrying Molly, hampered by the vest Frankie insisted she wear, they'd put some ground between them and Ryan's cabin.

"Okay, Molly. Get behind that big tree. We can hide here now."

"This is *not* hide and seek," Molly insisted. "You're not allowed to change hiding places."

"Shh," Frankie said. "I told you grownups play different."

Molly fisted her little hands on her hips, then shrugged out of the clumsy vest. "Well, I don't want to play anymore. I want to go home."

Much as she'd wanted to get into the car and race off the mountain, her gut told Frankie she'd be safer on foot for now. More places to hide. They'd spend the night in the woods if they had to. She'd raided Ryan's supply of blankets, and the two of them had stolen away like gunmetal-gray ghosts.

In the distance, she heard gunfire, then another sound, much louder and closer. She crept from behind the bushes and gaped at the heavens ablaze with color. Bits and pieces of what had to be Ryan's cabin drifted from the sky.

Molly covered her ears. "Is it fireworks? Can we see?"

She pulled Molly against her. "It sure looks like it. But we have to find another place to hide. Remember to stay very close to me, and no talking."

This time Molly seemed to understand, because she did exactly as Frankie asked. They walked, using the glow of the sky to pick their way through the trees, avoiding the easier footing on the road. Molly stopped whining about being tired and hungry, but Frankie knew she had to be exhausted. What had seemed a reckless move at the time, sneaking out the back door of the cabin, had saved their lives.

They were back in the shadows, and her fear that one of them would trip and twist an ankle, or worse, made her call a halt. "We're going to hide in the woods until it's morning and we can see again. Ryan wanted us to hide, and we have to be nice and do what he asked."

Using what little light the fire cast, she found a clear spot, kicked rocks and sticks out of her way and spread a blanket on the ground. "Lie down. You can sleep here. I'll snuggle with you and we'll stay warm."

"Are we going to die, Mommy?"

Frankie blinked back tears. "Of course not, Peanut. Go to sleep, and it'll be morning before you know it." What they'd do then wasn't clear yet, but she'd think of something. Ryan would find them. She gazed at the sky. If he hadn't been blown up.

Molly curled up on the blanket, and Frankie covered her with another one. Soon, Molly's breathing evened. Frankie wondered if she'd made a really stupid mistake. One more look at the fading glow in the sky told her no. She might not be in the best situation right now, but it sure as heck beat being burned to a crisp.

Somewhere far above, a helicopter circled, illuminating bits of the forest with its searchlight. Frankie huddled in the last blanket, one hand holding Molly still, trying to look like a rock, trying not to breathe. The lights moved away and the whup-whupping faded into the distance. She counted to a hundred before daring to stretch her cramped legs.

She listened to the night noises, trying to filter out normal woodsy sounds from approaching danger. Then again, some of those normal woodsy things could be dangerous, too. When one of those noises got closer, she thought her heart would explode through her chest. She reached for Molly. Or should she move and lure whatever it was away? While she'd gladly sacrifice herself for her daughter, how would Molly get back to civilization alone?

No time to think.

Trusting her instinct, she moved close to Molly and lay flat, pulling the blanket over them. Her heart pounded into the ground beneath her, its drumbeat echoing in her ears.

She remembered Ryan protecting her with his own body. His warm, hard body. Was it this afternoon? And last night they'd made glorious love. New thoughts of Ryan surged like a tidal wave through her brain. This was normal for him. Before she could sort her thoughts, she felt a tug on the blanket.

A cold nose tickled the back of her neck. She swallowed a scream. The creature whined. She smelled dog. Definitely dog. She braved a peek from under the blanket.

"Wolf. You do have a way of showing up when you're needed, don't you, boy?"

She crawled out from under the blanket and wrapped her arms around his warm, furry body. He licked her face and sat beside her.

"I guess we should all get some sleep."

He thumped his tail and curled up between her and Molly. Knowing she had a sentry on guard, she relaxed. "In the morning, you can lead us out of here, right?"

With the dog's added warmth, she let her exhaustion take over and drifted in and out of a fitful doze.

Whether it had been seconds, minutes or hours, she wasn't

sure, but Wolf sat up and barked. She strained her eyes into the darkness.

"Wolf." Molly's voice was a sleepy mumble.

"Shh." Frankie grasped Wolf's neck. He shook free and trotted a few paces away, still barking. She fumbled for the Kevlar vest and covered Molly. "Don't move, Peanut."

"You're positive they're still there, Grinch?" Ryan crouched behind Grinciewicz and checked the display one more time, needing to see the two forms in the trees. The helo circled a small clearing about fifty feet from the spot Fozzie had reporting finding Frankie and Molly.

"What's the matter, Harper?" Grinch pointed to the blobs of color on the screen. "A little time off and you forget how to do the job?"

"Step on it, will you," Ryan said. "It's cold out there."

"You sure you're up for this? Manny or Hotshot would be happy to do it. Nothing like being harnessed to a woman to wrap up a mission."

Ryan adjusted the jump suit Manny had given him. "I told you I'm going. You keep the damn bird steady."

"Now you're hurtin' my feelings," Grinch said. "Have I ever let you down?"

"I'm more concerned with you getting me back up," Ryan muttered. Dangling below the belly of a helo ranked about a minus three on his ten least favorite ops list, but he damn well knew what he was doing. It wasn't jealousy that kept him from allowing anyone else to do the rescue. Never mind that to hoist them up, they'd be strapped together belly to belly. Manny and Hotshot might be more experienced in helo rescues, but this mission was his.

When Fozzie had reported locating two individuals, alive, Ryan's world stopped. His throat tightened. Blood rushed in his ears. Dalt had forced him to the ground and shoved his head between his knees before he'd actually passed out. When Ryan could breathe again, he insisted Fozzie delay the rescue long enough to come back for him.

Fozzie hadn't exactly identified them as Frankie and Molly, but it had to be them. Apparently they were hiding, and quite effectively, unless someone looking had a helo with night vision, infra-red and God-knows-what-else that could pinpoint a squirrel's balls at a hundred yards. But Wolf, bless the dog's heart, had given their location away. The dog would eat steak for the rest of his life.

Ryan quelled the butterflies zipping in formation through his gut. Frankie and Molly were alive. But until he was standing in front of them, until he could touch them, it wasn't real.

He crouched by the helo's open bay, checked his harness and the one he'd use for Frankie. Again. He sent his mind elsewhere while the preparations continued. The noise of the helo made conversation difficult, even with the radio sets, but they didn't need words to communicate. Everyone had a job to do, and the routine eased Ryan's anxiety.

Hotshot snapped glowsticks and taped them to Ryan's hands, boots and helmet. He clapped him on the shoulder and tugged on the line attached to his harness. Ryan gave him a thumbs up and circled his hands. The glow sticks, which would give Fozzie a way to track him and make hand signals visible, painted green loops in the darkness.

Hotshot leaned his helmet against Ryan's. "Chill. The tangos are gone. This is no HALO op. Not even fast roping. Sit back and relax. The winch will do it all."

Knowing didn't make him like it. So what if he wasn't free-falling from 30,000 feet? He couldn't shake the nerves. Thinking about Frankie made breathing an effort. He tapped his helmet to Hotshot's as if toasting the mission. With one last deep inhale, he clutched the rescue bag to his belly and slid into the night.

Trusting his buddies to lower him at a rate appropriate to the terrain, he stared straight ahead until tree trunks told him he was near the ground. He made sure of a clear spot beneath him and signaled to the helo. Line played out and he'd barely hit bottom when Wolf raced to him, barking a frantic welcome.

He signaled Grinch to hold steady and broke into a run, almost before he unclipped his line and grabbed his Maglite. "Frankie! Molly! Come on out. It's over."

"Two o'clock, about fifty meters," came over his headset. He veered right, still calling their names. Wolf led the way. Ryan turned on the light and kicked up his pace.

Frankie, wrapped in a blanket, stood huddled behind a stand of trees. He shone the light over her. She was standing. Not lying battered and bleeding like in the picture that had played over and over in his head. She took a tentative step forward, hands shielding her eyes.

Damn, in the dark, he must look like some sort of a monster. He lowered the beam. "It's me. Ryan."

Altogether too slowly, she stepped forward. "It's really you? You're alive?"

This was not the two lovers racing into each other's arms he'd imagined. He waited.

When she stopped five feet away, holding Molly to her side, his gut twisted. In that instant, he'd seen a flash of relief in her eyes, but he'd caught a flicker of unease, quickly hidden, replaced by absolute neutrality. He'd been an idiot to assume she loved him. After what had gone down, she probably never wanted to see him again. One night of sex, even terrific sex, didn't make it easy to love someone who'd nearly gotten you and your kid killed.

Fighting his need to embrace her, he swallowed the tide of

emotions that surged through him. "Of course I'm alive. I told you I'd be back."

"Your cabin? Dalton?"

"Later. Let's go." He peeked around her where Molly clung to Frankie's legs. "Hey, Angel. Have you ever been in a helicopter?"

"Helicopter? What are you talking about?" Frankie said. "I don't see a landing pad."

He pointed skyward. "That's as low as she gets." He reached into his bag and removed two more glow sticks. "You know how these work?" he asked Molly.

She nodded.

"Good girl. You can be my assistant. Crack them, shake them, and let's go for a ride."

"Do you mean to tell me you're taking my daughter up . . . there?" Frankie pointed in the direction of the helo's sounds.

"We're all going. Fastest way out, and we need to get moving." He scooped Molly up and trotted toward the clearing, sliding into hostage rescue mode. Move quickly, reassure them they're all right, and don't let them argue.

He demonstrated the harness, helped Frankie into it, securing the buckles and straps and wondering if their contact electrified her as much as it did him. If so, she had Dalton beat out for the best poker face on the team. Molly, wide-eyed, took direction without hesitation.

Before he fastened them together, he knelt down and buried his face in Wolf's ruff. After giving the dog an energetic scratch behind the ears and a hearty pat to his chest, he straightened. "Home, boy. Good job." Wolf sat. Ryan knew he'd go home once they took off.

"Do heights bother you?" he asked Frankie.

She looked at the helo overhead. "I guess I'm going to find out."

"Okay, Molly," he said. "Got your braves ready?"

She patted her tummy.

"You're going to be the peanut butter in the sandwich. But first, make a circle with the glow sticks. That will tell Fozzie we're almost ready to go. Then I want you to hold on to me like this." He took her hands and wrapped her arms around his waist.

She did, and he retightened all the buckles. Better with Molly as a buffer between him and Frankie. They were safe. He told himself that's all that mattered.

He spiraled his hand above his head, giving the go. Then he embraced Frankie, holding her tight, and wondered if it was for the last time as the earth dropped away beneath them.

Avoiding Frankie's eyes on the ascent, he focused on Molly. Instead of fear, a grin spread across her face. Although the helo's rotors drowned out any other sounds, he swore she was giggling.

Once they'd reached the helo, Ryan braced his legs below the open door. Without a wasted movement, Hotshot and Manny hoisted Frankie and Molly inside. Fozzie assisted Ryan with getting in and closing the door, while Grinch whisked them away toward the nearest airport.

With practiced ease, Hotshot had Frankie and Molly out of their harnesses and belted into their seats. Seconds later, he'd outfitted them with headsets. Ryan watched him demonstrate how to listen and talk. Dammit, Hotshot didn't need to hold Frankie's hand to do it.

Molly twisted until she spied Ryan standing behind Manny. "Can we do that again?"

His insides loosened at the child's innocent grin. He stepped to her side and sat in the seat across from her. "Not today."

"But someday, okay?"

Frankie glared at him. Did she think he'd make promises he couldn't keep? She leaned forward, her face inches from Molly's. "Ryan and his friends have important jobs to do. They're probably not going to come back for a long, long time."

That answered his question. He levered himself out of his seat to find a private spot in the back of the helo.

"Ryan, wait."

He spun around at the sound of her voice.

Her eyes implored him to come closer. He was back in half a heartbeat. "Yes?"

"The disc. In your computer. The files. I think I figured out where the information is hidden."

He heard a collective intake of breath through his headset. He could feel everyone's eyes on them. "What did you find?"

"It's in the pictures. At least I think it is. I looked at a few of them, and there's something wrong."

"What do you mean, wrong?" She gazed above his head, and he sensed Hotshot behind him.

She didn't return her eyes to his as she went on. "I was enlarging some of them to entertain Molly while we waited. Some of the pixels didn't match."

"What does that mean?"

"I don't know exactly. I wanted to check it out in Photoshop. But now that it's all over, I suppose your people have much fancier technology."

Ryan stopped himself before he touched her thigh, afraid she'd recoil at his touch. "All the CDs were destroyed in the fire."

For an instant, her eyes sparkled. "But I took it with me. I thought it was important."

Manny stepped in. "Way to go. You want a job with Blackthorne?"

Frankie reached inside her parka. She pulled out fragments

of a CD and a jagged rock. "Oh, dear." Her face crumpled.
"I'm sorry. I'm so sorry."

CHAPTER 29

Frankie dropped the shards of the CD into Ryan's outstretched hand. "Do you think you can recover the data?"

He examined the gouged pieces. "I doubt it, but I'll send it to the techies."

"I am *so* sorry. It must have snapped when you buckled the harness. I forgot I'd picked up that rock. I thought I might use it in case someone—"

"Hey, stop it. We might not have the file, but neither do the bad guys. You did great."

She studied the faces hovering around her. The one who'd helped them into the helicopter. Hotshot, he'd called himself. His blue eyes didn't seem angry. Neither did Manny's brown ones. Both men gave her reassuring smiles.

She spoke to them, avoiding Ryan's eyes. "But I ruined your mission. You were supposed to get the information, right?"

"Let it go, Frankie," Manny said. "Harper's right. Our mission was to make sure the tangos didn't get the intel, and we did that. If you hadn't taken the disc, it would have been destroyed in the fire, so either way, it's gone."

"Tangos?" she asked.

"Terrorists," Hotshot said. "Tango's the call sign for the letter T."

She nodded. Still, her one chance to create a bright side from tonight's mess was nothing more than bits and pieces of plastic. Shaking off the whirling confusion of emotions plowing through her, she put a hand on Molly's shoulder. In the end, Molly's safety was all that mattered. There might be a big, bad world outside, but hers was in Broken Bow with her family.

Oh, God, her family. Mom. Bob. Brenda and the money. And Angus Harper's land access. Out of the fire, into the frying pan. Someone's voice barked in her headset, and the men scattered to seats. Molly looked up, startled.

"It's okay," Ryan said. "We're getting ready to land."

"Like on the ground?" Frankie said. "No ropes?"

"No ropes. Missoula airport. Dalton will be waiting."

Missoula. She had no transportation, no money. "How will we get home?"

Ryan's expression was flat. "You'll spend tonight in a hotel. And we'll watch your house, to be safe."

"But—"

"No buts, Frankie. Until we make sure everything is under control, you're going to have to do as we say."

Too exhausted to argue, too confused to deal with it, she nodded her assent. A night in a hotel would give her time to think. With a dull thud, they landed.

"Oh, my," she said when she peered out the open door. A black limo waited on the tarmac, the passenger doors open. Like dominoes, the crew exited the helicopter. Hotshot turned and stretched his arms toward her. His hands at her waist, hers on his shoulders, he swept her to the ground like a ballroom dancer. Molly dove into Manny's waiting arms.

With a hand at her back, Hotshot guided her, and Manny carried Molly. They were whisked into the limo, Grinch bringing up the rear.

"Wow," Molly said. "This is so cool."

Hotshot, Manny and Grinch joined her in back. Ryan went directly to the front passenger seat without a word. Dalton leaned over from the driver's seat. "Everyone set?" Seatbelts clicked into place, and with barely a whisper, the limo glided away.

"Wait here, Frankie," Dalton said when they arrived at the Holiday Inn. "Be right back."

Hotshot and Manny waited with her while Dalton, Ryan and Grinch strode toward the hotel entrance.

Molly scrambled from one side of the car to the other, trying to peek out the windows.

"Come here, kiddo," Hotshot said. "How old are you?" He pulled Molly next to him.

When she realized the men were putting their bodies between Molly and the window, her breath hitched. Maybe Ryan's earlier, "Everything's okay" hadn't been a hundred percent accurate.

"Isn't a limo kind of conspicuous?" she asked.

"Not if you're a big Hollywood film mogul come to scout locations," Manny said. "Dalton's feeding them a line about this being a hush-hush deal. If the staff respects our privacy, maybe we'll bring the big stars here, yada, yada, yada. He's first rate with the charm. And anyone looking for us would expect more conventional transportation."

Frankie marveled at the complexity of this world, and how easily these men seemed to slip from one persona to another. She was just a small town schoolteacher with aspirations of being a photographer. She'd had her big adventure, nearly lost her daughter, and it had scared the daylights out of her. The exhilaration—that was an emotion she'd deal with another time, when she could think again.

Dalton appeared. He pulled a suitcase from the trunk. "All set."

They slid out of the limo and were inside the lobby before she realized that she and Molly were flanked by four men. Big, strong—and, okay, handsome—bodyguards. Bodyguards who herded them into the elevator.

Dalton handed her two small paper bags with the Holiday Inn logo. Warm, and emitting an aroma that had her mouth watering. Chocolate chip cookies. She handed one to Molly, who ripped the bag open and devoured the treat inside. Glancing up at her entourage, Frankie saw smiles—and cookie crumbs—on their faces. She looked again, only then realizing Ryan wasn't part of the group.

"Okay, little lady," Dalton said when they reached what she assumed was her room. He unlocked the door and ushered them inside, immediately crossing to the window and drawing the drapes. He set the suitcase he'd been carrying onto one of the two double beds.

"Here's your key. We've got the rooms on either side and the one across the hall. If you want anything to eat, call room service. Feel free to hit the mini bar. If you need company, call one of us." He recited the room numbers and watched her write them on the pad by the phone. "Please don't leave the room."

She hadn't noticed who'd gone into which room, but she supposed it didn't matter. What had he meant by company? "I'm fine. We're fine. Thanks."

"There's clothes and stuff in the suitcase. Hope they fit."

Somehow, she knew whatever was in there would fit perfectly. She shook her head. Dalton turned to leave. At the door, he stopped. "I meant it, Frankie. Things can get scary after it's all over. If you or the little one need to talk about it, any one of us will listen. We've all been there."

She mustered a smile. "I think we're both too tired for that. But thanks for the offer."

"Then good night. Sleep well." He pulled the door open.

"Dalton, wait."

Closing the door behind him, he winged his eyebrows.

"Ryan. Where is he?" she asked.

"On his way to your place."

"If you talk to him, would you tell him thanks for everything?"

"I'll tell him."

"I think . . . you know, he has . . . feelings for me. Please tell him I'm not ready to deal with that yet. I have to sort things out." Did she ever. Thinking about him and what had happened today made her feel like firecrackers were exploding in her belly.

He pressed his lips together before he spoke. "That's between the two of you. Not my place to get involved."

Frankie's face grew hot. "You're right. I didn't mean—"

"You're beat. Get some sleep." He slipped out the door, but before he let it close, he poked his head back in. "Throw the latch."

She heard the click as the automatic lock caught. On legs that wobbled like Jell-O, she crossed the room and did as Dalton asked. Her eyes burned, and she blinked back the tears before turning around. "Okay, Molly. Let's get ready for bed."

An hour later, Frankie lay in bed, staring at the ceiling, concentrating on Molly's steady breathing. The room heater hummed. Traffic noises whooshed from the street four stories below. Normal, everyday sounds.

She pulled back the covers and padded to the other bed. Tucked against her daughter's warm body, she inhaled the scent of herbal soap and shampoo and waited for sleep. Nothing, she knew, would ever be normal again. From beyond the wall, she heard a phone ring once. A deep, male voice answered, but the words were unintelligible.

Ryan stepped from behind an oak tree in Frankie's yard. "What are you doing here?" He zipped his parka and shoved his hands into the pockets. "I called Grinch."

Dalton lowered himself to the ground next to Ryan. "And Grinch called me. Which, if you remember the way things work, is because I give the orders on this op, not you."

Ryan paced. "This op. As long as you're here, how about you fill me in on what the hell this op is."

"Long story."

"Well, unless another batch of tangos comes calling, we've got about six hours until sunrise. That enough time?" Ryan didn't disguise the anger in his tone. Anger was all that held him together. Dalton, *damn him*, would know that. At least it was dark, and he didn't have to deal with Dalton's penetrating stare.

Which was why he'd called Grinch, not Dalton. Dalt always knew every fucking thing whirling through his head. All he'd wanted was backup—so they could cover front and back of the house. Someone to help him stay awake. Definitely not someone playing shrink.

"Sit down." Dalton's drawl had changed to a growl. "Don't need the neighbors calling the cops."

Ryan sank to the lawn on the other side of the oak tree. He plucked blades of grass and threw them into the night. "You rigged my car, didn't you, you bastard? You almost killed my father. And then you drugged me so you could search my cabin. Oh, and let's not forget setting me up for that little punching bag job with those two thugs."

There was a long silence. "God's truth, I only tweaked the steering. I had no clue your daddy would drive away, or what happened for him to crash like that. I figured you'd take the car to the shop, and I could search your place."

"You could have asked, you know."

Another silence. Longer this time. "Blackie said no. You'd walked out. I couldn't believe you'd turn, but then, you thought *I* had, didn't you?"

This time it was Ryan who was silent. He uprooted a clump of grass and crushed it in his fist.

Dalton went on, his voice a low monotone. The kind that wouldn't carry beyond Ryan's ears. "The Alvarez assignment. It was supposed to be mine. Only I got stuck on another mission, so Blackie sent you."

"With no clue about what I was really after." His gut clenched at how vulnerable he'd been. "He didn't trust me enough to tell me?"

"Bad call, I agree. He said it was 'need to know.' He figured if you thought you were on a cakewalk, you couldn't give anything away. But he should have had backup closer. He didn't want to alert anyone that the mission was more than it appeared to be."

"So, tell me. When did Blackthorne start trusting me again?"

"I think he always did. It threw him when you quit like that, though. You didn't think it was strange when you got into Blackthorne's computer system so easily?"

"Shit." So much for his so-called clever way around Blackthorne security. They'd left the door wide open for him. God, his head had been totally fucked up, or he'd have noticed. He let the dirt dribble between his fingers. "What about the Forcadas?"

Dalton whistled softly through his teeth. "Someone intercepted our intel. Got through our encryption codes."

"Not an internal leak?"

"Nope. A damn good hacker. It's been fire-walled."

So there were no connections between the two cases. His dumb luck to be in the wrong place twice.

Headlights cruised by, and they waited in silence. Above, an owl hooted. From down the street, a dog barked. The car didn't come back. The wind picked up.

"It's getting cold," Dalton said. "What do you say we move inside?"

Ryan didn't bother to ask if he had a key. He trailed Dalton to the back porch, up the steps, and stood behind him while Dalt worked the lock. The door swung open.

"After you," Dalton said.

"That was quick, even for you."

"Yeah, well it helps that nobody bothered to lock the door."

Smiling despite himself, Ryan moved across the porch, through the kitchen, and into the now-empty bedroom that had once been Brenda's. He drew the curtains. In this room, shrouded by trees, they'd be away from any insomniac neighbor's eyes. He felt his way to the bed and sank onto the soft mattress. The frame squeaked as he lay down on his back. Hands clasped behind his head, he heard the scrape of a chair across the floor, and then a quiet creak as Dalton settled himself facing the door. Without having to see it, Ryan knew Dalton would have his pistol on his lap.

An unwarranted precaution, he told himself. Everything indicated it was over. Tonight was a formality. In the morning, Frankie and Molly would return home. Anyone who could ID her was dead.

He put a mental lid on that thought. "You think the new smallpox virus is out there?"

"Everything's out there. If not today, then tomorrow, or a week from Tuesday. Maybe a year. All we did was slow things down."

Which, Ryan knew as well as he knew the sun would rise, was all they ever did. "Do you think *we* have it tucked away in some laboratory? The CDC, or some secret medical research complex?"

"I don't know. But for what it's worth, I think if we *do* have it, tonight we showed the muckity-mucks that we need to make sure we can cure it. Pronto. Hell, we don't have enough vaccine for the normal, everyday smallpox."

He closed his eyes. "Ever wonder about man's inhumanity

and all that? You think it'll stop someday?"

Dalton snorted. "Yeah, right. But we'd be out of a job if that ever happened."

Job. Another thought he relegated to his mental strongbox. "What about Smith and Jones? How did you hook up with them?"

Dalton shifted in his chair. "Word on the street was you had Alvarez's files. Everyone wanted them. Smith and Jones, as you called them, were first to arrive. Since I was already here, I convinced them they couldn't do it without me, what with me having the inside track on my former partner's defection and all. They didn't believe me, so I had to convince them."

"I can accept you handing me over. But Frankie and Molly?" The thoughts he'd locked away hammered at the lid of his strongbox.

"Hey, I told you, I didn't let anyone hurt the kid. And if your brain wasn't so scrambled, you'd have noticed things. Like Frankie wasn't tied up, for starters. I did what I could to leave you a trail. I snuck a little surprise into Jones' food to slow them down. Short of handing you a map and a key, I fixed it so you'd get out and find us."

"So I should be thanking you, I suppose."

"It wasn't pretty, but it's done. Why don't you crash for a couple of hours? I'll be in the other room."

"No." The word spewed out too fast. "I mean, you haven't told me about the Phantom. You seemed to be where he was a lot of the time."

Dalton responded with another prolonged silence.

"Shit, man. Your nose is out of joint because I checked up? I didn't know what the hell was going on, and all of a sudden the man I thought was my friend seemed to have his own agenda. I called Debbie about the car parts, you know."

"Dammit. I got called out before I could give her the line to feed you."

"The Phantom. Tell me."

"Not a lot to tell. Idea was I could infiltrate, find out how he was getting his information. Nobody could get a handle on him, so Blackie switched tactics. I was laying the foundation for cover as a new competitor."

"You ID him?"

"No. Half the time the intel was off, and I wasn't where I needed to be when I needed to be there. He's still out there, somewhere."

"As long as we're having this heart-to-heart, I've got one more question."

"Shoot."

"How come you're the only person who calls Horace Blackthorne Blackie?"

Dalton's laugh echoed in the small room. "He's my momma's cousin. I've known him since I was a kid."

"No shit."

"I'd prefer nobody know. Can't have them think I'm getting special favors."

"Your secret's safe."

The crickets outside and the ticking of the Grandfather clock in the living room created a soothing background rhythm. Ryan relaxed. Maybe he *could* catch a quick nap. But relaxation after a mission was always short-lived. Memories encroached, and the adrenaline pumped anew. His eyes snapped open.

"How's Frankie holding up?" he asked. "And Molly?" *Did Frankie ask about me? Did she seem to care? Even notice I'd left?*

"They seemed fine."

"Come on, Dalt. Fine? After what they went through? I can believe she never wants to see me again. She's an elementary school teacher, for Christ's sake. She doesn't fall for guys who kill people."

"She's got guts. I think she knows we had to do what we did. And the kid was so excited about the helo and the limo, she's probably forgotten everything else."

"When you see them, tell Frankie I'm glad they're all right, okay? Tell her I'm sorry things turned out the way they did." *Tell her I love her.*

Dalton stood. His shadow towered over the bed. "Two things I don't do, pardner. One is poach. The other is play go-between for a man and a woman. You want to tell her anything, do it yourself."

The shadow moved away, and he heard the door open. Before it closed, Dalton spoke again. "You want my opinion? You've been doing a lot of running away lately. It doesn't solve your problems, just lets 'em fester. You've gotta decide what you're gonna do."

The door closed. Ryan stared at the ceiling, sorting his thoughts, knowing sleep wouldn't come.

Eventually, faint fingers of light slipped through the curtains. He rubbed his eyes and stumbled out to the living room. Dalton looked up at his approach.

"Thanks for everything," Ryan said. "I've got to go."

Outside, he paced around the Blackthorne SUV. Remembering Frankie. How she paced when she needed to think. Pushing the thought from his head, he opened the driver's door and sat sideways in the seat. He punched his father's number into his cell phone. Pop answered on the first ring.

"Hey, Pop. It's me. I'm fine."

After a pause, his father spoke. "Glad to hear that. Bit of a ruckus last night. You comin' home?"

"Not right now, Pop. I've got things to take care of."

"Your lady friend okay? The little one?"

"They're all right. They'll be home in Broken Bow later today."

Pop cleared his throat. Twice. "Don't do nothing stupid, son. Someone special comes along, you've got to grab her and hang on. Your mama was that kind of a woman. I nearly didn't go after her, afraid she wouldn't hook up with a poor rancher. We didn't have enough time together, but there's never been anyone else like her."

Ryan realized he was pacing again. "I'm not sure this is the same, Pop, but thanks. Frankie doesn't want . . ." His voice caught. "I'll try to get back. But first, I have some unfinished business in San Francisco." He almost ended the call, then brought it back to his ear. "I love you, Pop."

"Take care, son."

He stared at the phone for a long time before he drove away.

The teller's eyebrows lifted and his pinched nostrils flared before he motioned Ryan to the end of the counter. Ryan knew he looked like shit. He'd driven straight through, and hadn't bothered to change his shirt, much less shower, when he'd stopped at his San Francisco apartment for the emergency ID he kept stashed in a floor safe.

Now, at the bank, the two of them performed the rituals necessary to enter the sanctum of the safe deposit boxes, and finally, the man removed the small steel box. He handed it to Ryan, unlocked yet another door and stepped aside.

"You can press this button when you're through, Mr. Randall. I, or someone on staff will return."

"Thank you," Ryan said. Once the door clicked shut, he sat at the small table and released the catch on the box. A faint aroma of tobacco wafted up. He sat there, staring at Alvarez's flash drive. Although he'd thought about little else for the past two days, he hadn't been sure what he was going to do until he saw it. Ryan picked up the drive, running his fingers over its smooth surface. He closed the box and buzzed for the teller.

CHAPTER 30

"Hold still, Molly." Frankie straightened the pink ribbon on Molly's French braid.

"But they're starting the Taco Bell cannon song. That's my turn."

"Pachelbel," Frankie corrected. "Canon in D. You remember what to do?"

Molly rolled her eyes. "Step-together-step. Sprinkle flowers one way," she chanted in a singsong. "Step-together-step. Sprinkle them the other way."

"Good. And remember—"

"Don't throw them, let them float. I know."

Frankie kissed her daughter on the forehead. "You're the best." She stood in the church entryway and watched Molly shower pink and white rose petals along the white runner. She smoothed her dress. "Ready, Mom?"

Frankie adjusted the corsage on her mother's cast and crooked her elbow. "You look beautiful." The music shifted to Wagner's familiar strains. "Let's go."

Arm in arm, she and her mother walked down the aisle. At the front pew, Frankie stopped, kissed her mother on the cheek and took her seat on the sleek wood. Any doubts about Mom's judgment fled at the look of pure love in Bob's eyes as he clasped her hand.

Later, at the house, after the reception guests had left, Meg Winthrop stayed to help clean up. She handed Frankie a glass of champagne. "I don't see how you put this together in a week. Did someone give you thirty-hour days while the rest of us are stuck with the usual twenty-four?"

Frankie set the glass aside and squeezed her neighbor's hand. She didn't want to think of the days ahead now that the hectic planning was a thing of the past. Keeping busy had been her salvation.

"It wasn't a big deal, and I know Mom wanted it, even though she denied it. Why put it off? Like she and Bob said, at their age, they don't buy green bananas. Almost everyone in town pitched in."

"Now that the wedding is over, are you going to tell me what happened before? All the juicy details? Molly keeps talking about a helicopter ride and a big limousine. And some big, strong men."

"Another time, okay? I'm beat."

Meg looked disappointed as she flipped the latch on the dishwasher and pressed the start button. "I'm going to hold you to that."

"Fair enough." When the time came, she was sure she'd conjure up a nicely sanitized version of what happened. She'd watched the news, scoured the papers, but hadn't seen anything about terrorists in the Montana mountains. Or heard from Ryan. Which was what she wanted. She'd had her adventure, and it was plenty. It was time to get back to the reality of being a schoolteacher in Broken Bow, Montana.

After Meg left, Frankie wandered out to the front yard, bagging stray plastic champagne glasses and paper plates that hadn't made it to the trash. She lingered at the oak tree in the front yard, re-tying the yellow ribbon she and Molly had tied in memory of Mr. Snuggles. Frankie was pleased at the way Molly had accepted the loss after Ryan's cabin had been destroyed, and the memorial seemed to be all her daughter needed.

On the way to the trashcan, she straightened the "For Sale" sign in the yard. With Mom and Bob moving to Santa Rosa, the house was too big for her and Molly. And too expensive to maintain.

She smiled. Selling the house meant Mom didn't need to sell the mountain property, and Angus Harper could keep his trail ride business. That left Brenda. Mom's elephant pin had turned up in an Arizona pawnshop, and the police were confident they'd find Brenda.

Once she knew she'd get her pin back, Mom had hardly been upset about the missing savings.

"It's only money. In the grand scheme of things, that's not high on my list," she'd said. "Most of my assets are invested, so all she got was my 'just in case' cash account."

Nevertheless, Frankie hoped they'd recover Mom's cash. She sighed. If she'd confronted Mom sooner, she'd have known there wasn't any real financial crisis, and she wouldn't have taken the job at Three Elks. Which meant she'd never have met Ryan. Of course, he'd nearly got her and Molly killed, but they were fine, so despite everything that happened, she was glad he'd been part of her life, even for that short while. She went inside, a mere shade away from content.

She and Molly were sharing a dinner of leftover finger sandwiches in front of the television when the doorbell rang.

"I'll get it." Molly jumped up.

"Wait for me." Getting up from the couch was an effort, and only then did she realize how exhausted she was. She checked the clock. Seven-thirty? It felt like midnight.

"Who is it?" Molly called from halfway across the living room. She gave Frankie her "I know the rules" smirk. She darted to the door and had one hand on the knob before Frankie stopped her with a hand to the shoulder. She stepped in front of Molly.

Frankie checked the peephole. Her heart leapfrogged to her

throat. She licked her lips, her mouth suddenly dry, and pulled the door open.

"It's Mister Ryan!" Molly squealed. She wriggled past him onto the porch and searched the skies. "Did you come in a helicopter?"

"No, Angel. A regular car."

His whiskey-colored eyes showed almost as much misery as they had the first night she'd seen him at the Three Elks. "Come in." Frankie stepped back and motioned him inside. "How have you been?"

"Fine," he said. "Busy. You?"

"Busy, too." Awkwardness hung in the air between them. "Come inside, Molly. You can finish watching the movie. Ryan and I are going to have some grown-up talking time."

"Wait," Ryan said. "I'll be right back." He jogged to the street. A car door opened, then closed, and he jogged back with a blue-and-white polka-dotted shopping bag in one hand.

"Did he bring Gramma a wedding present?" Molly asked. "Can we open it for her?"

"I don't know, Peanut. Let's wait and see." All week, as she'd been busy throwing a wedding together, she'd thought about how she'd respond if she ever saw Ryan again. Cool and aloof, she'd decided. Friends, for sure. They'd been through hell and back together. But nothing more. Maybe brother-sister. Then why were her breasts aching? She folded her arms across her chest to hide the nipples straining against her bra. Forget what she was feeling lower.

Ryan trotted up the steps. He stopped at the doorway and raked his fingers through his hair. He'd cut it much shorter, and it stood up, as if he'd been fingering it a lot recently. Freshly shaven, too, and she smelled his aftershave, mixed with his own Ryan scent.

His gaze held hers for an instant before fixing on some distant place over her head. "I hope you don't mind, but I brought you each something." Before Frankie could respond, he reached into the bag and pulled out a box and handed it to Molly. She tugged on the ribbon.

"Molly. What do you say?" Frankie asked.

"Thank you," she said without looking up.

"That's better. But let's go indoors." She moved aside, and Ryan stepped into the room, still not making eye contact.

Molly ripped the paper off the box. "Mommy, look. It's a little Wolf!" She held up a small stuffed German Shepherd.

Ryan cleared his throat. "I know it's not Mr. Snuggles. I hope it's all right." He lowered his voice. "It's not one of those bribe things. Honest."

"Look at her. Of course it's all right." She made a production of checking out the toy for Molly's sake, then gave it back to her. "Why don't you take Little Wolf to the den and watch the movie together?"

Molly barreled into Ryan and hugged him around the legs. "Thank you." She skipped out of the room. The raw emotion that crossed Ryan's face sent a lump to Frankie's throat. This was not a good thing. She'd played this tape in her head for days. The world needed people like Ryan. People who would put their lives on the line. Molly needed someone she could count on to be there. Ryan couldn't be both.

"Sit down," she said. "We should talk."

We should talk.

Those words chilled Ryan more than seeing the For Sale sign in Frankie's yard. More than marching into an ambush. "Yeah."

"Would you like some coffee?"

Grateful for the time it would buy him, he nodded. Frankie retreated to the kitchen. After half a minute that lasted half a year, he picked up the bag and followed.

He stood in the kitchen doorway as he had a lifetime ago. Instead of jeans, this time she wore a silky pink dress that clung to her curves. No shoes, but the shimmer on her legs made him ache to run his fingers down the sleek nylon.

Her hair was done in another French braid, not hanging loose around her shoulders. He imagined releasing it, knowing how soft it would feel beneath his fingers.

She wore a different perfume tonight. It had hit him as soon as she'd opened the door. But underneath the exotic scent, she still smelled like Frankie, which had almost undone him on the porch.

She pressed a button on the coffee maker and turned around. Her eyes, blue as he remembered, flew open and a hand clapped against her chest. "You scared me."

"I wanted to give you this." He set the bag on the table and removed the package.

"You didn't need to bring me anything."

"I think I did. Open it."

Eyeing him with curiosity, she took the box. "It's heavy. Is it a book?"

"Open it already."

He watched her slender fingers untie the bow, then carefully pry the tape at the ends of the package. She removed the paper. Her mouth dropped open and the paper fluttered onto the floor. "If this is for real, you shouldn't have. I can't accept this, Ryan. It's much too expensive."

"It's for real, and I know what I can afford. If you can't think of it as a gift, then think of it as a replacement for what I broke."

She sank into a chair, turning the Nikon box round and round on the table in front of her. "You didn't break mine. I left it behind."

"To save something more important."

"Which I broke."

"Stop it, Frankie. You're a damn fine photographer, and you deserve a decent camera."

She burst out laughing, and he looked around the room, expecting to see Molly. When there was no sign of her, or anything else the least bit amusing, he yanked a chair away from the table and sat across from her. "What's so funny?"

"Nothing. I was going to say you owed me a quarter, but after last week—never mind."

She scooted her chair back. "Coffee's almost ready. Black, right?"

He nodded. The need to move welled up in him like a hot air balloon. Slowly, the room beyond Frankie registered. Platters in the draining rack. Three big plastic trash bags by the door, one revealing bits of silver and white wrapping paper and a number of bows. Which explained Frankie's attire. Real observant. In the field, he'd be dead by now.

"You had a party." When he noticed the empty case of champagne, his eyes darted to her left hand. He wasn't *that* blind. He'd have noticed a ring. His breathing steadied a little.

"Mom and Bob got married this afternoon. We had the reception here."

"I'm sure they'll be happy."

"They are."

In the kitchen light, he looked more closely and saw the strain, the shadows under Frankie's eyes her carefully applied makeup hadn't hidden.

"Okay, Frankie." He got up and went to the cabinet for mugs. She rose, but he motioned her down. "I'll get it. You said we needed to talk. So start talking." The gruffness in his tone surprised him, and he almost apologized. Almost.

"I'm not sure where to start." She laughed a quiet laugh. "You'd think I'd be babbling a mile a minute, because it's obvious we're both nervous."

He set both mugs on the table and sat next to her this time. "Okay, I'll start. Why did you push me away? Was it because of my job?"

She shook her head. "You were the one who disappeared, you know. I was confused. I needed to think, but you didn't even call."

He lowered his head and put his hands over hers. They were cold and trembled a little. "I was hurt. I ran."

"Hurt? What happened? I thought you were all right."

The alarm that crossed her face touched him. "Not that kind of hurt. You made it clear you didn't want to see me. I believe your exact words were, 'Ryan and his friends have important jobs to do. They're probably not going to come back for a long, long time.' I've heard them in my head since the helo landed."

"But you came back."

"I did. I've also been hearing something Dalton said to me."

"Which was?"

"That I've been doing a lot of running away lately. And it doesn't solve problems. So I'm not running anymore. I'm here, and we're going to work out what we're both trying to ignore."

"Which is?"

"I'm in love with you. That one way or another, I'm going to spend the rest of my life loving you. You're the reason my heart beats, you're the next breath I take. I'm not giving up. And you might have noticed, when I decide to fight, I don't back down."

A corner of her mouth turned up. "I've noticed. But—"

"No buts. We'll talk, we'll figure it out. Maybe not today. Maybe not tomorrow or next week, or six months from now, but I'm not letting you out of my life. Or Molly. You're both too much a part of me."

"Why didn't you say it before? That you loved me?"

He backed off and regrouped, organizing his thoughts. "Because I was afraid to admit it. Afraid to let anyone too close.

Afraid of the pain. But the emptiness hurts worse." He looked into her eyes. This was where she was supposed to throw her arms around him, kiss him and say she loved him, too, and she'd follow him to the ends of the earth. Instead, she pulled her hands out from under his and picked up her coffee mug.

He waited, afraid of what he'd hear. Which turned out to be the all too familiar sound of feet scampering across the floor. He took a deep breath and found a smile. "Hello, Molly. Is the movie over already?"

She climbed into a chair across from them. "I'm tired of it. Are you done doing grown-up talking? I want some chocolate milk."

Frankie looked at him as if to say, *You want to change your mind?*

He shook his head. *No way. Can't scare me off that easily.*

"I don't know," Frankie said. "You've had lots of sweets today."

"A little glass? Please?"

Frankie made a Mom face he recognized. The one that said, "You win, but I'm not a pushover."

She sighed. "Okay, the blue cup. Half. Then a bath, then bed."

Molly seemed satisfied with the compromise. She looked at him and he melted at her round, blue eyes.

"Can Mr. Ryan read me a story? And Little Wolf, too?"

He pushed his chair back. "I'd love it, Angel. Now, you can show me how to make chocolate milk. Your mom's tired, and we should let her rest."

Molly pointed him to the cabinet where he found a small blue plastic cup. She opened the refrigerator and carried a bottle of chocolate syrup to the table. He brought the milk, and poured and squirted under her supervision. He handed her the spoon. "You stir."

She did, then licked the coating of syrup off the spoon. He eyed Frankie, who was watching with a bemused expression.

"Bath next," he said. "Right?"

"Can you do bubbles?"

He gave Frankie a questioning look. She nodded. "She knows where everything is. Just make sure the tub doesn't overflow."

"Come on." Molly tugged at his arm, and he followed her upstairs.

Half an hour later, with Molly bathed, storied, and already asleep, Ryan went downstairs. He found Frankie on the couch in the den, studying the new camera. When he sat next to her, she set it between them like a shield.

"She's out," he said. "I didn't even finish the story."

"She's had a busy day." She tapped the camera. "Thank you again. I think it'll do everything but cook dinner."

"It's the eye of the person behind the lens that makes the picture."

When her eyebrows lifted, he confessed. "My brother's words."

"Your brother. His cabin. Does he know? His pictures? Are they all gone?"

"Yeah. But he's got the negatives in storage, so it's not a total loss. And I never said thanks for fixing the trail access for Pop."

"Don't worry about it. I'm glad I could help. I like your father."

Ryan recalled his father's words. "I do, too. He told me there were some things worth fighting for." He moved the camera to the coffee table. "Talk to me."

"About?"

"Us."

She stared at the ceiling. "I'm trying to get a handle on things."

"What things?"

"Who I am. What I want. Nothing is the same. I've been thinking, too."

Ryan forced himself to stay calm and hear her out. Then he'd argue her into seeing his side. "Go on."

"I've always lived my life for someone else. I had to fix things for people. They had to be happy. But I never really thought about what made *me* happy."

"Let me make you happy."

"That's not all of it." She got up and paced. "I always figured I'd fall in love with someone who would be a father for Molly—that was always what I looked for. I never really considered what *I* wanted for *me*. And in your line of work, you wouldn't be around. And there would always be the chance you wouldn't come back."

"I could get hit by a bus crossing the street to an office job, you know."

"Don't try to make fun of me. This is hard."

"Sorry." He repressed the desire to intercept her pacing so he could hold her.

"Well, I keep thinking how important your job is. You can save so many lives. But Molly is the one life I put above all the others."

"I understand."

She flopped into one of the easy chairs across from the couch. "After everything that happened last week, I realized how trivial my own problems were. Mom's happy, she doesn't care about the missing money, which it turns out wasn't much of her savings after all, and things are set for your father and his trail rides.

"I'm in love with you, too, Ryan. And I was worried for nothing, except when they kidnapped Molly, and then I was really scared and—"

She'd said it out loud. In the middle of a Frankie-babble, but she'd said it. She loved him, too. "Whoa. Take a breath."

She gave a sheepish grin. "Guess I'm back to normal."

"Normal enough to sit next to me?"

She curled up next to him, and he inhaled her scent. Spicy, musky, and Frankie, with an undercurrent of coffee. The erection he'd been trying to ignore strained against his zipper.

She fingered the buttons on his shirt. "But the real reason I couldn't deal with you wasn't you. It was me."

"What do you mean?"

"When everything was happening, after Molly was safe, I *liked* the feeling of power. Being in charge of those two men. Pointing a rifle at them. The rush, you called it. And I didn't like that I liked it. I've never liked violence. A little fantasy adventure, but this was real, and everyone could have been killed, and I *liked* it. When I decided to leave the cabin, even though you said to wait, I felt in control. Scared to death at the same time."

Her lips were parted, her eyes deep blue pools. "And how do you feel right now?" he whispered into her neck.

"Hot. On fire. Aroused. I want you to touch me everywhere. I want to touch you everywhere. I want you inside me, and I want—"

"Frankie." He covered her lips with his. It seemed the best way to stop her babbling.

Her tongue delved into his mouth. One hand fumbled at the waist of his pants. The other worked to unbutton his shirt.

"Upstairs?" he said, when she gasped for breath.

"Too far. Brenda's old room."

With a bed. And a door that locked. He unzipped her dress along the way.

He flipped the light switch, illuminating the room. Unlike a week ago, the bed was made. "This time, I want to see you. I want to watch you come."

"Then look at me." She ground her hips at his groin.

Finding restraint he didn't know he possessed, he broke the connection. "Slow down, honey. Let's not rush this."

He sat her on the bed and knelt behind her. Lifting her braid out of the way, he planted kisses down her neck. She tilted her head. The pulse at her throat danced. He lowered the sleeves of her dress and kissed her shoulders. The thin straps of her bra were next. His fingers found the clasp at the back and flipped it open. He reached around her, his hands caressing her breasts.

"I love you, Frankie. You and Molly rescued me from a life of emptiness."

She arched against him. "I fell in love with you when you paid more attention to Molly than to me at the ranch."

He slid the dress down to her waist. She started to stand, but he pressed on her shoulders. "Wait." He untied the ribbon at the end of her braid, then slid the rubber band off. One strand at a time, he undid the plait, running his fingers through her hair when the braid reached her scalp. He buried his nose in her hair. The fruity smell was pure, unadulterated Frankie. She may have changed her perfume, but she used the same shampoo. "Lie back. I want to enjoy you."

He took her nipple into his mouth, tugging it into a taut peak. She writhed, tossing her head from side to side. She made little sounds, half groan, half squeak, that had him stiffer than he thought possible.

"Mmm." He laved her other breast. "You taste delicious. Tonight, I want to taste you all over." He raised her hips and slid the dress past a tiny triangle of silk covering her delta of golden curls.

Her scent ratcheted his own arousal up another five notches. If he wasn't careful, his fantasy of slow, languorous lovemaking would be shot to hell. His fingers toyed with the inches of bare flesh between her panties—if that scrap could be called panties—and the elastic tops of her stockings.

She kicked at the dress, and he eased it down, letting it caress her legs as it traveled down their nylon-clad lengths.

"Ryan," she gasped. "I'm going crazy."

"Good. That's part of my plan." One at a time, he unrolled the stockings from her legs, then kissed his way north. He tugged at the scrap of silk with his teeth. "I want this perfect for you."

She yanked at his hair, trying to push him away from his target. "I'm not sure I want—"

"You tell me to stop and I will. But this is my fantasy. Later, we can do yours, okay?"

"But I don't have a fantasy."

"Of course you do. Everyone does." His tongue found the nubbin it was looking for and twirled circles around its base.

"Oh . . . my." Her hands stopped pushing and started pulling him closer. Her hips bucked, and he followed the rhythm she set. "Oh, my . . . ohmyohmy."

Her thighs gripped him. He suckled her core, and she arched her hips one more time, then shuddered.

He scooted up beside her, his fingers tracing lazy circles around her navel. "Dang it."

"What?" She sucked in deep gulps of air.

"I forgot to watch. Guess we'll have to do it again." He grinned.

"What about my fantasy?" she said, grinning back. She shoved him onto his back and popped the button of his pants.

CHAPTER 31

Frankie reached for Ryan's zipper. His eyes twinkled, his mouth turned up, but there was an undercurrent of unease.

"You're not afraid, are you?" she asked.

He brought her hand to his lips and kissed her knuckles. "No. But be careful, okay?"

When she tried to lower the zipper over the bulge at his fly, she knew why he was nervous. "Maybe I should let you do this."

"It's your fantasy. Do whatever you like."

She hitched herself to the head of the bed and arranged the pillows behind her back. Crossing her hands behind her head, she leaned against the headboard. "Let me think for a minute."

"Thinking kind of spoils things." He scooted up next to her and nuzzled her breast. "Times like these, action is a better approach."

She nodded in agreement. "But I'm learning as I go here. Until a few minutes ago, I'd never fantasized about what you just did. If I even thought about it, it was, like . . . gross."

"And now?" She detected a trace of concern in his voice.

With a forefinger, she traced his eyebrows. "I never imagined I could feel like that." She shook her head, enjoying the sensation of her hair floating free after being confined all day. Each strand ignited a spark under her skin. She recognized the jittery sensation as the same one she'd felt when she'd held a gun on Smith and Jones. Control. Power. But now, it didn't frighten or confuse her. With the same voice she'd used then, she said, "All right, cowboy. You're going to do what I say, understand."

He cocked an eyebrow. "I think you're scaring me."

"Good." She leaned forward. "First, only one of us is naked. That's not in my fantasy."

"I can take care of that." He reached over his head for his shirt collar.

"No. Stop."

He let go of his shirt, obviously confused. "Okay, now I *know* you're scaring me."

"No talking. Get off the bed. Stand back."

The expression on his face was half amused, but he complied.

"Strip. But slow. Real slow," she commanded. "And seductive." Her pulse throbbed as she watched him undo the remaining buttons on his shirt. "Don't look down. Put those eyeballs right here." She made a V with her fingers and pointed to her own eyes, clenching her teeth to keep from laughing when Ryan's mouth dropped open.

She shrugged. "Hey, I found out I like being in control. Now, a little hip action, please."

"Frankie," he croaked.

"I said no talking. I'd put on some music, but there's no player in this room, so you'll have to provide it. Humming is acceptable."

"You've got to be kidding," he mumbled.

"Hey, you said you'd act out my fantasy. I'm kind of making it up as I go along. Improvising, you know. Haven't you ever been to a strip club?"

His face reddened. "Yes, but they were women."

"So, I'm sure you can make the necessary adjustments. Pretend it's an undercover assignment." She crossed her legs at the ankles. "I'm waiting."

He swore under his breath, but she let it pass. His back was to her now, his head bowed, and she could see his ribcage expand and contract as he took several deep breaths. For an instant, she wondered if she'd gone too far, but the delight that filled her made stopping impossible.

When Ryan turned around, his shirt was buttoned to the neck. His thumbs were hooked into the belt loops of his khakis. His eyes bored into hers like glowing embers. He licked his lips. Her temperature escalated along with her heart rate. Somewhere beneath the pounding in her ears, she thought she heard the melody of *Let Me Entertain You*. She wasn't a hundred percent sure which of them hummed it.

His hips gyrated from side to side while his fingers toyed with the top button of his shirt. One by one, he unbuttoned them, with a forward jerk of his hips as each inch of chest became visible.

Once he reached the last button, he spun around, shrugged the shirt off, twirled it above his head and tossed it on the floor. She was having trouble breathing. His hands met at his waist, dropping to his zipper. She gave up on breathing while he released himself. It dawned on her that he wasn't wearing anything under his pants, and she gasped.

"Come here," she whispered, reaching for him. "Forget the slow part. Get those pants off. Now."

Before he did, he dug into a pocket and showered her with a handful of foil condom packets like so much confetti. Gloriously naked, he closed the remaining distance to the bed, stopping inches from her, his erection towering from his groin. She found her breath, and with trembling fingers, cupped him. Stroked him. And with no more hesitation, took him into her mouth.

Her tongue explored his length. Smooth as satin, rigid as steel. He groaned, and she anchored him with her hands at his hips.

"Am I doing this right?" she asked.

He groaned. "Honey, it's your fantasy, but yeah, you're doing fine."

She shifted to her knees and took more of him into her mouth. His hands at her head set the rhythm. His gasps of pleasure enflamed her.

"Hon, unless your fantasy is supposed to end in about ten seconds, I'm begging you. Stop. I want to finish in . . . um . . . the more . . . Oh, God . . . more . . . traditional . . ."

She wanted him there, too. She relinquished her hold on him. He was sheened in sweat, and his eyes were glazed. But in their depths, she saw what she'd seen in Bob's eyes this afternoon. Love. She fumbled on the bed for a condom.

Ryan snatched it from her hands, tore the packet open and sheathed himself.

He slid inside her, and when the earth shattered around her, she kept her eyes open and watched him come.

Frankie pillowed her head on Ryan's chest, twirling her fingers through the coarse hair. "You begged."

"Like a man on death row."

"I liked that. Big strong cowboy begging the schoolmarm." She rose to one elbow and searched his face as he lay there, relaxed and sated, and wished they could stay that way. All the 'what if's' she'd been sorting through jostled for position in her brain. Resigned to reality, she settled back onto his chest, where she couldn't see his eyes. When she looked at him, all the reasons it couldn't work scattered like a flock of pigeons in the park. "All right. Fantasy time is over. We haven't finished talking."

His chest rose beneath her head, then collapsed down. "We can make it work. We're good together."

"Great sex isn't enough for a relationship."

"It wasn't just great sex. We made *love*, Frankie. There's a difference. But there's more than the physical side." His fingers drew feather-light strokes along her back. "You're smart, you're talented, and you're strong. You chase away my nightmares. And you make me laugh. In my world, there's not enough laughter. I'm not giving up on us."

"Us. That's the biggie. The way I see it, there would be a lot of time when the 'us' is me and Molly."

"And her brother or sister. Or both."

Frankie raised her head. "Whoa. That's kind of jumping ahead."

"I'm still in fantasyland." He stroked her hair, and she settled back onto his chest, listening to the rhythmic thumping of his heart.

"You sure are. For once, I'm looking ahead further than next week. Considering long-range plans. Dealing with what *I* want. I refuse to think of Molly as a mistake, but getting pregnant changed my life. I took a job I didn't really like because it was the best thing for Molly. I gave it up to come home and take care of Mom, who never even asked me to. Bob wants to be near his sister. She'll need long-term care, but he wants to be close, and Mom agrees."

His heart thudded a little faster. "Your mom. She'll want to be close to you and Molly, won't she? Will you go with her? I saw the 'For Sale' sign, and I almost had a heart attack thinking you were already gone."

"Not yet. Bob makes Mom happy. He made her go to a different doctor, and it turns out her medications were causing her memory problems. But even if she really was losing it, he wouldn't care. She told me he loves her a minute at a time."

"But you're still leaving?" His hand stopped moving.

She hesitated. "Yes, but not right away. I'm going to finish out the school term. Molly's been uprooted once this year already. No more Three Elks, though. It'll be tight for a while, but we'll manage. Once the house sells, I'll get a third of the proceeds. And I want to pursue photography for real."

Ryan wrapped his arms around her and pulled her on top of him. "Could you do it around San Francisco instead?"

"Why? What's there?"

"Me. Blackthorne." He tucked her hair behind her ears.

Even though she'd expected them, hearing the words out loud made her heart drop to her stomach. "You're going back to work for them?" She rolled beside him and arranged the covers over her.

"My job's available. I can do good."

She twisted the sheet in her hands. "Would you quit your job for me? Find a normal occupation? Something safe? Come home for dinner at the same time every night? Be at school plays and ballet recitals?"

He sobered. "Is that what you want?"

"What I want is the answer to my question. Would you quit saving the world for me and Molly?"

"Is this a test?" His voice lost its dreamy quality and took on a hardened edge.

"Think about it. You came in here *telling* me how it would be, like it was a done deal. Don't you think you should *ask* me first? Find out what *I* want?"

He stared into the distance for a long time. She waited, knowing tonight might be the last night they'd have together. She studied him, wanting to memorize every hair on his head, the creases at the edges of his eyes, the dimple in his cheek. Her gaze took in the scars, those reminders of his sacrifices for what he believed in.

When he spoke, his voice was thick. "I don't think I can quit, Frankie. I walked out once, and it was for a stupid reason. I need to do what I think is right. I hope you understand that. I love you. You're the most important thing in my life, but I have to think of the lives of other people. They're important, too. And knowing you'd be home waiting would make the job even more meaningful."

Her emotions roiled at the thought of what he did. She respected it. Admired it. Envied it, maybe. But could she live with it? The ugly reality was Ryan killed people. Bad people, to be sure. She chided herself. She'd have done it too, to save her child. Ryan saved everyone's children.

"I've thought about it. A lot. What it would be like to live with someone who might walk out the door in the morning and never come home. Sitting at the dinner table, and not being able to do the basics, like, 'Tell me about your day, dear.' All the uncertainty. And what about Molly? If she loves you, and you . . . go away . . . it would be devastating."

"No life comes with guarantees. You know that. But there are a lot of family guys at Blackthorne, and countless military families who deal with separation all the time. It's not easy, but they pull it off. You could, too. You've never *needed* someone to be around all the time."

She moved to get out of bed, but he held her back. "No pacing. We're going to talk this out, face to face, eye to eye." He turned on his side and his determined gaze trapped her. She sifted through her thoughts, searching for the words she'd rehearsed all week.

"Would it help if I begged?" he said. The hint of humor in his tone didn't reach his eyes.

"No begging. Not for this. Your work is important. To you, and to so many people. Mine might not be 'save the world' stuff, but it means a lot to me. If it's going to work between us, we'll both have to sacrifice. Compromise. I can't do this only for you."

"So, are you saying you'd accept me as a field agent?" He

couldn't disguise the hope in his eyes.

"I've played out all the alternatives, and I can't see you happy being anything else."

"So, did I pass your test? I'm not hearing the answer."

"You haven't asked the right question."

He cradled her face and kissed her. A soft, gentle kiss. "Frankie—"

"Wait," she said. "Please don't ask yet. I don't want to hurt you when I say I have to wait a while longer before I'll know for sure."

He grinned. "You'll wait? I can do waiting. Waiting's not the same as 'Go to hell, Ryan'—oops. I meant, 'Go to blazes, Ryan.' I told you I wouldn't go away."

She tousled his hair. "That's borderline babbling, you know."

"You've unearthed a whole new me."

"Not a new you. A part you could never show. You're a warrior. A warrior with a layer of marshmallow fluff hidden inside, but a warrior all the same."

He burst out laughing. "God, I love you."

"I love you, too. And for what it's worth, you gave me the right answer. Giving up what you love would make us both resent each other."

"If it helps, my days in the field are probably going to end sooner than I'd planned. I saw the doctor, and the knee is never going to be a hundred percent. Once I start slowing down a team, I'd quit the field work. They need people behind the scenes coordinating operations, and I can do good there, too."

"You didn't mention that part. So you were testing me, too?" She tried, but couldn't summon up any resentment. She'd done the same to him.

He kissed the top of her head. "I think we're both using our brains here, instead of our hormones for a change. Neither of us would be happy knowing the other one sacrificed their dreams."

She smiled. "So, if I want to travel for my photography, you'd be okay with that?"

"All the way." His eyes widened. "You're not going to want to photograph combat zones, or political uprisings, or things like that, are you?"

"Maybe. It might be interesting." At his look of panic, she smiled. "Nah. I think I'll leave that to your brother. I'll stick to nature." She threw back the covers and ran her finger down his naked torso. "You're a natural subject right now. Maybe I should test my new camera."

His eyebrows shot up and he yanked the sheet up to his waist. "No way. I have one more present for you." He kissed her forehead and leaned over the edge of the bed. She watched his tight behind as he fished on the floor for his pants. When he brought up a small velvet box, her pulse raced.

"Ryan, this isn't right. I said—"

"Open it."

With trembling fingers, she pried the lid open. Inside was a gold, heart-shaped pendant with a diamond in the center. She traced the surface with a fingertip. "It's beautiful."

"Come here." He took the box and lifted the necklace, dangling it from its fine gold chain. "You've got my heart, Frankie. Wear this and remember, no matter where I am, you've got the most important part of me with you all the time. I'll always come back."

When he fastened it around her neck, tears welled and her throat closed. "You're making me cry. I never cry."

With his thumb, he wiped the tears from her cheeks. "You promise never to say another word about marshmallow fluff, and my lips are sealed."

She pressed her mouth to his.

"Bad choice of words," he mumbled as he opened to her probing tongue.

"And there's a part of you that's definitely not marshmallow fluff."

"If you'd like, I've got a few more fantasies we can try."

She reached for him. When he put his arms around her, she knew this was where she belonged. With Ryan. Who had her heart.

ABOUT THE AUTHOR

Terry Odell was born in Los Angeles and now makes her home in Orlando, Florida. An avid reader (her parents tell everyone they had to move from their first home because she finished the local library), she always wanted to "fix" stories so the characters did what she wanted. Once she began writing, she found this wasn't always possible, as evidenced when the mystery she intended to write rapidly became a romance.

With her degree in Psychology from UCLA, and a Biology minor, she loves getting into the minds of her characters, turning them loose in tight spots and seeing what they do. Too often, they surprise her.

Terry has published numerous contemporary romance short stories and three romantic suspense novels. She is a member of the Romance Writers of America, an active member of the Central Florida chapter and the Kiss of Death chapter, as well as the Mystery Writers of America. When she's not writing, she's probably reading. Visit her at www.terryodell.com.